Kate Coscarelli launched her spectacular career as a bestselling author with her very first novel, *Fame and Fortune*, and continued it with *Perfect Order* and *Living Color*. As the young bride of an Air Force officer, she spent three years in Tripoli, Libya. She and her husband now live in Los Angeles and Rancho Mirage, California.

By the same author

Fame and Fortune
Perfect Order
Living Color

KATE COSCARELLI

Pretty Women

First published in Great Britain by
Severn House Publishers Ltd 1990
by arrangement with Grafton Books.
A Grafton UK Paperback Original 1990

This edition published 1993 by
Diamond Books
77-85 Fulham Palace Road
Hammersmith, London, W6 8JB

Grateful acknowledgment is made for permission to quote from
'Pretty Women,' music and lyrics by Stephen Sondheim, ©
1978 Revelation Music Publishing Corp. and Rilting Music Inc.
A Tommy Valando Publication.

Printed and bound in Great Britain by
BPCC Hazells Ltd
Member of BPCC Ltd

This book is dedicated with love to Don,
my traveling companion from one end
of the world to the other, through
this life to the next . . .
and to all the pretty women who stand
beside their men in uniform.

Acknowledgments

Thanks for the memories: Beti and Dale, Monica and Frank, Gerty and Chuck, Mary Beth and Horace, Beth and Wick, Jane and John, Stella and Dick.

A special word of appreciation to Joan Stewart, Maureen Baron, and Michaela Hamilton, as well as to Stephen Sondheim, whose genius and artistry are an inspiration to all who love words . . . and music.

'Pretty women,
Blowing out their candles or
Combing out their hair,
Even when they leave,
They still are there.'

– from 'Pretty Women,'
music and lyrics
by Stephen Sondheim

1

1976

As Tess Kipling crossed the quadrangle, she found it almost impossible to resist skipping. But she certainly couldn't be seen doing something so gloriously undergraduate as that. She had an image to protect, now more than ever. After all, she was not only the dean of women, she was also, glory hallelujah, now one of the two top candidates for the position of chancellor of this august and revered institution!

For the past year, ever since Chancellor Harris had informed the board of trustees that he intended to retire, Tess had hoped, oh Lord how she had hoped, but she had not expected to receive serious consideration to be his successor. In spite of the women's movement, the antiwar protests, Watergate, hippies, Yippies, and hair, Christopher University was still a staunchly conservative, private California university, and there was a ceiling hanging over the heads of all women faculty members, a glass ceiling that permitted them to look up but never climb higher than the position Tess held. Until now.

When she arrived at her office in Hayward Hall, she hurried through the door and closed it sharply behind her. Wilma Burns, her secretary, looked at her quizzically. 'You okay, Dean Kipling?' she asked.

Suddenly Tess knew she could not keep her promise to Chancellor Harris. She had to tell somebody or she would simply explode with excitement.

'Is there anyone waiting to see me?'

Wilma shook her head. 'Marcy Clinton was here again, but I told her you wouldn't be back until after lunch.'

'Good,' Tess said emphatically, turning the key and locking the door so they wouldn't be disturbed.

'Wilma, I'm going to tell you something in the strictest confidence. You must not tell anybody, understand?'

Wilma, who had worked for Tess Kipling for her entire four-year tenure as dean, was miffed. 'I never tell anybody anything. You know that.'

'Of course you don't,' Tess quickly agreed, and perched on the edge of her secretary's desk so she would be close enough to speak in a conspiratorial whisper, as if it would perhaps exculpate her for breaking her vow of silence. 'I just had a talk with Chancellor Harris. He invited me to a dinner party at his house on Thursday.'

'So?' Wilma asked curiously.

'Frank Higbee has been invited too,' Tess added, hoping that perhaps Wilma would make the connection, but she didn't. She just continued to look blank, waiting patiently for the revelation.

'It seems that the field of candidates to replace Chancellor Harris next year has been narrowed down to two,' Tess finished.

'So? Who are they?'

'I'm one of them,' Tess said gleefully.

Wilma gasped in surprise. 'Oh, my God, that's wonderful!'

'Isn't it, though?' Tess replied, her eyes sparkling with the excitement of it all.

'It's just . . . it's just . . . great, that's all. I can hardly believe it.' Suddenly Wilma's eyes narrowed suspiciously. 'Can we believe it? Are they really considering a woman?' she asked, her voice now heavy with disbelief.

'Harris said they were. When I applied, I did it without

any real hope, you know. It was a gesture I felt I had to make,' Tess explained. 'Somewhere along the line they're going to have to stop overlooking us, Wilma. And we've got to stop pretending it's okay. Nobody's going to do anything for us if we don't insist.'

Wilma took off her horn-rimmed glasses and set them down on the desk. She was almost thirty years old and had a master's degree in political science, but the only job she had been able to find after graduation was as a secretary. All the excitement had faded from her demeanor as she closed her eyes and pinched the bridge of her nose in a gesture of frustration. 'Has it occurred to you that they might just possibly be using you?' she asked in a monotone.

'As a token candidate, you mean, to take off the pressure? That was my very first reaction, Wilma. I told him I would not be used as a shill, but he assured me that I was being seriously considered. In fact, he admitted in confidence that he had already told the board that I was his first preference and Professor Higbee was a distant second.'

'Frank Higbee's family has donated a ton of money to the school, and he's extremely popular with the athletic department,' Wilma pointed out warily.

'True, but he blew his cool with the student body during that protest last year by threatening to send them all to jail, remember?' Tess reminded her.

'Not exactly his finest hour,' Wilma giggled. Her face lit up as she recalled the speech. 'He turned the most apathetic students into militants.'

'Chancellor Harris mentioned that, as a matter of fact, and he said that my popularity with the students was the reason I was being seriously considered. There's been so much protest and disorder on campuses all over the country for the past few years that they want someone who can keep things peaceful.'

'And I'm sure it doesn't hurt that you have a son graduating from the Air Force Academy in June who is a straight arrow, either.' Wilma put her glasses back on and returned to her typewriter. 'Well, just don't be disappointed when things don't turn out as you hope.'

Tess put her hand on Wilma's shoulder. 'Don't be cynical, Wilma. We've got to keep trying, even if we fail. We can't settle for the status quo.'

'True, but suppose you do get the job . . . then what? You'll be duty-bound to carry out the wishes of the board, and you've been one of their severest critics, not in public maybe, but certainly in private.'

'Life is supposed to be a challenge,' Tess retorted, and marched into her office to think things through. She had no time for her secretary's pessimism. She had to concentrate on her performance at that dinner party on Thursday night. How strange life is, she thought, knowing that her whole career would be on the line that evening. She'd have just a few hours of social chitchat in which to convince the board of trustees that she was the best candidate for the position. Until then it would be useless to speculate about how she would handle the job if she got it.

Chancellor Harris had warned her that several of the trustees were extremely cool to the idea of a woman heading the university, but he had persuaded them to give her consideration. He said he was confident that by seeing Frank and her side by side in the same room, the board members would have to admit to themselves that she was the better choice. But would they? Could they look past her pretty face and trim figure and see the strong leader they were seeking? God, it wasn't going to be easy.

12

Mentally ticking off the names of all the trustees, she tried to recall every tidbit of information she had ever heard about each of them. Wilma interrupted to tell her that there was a long-distance call on line one. When she picked up the telephone, she heard a vaguely familiar woman's voice reaching across twenty years.

'Tess? Hi, it's Beth Cellini from Tripoli. Remember me?'

'Beth! My Lord, yes! How are you? How's Joe?'

'Joe died last December, Tess,' she replied softly.

'Oh, Beth . . . I'm so sorry. Was it sudden?'

'Not really. He retired from active duty last year when he found out he had lung cancer. He wanted to spend his last months near our daughter, Angela, out here in Colorado Springs,' Beth explained, her words rimmed by sadness. 'She married an Air Force officer too. He's a math instructor here at the Academy, and your son is one of his students.'

'Really? How nice. I must write and tell him,' Tess responded politely, wondering why Beth was calling her now. Except for their annual exchange of Christmas cards and short notes, they had had no personal contact since Tess had left Tripoli twenty years before.

They chatted briefly, and then Beth explained the reason for her call.

'Tess, I need your help. I just got an upsetting letter from Nell Carson that concerns you and Kip, Samara Mulhare . . . and Chili. I was even more disturbed after talking to Nell on the telephone. Did you know, by the way, that Howard was killed in Vietnam?'

'No, I haven't had any contact with Nell since I left Tripoli. You sound so mysterious, Beth. What's this letter all about?'

'I can't tell you on the telephone, because it sounds too

13

farfetched and unbelievable unless you read the letter for yourself. It's not pleasant, Tess, but it's very important. We need your help desperately in sorting things out and deciding what to do. I've already talked to Sam in Los Angeles, and she's agreed to meet with me at the Broadmoor Hotel here on Wednesday.'

'That's day after tomorrow!' Tess exclaimed.

'I know it's awfully short notice, and you're probably thinking of reasons why you can't possibly come, but please don't refuse. There are decisions to be made that might affect all of our lives. We need you with us.'

'This week is really bad for me. Could we possibly postpone it until next week?' Tess asked, wanting to be responsive to Beth's request but thinking that a quick trip to Colorado Springs might impinge on her important meeting on Thursday.

'No, we can't,' Beth retorted adamantly. 'Believe me, Tess, this is important and very urgent, not only to us but maybe to our country. I just wish that Nell hadn't waited so long to tell somebody. Do you think you could possibly get Kip to come with you? We could really use his help and advice.'

'He's in Washington, but I'll call him and ask,' Tess replied, capitulating. If Beth was the same woman she had known in Tripoli, she was no alarmist. If she said it was important, it was urgent, and Tess found it impossible to refuse her request.

'I'll make all the arrangements,' Beth responded quickly, before Tess could change her mind or ask any further questions. 'I knew I could count on you.'

When the call ended, and Tess was alone again with her thoughts, the elation that had filled her heart and her mind just minutes before had evaporated. She remembered Beth Cellini as being a thoroughly sensible, sensitive woman, devoted to her husband and daughter, and a

14

devout Catholic. Tess closed her eyes briefly to reflect on the mystical process of life. One brief telephone call, and her happily ordered world, which moments before had been replete with the joy of challenge and accomplishment, was now filled with mystery and uncertainty. The meeting in Colorado might very possibly slam the door on her aspirations to be chancellor if it kept her from going to that most important dinner Thursday night. The chances of their choosing a no-show candidate to be the chancellor were almost nonexistent, but she had no choice.

She called Wilma on the intercom and instructed her to track Kip down. He would react impatiently to the utter secrecy of it all, but he would probably agree to go because it would give him an excuse to visit his son.

Standing at the leaded glass window, looking down on the quadrangle below, she was oblivious of the students hurrying to class across the cobblestone path. The telephone call from Beth had opened doors in her mind that she thought had been shut forever, and now her thoughts were taking her back through the years to a place far away and long ago to an adventure that had reached across time to alter her life.

'This meeting better be important, Beth, my friend,' she muttered. 'It's going to cost me dearly to be there.'

She picked up the telephone to call Chancellor Harris to tell him she was being called out of town on an emergency, and although she planned to be back on Thursday for the dinner, there was a remote chance that she might not make it. She just hoped he wouldn't think she was backing away from the competition.

15

2

Helen knocked on the door before entering her employer's office. Even though she had worked for Samara Silverman Mulhare for more than ten years and knew more about her than anyone else inside or outside of Hollywood, she still treated her employer with as much respect and deference as she had on the day she was hired.

'I didn't want to disturb you while you were on the telephone, but the attorneys said they had a new offer prepared, and they'd like you to take a look at it,' Helen announced as she entered the spacious and elegantly furnished office and laid the document on the large, sleekly modern desk. Samara Silverman Mulhare had learned early on from her father that it was important to convey an image of power in an industry built entirely on illusion. And so when she became president of Silverstone Studios after her father's death, she did not merely occupy his office, she brought in a top designer to create a dynamic setting that would make a statement. Gone from the walls were the dark nineteenth-century paintings – they were presently on loan to the Los Angeles County Art Museum. In their place there hung the bold paintings and strong colors of Mondrian and Miró and the densely covered oversize canvases of Jackson Pollock. She had chosen modern art because most people were intimidated by bare-bones abstraction and were impressed by those who understood and appreciated it enough to spend vast sums of money to acquire it.

Sam looked up from the papers detailing her company's latest offer in the current contract negotiations with the technical unions and sighed in exasperation. 'Why can't these people understand that if hourly wages go much higher we'll all be out of work?'

She tried to concentrate on the paper before her, but the earlier telephone call from Beth Cellini now began to distract her. Sam's life had been so full and demanding that most of her past had been bleached out to pale, rarely recalled memories. She looked up from the paper and caught a glimpse of herself in the shining steel facade on the fireplace. How different she was from the young woman who had left Tripoli all those years ago.

Unlike most of the women in the movie industry, Sam had allowed her dark hair to whiten naturally, and wore it long and twisted into a tight knot at the nape of her neck. She was still reed-thin, and her black-and-white Chanel suit enhanced the whiteness of her hair and the darkness of her deep-set eyes, eyes that revealed nothing to anyone. In an industry where pretty women had always been expendable commodities, expected to shine briefly and then make way for a younger generation of lovelies, Samara Mulhare had started at the top and stayed there.

She got up from the white leather chair that had been upholstered to fit her spare frame and walked over to the expanse of windows looking out toward the San Fernando Valley. Below her were spread the acres of soundstages and back lot of the studio that had been built by her family. For more than fifteen years the responsibility for the fiscal and creative health and well-being of that gargantuan company had been her responsiblity, but it had also been her salvation and her redemption. Because the task had been so vast, it had consumed her and kept her from dwelling too long on what might have been.

17

But her old friend's call had summoned her back, demanding that she return once more to the sorrows and the tragedy of another time and another place.

She closed her eyes, and suddenly it was the morning of April 12, 1945, the day her life was to be changed forever. Someone was shaking her, trying to awaken her from the deep and satisfying slumber of a nineteen-year-old student who had spent most of the night cramming for a history exam.

'Go away,' she mumbled, and tried to bury her face deeper into her pillow, but the earthquake continued to shake her bed.

'Silverman, for God's sake, wake up! There's a long-distance call for you!' It was the voice of Cheryl, her roommate at Sarah Lawrence, where both girls were just finishing their freshman year.

Samara was instantly awake. 'Who the devil is calling me at this hour?' she asked grumpily.

'It's past eleven, lazybones. I knew how late you were up last night, so I let you sleep in. I figured it was better for you to miss your English class and be rested for Madame Bitch's exam this afternoon.'

'Thanks. Lend me your robe, will you?' Without waiting for consent, Sam grabbed the faded pink chenille robe, wrapped it around her shoulders, and trotted out to the telephone in the hallway.

At first the voice she heard didn't sound much like her father's. It was too strained and muffled.

'Princess?' he asked.

'Dad . . . is that you?'

'Baby, come home . . . as fast as you can.'

'Daddy, what's wrong? Is Mom all right?' she asked, and her heart began to hammer away at the walls of her

18

chest, threatening to break its way through her rib cage. Something awful had happened.

'It's David.'

'David?' My God, Dad, what's happened to David?' she asked, trying to control the sudden fear twisting inside her and threatening to cut off her air. It was wartime. Every day somebody got terrible news about a loved one, but nothing could happen to her brother, David. David was pure, invulnerable, flawless. God had blessed him with beauty, intelligence, and grace. He was the most perfect human being on earth. Nothing bad could happen to him.

'Okinawa . . . he died at Okinawa. Come home, honey. We need you.' Her father's voice broke, and the conversation was over.

On the way back to her room, Sam felt exactly as she had the day she had fallen through the ice on the lake up in the mountains and was trapped in the freezing water. She felt as cold and near suffocation as she had felt then, beating her little ten-year-old hands on the crust of ice above her. She began to tremble, and although Cheryl put her arms around her to try to comfort her, it was more than two hours before Samara was able to stop shaking enough to tell her roommate what she had just heard.

With the help of her friends, Sam stumbled her way to Grand Central Station in New York. While she was waiting to board the train that would take her home to Los Angeles, she watched, glazed and dry-eyed, the servicemen in their uniforms passing before her. She had not yet shed a single tear, because if she cried then she would have to admit it was true, and it couldn't be. It had to be a terrible mistake. David could not be dead. It was simply not possible that her brother could have been killed without her having felt something at the moment of his death. She loved David more than anyone else in the world. Life could never be the same without him.

Emotionally numb, Sam at last boarded the crowded train, unaware that she had gotten a reservation in the Pullman car solely because of her father's influence. Because of the war effort, few citizens had priority over servicemen. All around her, people were huddling in groups, talking in hushed tones, many of them weeping. Locked in her own personal haze of misery, it did not penetrate to her consciousness until they reached Chicago, that the whole world was in mourning, not for David, but for the smiling President in a wheelchair, who had led them out of the depression and through most of a bloody war. David, with his whole life before him, and Franklin Delano Roosevelt, whose glories were past, were both gone. The President had died in Warm Springs, Georgia, only a few hours before.

Four days later, Samara stepped off the train and into her father's arms. Jules Silverman, head of Silverstone Studios, the most successful privately held studio in Hollywood, had suddenly lost control of his world. Destiny had taken over his life and usurped his power. He had lost his son.

Suddenly the elusive tears rose in her eyes and Samara finally was able to cry in the shelter of her father's arms. 'Oh, Daddy, what are we going to do without David?' she wailed, but she found scant comfort in the husky words dredged from the depths of his pain. 'We're going to carry on,' he said hoarsely. 'That's what he'd want us to do, Samara.'

The sound of her name as it passed his lips startled her. She couldn't remember her father ever using her given name. He had always called her Princess. In that moment,

Sam knew that her life would never be the same again. David was gone forever, as was the pampered and indulged daughter of a wealthy and powerful man. She was not a princess anymore; she had become the heir to a throne. From that day until he died, Jules Silverman never called his daughter anything but Samara.

3

1945

Tess watched her father's face closely as he sat next to the Philco console radio and twisted the dial until the unctuous tones of Gabriel Heatter floated from its speaker and filled the room with the unsettling news that the President of the United States had just died at Warm Springs, Georgia. She sat quietly and waited for her father to make some comment. It was so unlike him to listen to anything on the radio in silence. He was always talking back to the faceless voices emanating from the highly polished Philco radio in the living room of their big house on Lake Street, but not tonight, and she wondered why. He had often been critical of the administration of Franklin Delano Roosevelt. Why, then, did he seem so disturbed by the news of his death?

Her mother, too, was unusually quiet. Martha Godwin Marshall was a woman with much on her mind and a tongue to match. That was why George Milton Marshall, M.D., often retreated to his study, the only place he could be free of his garrulous wife's need to fill every available moment with conversation. One could hardly blame Martha, for her husband was a devoted family physician, on call at any hour of the day or night for his patients, a fact of life that his wife accepted with patience and forbearance. She just liked to make full use of every moment he was available to her. But not tonight. The details of the President's death were more important than anything else in her world that evening.

Finally, when they had heard the remarks of every

commentator and newscaster on all the networks, Dr Marshall turned off the radio and stood up. It was now almost ten o'clock, and Tess and her father still had not had their usual quiet conference in his study.

'It's late, George, Tess ought to be getting to bed – ' his wife began, but he lifted his hand to silence her. 'Martha, this is a historical night, and I don't think either of us is ready to retire. Why don't you make us a nice cup of hot Ovaltine and put in some of those marshmallows I saw in the cabinet, while Tess and I talk? She's almost fourteen years old now. I see no reason why she has to rush to bed so early every night.'

Tess tried to avoid her mother's eyes. Martha Marshall had always had complete control of her two elder daughters, who were now away at college, but Tess had never really been hers to command. George Marshall had been too busy building his practice to participate much in his first two children's upbringing, but when Tess came along, he was older and knew that she would be his last chance, for Martha could have no more children. He lavished attention on Tess and found in her a companion closer to him in spirit than any person he'd ever known. Tess was extraordinarily bright, and she loved to ask questions and debate ideas. He had taught her not to be afraid of defending her views, and in fact he encouraged her to be argumentative. Above all, he instilled in her a love of learning, a devotion to language, and a respect for her own abilities.

When they were alone in his study, Tess curled up in the big leather wing chair and he sat in his chair behind his desk. He fiddled with his pipe and tried to light it, but he never succeeded in keeping it lit longer than a minute or two.

'Dad, why are you so upset about Roosevelt's death?

You've been irked ever since he ran for a third term, and you were furious when he ran for a fourth,' she reminded him.

'Just because I think he made a mistake doesn't mean I hated him. Franklin Roosevelt was a great President for two terms, but he should have stepped down then. Nations get into trouble when they start considering their leaders to be indispensable. That's how dictators are made – not, mind you, that I think F. D. R. had such aspirations. But the preservation of freedom as we know it is based on an orderly transition of power. That's what has made our country different.'

'He's the only President I've ever known. It'll seem strange to say President Truman. Who is he, anyway?'

Dr Marshall leaned back and took a long draw on his pipe, but it had already gone out, as usual. She had decided years ago that her father just liked to clench it between his teeth because it made him look professorial and scholarly.

'That's what worries me, my dear. We choose vice-presidents solely on their ability to help win elections. What kind of Presidents they might make is never even considered. They become forgotten men until something like this happens, and now, God help us. The war isn't over yet, and I'll just bet that F. D. R. never told the little guy from Missouri a damned thing about what's going on. That's why I'm upset.'

Martha brought in a tray with three cups of hot Oval-tine, and the conversation turned to the war effort. Tess and her family had been only marginally inconvenienced by it. Because George was a doctor, he had plenty of gasoline coupons, and the grocer and the butcher were patients who took as good care of him as he did of them. More important, however, George and Martha had not sacrificed any children to the conflict. Martha Marshall's regret that she had never borne a son was soon turned to thanksgiving when she saw her friends hanging gold stars in their windows. Each night she said a prayer of gratitude that she would never have to send one of her children to die on a faraway battlefield.

When Tess went to bed that night, she wondered if life would be any different with a new man in the White House.

4

1948

Jules Silverman stood beside his wife in the hot sun on the campus at UCLA and watched his slender, dark-haired daughter move among her friends in her cap and gown and receive hugs and kisses and congratulations. He was proud of her graceful young beauty and even prouder that she was so bright. He tried not to think about how much she resembled David, but the comparison was inescapable, especially with her eyes, which were the same deep brown as her brother's, so dark that it was almost impossible to see the irises. She was tall and angularly thin, just as David had been, and her hands had the same long tapering fingers. In spite of his love and pride, she was also, unfortunately, an ever-present reminder of the loss of his son.

Three years had passed since David's death, but the hurt still ate at his insides like a cancer. Jules had returned to the practice of his faith, finding comfort in attending services at the temple regularly. He had also begun to keep the sabbath, because it pleased his wife. Reba had been his rock and his support, for she had found strength and solace in her firm belief that what had happened was part of God's plan. He wanted the practice of his religion to being him the blessing of faith too, but it eluded him. If He really existed and was a merciful God, why would He allow six million innocent people to be slaughtered? Why would He take away Jules's and Reba's only son?

Flushed with excitement, Sam returned to her parents' side and hugged them. She had graduated with honors in a business major, aware of the unspoken agreement that she would step into her brother's shoes and enter the movie business. Jules Silverman had no other heirs, and his partner, Abe Stone, had never married. Determined to fill the awful vacancy left in the family by her brother's death, Sam had studied hard and learned much about economics and accounting and had taken additional courses in business law. Now that school was behind her, she hoped to take a few weeks of rest before she started work at the studio. She still hadn't the slightest idea what she would be doing once she got there.

The limousine drove up the long driveway to the great gray stone house on top of the hill on Sunset Boulevard and proceeded past the circular driveway to the large terrace in the back. Gala pink-striped canopies dotted the broad expanse of lawn, and there were long tables covered with mammoth silver bowls of iced seafood and caviar. Platters of fresh fruit, salads, and pâtés abounded, as well as hot tables on which rested freshly roasted turkeys and barons of beef ready for carving. Large silver tubs were filled with mounds of ice and bottles of Dom Perignon. The war was over, Jules's only living child had just graduated from college, and he was honoring her accomplishment with the most lavish party money could buy.

Sam scooted upstairs to change into a white Irish lace dress, created for her by Edith Head as a graduation present. She ran a comb through her thick hair, curled under into a pageboy style, and pulled it back on one side with a spray of white orchids from their greenhouse. She stepped into a pair of high-heeled sandals, applied a bright red Max Factor lipstick to her full lips, and then checked her appearance in the tall three-way mirror in the corner of her dressing room. As she handed Samara a white lace handkerchief, her personal maid, Beldonna, smiled and said, 'You look like a young bride, Miss Samara.'

Sam smirked. 'This is probably as close as I'm ever going to get to a bridal gown, Bel. What kind of man would want to marry a woman who's going to run a movie studio?'

'Miss Samara, you have lots of boyfriends. You could have anybody you wanted.'

The smile on Sam's face dissolved. 'Quantity, Bel, is not the same as quality. I've never dated a guy who didn't want something from my dad. Never. They think because I'm pretty I'm also dumb. And the actors are the worst of all. They're so full of themselves they don't know what romance is. They not only expect me to hop into bed with them, they also expect me to feel flattered that they asked.'

Beldonna just smiled. 'Don't you worry. The right man will come along someday, and then you'll be singing a different tune.'

'Bel, I don't want a man, understand? I've got too many things to do before I can settle down to being somebody's little wifey. In fact, I just might never get married.' As she protested, Sam glanced through the open French windows to the garden below. 'Oh, God, there are people all over the place already. I better dash downstairs.'

Sam moved across the terrace slowly, accepting congratulations from the smartly dressed crowd. Everyone was there, even Clark Gable, who kissed her on the cheek and told her she was beautiful enough to be an actress. Unlike other young girls her age, Sam was not impressed by the King or any of the other stars, except Gregory Peck, whom she considered very special. His manner was gracious and gentlemanly as he took her hand and told her in his distinctively deep and velvety voice how lovely she looked.

'Thanks, Greg. You know, I haven't seen you to tell you how much I loved what you did in *Gentleman's Agreement*.'

'Thanks. It was a film I really wanted to make, and I'm proud of it.'

'What are you doing now?'

'It's been a busy year for me, but I'm thinking of doing *The Gunfighter*.'

The tall, deep-voiced young Howard Keel came over to greet her, and she asked him if he was learning to shoot for the part of Frank Butler in *Annie Get Your Gun*.

He laughed and pointed his gun-finger at her. 'It's a great role, and Berlin's songs are wonderful. Did you see the show on Broadway?'

'Sure. My favorite song was "You Can't Get a Man with a Gun."'

'Wrong song, Samara, my sweet. That's Betty Hutton's number, not mine.'

'I know, but I also love "The Girl That I Marry." I don't suppose you'd be interested in singing it, would you? Just for me?'

'My pleasure.' He bent down, kissed her on the cheek, and then strode to the bandstand, where he spoke briefly to the conductor before taking the microphone in his hand to begin the song. Not once throughout the entire rendition did his eyes stray from Sam's. Romantic as it was, she was not unduly impressed. Everybody who was anybody in the movie industry was in attendance, and she knew that any singer would sell his soul to perform for this crowd. Sam had simply given Howard his chance. Her father had taught her to do favors for people,

29

especially when it didn't cost anything. They were like money in the bank, he said, and someday you might have to make a withdrawal.

Sam slept in late the next morning, and when she awakened, Beldonna brought her a tray with fresh orange juice, a bowl of Grape Nuts with bananas, and black coffee. Sam loved champagne, and the night before, she had drunk more than she was used to drinking. She was sure that all the bubbles were still floating around in her head, because it felt as if it might drift right off her neck. She hoped she hadn't gotten too flip with her remarks, although she vaguely remembered telling somebody to go to hell. She had no idea who it was.

As she sipped her orange juice, Beldonna propped pillows behind her head. 'Bel, get me a couple of aspirin, will you?' she asked, massaging her forehead.

'There are two on the tray under your saucer,' the young maid said with a slight smirk. 'You better take them pretty quick. Your father is waiting downstairs for you to get up.'

Sam sat upright in bed and looked at the tiny jeweled clock on her bedside table. 'Good Lord, it's after twelve! What's he doing still at home?'

'Waiting for you. Better get moving. I've filled the tub and laid out your pink linen skirt and blouse.'

Sam pulled herself out of bed and tottered into the bathroom on shaky legs. Ugh, she felt awful.

Half an hour later, treading gingerly so as not to jostle her aching head, she walked into her father's study. Her mother was there too.

'What's cooking, Dad? It's not like you to stay away from the office,' she remarked, trying her best to sound chipper and bright.

'Samara, your mother and I have been talking about

30

your future. She feels that I have given you no options . . . that you really have no interest in the movie business. Is that true?'

'Mama! Why would you say a thing like that? I love the business,' Sam replied with indignation.

Reba looked down at her hands, and Sam could see the corners of her mouth tightening. Her mother was upset about something. Finally, choosing her words carefully, Reba expressed her feelings.

'I think it's time we brought things out into the open. Samara, my dear, you are not suited to run a big business like Silverstone. I know how much your father would like to pass the studio into the hands of one of his children, but I am against it. I want you to have a normal life – marriage, children, a fine home.'

'You think I can't handle it, right, Mama? Because I'm a girl.'

Reba nodded, her lips pressed tightly together in a thin line that etched wrinkles into the flesh around them.

Sam turned to her father. 'Is that what you think too, Daddy?'

'Samara, I think you can do anything you want to do, but I'm not sure it's fair to ask you to take on something that might bring you nothing but unhappiness,' he replied. 'This town isn't used to seeing women in executive offices, you know. They might make it rough for you.'

'Don't you think I know that? Besides, marriage isn't an option for me yet. I haven't met anyone I'd want to spend my life with. So let's make a deal. How about letting me start at the studio to see if I like it? I promise that if something better comes along, or if I'm at all unhappy, I'll let you know. What do you say?'

Jules agreed immediately. 'I'll buy that, sweetheart. What do you say, Reba?'

'Just as long as you feel free to leave it the minute you're not enjoying yourself, honey. This can be a very tough business, and I don't want to see my sweet little girl turned into a hard businesswoman,' Reba said softly, nervously twisting her lace handkerchief. Reba rarely commented on her husband's work, but when she did, he always listened. He not only loved and cherished his wife, he respected her opinions.

Jules sighed with relief. The idea that the studio he had so lovingly built and tended for most of his lifetime might pass into strange and unappreciative hands worried him. In spite of her sex, he knew that Samara had the guts and the toughness to carry on, but he was concerned that she might not have the will and the desire. He just hoped Reba was wrong and that a woman didn't have to have a home and a family to be happy, because it would be damned near impossible for Samara to handle both a marriage and this career.

'Everybody thinks making movies is all glitter and glamour, but the truth is, it's a lot like watching cement harden,' Jules began. 'It takes time and a lot of hard work and effort. Next week Tom Buffum starts shooting *Storm in the Sky* on location at Edwards Air Force Base, and I've arranged for you to sit in with his script girl, Shirley Pinkston, and learn how it's done. When you're ready, you can have that job on another film. The script girl is right there on top of everything, and you can learn a lot. What do you say?'

Sam did not let her disappointment show on her face. Several of her friends were sailing to Europe on the *Queen Elizabeth* for a few weeks, and she had hoped to go with them, but that, of course, would not be possible now. 'Sounds great,' she responded, feigning enthusiasm.

Ever since her brother had died, Samara had found it impossible to deny her parents anything.

Jules got up from his chair and put his arm around her. 'Good girl. I'll call Tom and tell him you'll be there. Well, gotta get cracking . . . the day's almost shot and I've got a lot to do. Reba, don't forget that I've invited some folks over for dinner tonight.'

Reba sighed. 'Jules, dear, the staff is exhausted after cleaning up from last night's party. I know Martin is the best butler in town, but he's getting tired, and if we're not careful, we'll lose him.'

'Don't let him kerflummox you, Reba. Just raise his salary and see how fast he gets rested,' he proclaimed, striding into the hallway, where the butler was waiting with a panama hat in his hand. Jules set it on his balding head at a jaunty angle and marched out the door to his waiting limousine. That daughter of his was something, he thought as the big car pulled out of the driveway. She never failed him.

33

5

Tess opened the mail excitedly. There were two letters
for her, one from Vassar and the other from the University of Illinois, both accepting her application for admission. She squeezed her eyes shut and let out a yelp of
triumph, which brought her mother racing into the hall to
find out what was wrong.

'Mom, I got accepted at both places,' she said, waving
the letters under her mother's unimpressed nose.

'Well, I would think so. After all, you have a straight-
A average, and you scored in the top five percent in the
entrance exams, why in the world wouldn't they want
you?'

'But, Mom, it's tough to get into any university nowadays. The schools are flooded with men on the GI bill.'

'Not at Vassar, darling. That's a girls' college.'

'True, but I'm not going there anyway, you know that.
I just applied because that's where my friends Ruth and
Brenda are going,' she answered, and her mother
detected a note of wistfulness in her voice.

'And you want to go with them, don't you, honey?'

'Sometimes I do . . . sometimes I don't. Dad says he
thinks I'm too young to leave home, and he's probably
right.'

Martha frowned. Her husband had no right to dictate
to Tess the way he did, especially since he had all but
ignored his two elder daughters, Marie and Phyllis, both
of whom he had allowed to attend colleges away from

34

home. Tess needed to get out from under his heavy-handed influence. She had become entirely too serious and bookish, and it worried her mother that she had so few dates. She was pretty enough, but she seemed to have no flair for flirting or getting a young man interested in her.

'Well, I intend to talk to your father about this, honey. If you want to go to Vassar with your friends, there's no reason for you to stay here.'

When she brought the subject up at dinner that evening, Tess herself scuttled it. 'Dad's right, Mom. In the long run, I probably should stay here. The English-lit department is first-rate, and I may have a better crack at the graduate program if I do my undergraduate work here.'

Martha Marshall did not retreat gracefully. 'Good Lord, George, she's not eighteen yet and you've already got her life mapped out for her.'

Dr Marshall smiled with satisfaction and got up from his chair, his pipe in his hand. 'Come on, everybody, let's go out and celebrate tonight. How about a movie?'

'What's playing?' Tess asked.

'*Sitting Pretty*, which all my patients are raving about. It stars Clifton Webb,' he replied.

'Who's he?' Martha asked doubtfully.

'That stage actor from *Laura*, but it's a comedy, and Robert Young is in it too. Come on, let's go,' he insisted.

'What about dessert?' Martha asked.

'Let's skip it and treat ourselves to some candy at the show,' Tess suggested.

'I prefer popcorn myself,' George replied. 'Now, hurry up, Martha. You don't want to miss any of Robert Young's scenes, do you?'

35

Martha made a face at him. 'And you don't want to miss any of Maureen O'Hara's either, now do you?'

George lifted his eyebrows in mock surprise. 'Oh, is she in it?'

'You knew darn well she was in it before you suggested we go to the movies, George. But I don't mind. She really is a beautiful woman.'

Tess watched her mother and father teasing each other as they often did, and she wondered how they behaved when they were alone together in their bedroom. Her father was a loving and affectionate man, but he never seemed to want to talk much to her mother. Whenever Martha tried to get him involved in a conversation about something in the newspaper or on the radio, he always brushed her off, yet he was eager to talk about almost anything with Tess. It was strange, Tess thought, putting on her coat. She'd certainly hate to be married to a man who wasn't the least bit interested in anything she had to say, but her mother seemed to be happy enough. Marriage was a strange relationship. She couldn't imagine ever giving up her independence and letting a man dictate what she would do with her life.

6

Sam was sitting beside Shirley Pinkston watching her lay out the pages of her notebook in preparation for the flying scenes in *Storm in the Sky*. The United States Air Force was giving the production cooperation and support because now that the war was over, Congress was cutting back drastically on military funds, and the services were scrambling to get their share of much smaller allocations. A little publicity for the Air Force in a big studio picture couldn't hurt them a bit.

'The job of a script girl is to keep track of everything that goes on in a scene and make notes about it. See, you put the footage here . . . and here. The last thing the director wants is for the camera to run out of film in the middle of a take, especially in a big production scene like the ones that will be shot today,' Shirley explained.

'Is that all?' Sam asked ruefully.

'Not by a long shot. You have to make detailed notes about how the actors are dressed and what they're doing, especially if they're holding props, so that a guy won't have a hammer in his left hand on one setup and in his right on another, see?'

'Sounds pretty complicated to me,' a deep voice said into Sam's ear, startling her. She turned around and found herself staring into the deepest, most joyfully blue eyes she had ever before seen, eyes set in a roguishly handsome face capped by dark brown hair so curly that even a short crew haircut could not straighten it.

'Oh, hi,' she said to the smiling young man in a flier's

suit hovering over her. 'It does seem like a difficult job, doesn't it?'

'What a pretty lady you are,' he said softly into her ear.

Sam was startled at the sudden rush of feeling his words and his physical nearness precipitated in her. Her cheeks flushed, and she felt nervous and ill-at-ease. 'Why, thank you,' she replied, and although she groped for something witty and bright to say, she could think of nothing. What was there about this young man that made her feel awkward and stumbling? All her life she had been surrounded by the world's great lovers, matinee idols who teased and complimented her, and she had always been able to return their banter easily, but this man was like none of them. He radiated masculinity, but with a manner that did not seem to take itself too seriously.

'Now, tell me your name, lovely lady, so that I can have it on my lips while I perform the death-defying stunts your director has asked me to do, all for the greater glory of Hollywood and the United States Air Force,' he said, his words teasing but his eyes fixed meaningfully on hers.

'Samara,' she replied softly, but before she could tell him her last name, he slapped himself on the forehead and exclaimed in mock astonishment, 'Glory be, my favorite saint . . . I should have known! Now, promise me, St Samara, that you will be here when . . . and if – I return. These are very dangerous things I'm going to do, you know. You wouldn't be inclined to maybe give these lips a kiss good-bye, just in case . . . ah, I can see by your eyes, you wouldn't. Well, we'll just have to have dinner together tonight at the officers' club. We'll drink spirits and dine and whisper our innermost thoughts and yearnings. You're not a married girl, now, are you?'

Sam shook her head mutely. What was there to say to this impertinently attractive man? No, he wasn't just attractive, he was downright irresistible. She had all she could do to keep herself from falling into his arms then and there.

He put his hands together and looked heavenward. 'Thank you, God, I knew you wouldn't have sent this lovely creature to me with a wedding band on her finger,' he murmured loud enough for everyone to hear. He reached his hand toward her and ran his fingertips lightly along the curve of her chin. 'Now, if anybody asks you, tell them that Captain Robert Mulhare has claimed you for his own.'

He turned and walked jauntily toward the P-80 that was being rolled out of a hangar.

'Watch out, honey,' Shirley remarked, 'that one's going to be tough to handle.'

Arousing herself from his spell, Sam laughed self-consciously, trying to toss off the girlish awkwardness she had felt while Captain Mulhare's eyes were fixed on hers.

'After some of the lotharios I've encountered in Hollywood, this one will be a cinch,' she remarked offhandedly, but in truth she was far less confident than she pretended to be. Captain Mulhare did not know that her father was Jules Silverman, and even if he did, she suspected he wouldn't give a damn.

That night the officers' club was packed. They were having a lobster and champagne dinner, and everyone was there, including the film crew. Bob Mulhare kept his hand on Sam's arm as he guided her through the crowd, introducing her to everyone as Samara, his patron saint. It was a gentle joke and accepted as such. Bob seemed to know everyone, but most important, everyone seemed to know and like him.

When, at last, they were sitting alone at a small table

he had apparently arranged to have for himself, Sam finally found her voice.

'That was spectacular flying you did today. The director's thrilled with the footage they shot.'

'Good. I showed off a bit, knowing you were watching . . . and also hoping that the director would be impressed enough to ask me to stay with the production for a while and be near you. What do you think?'

'About what?'

'Would you like to have me around for a while?'

Sam looked up into his eyes and was reminded of the long hours she had spent aboard her father's yacht, lying on the prow and staring down into the dark blue waters of the ocean, imagining the wonders just below that were too deep for her to see. There was much more to Bob Mulhare than the joking fellow he played.

'I'd like that very much,' she replied seriously.

Bob covered her hand with his and said softly, 'Tell me your thoughts . . . not just now, not just this moment. I want to know everything you've ever thought about anything in this world,' but the words spoken between them had no substance, no reality, no meaning. All that seemed to matter that night was the physical and spiritual presence they felt in each other. Perhaps if they had listened to the words they were saying, if they had found out more about each other, the fascinating spell that gathered them in might not have been so intense, but they were beyond reality. The murmured words were just sounds in the night, fluttering about them like petals in the breeze, perfuming the air, heightening their sensitivity and nourishing their growing desire for each other.

Never in her life had Sam been affected so completely by another person's sexuality. Although she had occasionally teetered on the edge of consent in the back seat of a car during college out of curiosity, she had never before felt an urge strong enough to make her forget the dangers of becoming pregnant or being considered an easy conquest. There had even been times when she wondered if perhaps she had been born lacking the powerful emotion that drove so many of her friends to risk everything for the moment. The sensations aroused by Bob Mulhare, however, were quickening her and coloring the virginity of her emotions with a consuming passion.

As they sipped the cheap champagne and picked at the overcooked lobsters, their bodies moved closer and closer together. Soon his arm was around her shoulders, and he was brushing his lips softly against her cheek. Sam felt herself responding, aching to open herself to him, wanting to gather him into her and never let him go.

On the dance floor, with their bodies pressed close together, the unspoken desire gained momentum, and they found themselves carried along on a silent promise of ecstasy. Their overwhelming desire to experience and possess one another carried them out of the club. Standing beside his car, Bob spoke the first words: 'Where should we go?'

As Sam turned to look up at him, he pulled her close to him and their lips touched only briefly. 'I don't dare kiss you here, Samara my love, because I'm afraid that once I start, I won't be able to stop.'

'The crew is quartered at the Cloud Motel on the highway . . . I have my own room,' she said softly, knowing that she had just made a contract that could not be broken.

He smiled and nodded. They got into his green Nash and drove to the motel.

He had been right. Once they were alone inside the room and he kissed her, there was no way that either of them could have halted the urgency of their passion. Samara felt as if she had been caught up in a storm of emotions over which she had no control, nor did she seek any. Between them there was no lover and loved, for they both gave and received in an equal exchange of hunger and thirst. The initial softness of their kisses, the gentle stroking of the fingers over each other's bodies, soon gave way to demand and fulfillment. When they could no longer hold themselves back, she opened herself to him and he pressed himself toward her. At first, her body resisted, but with both of them straining toward each other eagerly, their bodies demanding to be joined and satisfied, her virginity gave way. In spite of the sudden pain, Sam felt exultant that they were one, and her body responded in a climax in which Bob shared. Breathlessly they held each other tightly, their hearts beating against each other, their breaths coming in gasps of release and joy.

When the passionate moment began to settle into bliss, Bob brushed his lips across her face and kissed the tears that ran from her eyes down her temples and into her hair.

'Good God, love, you saved yourself for me,' he whispered.

'Somehow I must have known you were there and that someday we'd be together, she whispered, clinging to him. When they separated and she sat up, they were both startled to see a large red stain on the sheets, and there was fresh blood smeared on her thighs.

Suddenly Bob reached out, took her arm, and pulled her to him again. Softly he kissed her and then whispered teasingly into her ear, 'I believe you, darling. You don't have to overdo it.'

They kissed again, their mouths searching and exploring each other's, and it was soon evident that their bodies demanded to be joined again. 'Let's see what it's like now that I know how it's done,' Sam said softly.

'Not till you promise to marry me, my darling St Samara. After tonight, no other woman could ever possibly interest me. Will you . . . as soon as possible?'

Because his lips were covering hers, Sam agreed without words. In the years to come, she never regretted her answer in spite of the heartbreak her marriage to Bob Mulhare brought to her family and to herself. As she lay in her lover's arms, Sam was utterly certain that here was where her future would begin, and she would never look back. She belonged to Bob Mulhare for all of eternity, as he belonged to her.

7

Chili Lou Harris made a quick check of her appearance in the scratched and cracked mirror in the rest room at Handy's Café in San Antonio. A glance at the clock reminded her that the allotted five-minute toilet break for waitresses was about up, so she quickly pulled a tube of Flame-Glo lipstick from the pocket of her green-and-white starched uniform to add a little color to her full pouty lips. No sooner had she smeared her mouth with the bright orange grease and pursed her lips to even the color than she changed her mind. She went into the toilet stall, pulled a square of the harsh, slick paper from its dispenser, and wiped her mouth clean. There. Better, much better. The lipstick had left enough of a residue of color to satisfy her. Pushing a wandering curl back into the hairnet, which she was required by law to wear while serving food, she tidied the starched white handkerchief in her breast pocket. One more item needed attention. Reaching into her Hollywood Maidenform brassiere, Chili pulled each of her full breasts up so that her already considerable cleavage was in even greater evidence.

Except for the tiny chip on her fingernail polish, she had done the best she could. If Captain Gamal Shaheen didn't come through tonight, she was in big trouble. She had been dating him for two months now, restricting him to heavy petting, making it clear that she was a virgin waiting for marriage, but her resistance was getting low.

For the first time in her life, Chili was using her abundant sexuality to get something for herself – a husband. All her life, she had given sex away, not counting her stepfather, of course, who had taken it from her forcibly by threats and coercion. She had given it to her first boyfriend and his friends and every other man who expected to be paid for a cheap meal or a movie, but not anymore. Even if she never screwed another man for the rest of her life, she was finished being an open bottle ready for every man to cork with his cock. Finished. Period. Exclamation point. And all because of Jimmyjohn. Dear Jimmyjohn Jensen, her first cousin on her mother's side, had come into the grill for a meal one day, and they recognized one another right away even though they hadn't been together since they were just kids in Whitewater.

Poor Jimmyjohn. He'd been almost blown to bits in the Battle of the Bulge. He was blind in one eye and had lost his right leg, but he still had his sense of humor and more brains than any man she'd ever met. He was special, Jimmyjohn was, because even with all his problems, he didn't feel one bit sorry for himself. He was proud of his medals and the sacrifice he had made for his country. Lucky for her, he'd come to San Antonio to live instead of going back home. But the poor guy was always in a lot of pain.

He and Chili hit it off so well that he started eating dinner at Handy's several times a week. Long after she was off work, they'd sit in the back booth and talk and drink gallons of coffee. Jimmyjohn made her feel good about herself, telling her she was the most beautiful woman he had ever seen and that she shouldn't be throwing herself away on the scum she was dating. 'Save yourself, Chili Lou. A guy won't buy a cow if he can get milk for free,' he told her. 'You can't hook a man by bein' free and easy. Make the asshole pay.'

'I'm not a hooker, Jimmyjohn,' she had protested, but he just hooted and wagged his finger at her.

'Don't be a dumbbell, Chili. All gals are hookers one way or another. That's the way God made things. Women got it, men want it. There wouldn't be no such thing as marriage if it were up to men. Smarten up.'

Chili gave Jimmyjohn's ideas a lot of thought and figured maybe he was right. She'd give it a try. What the hell. She didn't have anything to lose that she hadn't already lost many times over.

So Chili had been celibate for almost four months now, and although a few of the guys pushed her around because she wouldn't come across like they expected, life had become a whole hell of a lot easier. She didn't have to worry about getting pregnant anymore or catching syphilis, and she didn't miss the sex, not much, anyway. Maybe that was because she had Jimmyjohn to talk to, and she didn't need someone groping her in the dark to keep from being lonely anymore. Then, just like Jimmyjohn said he would, Mr Right came into the grill one night, big as life.

She knew the minute she saw him. She had always been a sucker for men with dark eyes and black hair, and Gam had them both. He was tall, real slim, but strong, and he had a nose that was royal, pure and simple. Somebody once told her the size of a man's nose was a key to the size of something else important. He was soft-spoken and gentlemanly, and to ice the cake, he was a captain in the Air Force.

With Jimmyjohn coaching her every step of the way, Chili began her campaign. Just to be safe, Jimmyjohn had checked at Randolph Air Force Base to make sure the guy wasn't married. Then Jimmyjohn insisted that she start taking better care of herself. She sent her uniforms to the laundry so they would be starched and done up right, and she wore a clean one every day. He made her stop wearing any makeup on her face except for a little powder on her nose and the tiniest bit of rouge on her cheeks.

'You not only need to look like a virgin, Chili, but you gotta start actin' like one. And your story is that you had to quit college when your mama died and go to work to support yourself, got it?'

'And just what kind of college studyin' was I supposed to be doin', Jimmyjohn? Nobody would believe that baloney. I quit high school in the tenth grade,' she protested.

'You was studyin' home economics, sugar. Learnin' how to cook and clean and sew and make some lucky fella a good wife . . . that's what you were studyin',' Jimmyjohn said with a chuckle, taking a swig from the bottle of beer he brought in with him, wrapped in a brown bag.

'Nobody's gonna believe it. Why, if I ever walked inside a college, the roof'd probably fall in.'

'Trust me, babydoll. I had a girlfriend who was studyin' that stuff back in Missouri when I was stationed at Jefferson Barracks. Now, did you get those lace panties I told you to get?'

'Sure did. I got 'em on. I bought two pairs, and I been washin' 'em out every night just like you told me.'

'Well, be sure you keep 'em on, but it won't hurt to let him get a teeny-weeny peek, okay? Maybe even a little feel. But that's all, understand?'

And that's all Gam had ever gotten – a little peek and a little feel. It hadn't been easy to torture him like that, but she kept resisting because he was treating her nicer than any man had ever treated her before. Every time they'd come close to actually doing it, she'd pull back and

47

say, just as Jimmyjohn had coached her, that she promised her dying mama that she'd save herself for the man she married.

It was getting close to quitting time now. The dinner rush was over, and there were just a few stragglers at the tables sucking on their coffee cups. Where in God's name was Gam? He always arrived in time to have a Coke while he waited for her to get off work. As the time passed, she fretted. Jimmyjohn wasn't sitting in his usual booth in the back because he was home in bed having one of his bad days. She needed him to convince her one more time that what she was doing was absolutely necessary.

Everything seemed just fine when Gam was around, telling her how beautiful she was and how much he loved her, but her courage failed when he was late, and guilt overwhelmed her. It just didn't seem right to hold out on Gam, the one person who treated her nicer than any man ever had, especially since in the past she'd spread her legs for so many other jerks who treated her like dirt. She was also afraid he might just never show up again. Suppose Gam had gotten fed up and tired of waiting? Maybe she had pushed him too far. Oh, God, where was Jimmyjohn now that she needed someone to shore up her determination?

The last patron got up and left, and Handy put up the sign that said the table area was closed for the night. It was almost ten o'clock.

'Where's your boyfriend, toots?' Handy asked in a voice that had been ground to gravel by forty years of booze and tobacco.

Glumly Chili wiped up the tables and replied, 'Just late, I guess.'

'Yeah, well, you were lucky he stayed around longer than most. Must like that nooky of yours.'

48

Chili lashed out with a bravado she did not feel.

'He's comin' back, Handy! You just wait and see. We're gonna get married! So don't go makin' any of those nasty remarks about him and me.'

The round-bodied, bald, crimson-faced man turned to look at her in astonishment. 'Jesus, Chili, what've you been smokin'? Christ, that guy's an officer. Why the hell would he want to marry you?'

'Because I'm pretty and I've got a great body . . . and I'm a nice girl!' she flashed back.

'Nice girl? Are you crazy or somethin'? You're a cunt, Chili . . . that's all you ever were, and that's all you'll ever be. Who you trying to kid?'

Although his words were vicious, his tone of voice was matter-of-fact. He had simply told the truth as he saw it, but Chili reacted furiously. She picked up the heavy glass sugar pourer and threw it at his head. Although she missed him, the missile sailed across the counter and smashed into the row of glasses on the shelf in front of the mirror, splattering sugar and sending lethal shards of glass rocketing everywhere.

Handy too exploded in fury. He grabbed an empty Coke bottle, smashed it on the edge of the sink, and turned toward her waving the jagged edge of the glass.

'You little bitch! I'm going to carve up that pretty white skin of yours so bad that no man will ever even look at you again without puking!' he screamed, advancing on her, infuriated at the mess she'd made of his grill.

Chili was in a panic. They were all alone, and she knew that Handy meant what he said. She'd seen him lose his temper before, and he was mean when he was mad. He relished beating up unruly customers. If he said he was going to cut her, he would slice her to ribbons.

Shaking and weeping, she begged him to let her go as

49

she edged away, trying to change positions so that he was not between her and the door. She knew she didn't have much of a chance to escape, but she had to try or she'd be dead or wish she was.

'Please, Handy, I'm sorry . . . honest to God, I am. I'll clean everything up, and I'll pay for it . . . don't hurt me, Handy, please.'

But Handy did not hear. He only knew that he was going to pay her back. No dumb broad was going to get away with breaking up his place. He was not moving fast. There was no need to hurry. Nobody was going to stop him. What a mess she was – tears running down her face, and her body contorted with terror. As he came into striking range, he lashed out with the jagged bottle, but she lifted her arms to protect her face, and the sharp heavy glass sliced through her right forearm. Blood spurted from the deep gash, and she screamed in pain and terror. Instinctively she dropped to the floor and coiled her body tightly into a fetal position so that the blows would fall on her back, and that enraged him even more. He wanted to carve up her face, destroy that simpering pretty smile, fix her good. He grabbed the back of her collar and pulled her to her feet as she whimpered and wept hysterically. Her fear fed his fury. He waved the bottle under her face, trying to get a clean stroke.

Suddenly he released his hold and she dropped back to the floor. Curling herself up again, she heard another voice and some scuffling, but she was afraid to look up and see what was going on. The noise became louder. There were more men in the room now, and they were shouting and fighting and swearing and cursing, but after a while the noise settled down. Someone's hand took her arm and tried to lift her up, but she resisted, keeping her face and her legs tucked tightly together. Even had she

50

wanted to open up, she couldn't have, she was so frozen in terror.

'Baby, it's me, Gamal. It's okay. He can't hurt you anymore. Come on, now. You're bleeding. We've got to get you to the hospital.'

The soft, loving tone of his voice at last traveled from her ears to her arms and legs, and to her soul. She looked up and saw the face of the man she loved and wanted more than anything else in the world.

Gently Gamal picked her up and carried her to his car. Although she was told later that they had passed several young airmen who were sitting on Handy and holding him down while they waited for the police to arrive, she remembered nothing of it. All she remembered was being cradled in Gam's arms and feeling safe, really safe, for the first time in her life.

Because she had lost a lot of blood, they kept her in the hospital that night under sedation. It took fifty-six stitches to close the gash in her arm, and when the doctor finished, he warned her that there was probably some nerve damage.

'You're never going to play at Wimbledon, honey, but with a little therapy your arm will be usable but pretty weak,' the nice young intern in the emergency room had told her.

Chili didn't complain. She was grateful that the bottle had not connected with her face. She thanked the doctor sleepily and asked if he'd see that Jimmyjohn was called and told where she was. His was the first call she received when she awakened the next morning.

After she had told him as much of the story as she could remember, Jimmyjohn asked, 'Have you told Prince Charming what the fight with Handy was all about?'

51

'I don't think so. I was too out of it last night.'

'Good. Now, here's what you tell your knight in shining armor. Tell him that Handy attacked you and tried to rape you. When you fought him off, throwing the sugar jar at him, he tried to kill you in a rage. Understand?'

'I can't do that, Jimmyjohn. The nurse told me that the police were waiting for me to give them a statement. Handy's in the pokey.'

'He should be. The bastard tried to kill you.'

'But I can't lie under oath, and I can't very well tell the police one story and Gam another, can I?'

'Okay, okay. Let me think a minute . . . Look, what's more important to you, marrying Gam or putting Handy away?'

The question shocked her. 'Jesus, Jimmyjohn, do I have to make a choice?'

'Yep, you sure as hell do. If you try to nail Handy, he'll haul every joe who ever had a meal in his café to testify that you're the neighborhood mattress.'

The cold reality of it all sent a chill through her. 'I don't want to hear that,' she protested feebly.

'Nobody ever chooses to be born a woman, honeypie. That's just the way things are. You haven't got much time to decide.'

'What'll I say, Jimmyjohn? What do I say?' she asked as tears streamed down her face.

'Tell the police it was all a misunderstanding. Handy had been drinkin' from that bottle he keeps under the counter and he got fresh and you started the fracas by throwing the sugar jar at him. Say you don't think he really meant to hurt you and you want 'em to let 'im go.'

'Gam will think I'm crazy. He risked his life to save me from that animal! I'll lose him, Jimmyjohn. I just know it.'

'No, you won't, either, 'cause you're gonna tell lover-boy a different story. You're gonna tell him that Handy's been pestering you for a long time, trying to get into your pants, but you needed the job and just kept joshing him and putting him off. Say you're afraid that if you don't let Handy off the hook, he'll send some of his friends after Gam as well as you. You don't dare press charges because you're afraid Gam'll get hurt. Tell 'im that Handy's got friends in the rackets, and you've heard him brag about havin' people knocked off.' Jimmyjohn was relishing the story. He had always loved making up schemes and telling stories.

'Will he believe that stuff? Handy hasn't got any friends in the rackets. He's always getting into trouble with that temper of his. It'll never work.'

'Baby, I know it will, especially when you tell him that you even have to go back to work at the café because you need the job so bad.'

'Jesus Christ, are you nuts, Jimmyjohn? I won't ever go near that place again!'

'Calm yourself down, I know that. Let's just hope Gam has a better idea. Now, you got it straight?'

'I think so, Jimmyjohn. But it's not gonna be easy,' she replied uncertainly.

'Life's just a big game, kiddo. Last night you almost died, but today you're alive and kickin'. Believe me, I know exactly how it feels. We all get some scars, but that can't keep you from tryin' to get as much outta life as you can. Look at me. You've still got both your eyes and your legs, as well as the best-lookin pair of tits in town.'

'I love you, Jimmyjohn. You're the only friend I've ever had.'

Chili Lou did just as her cousin had advised her and was startled that nobody, but nobody, questioned her about it. Instead of being called a whore, she was praised by one and all for being a compassionate, forgiving lady, and just as Jimmyjohn said it would, everything went perfectly. Two weeks after she got out of the hospital, she and Gamal were married by a justice of the peace, with Jimmyjohn in his wheelchair as their only attendant.

Although her new husband had a few suspicions about her virginity, he never questioned her, and their wedding night was a triumph. When he went to sleep that night, Gam thought of himself as the world's greatest stud. God, he'd never known a woman could have that many orgasms. It would have been intimidating if she hadn't kept thanking him for giving her so much pleasure.

8

After their first night of lovemaking and discovery of one another, Samara and Bob slept soundly in each other's arms, but they awakened late and had to hurry from bed to get ready to report to the set.

Bob followed her into the bathroom, reluctant to let her out of his sight for even a moment. 'At least we can shower together . . . the rest will have to wait until we've finished our work,' he said, and then asked huskily, 'Would you like me to wash your back, Miss . . .? My God!' he exclaimed, slapping his forehead in exaggerated chagrin. 'I've asked you to marry me, and I'm not sure, but I don't think I ever really heard your full name. Now, is that a good one! Are you going to tell me, dearie, or should we just skip over it altogether and call you Samara Mulhare, which you'll soon be?'

A premonition of danger caused Sam to hesitate briefly before answering him. Bob was quite obviously a Christian and she was a Jew, and marriage between Jews and Christians was frowned on by both faiths.

'Silverman . . . my father is Jules Silverman,' she said softly, her back turned to him as he gently lathered the flesh between her shoulder blades.

'Jules Silverman . . .' Bob mused. 'Where have I heard that name before?'

'He's the head of Silverstone Studios,' Sam answered, wondering how much her father's position in life would affect him, hoping desperately that it would make no difference.

Suddenly he took her arm and pulled her around to face him. 'Good God, girl, don't tell me now that you're rich?' he asked accusingly.

Sam looked up into his perceptive blue eyes and winced. Why couldn't her father have been a grocer or a shoemaker? She nodded and replied, 'My father is.'

'Well, well, we're even then. So is mine. Old Dad's a successful lawyer, and Mom's one of the Connor Department Store heirs. Danny, my older brother, did his tour in the Navy and got out of the service right after VJ day. He's heading up the big store in Chicago already. They keep trying to lure me back home to join him, but I love the Air Force and flying planes, and I can't do that in a department store.'

As he spoke, his eyes traveled down from hers to the circle of suds he was tracing around her left nipple. 'Dear old Dad was proud as punch of me when I was the hero flyboy defending the nation during the war; now he thinks of me as an adolescent ass. Making money has always been very important to him, although God knows it's never bought him any real happiness. He can't seem to understand why I prefer doing something I enjoy to being rich.' Bob looked into her eyes and saw that they were glistening with tears. Sam leaned into him and put arms around his wet, tightly muscled waist. She was happier than she had ever thought she could be.

Bob slid his hands down her slippery back and cupped each of her buttocks in his hands as he whispered, 'Consequently, I'm a man of rather modest means. They don't pay captains very much. Do you mind?'

Sam was exultant. Bob was not interested in her father or his money or position! He didn't care about any of that. There was only one other hill to climb.

'Bob, I'm Jewish.'

He kissed her lightly on the lips as he ran his soapy fingers from the point of her chin down to the cleft of her mons. 'Do tell, and I'm Catholic, so it seems we both believe in Him, don't we? And wasn't it nice of the Good Lord to help us find each other?' he said with a smile that signaled they were going to be late to work that day, very late. 'Ah, dear, then I suppose you're the only St Samara, mmh?'

'I would think so. Samara is a Hebrew name. It means "guarded by God,"' she replied huskily, her lips moving closer to his, her body trembling as she swayed it sensually against his, her slippery, soapy softness encapsulating his imposing hardness.

'It's the most beautiful name I ever heard . . . Samara, Samara,' he whispered, his warm breath caressing her lips.

'Bob, what will our parents say?'

'When the screaming and the shouting and the wailing are all over, they'll settle down and accept the inevitable,' he whispered, his voice hoarse with desire. 'They'll have to.'

'Bob, I can't convert to Catholicism,' she said faintly, her limbs already beginning to grow weak with the longing his wandering fingers were arousing deep inside her.

'I wouldn't dare ask a saint as lovely as you to change a thing. You're perfect just as you are.'

'It isn't going to be easy, Bob,' she whispered as his arms enfolded her and his body pressed into hers.

'Nothing between us can ever be hard, sweetheart, except this,' he murmured, lifting her body so that he could slip easily inside her.

They were half an hour late reporting to the set, but everyone was so titillated by the obvious electricity between them that no comment was made, although there were a lot of significant glances and raised eyebrows.

They spent the next three weeks working on the film during the day, experiencing each other insatiably throughout the nights that never seemed long enough. Since the set was in a constant buzz of gossip about the romance, the word eventually made its way back to the main offices of Jules Silverman, who was not pleased. In fact, news of his daughter's romantic dalliance could not have come at a worse time in his life. The House Un-American Activities Committee had subpoenaed everyone in Hollywood some months before to testify about Communist affiliations, and now he was unable to stem the tide of fear it was engendering at the top level of all the studios. He found himself forbidden to hire some of the most talented people in the industry, and although his gut instincts told him to resist, to refuse to capitulate, he was afraid to try to fight them alone. The disease of fear had affected everyone, and he just couldn't take a chance on having everything that he'd worked so hard to build collapse under him. He had tried to convince his colleagues to stick together and resist, but he had failed. There was a hysterical stampede to be pro-American and anti-Communist, and it frightened him. This grand country whose citizens and government had pulled together in a magnificent effort to defeat the Axis powers had now turned inward and declared war on its own people.

Everything was in a mess, and Jules released his fury and frustration on his daughter for cheapening herself and becoming a target for gossip. He was determined that she would someday be the first woman to head a large movie studio, and he knew that she would need all the respect she could get to pull it off successfully.

There was only one thing to do: get her home and away from the pernicious influence that had caused her to behave so recklessly. He called the producer, and over his protests, ordered him to finish up and return to Los Angeles within the week.

When Sam came home, however, she brought Bob, and they confronted her father together.

'Dad, this is Captain Bob Mulhare, the man I love and plan to marry. We've come to ask your blessing,' she blurted out immediately, all of the carefully worded phrases she had practiced evaporating under her father's grim scrutiny.

Jules was accustomed to manipulating people with ease, but her abruptness and candor caught him completely off guard and he reacted savagely and out of character. 'Are you crazy, Samara? You hardly know this man!'

'I know that I love him, Dad. I'm a grown woman now. You've always trusted my instincts about people, and on this you should certainly have faith in my judgment. After all, it's my life we're talking about. Believe me, I know exactly what I'm doing.' Her voice had taken on an edge even harsher than her father's.

Bob interceded in an effort to slow the mounting hostilities. 'Please, sir, for Samara's sake, give yourself a chance to know me before you say anything more. I love your daughter more than life itself, and I promise you that I'll love and protect her as long as I live.' He paused, and there was a tense silence. Jules's eyes and those of his daughter were locked in anger and defiance. From the moment the couple had walked into the room, Jules could not being himself to look at the man who posed such an enormous threat to him and his family.

Bob continued, but his tone became less ameliorating

and more forceful as he sensed the hatred directed toward him.

'Please, sir, you know nothing about me. You've raised a beautiful, intelligent daughter, and you ought to have faith in her and trust her. We love each other dearly.'

'I know all about you that I need to know,' Jules said, finally turning his hostile gaze on the handsome young man before him. 'You love her, but you seduced her and made her look like a pushover in front of people who work for me.'

'We should have waited, sir, I know that, but we didn't, and I don't think either of us is sorry. We just got carried away by the intensity of the feelings we had for each other. You see, sir, I want Samara to be my wife. She's the only woman I've ever wanted to marry. I'm a Catholic, and marriage to me is sacred and eternal. I want Samara to be the mother of my children. Please, for her sake – and your own – give us your blessing. Because we will marry with or without it.'

Bob's words were eloquent, and a disinterested observer would not have doubted their veracity, but Jules Silverman was a stubborn man, accustomed to having his way. No smartass young punk was going to tell him what his daughter was going to do. Sam watched the animus rise in her father's eyes. Nobody had ever defied him so gently and yet so thoroughly.

'Well, flyboy, you don't have it! Not now, not ever! Neither her mother nor I will ever agree to such a match,' he declared, ignoring the voice inside him warning to proceed cautiously. When the words were said, they hung in the air like a sentence of exile over them all. Jules wanted to call them back, to unsay them, but his pride and his incredible need to control everything around him obliterated the love he had for his only living child.

60

Sam walked behind the desk and in a gesture of love put her arms around the stiffened figure of her father.

'Don't do this to us, Dad . . . please. At least give yourself a chance to know Bob . . . you have no idea what a wonderful person he is,' she pleaded, but her father pushed her away from him. He steeled himself to resist her entreaties in the vain belief that once Samara was convinced that she had no choice other than choosing between this stranger and her family, she would reconsider. He hoped, at the least, to buy some time for her to get to know the man better, time for the first blush of passion to fade so that she could put everything into perspective and think rationally. It was the most far-reaching misjudgment of his life.

'No! It's out of the question. I won't be a party to this. If you want to throw away your life, you'll do it without any help from me.'

Sam knew that having made the decision, he would never turn away from it. Sometimes the very strength that propels a man to success in the world can also be a weakness that destroys everything he has accomplished. Jules's will and tenacity had given him wealth and power, but now they would cause him to lose what he held most dear. Samara was his child, possessor of his traits and his determination, and she responded with a bitterness and fury he had never seen in her before.

'You may be my father, but you don't own me,' she said with a soft intensity that had the ring of determination. 'You may think you're God because everybody around here jumps when you frown, but you have no right to tell me whom I can love. Before you say anything else that you might regret for the rest of your life, Bob and I are going home to tell Mom about our plans. Maybe she can talk some sense into you.'

Sam took Bob's arm and rushed him out of the office, but he protested. 'Come on, now, darling, give the poor guy a chance to think this over before getting so mad at him. He's your dad, for God's sake! He just needs time to get used to the idea. There's no point in having a showdown just yet. You've both said things you'll regret when you've had time to think about them.'

'You don't know what a stubborn man my father is, Bob. Once he makes up his mind about something, nothing can change it, except my mother. Our only hope is to convince her. If she sides with us, he'll eventually come around. If she doesn't . . .'

To Samara's dismay, her mother was even more difficult. Jules had called her on the telephone and warned her about the coming encounter, and she refused to come out of her bedroom, insisting that Bob wait downstairs while she talked to her daughter alone.

When Samara walked into the lovely large sitting room where she had spent so many quiet hours with her mother, Reba Silverman was stretched out in her usual place on the chaise longue in front of the windows overlooking the garden below. For a long silent moment she ignored Samara's presence, and then with a shuddering sob she spoke without turning to look at her only daughter.

'How could you do this to us, Samara? After all we've been through? Isn't it enough that we lost our only son? Where are your loyalties?'

'Mom, please, listen,' Sam said, going to the chaise and dropping to her knees beside her mother. 'Don't judge Bob without meeting him. You'll love him, if you'll just give him a chance and get to know him. He's a lot like David, really. He's gentle and funny and bright . . .'

'He's not one of us,' her mother said softly, and Samara could see the tears rolling down her cheeks.

Sam put her arms around her and rested her head against her shoulder, but her mother did not respond. Sam could feel her stiffen and pull away.

'Please, Mom, don't let Dad tell you what to do and what to think. I love Bob as much as you love Daddy and me and David.'

Reba was insulted by the comparison. 'Don't you dare compare this cheap, shoddy little affair of yours with the love I have for my family. Love grows only with respect and consideration and duty. If you have any regard for your father and me . . . and for the memory of your poor dead brother, you will not marry this man.' Her tone of voice was now cold and threatening, and Sam was repelled by it. She got to her feet instantly.

'Mother, if that's the attitude you're going to take, there's no point in my staying under this roof with you. You're going to make all of us terribly unhappy . . . but that, of course, is your prerogative. Would you have treated David this way if he had decided to marry someone you didn't like?'

Reba's voice was cold. 'David had respect for us, for our family and for our traditions. He would never have deliberately hurt us as you are doing.' Her words had a deadly finality to them.

Samara had expected her father to rant and rage and try to dominate her. She was sure that her mother too would weep and cry at first, but it would be only a temporary thing. Her mother was an emotional and demonstrative person, but she was also generous and reasonable and warm. Sam had been sure that once she recovered from the initial shock and realized that her daughter meant what she said, her mother would come around, but she had made an enormous miscalculation. The cold fury on Reba's face was identical to that on her father's. She was being forced to make a choice between her parents and Bob, but dear God, how could she do that? Samara closed her eyes tightly to shut in the tears. She would rather die than live without Bob. What kind of choice was that?

Samara stood up, and as she looked around the lovely room, she wondered if she would ever see it again. Tears filled her eyes, and her words were shaky with emotion as she said tremulously, 'I'm sorry, Mom. You're asking me to do something I can't do. If you had any idea how much I love Bob, you would at least make some effort to understand.'

Reba was unable to speak. She was filled with rage and resentment toward the man who was taking her daughter from her. She could think of it no other way.

'Mom . . . I can't stay here. I have to be with Bob. If you think it over and change your mind . . . or want to talk to me, we'll be at the Beverly Hills Hotel. We can only wait there for two days, because Bob has to report to his new assignment on the tenth, and we're going to New Haven to tell his parents. I love you, Mom. I always will. Tell Daddy I love him too.'

Sam couldn't believe that she was actually issuing such a final, desperate ultimatum. In all of her life, she had never disobeyed her parents. She could not remember a single exchange of cross words with them, until this.

Her mother at last turned her eyes toward her weeping daughter. 'Samara, if you walk out that door and check into a hotel like a common slut, you'll be as dead to your father and me as David is.'

Shaken by the severity of her mother's words, Sam drew back as if she had just been struck across the face. How could her mother love her and make such a threat? 'Mother, you and Dad have given me no other choice. I want to stay here . . . to be married in this house, but you won't let me. I'm not leaving. You're sending me away,' she replied, barely able to control her weeping.

For the two days that they waited at the hotel, Samara did not leave the room, afraid that the call would come and she wouldn't be there to receive it. When it was finally time for them to leave, she was miserable. Bob tried to contact both her parents by telephone to effect some sort of conciliation, but they stubbornly would not take his calls.

In her pain, Sam began to conclude that perhaps her mother and father had never loved her as much as they had loved David. This was the first time she had put their love to a test, and they had failed her. Was it possible that they resented her because she had lived while their beloved son had died? Or had they loved her only because she was obedient and easy to bend to their will?

In the years to come, all Sam could remember of those miserable days in the hotel was the tears she had shed.

The young lovers took the train cross-country and arrived in New Haven to tell his family. This time, however, they were prepared for the storm of protest and anger that greeted their announcement. They were now battle-scarred veterans of the parent wars. The skirmish with Bob's family was different but just as bad as the cold ultimatums from Sam's parents, for the ordeal was dragged out over a period of days, while everyone, including the family priest, tried to dissuade them from marrying. When at last they gave up arguing and trying to appease Bob's parents and left his family amid threats of damnation and disownment, they felt very alone.

Bob reported to his new assignment at Luke Air Force Base in Phoenix, where they were married by the base chaplain, who was a Methodist. On their wedding day,

Sam realized that her period was two weeks overdue. The bittersweet realization that she was pregnant with a child who would never know the love of his grandparents brought sadness to an occasion that should have produced only joy.

9

1952

Tess was sitting at the desk in her bedroom typing the final pages of a paper for her class in American literature. She was just beginning the last semester of her senior year at the University of Illinois, and sometime in the next couple of months she expected to receive word from the English department about her application for graduate school. Though she had been assured by her adviser that there was nothing to worry about, since her grades were very high and she had scored well on the exams, Tess knew that her father would be upset if she was not accepted. She tried to ignore her own feelings of ambivalence, refusing to admit even to herself how really tired of school she was. Most of her friends were going into jobs teaching or getting married, and all she saw in her future was more of the same – classes, papers, exams, studying.

She finished the last page, scrolled her paper out of the Smith-Corona portable typewriter that had carried her through high school and college, and assembled the pages. She knew she should have used carbons so that she'd have a copy in case anything happened, but she hated using the stuff. It was so hard to correct mistakes, and she somehow always managed to get her fingers black and leave smudges on her papers. There ought to be a better way of making copies.

As she started reading for errors, she decided she was sick and tired of Oliver Wendell Holmes and his polished poetry. At the beginning, she had liked his work, especially 'The Deacon's Masterpiece,' but the more she read, the more he annoyed her. Like so many of the great authors, he seemed to think it was perfectly all right to describe women as being empty-headed and dumb. She had started a notebook of quotations putting women down, and the first one, and the one she most hated, was from 'The Professor at the Breakfast Table,' and she knew it by heart: ' "I love you" is all the secret that many, nay, most women have to tell. When that is said, they are like China crackers on the morning of the fifth of July.' The old goat. She had tried to change the subject of her thesis, but her adviser was a man, and he thought her ideas about the denigration of women in literature were silly. So was he, with that scruffy little goatee of his and his teeth covered with green tartar. She wondered if he ever brushed them. Probably not. He wore the same suit and shirt to class every single day.

She glanced up at the clock. It was almost six, her father would be home at any minute, and she hadn't even looked at the newspaper. Darn it!

She hurried downstairs and out the front door to get the afternoon paper from the veranda. She carried it inside and settled down on the mohair couch in the living room to scan it quickly. Her father liked to discuss the events of the day with her at dinner, and if she didn't know enough to hold up her end and defend some point of view, he would be disappointed and annoyed. She scanned the paper quickly. Nothing terribly exciting today. The proposed armistice had hit a snag in the Panmunjom peace talks because the Koreans had refused the ban on building air bases in the North.

That was about as far as she got before her father came in the door, stomping the cold January snow from his boots. He kissed his daughter on the cheek and asked, 'Where's your mother?'

'In the kitchen. She said dinner was ready and we should sit down immediately. She's going over to the Waites' house to watch television.'

'God, not again! That's the third night this week she's been over there. What's the big attraction tonight?'

'I'm not sure – *The Goldbergs,* I think. When are you going to relent and buy her a TV set, Dad? At least it would keep her home nights.'

'Never! I wouldn't have one of those silly things in my house. Watching that stupid tube is going to make everybody's eyes the size of cantaloupes and their brains the size of peas.'

'But, Dad, wouldn't you like to see the news in the evening?'

'I get all the news I need from the newspapers. I don't need some vacant-eyed actor reading the headlines for me. Mark my words, the television set is the biggest threat to conversation and intelligent thought that has ever been foisted off on a gullible public.'

Slyly but as innocently as possible, Tess asked, 'Do you feel that way about the radio too, Dad?'

'Of course not,' he snapped impatiently. 'The radio allows us to use our imaginations to conjure up pictures to go with the words. Television does it all for us, and quite badly, too. We become passive receptacles waiting to be filled . . . with garbage. It'll turn us into a nation of lazy, do-nothing spectators, swilling beer and getting fat, sitting on the sidelines watching the world pass us by.'

Martha, who had entered the room to greet her husband, pursed her lips and said nothing. To her, the secret of a successful marriage was to listen patiently to her husband's pronouncements and then do as she pleased.

Over pot roast and mashed potatoes, Dr Marshall expounded on Korea and the dangers of trying to police the world. He was particularly worried about a military hero like General Eisenhower running for President.

'Why?' Tess asked.

'It's important to keep our government in civilian hands. You can take a man out of the military, but I'm not sure you can take a lifetime of military service out of a man and make him a civilian.'

Martha got up to clear the dishes, interrupting his speech. 'There's some tapioca pudding in the Frigidaire if anybody wants dessert. Just stack your dishes in the sink, and I'll do them when I get back. I don't want to be late,' she declared, and Tess marveled at her mother's ability to tune out her husband's conversation.

George was irked. 'Martha, now, just come back here and sit down. I have something to say.'

She came back in with her apron off and her sweater on. 'George, I'll miss the show,' she complained.

'Well, if the show's more important to you than a letter I got from Stanton Horvath today, by all means, leave.'

Martha sat down. 'What did he have to say after all these years?' she asked, her eyes alive with fascination.

Dr Marshall took his pipe out of his vest pocket and put it in his mouth. 'Tess, Stan was my chief rival for your mother's affection. Lucky for me, he went off to the Military Academy at West Point and left the field wide open.'

'Come on, George, what did he say?' Martha demanded impatiently.

'Well, it seems he's the new commanding officer of Scott Air Force Base, and he's invited us over for dinner next week.'

'When?' Martha asked breathlessly, and Tess was

amused at her mother's ill-concealed excitement about an old beau.

'Friday. Peter Waters has agreed to cover for me.'

Martha got up from the table and briskly checked her appearance in the mirror. She ran a hand over her short, wavy brown hair lightly streaked with gray and smoothed the wrinkles from her skirt. 'Good, that will give me time to find something new to wear and get my hair done.'

'Aren't you jealous, Dad?' Tess teased.

George chuckled as he struggled to get his pipe lighted. 'It's good for a woman to have a little excitement in her life, honey. Keeps her young. Besides, Stan's a good friend, and I want you to go with us so he can see what a beautiful and intelligent daughter we have. Stan's been around, and your mother's not much of a conversationalist. I'm sure he'll want to talk about something other than the sales down at the department store.'

Tess said nothing, but she resented it when her father put down her mother like that.

The weather forecast promised a heavy snowstorm on Friday, and although George discussed postponing their visit until more clement weather, Martha would not hear of it. She had been to the beauty shop and had her hair freshly tinted to conceal the gray, she'd had her nails manicured and painted a clear bright red, and she had not only bought a new dress and shoes, but she had splurged and gotten an expensive new black wool coat with a silver-fox collar.

At noon they picked up Tess at the sorority house and started the long drive. Although the base was only 185 miles away, George took several wrong turns, and it was after five o'clock when they finally arrived at the gate.

71

The Air Police were expecting them, and they were given an escort to the commander's quarters.

Tess was amused at the flush on her mother's cheeks and the shine in her eyes. She had never seen her look younger or prettier. Dr Marshall was always teasing her about having been the most popular girl in school, and Tess often wondered why she was so different from her mother. She had only a few friends that she cared about, and she had little interest in the social life on campus. Most of the girls in her sorority were too obsessed with boys and dating, proms and parties. Tess found that she enjoyed herself more with the people who worked on the newspaper. She was the only sorority girl on the staff, and although the guys teased her a lot, they were interested in important things like politics and world events, and she could argue with the best of them. She knew it disturbed her mother, however, that she rarely had dates and almost never got invited to the big parties or proms.

Still, it was her own fault. Tess knew she was pretty, but she hated the awkward feeling that engulfed her whenever she tried to talk to attractive young men. She had long ago given up going to fraternity tea dances, because she found it humiliating to wait around awkwardly for someone to ask her to dance. Being tall didn't help, either, since most of the guys were not interested in dancing with girls who towered over them. And no matter how she tried, the art of flirting was totally beyond her. Her father had raised her to have serious, meaningful conversations, and most of the young men she dated avoided any but the dumbest kind of talk. All they ever wanted to do, it seemed, was drink beer and try to grope her in the car on the way home.

General Horvath came down the steps of his house to greet the Marshalls as their car drove up. Snowflakes had

72

begun to fall gently into the darkness of the night, and Tess was struck by the man's stature as she looked up at him and saw the feathery flakes of moisture settling on his head. Although he was only of medium height, he carried himself with so much assurance and authority that he seemed to tower over everyone around him. He took her father's hand first and shook it warmly, and Tess realized that a strong friendship existed between the men, though they hadn't seen each other for years.

'George, you lucky devil, you kept all your hair!' he said teasingly, and her father responded in kind. 'Your hair might be a little thinner, Stan, but then, so's your waistline.'

The general then turned to her mother. He started to take her hand and then their eyes met and suddenly they were in each other's arms hugging and laughing. 'God, Martha, you're as beautiful as ever,' he exclaimed. Then it was Tess's turn.

'And you must be Tess. I'm sure glad to see that you have your mother's looks, young lady, because I promised one of my young officers that if he came to dinner tonight, he'd probably meet the girl of his dreams. Come in, come in. I mustn't keep you waiting out here in the cold.'

As they walked into his spacious and comfortable quarters, Tess was angry with herself for coming. Dammit all, she hated blind dates! She should have stayed home to study.

Jean Horvath, the general's wife, greeted them at the entry, and although she was friendly enough, there was a brittle edge to her. She was extremely thin, and her hair was tinted a strawberry blond. Her royal-blue rayon crepe dress was cut a little too low, revealing a bony chest and a bustline that looked padded, and Tess found the difference between her mother and this woman striking.

73

Martha was all curves and softness, and Mrs Horvath was all angles and points.

They took off their coats in the hall, and when they entered the living room, a tall young officer who had been sitting in front of the fire with a highball in his hand got to his feet. Oh, Lord, Tess thought anxiously, he's gorgeous. He's probably accustomed to women falling all over him. He had to be at least six-feet-four, and his shoulders looked a yard wide. He had a short crew cut, but his hair was thick and sand-colored, and his complexion looked tan and outdoorsy. When he smiled, she could see that his teeth were even and perfect. He'd probably been the captain of the basketball team and maybe even the football team.

Jean Horvath introduced them. 'Tess, sweetie, we thought you might get bored listening to us old folks reminisce about the good old days, so we asked Lieutenant Kipling to join us. After dinner, he'll take you over to the officers' club, where there's a nice little band. Would you like that?'

Tess nodded mutely with a smile fixed on her face as the lieutenant stretched his hand toward her. 'Nice to meet you, Tess. Please call me Kip, everybody else does.'

Tess was annoyed at the small flutter her heart gave as they clasped hands, and she murmured, 'Nice to meet you.' As she looked into his deep green eyes, she felt sorry for him. The poor guy had undoubtedly been ordered to be here, and it would probably be an excruciatingly dull evening for him. There must be loads of more interesting girls he'd rather be with tonight, she thought, trying to ignore the little flicker of hope she felt deep inside her.

An orderly passed trays of martinis and manhattans, and since her parents did not seem to be paying attention to her, Tess took a manhattan. Although she had drunk occasionally at fraternity parties, she had never taken a drink in front of her parents before. She took a big swallow that tasted both sharp and sweet at the same time, and the fiery bourbon laced with sweet vermouth stormed its way down her throat, setting it ablaze and warming her. After three sips of the cocktail, Tess began to relax a little and see things from a better perspective. Why should she try to make an impression on this person? She'd never see him again anyway. Let him entertain her, she thought arrogantly. That's what he'd been ordered to do. Let him do it.

The lieutenant guided her over to the bay window and they sat down across from each other on high-backed wing chairs covered in a bright floral chintz.

'The snow's coming down pretty heavily. Your dad's not going to try to drive back tonight, is he?' Kip asked.

'He has to. He's in private practice, and the doctor who's covering for him goes off duty at six in the morning.'

Kip laughed. 'Well, I hope nobody gets sick tomorrow morning, because I have a feeling you're all going to be occupying the base's guest quarters. Didn't you check the weather forecast before you started out?'

'Dad wanted to postpone, but Mom wouldn't let him. Besides, we have chains in the car,' Tess replied with an assurance she didn't feel as she looked out the window at the snow that was falling heavily, turning the night into a white blur.

'Take my word as a pilot, you're not going home for a while. This is a full-blown blizzard, maybe the biggest of the year.' He grinned, amused at her discomfiture. 'I hope you brought a toothbrush.'

Tess turned her eyes from the window to appraise him

and noticed an air of assurance and authority about him that almost equaled the general's, yet he couldn't be more than a year or two older than she was. Maybe he was an old soul in a young man's body, she thought, and immediately felt more comfortable with him. Old souls, she understood. It was the young ones that disconcerted her.

She lifted her cocktail and grinned. 'Well, here's to a long stay. I'm glad I turned in my paper on Oliver Wendell Holmes this morning.'

'So you're a fan of Oliver Wendell Holmes?'

'Not really,' she said, curling her lip slightly.

'Good, neither am I,' he replied, and as they clinked glasses, Kip leaned toward her and whispered conspiratorially, 'This is the best duty I've ever pulled.'

Was he making fun of her? Or was he by any chance telling the truth? Well, let's find out what he thinks of the real me, she thought, and said, 'Tell me, as a military man, what did you think of Douglas MacArthur's problems with Truman?'

Startled at the suddenly serious turn of the conversation, Kip replied, 'Well, he's an Academy man, as I am, and a military genius, but I believe the power in our country has to remain in civilian hands,' he began, and they were off and running in a conversation that interested them both.

Social custom in the military places an undue emphasis on a cocktail hour so protracted that the food, by the time it is served, is usually irrelevant. Stan Horvath had not achieved rank by flouting custom, and so the conversation and the booze both flowed interminably.

Before they finally joined the others at the dinner table, Kip and Tess had exhausted the subject of General MacArthur, the Korean War, George Orwell's 1984, the Atomic Age, and the North Atlantic Treaty. They had

76

just begun a titillating discussion of Alfred Kinsey's *Report on the Sexual Behavior of the Human Male,* which they had both read, when they were called to dinner, and they went reluctantly. For the first time in her life, Tess had enjoyed the complete and undivided attention of a handsome young man, who was not only attractive and intelligent, but who could converse as well as her father. She was enthralled.

Kip was equally impressed. A serious and ambitious young officer, he had never before dated a girl who knew almost as much about the world around her as he did. Her knowledge was not superficial, either. She seemed to have a deep understanding of issues, and she expressed herself eloquently and with intelligent conviction. Not only that, but she was beautiful.

They sat next to each other during dinner, and only occasionally joined in the general conversation, content to talk quietly to each other. All through the meal, Kip kept looking at Tess's long blond hair, wishing they were alone so that he could touch it. Her complexion was pink and glowing, and her blue eyes sparkled when she spoke. He admired the trimness of her long body and the graceful way she held her fork. She was pretty, yet she was the brightest girl he had ever met.

When Jean announced that coffee would be served in the living room, Kip whispered, 'Let's have coffee at the club, okay?' Tess agreed eagerly, and they donned their coats and left.

As the door closed behind them, George Marshall felt the future blowing its cold breath on his face, and it had nothing to do with the burst of snowy air that rushed into the house as the young couple departed.

10

Chili had spent all her time making Gamal happy in bed and trying to prepare herself to be the best wife she could be. She was a pretty good cook, she could scrub and clean with the best of them, and she had enough energy to spare for that kind of thing, but she knew that what she really needed to do was learn about manners and stuff like that. So she went to the San Antonio library and took out the book by Emily Post, and she forced herself to wade through the whole newspaper every day. *Time* magazine was read cover to cover each week, and she subscribed to the *Ladies' Home Journal* and *Good Housekeeping*.

But it wasn't enough. She stood looking at her reflection in despair. God, no matter what she did to herself, she still looked like a sexy hooker on the prowl. Her breasts were too big, her waist too tiny, her lips too full, and her hair too bright and unruly. She took a deep breath. Even the black rayon crepe dress she had just bought, with its high neck and long sleeves, still didn't turn her into a lady. Besides, she hated black. It was so grim and dead.

Chili stood in front of the full-length mirror she had hung on the back of the closet door in the spare room of their apartment, and pondered her problem. She and Gamal had been married for almost six months, and she had yet to make an appearance at the officers' club. Every time Gamal broached the subject, she managed to divert him. At first, she used sex, the most powerful distraction at her command. All she had to do was rub up against him or touch his privates, and he was ready to go. For a man she had kept at bay for weeks of courtship, he was mighty easily stimulated. Even now, she wondered how she had ever managed for so long to keep his cock in his own pants instead of in hers.

The time of reckoning was close at hand, however, and no amount of screwing or feigning a headache or menstrual cramps was going to postpone the inevitable. Gamal had been assigned to Germany, and one of his fellow officers was throwing a going-away bash for him. If she missed this, Gamal would suspect something for sure, for damn sure.

Chili was terrified of being recognized by one of the guys she'd screwed around with, and if there was one thing of which she was perfectly sure, it was that men were a lot more talkative about sex than women were. All she needed was for some joker to tell Gam or even let on that he knew her, and she'd be in big trouble with her husband. Very big trouble. Terminal trouble. She'd been learning a lot about the man she married, and she'd found out, much to her dismay, that for Gamal, who was a Moslem, a woman's chastity was her most important virtue.

As she always did, she'd called up Jimmyjohn and told him about the party, but he wasn't any help at all. Ever since she'd gotten married, he'd been different. Not at all the friendly, helpful person he'd been. He acted kind of like he didn't care much about her problems anymore. He was particularly distant when she told him how happy she was they were getting out of Texas and going to a faraway place like Germany. His response hadn't made her feel a bit good about herself. 'Look, Chili, you might as well face it and get it over with. You're just as likely to run into one of your old boyfriends in Germany as you are in Texas.'

She'd tried to point out that it would be different there, that maybe people wouldn't recognize her outside of San Antone, but Jimmyjohn had given her that down-and-dirty little laugh of his and said, 'Any guy who's slept with you, Chili girl, ain't gonna forget you. No way.'

Chili sighed and grabbed a hairbrush. She began to brush the unruly tangle of rich auburn curls. Pulling it together tightly with a rubber band, she succeeded in taming the hair enough to wrap it into a prim knot at the base of her skull, and suddenly she looked different, very different. The eyes were just as big and bright, the mouth just as sensuous, but she looked more subdued without that wild mane of hair framing her face. Now, if Gamal didn't object, she'd be in good shape, particularly if she wore the reading glasses she'd gotten at the drugstore. She put on the rimless spectacles, and the effect was perfect, subdued and spinsterish, but there was no way she could walk around in them. Everything more than two feet away was all blurred. So much for that.

When Gamal got home that evening, she was all ready. She had a terrible feeling he would not like her new image, but she couldn't have been more wrong.

'Sweetheart, you look gorgeous!' he exclaimed, kissing her unpainted lips and appraising her new dress and hairdo with admiration.

'You really think so?' she asked suspiciously. She thought she looked perfectly grim and sexless.

'It's a beautiful dress. I love it, and your hair looks terrific that way. You look aloof and sophisticated. And very much, I might add, the lady.'

'I do? Really?' she said, turning from him to look in the mirror over the hall table.

80

'You bet. Did you have a chance to press my good uniform?' he asked, checking through the mail.

'It's all ready, and I washed and ironed your new blue shirt. I was afraid that it would be too rough on your neck if you wore it brand new.'

'Good girl. I'll take a quick shower and be ready in a jiffy.'

While she waited for him, she stood at the mirror staring at herself. The more familiar she became with her new image, the better it looked to her. She refused to listen to the nasty little voice inside her declaring that Gamal liked the change in her only because it made her look dull and dowdy and undesirable.

When they walked into the club, she was reassured. Although she was treated with respect by the men she met, she could still see the old gleam in their eyes. No doubt about it. As the evening progressed and she saw no one she had ever met before, she relaxed and began to joke and laugh. Chili had a great sense of humor, which got a little racy when she had something to drink, and they were serving champagne, domestic and inexpensive, but her very favorite drink. She was about to accept her third glass when she felt Gamal squeezing her arm tightly.

'You've had quite enough, darling. You know you can't drink,' he said aloud, his eyes glittering with disapproval.

'I'm not drunk, Gam honey, honest I'm not,' she protested softly. 'I'm just having a good time.'

'If I catch you with another glass in your hand, I'll take you home,' he whispered threateningly. 'Now, go sit down at the table with the other wives.'

Chili did just as she was told, feeling embarrassed and miserable. For the rest of the evening she sat in her chair quietly, getting up only to dance with Gamal's commanding officer, who was a sweet older man almost ready for

81

retirement. If her earlier demeanor irritated him, Gamal was pleased with the manner in which she deported herself after his warning, but later, when they were in bed together, his caresses did nothing to arouse her. It was the first time in her marriage that she went through the motions without feeling a thing.

11

Although they intended to continue their animated discussion over coffee at the officers' club, something happened that curtailed all serious talk for the rest of the evening. Kip asked Tess to dance, and once they were in each other's arms, moving slowly to the strains of 'Tenderly,' their relationship moved into another phase that was even more exciting.

Kip held her close to him, and as their bodies moved rhythmically together, he buried his face in her thick hair, scented only by shampoo. Tess was the first girl he had ever held who did not reek of perfume but radiated cleanliness and naturalness.

Tess had never felt quite so at home in anyone's arms as she did in Kip's. She comfortably tucked her head into his shoulder and let her body blend with his. She wanted the music never to end.

When it did, however, they pulled away from each other with reluctance, and he held her hand as they walked off the dance floor. Even when they sat down at the table, he continued to hold her hand, and when they looked at each other across the small hurricane lamp, they saw a light in each other's eyes that neither had ever seen before. Kip lifted her hand to his lips, kissed it, and murmured, 'I can't seem to let go of your hand.'

'I don't want you to.'

Smiling, Kip replied softly, 'I don't think I ever enjoyed dancing with anyone as much as I do with you.'

Tess smiled mischievously. 'They say that ballroom

dancing is really only a mating ritual. Do you believe that?'

'I do now,' he replied, squeezing her hand.

Tess smiled and looked down shyly. Good heavens, she thought, I'm flirting with him, and it's wonderful! As soon as the music started again, they were in each other's arms once more, and they didn't stop dancing until the combo signed off for the night. Still holding hands, they returned to General Horvath's quarters.

Just before they went inside, Kip said, 'I hope you get snowed in here until spring.'

'So do I,' Tess said, her lips turned up toward his, waiting, hoping he would kiss them. As his mouth moved toward hers, slowly, tentatively, she thought she would always remember this moment in her life, for she had never experienced such a deep, rapturous longing as she felt then, standing in the freezing night air with the snowflakes caressing her face and his warm, soft lips brushing hers.

Suddenly the door opened, and a warm shaft of light sprang through the cold white darkness, spotlighting their first kiss.

Dr Marshall was the first one out the door, upset and angered at the spectacle his daughter was making of herself.

As the young couple moved apart, not slowly or guiltily, and continuing to hold hands, Tess's father barked, 'Well, we were on our way over to the club to find out what happened to you.'

Tess's mother was close behind her husband, but she was not upset in the least. 'Tess, honey, we're going to have to spend the night in the base VIP quarters. It seems the highway is closed for the night. Stan is having the base exchange opened so we can buy a few things to tide us

over, and Jean has graciously lent us some nightclothes.'
As she spoke, her eyes moved rapidly from one to the
other of the young people, appraising them and coming
to some exciting conclusions. Her bookworm daughter
might just have snagged herself a handsome young man,
Martha decided exultantly.

Kip and Tess looked at each other with unabashed glee.
'It looks like I won't have to fly tomorrow either, so I'll
pick you up for breakfast. What time?'

General Horvath emerged from the house just in time
to add his arrow to Cupid's pouch. 'Kipling, I'm going to
put you in charge of seeing that this young lady enjoys
her visit. If, by some chance, they're still weathered in on
Monday, I'll see that you're relieved of any other duties
while she's here. Take good care of her,' he said with a
wink at Martha. 'Jean and I will entertain her folks.'

If George Marshall ever wanted to shoot someone, it
was his old school rival. He looked up at the snow falling
faster and thicker than ever and silently implored it to dry
up. Even the gods seemed to be conspiring against him.

George stewed and fretted for three full days, worrying
about his patients, forced to stand by helplessly and watch
his daughter slip from his grasp.

Although Kip and Tess behaved in a perfectly proper
manner, there was no denying the erotic tension between
them. When they looked at each other, they seemed to
be drowning in each other's eyes.

Martha was elated. Kip Kipling was all a mother could
wish for her daughter. He was handsome, well-educated,
ambitious, and polite. He was a graduate of West Point;
both his father and his grandfather had been generals and
he would undoubtedly achieve that distinction himself.
Much to George's dismay, Martha began talking about a
wedding when she and her husband were alone.

'Stop that kind of talk, Martha. Right this minute! Tess would never let herself get involved with a military man. It's a rotten life for a woman, getting dragged from pillar to post, never settling down in any one place. She's not that stupid,' he declared, hoping it was true.

For the next three months, Kip made the trip every Friday evening to the Marshall house, where he spent the weekend in the guest room, and just when everyone had adjusted to the routine, he received orders to report to Wheelus Field in Tripoli, Libya, for duty.

As soon as they got in the car on their way to the movies, Tess and Kip fell into each other's arms.

'Oh, Kip, I can't stand the thought that you'll be so far away,' Tess whispered, destroyed at the prospect of his leaving.

He held her close, and their bodies ached for each other. He covered her mouth with his, and their kisses were long and deep. When at last they pulled apart, he said softly, 'I want you to marry me, Tess. Come live with me in Tripoli.'

All Tess could think about was that she had to be with him, no matter where he was. 'I love you, Kip. I'll go wherever you go.'

That night, instead of seeing Hepburn and Bogart in *The African Queen*, they went home to tell her parents of their decision.

George's response was directed toward his wife. 'Well, are you satisfied now, Martha?' he exploded in anger.

Even she was shocked. 'Where, for goodness sake, is Tripoli?' she asked.

'Libya-. . . North Africa, Mrs Marshall. On the Mediterranean. I hear it's good duty for families, although it's a thirty-month tour with dependents,' Kip replied. 'Eighteen months if you go alone.'

'You hardly know him, Tess, and you're thinking of living in some godforsaken – ' George began to protest, but Martha would have none of his bullying.

Getting up from her chair, she moved quickly across the room. Giving both Kip and Tess a quick kiss of approval, she murmured sweetly, 'Congratulations to you both. You'll be my first son, one I can be very proud of.'

Then with more defiance than she had ever before displayed, she looked directly at her husband and declared forthrightly, 'They have our blessing . . . don't they, dear?'

George Marshall looked at the handsome, virile young man and knew that he was no match for him. No matter how much he had prepared his daughter for a life of the intellect, in the end, it was always the hormones that won. Aware that if he opposed the marriage he might alienate his favored child for all time, he smiled bleakly and said, 'Dammit all to hell, how come we always lose our children as soon as they're old enough to enjoy having around? Congratulations, Kip.' He then shook his enemy's hand with a cordiality he did not feel. 'You're a very lucky young man.'

'George, get the sherry,' Martha commanded. 'Let's all sit down at the dining-room table and talk about the wedding.'

12

The passengers felt as if they were riding a wild, bucking bronco high in the sky, trying to hold on but being thrown and tossed about helplessly, strapped to a creature that was violently out of control. The engines of the C-54 strained to pull it upward, but just when they seemed about to succeed, the plane was pitched down into a sickening drop, the fuselage shuddering and creaking. The handful of people fastened inside the fuselage on bucket seats shivered and gasped and held on to their seats and their stomachs, expecting every plunge to be the one that would deliver them straight into the Atlantic Ocean below.

Most of the twenty suffering passengers aboard were young airmen on their way to assignments in North Africa, but sitting among them was a lone young woman, the bride of an Air Force officer. After three months of a marriage in which they had been separated for all but two weeks, Tess was finally on her way to join Kip at Wheelus Air Force Base in Tripoli, Libya.

'Oh, God, I'm too sick to be scared,' Tess moaned.

'And I'm too scared to be sick,' the young airman strapped in beside her remarked huskily.

It had been a long flight from Westover Air Force Base in Massachusetts, where Tess had seen scores of desperate, distracted women caring for tired and crying children. She had been dismayed to learn that many of them had been there for weeks waiting to get seats on planes that would take them to join their husbands and fathers at overseas assignments. She considered herself extremely lucky to have been assigned to a flight scheduled to leave the morning after her arrival at the base.

Luck, as Tess was to learn, was a relative term, however. Because of her short stay at Westover, there had been no time for a briefing, and consequently she was totally ignorant of the protocol of traveling by military aircraft. She had carefully selected the clothes in which she would first greet her romantic new husband: a black linen suit with a white rayon blouse, a little black straw pillbox hat with a tiny black eye veil, black pumps, a girdle and hose, and, of course, white cotton shorty gloves. At the dawn of the Eisenhower Era, she was properly attired for a trip by plane.

As she teetered toward the aircraft on her high-heeled shoes, she mistook the amazed stares of the attending airmen to be appreciation of her appearance and feminity. The moment she stepped into the plane, however, she realized she was ridiculously unprepared for the long, arduous journey.

'Good Lord, didn't anybody tell you to wear slacks?' the copilot bellowed when he saw her. 'The life jackets we have on board have straps that go between your legs.'

One glance at the interior of the plane, and she felt utterly undone. There were no traditional seats, just narrow lengths of canvas stretched along the sides of the cabin, equipped at regular intervals with seat belts. Bucket seats, in the jargon of the military. To make matters worse, cargo was stacked and strapped down the middle of the cabin. There was no insulation of any kind covering the skeleton of the fuselage. At the rear was a solitary toilet, freestanding and with the briefest of curtains to provide a laughable bit of privacy.

'I just arrived at Westover last night. Nobody told me

89

'anything,' Tess apologized feebly as young men in uniform began pouring into the cabin.

'Well, we don't ordinarily do this, but since you're the only dependent aboard, we'll let you use the head up in the crew compartment. It's got a door on it. Now, you better sit down and buckle up. We're taking off for Gander, Newfoundland, as soon as we get clearance. We want to beat a weather front closing in up there.' He whirled around and returned to the cockpit.

Humbled by her circumstances, Tess sat down between two young airmen, and after a bit of fumbling managed to fasten her seat belt.

Fifteen hours later, after a six-hour delay in Newfoundland, they were caught now in turbulence over the Atlantic Ocean. The young airman who was the flight attendant was out of his seat and risking his life to hand out airsick bags. Tess closed her eyes and was thankful that she had been too nauseous to eat the cold chicken and ham sandwiches in the box lunches distributed early in the flight.

God, what was Kip going to say when he found out she was pregnant already . . . almost three months to the day of their wedding? She'd had to beg her doctor not to tell her parents. She was not yet twenty-two, and her father still hadn't accepted the fact that she was going to a country they knew little about, and he would have raised a storm of protest if he'd learned of her condition. For more than a month now, as they'd helped her get things together to start a household on the other side of the world, she had been hiding her nausea from her parents, and it hadn't been easy.

Suddenly the lights in the cabin went out, and the attendant said, 'Brace for a landing . . . let's hope it's not on water.'

With a snap and a bump and a grinding of wheels on pavement, they arrived at Lajes Air Force Base in the Azore Islands. As the copilot deplaned, he informed her that a jeep would pick her up and take her to the officers' club, where she could relax and freshen up. The enlisted men clambered out of the plane and headed for the mess hall.

The promised transportation never arrived, and as she reboarded the flight with the airmen, who'd had the benefit of a visit to the rest rooms and a snack, Tess began to realize uneasily that life as a dependent military wife was not going to be one of priority and privilege.

It was breakfast time before they landed in Nouasseur, on the coast of North Africa near exotic Casablanca. Neither Ingrid Bergman nor Humphrey Bogart greeted the plane, nor did the phantom jeep appear as promised. This time, however, Tess knew better than to wait on the tarmac, and so she joined her fellow passengers in the mess-hall line. While she stood and waited her turn, she had begun to feel weak and dizzy. Bub, a paratrooper who had earlier rousted the guys out of their seats and onto the floor of the plane so that she could stretch out and take a nap, realized that she was about to pass out.

'Look, ma'am, go sit down at that table over there, and I'll get some coffee for you, okay?'

'No . . . no coffee, please. What I really need to settle my stomach is a cup of tea.'

'Tea?' Bub asked in horror. 'You want I should go up there and ask them guys for tea?' Then, seeing how tired and pale she was, he capitulated. 'Yeah, sure. I'll get some for you.'

He strode off toward the kitchen. A few minutes later, a triumphant Bub returned carrying a heavy china mug filled with hot water in which floated a tea bag.

Tess took the mug and sniffed the welcome, smoky fragrance. 'Thanks so much, Bub. I really needed this. I hope it didn't cause you too much trouble.'

'Piece o' cake, 'though I almost had to punch out some wise guy's lights. Nobody says that kinda stuff to me! Look, I'm gonna get some chow. How about I bring you some toast? I been watchin', and you ain't had nothin' but a hard-boiled egg since we left the States.'

'Some toast would be great.'

For most of the trip, Tess had huddled under one of the stiff Air Force-issue wool blankets. Dressed in her summer clothes, she was not prepared for a flight in a plane that seemed never to have any heat. But on the last leg of their journey, as they were approaching their final destination, hot air suddenly began to fill the cabin and turn it into an oven.

'Oh, fine,' Tess complained, 'the pilot finally figured out how to turn on the heat.'

'No, ma'am,' the attendant said, 'we've started our descent, and the temperature down there is over ninety.'

'What time is it there?' Tess asked.

'About two in the morning,' he replied.

As the plane made its final approach, a sudden strange, overpowering odor filled the cabin. The passengers looked around at each other suspiciously, but the closer they got to the ground, the more pervasive it became.

'Good heavens, what's that strange smell?' Tess finally asked aloud.

The cabin attendant grinned and replied, 'That's Tripoli, ma'am.'

13

A thousand images sped through Tess's mind as she descended the steps from the plane into the darkness of the Libyan night, her eyes searching through the crowd of men below. What in the world was she doing here? This adventure had certainly never figured in her girlhood dreams and aspirations. She had grown up during World War II and had come to accept the presence of young men in military uniform everywhere she went, but it never once occurred to her that she might someday be part of that life. Now, here she was a world away from home, exhausted, sick, pregnant, and married to a military officer she had not known existed six months ago. Where, for God's sake, was he?

As her eyes scanned the crowd, suddenly they connected with the eyes that she remembered, and she took the last few steps in an instant, hurtling herself into the arms of the young man who had filled her life and her thoughts for the past few months. Tall, strong, muscular, clad in the short-sleeved khaki summer uniform of the United States Air Force, sandy hair clipped short, a jaunty blue cap on his head, First Lieutenant Andrew Roy Kipling held her close for a brief instant.

It was a moment she wanted to last forever but which was tantalizingly brief. There was no lingering, urgent kiss of welcome to assure her that the past three months had been hell for him too. Instead, he stepped back, smiled, and said, 'Welcome to Tripoli, Tess. I hope the flight wasn't too awful.' Dear God, for a moment she expected him to click his heels and salute, his greeting was so stiff and formal.

Tess looked up into his eyes and whispered tremulously, 'Oh, God, Kip, I'm so glad to see you.'

He smiled and took her arm. Softly he said, 'I'll get you out of here as fast as I can.'

Expecting to be whisked away to be alone, Tess was bewildered when instead he stopped to chat leisurely and to introduce her to several of the officers standing nearby.

'Colonel Baker, this is my wife, Tess.'

'Welcome to Tripoli,' the man greeted her, and as she was introduced to one officer after another, she tried to murmur proper responses, but she felt as if she were sleepwalking. She had been through a wretched forty-hour flight, she was nauseated, exhausted, and starved for comfort and affection, but she was being paraded about to meet people whose names and faces she would never remember.

At last it was over, and Kip retrieved her suitcase, loaded it into the trunk of the 1950 Ford he had bought the year he graduated from the Academy, and finally they were in the car alone, on their way to God knew where.

Kip reached over and took her hand in his. 'God, I missed you,' he said softly as they drove through the darkened streets of the air base. These were the words she'd been waiting to hear, and they were almost too exquisite to bear. She began to sob.

'What's wrong, honey?' he asked in bewilderment, but she couldn't reply, her sobs and her tears were coming too hard.

Suddenly he slammed on the brakes and turned off the engine. Without a word, he got out of the car. He ran around, opened the door on her side, and forcefully but gently pulled her out of the vehicle and into his arms. He

94

held her against him tightly, willing her to be as happy as he was to be holding her again, and he succeeded. Her crying stopped. What had carried her through the past miserable hours, weeks, months of separation was the memory of his strong body pressed to hers, now a reality at last. She looked up at him and his mouth was suddenly enclosing hers, kissing her deeply, longingly. The desire that had simmered inside them both over the past months erupted with an intensity that transcended anything that either of them had ever felt before.

When at last he took his lips from hers, he whispered, 'There's a blanket in the car.' Without releasing her, he pulled the olive-drab blanket from the back seat. He then dropped to his knees and removed her high-heeled shoes from her feet so that she could walk through the sand down toward the water's edge. Quickly Kip spread the blanket on the soft sand, and they stretched their longing bodies on it, side by side.

With urgency, they undressed each other only as much as necessary, and they joined their bodies passionately, gratefully, and joyfully there on that faraway beach, inches away from the warmth of the Mediterranean Sea. At last they were together again. When their desire had been momentarily satisfied, they lay quietly, touching with their arms, their torsos, their legs. Tess wanted to stay there forever; the thought of separating her flesh from his even for only a moment was almost unbearable.

'We better go,' Kip whispered.

'Not yet, Kip, please. I don't want this moment to end. The air's so warm, and I love the sound of the waves . . .'

'I know, hon, but we can't stay. This beach is on the base, and the Air Police patrol it regularly. We took a big chance as it was. Come on. Let's go. I've reserved a room for us at the Del Mehari Hotel in town. Tomorrow we'll get some temporary furniture from Supply and move into our own apartment.'

Reluctantly Tess allowed herself to be pulled to her feet. As she groped through the moonlit night to find her panties and hose, a light appeared in the distance.

'Damn, here comes their jeep. Hurry, let's get in the car before they see us,' Kip said as he snatched up the blanket. As fast as they could move, they raced toward the car, with Tess giggling at the ridiculousness of their predicament as she stumbled weakly through the soft sand.

They climbed into the car, and Kip just managed to get his shirt buttoned, although his fly was still unzipped, when the patrol pulled up alongside them. A young AP shone a flashlight at them, and the light picked up the silver bars on Kip's shirt collar.'

'Good evening, sir. Any problem?' the airman asked.

'Not at all, Corporal. My wife just arrived from the States, and I was showing her the Mediterranean,' Kip replied stiffly.

'Too bad we don't have a moon tonight, sir. Welcome to Wheelus, ma'am. I hope you enjoy your stay,' the young airman replied with a slight grin on his face, then turned the jeep's wheel and left them alone.

Tess giggled and swept her hand across her tousled hair. 'Kip, we didn't fool them for a minute, you know. My God, look at me . . . and look at you.'

'I'm sure we're not the first couple they've caught out here . . . but I'll bet we're the only married ones . . . to each other, I mean,' he laughed as he pulled his uniform together.

He started the car, and as they drove toward the main gate of Wheelus Field, Tess also made herself presentable.

Once out the gate, they traveled the five miles to town, holding hands and chatting comfortably with each other. Since the speed limit was twenty miles per hour, it was a leisurely drive. Kip pointed out the little town of Suk El Giuma as they drove through it.

'The name of the town means "Friday market," and it's a real mess to get through here on Friday mornings. All the Arabs are Moslems, and Friday is their holiday. There are some Berbers here too, and occasionally you'll see one. They're fair-skinned, but for the most part, they live in the little farm villages. They're also followers of Islam. Anyway, this place is cluttered with camels and flat-bedded horse-drawn carts and Arabs who come in from the desert and the small towns nearby. It's even worse when it rains, because the roadway is low and it gets flooded.'

'What happens then?' Tess asked, peering out the window and seeing nothing but small huts and no lights at all.

'Well, I've been told to drive slowly through the water and pray the engine doesn't stall. I've also heard that it's a smart idea to carry enough piastres so you can pay a bunch of Arabs to push you out if you get stuck.'

Tess shivered. 'Well, I'll just stay home if it rains.'

'Not a viable option, honey. It rains at least once every day during the winter.'

'Wonderful. Kip, what in the world is that funny smell in the air? I noticed it as the plane was landing.'

'Oh, yeah . . . well, most of the men insist it's the smell of camel dung, but the natives say it's a combination of eucalyptus, jasmine, and hot sand. You'll get used to it soon.'

Entering the sleeping city, they drove along the Lungomare, the boulevard, built and named by the Italians, that stretched along the coastline.

Tess was impressed by the beauty of the whitewashed buildings against the starry sky.

'Oh, Kip, I had no idea the city would be so beautiful. It looks like something out of the Arabian Nights.'

'Yeah . . . at night or from a distance, but wait till you get a closer look. There's a lot of poverty here . . . and flies. This country was dominated by outsiders for more than two thousand years, and they became an independent nation just last year. The main street was named Victor Emanuel by the Italians, but the Libyans changed it to the Avenue of the 24th of December, because that's the day they became the United Kingdom of Libya.'

When they arrived at a bulbous dome that looked much like an igloo, Kip announced, 'Well, here we are. The Del Mehari Hotel. It's not the Waldorf, but it's the best in town. The hotel proper is on the land side of the highway, and there's a tunnel under the boulevard to the open-air dance floor and restaurant by the sea. I've been told that the funny-shaped dome is a marabout's tomb. Seems a strange place to have a tomb, next to a dance floor, but then, this is a country of paradoxes.'

Kip signed them in at the desk, and a young Arab boy took them to their room. It was a tiny room on the first floor with one large window looking out into a garden area. There was a bed, a lamp on a table, and one chair. Kip saw the disappointed look on his wife's face.

'It's only for one night, honey. Half a night, actually now . . . and we'll be together.'

'It's stifling. Let's open the window,' Tess suggested.

'Not advisable. They don't believe in screens here in town. They just tolerate the flies, and if we leave the window open, somebody will probably climb in while we're asleep and make off with all of our clothes. But we have our own bathroom, see?' he announced trium-phantly, wanting her to be pleased.

Tess looked at the cramped, strange little bathroom with its half-size zinc tub and was not impressed, but Kip took her in his arms and held her close. 'I'm so happy to have you here. Don't let anything spoil our time together.'

When they were at last undressed and in bed, Kip soothed her and stroked her gently as he tried to kiss away all her doubts and fears. When at last he felt her begin to tremble with desire, he moved over and into her. Together, they began to move slowly, tentatively at first and then with more passion and power, until the bed suddenly swayed too far and crashed to the concrete floor, taking the surprised lovers with it.

Tess yelped and Kip swore. 'My God, what happened?' she asked, still under him.

'I don't know. Let's look,' Kip responded as they separated and scrambled to their feet.

'Good grief, will you look at that?' Kip said, lifting the mattress. 'They suspended a flat spring on two damn sawhorses.'

It was a funny moment, and holding each other in merriment, they laughed until they were weak.

Kip voted to leave the bed on the floor, but Tess dissented. 'Not a chance. I'll just bet there are lots of little things scurrying around down there. Come on, let's put it back together again,' she insisted.

'I've got a better idea,' Kip replied. 'Let's finish what we started, and then we'll put it back together again.'

Later, when they were cuddled in each other's arms, Tess decided it was time to share the news with him.

'Kip, I'm pregnant,' she said softly, her head resting on his shoulder, her leg thrown across his.

99

'How do you know, honey? We just did it,' he replied sleepily.

Tess giggled. 'It didn't happen tonight, silly. It happened on our honeymoon . . . probably at the Waldorf Hotel.'

Kip's eyes snapped open and he sat up in bed. Looking down at his wife, he said, 'Are you sure?'

Tess nodded and smiled. 'Very, but I didn't tell a soul. I wanted you to be the first to know.'

Kip seemed so genuinely startled that Tess had a moment of concern that he might not be pleased. She couldn't have been more wrong.

'Oh, God, that's great . . . next to marrying you, it's the best thing that's ever happened to me,' he said softly, leaning down to kiss her eyes, her nose, her cheeks, and finally her lips.

'I love you, Kip,' Tess said, her eyes gleaming with tears as she pulled her husband close to her.

Whispering words of love and joy to each other, they soon found themselves aroused again, and just as Kip was about to enter her welcoming pocket of joy, he hesitated. 'Is it okay? I mean . . . I don't want to hurt you.'

Pressing him deep inside her, she whispered, 'It's more than okay, darling . . . it's wonderful.'

14

Samara Mulhare looked at the cards in her hand without enthusiasm, and counted the points. There were three passes to her, and she had enough to bid. With very little support from her partner, they could probably make two easily, which would give them enough for the game and rubber. She looked across the table and thought how pleased her partner would be if they won. Veronica loved to win . . . at everything. She was the base commander's wife and a tough lady. All the officers' wives at Wheelus Field were thoroughly intimidated by her, as she expected them to be. Everybody except Sam, that was, because Sam clearly didn't give a damn about Veronica, the base commander, or the United States Air Force, except as they related to her husband.

Sam looked over at her opponents: Nell Carson, the wife of the major who frequently and sardonically referred to himself as the commander's pimp, although never within earshot of either his boss or Veronica, and Tess Kipling, a lieutenant's wife who had just arrived in Tripoli and who obviously hadn't played very much bridge. Veronica would hate to lose to these two women.

'Pass,' Sam said with a ghost of a smile tugging at the corner of her mouth, and they tossed their cards in.

It wasn't going to be easy to throw this game away, but it would be fun to try, Sam thought, amused. It would sure as hell mess up Veronica's day.

While the next hand was being dealt, Sam signaled the

Arab waiter and asked the women at the table, 'My treat . . . who'd like another round?'

Veronica shook her head. A tall woman with short brown hair flashed with gray, amply endowed with breasts and hips, Veronica was more muscular than most women. She was an excellent athlete, the best woman golfer on the base, and an aggressive bridge player. After years of being a proper officer's wife, she had finally reached the top at Wheelus, where her husband was the supreme commander. Although she was neither mean nor unkind, she expected tribute for the years she'd spent playing by the rules, toadying to the wives of her husband's superiors. It was her turn, and she was enjoying the power.

Sam didn't buy it, just as she didn't buy much of anything military. She was here only because she loved Bob with a passion that transcended all else, and she would do anything for him or their two small children, David and Melinda. She had been an Air Force wife for almost four years, and she had come to Tripoli only because Bob loved the Air Force and she couldn't bear to be separated from him. One of the few advantages about the assignment to Wheelus, as far as Samara was concerned, was that Bob's job here was primarily a nonflying one, and so for the first time in their marriage he was home almost every night. They were still as much in love as ever, although there had been no reconciliation with either of their families. They had both tried, but for some misbegotten reason, there had been no response from any of the grandparents, although telegrams had been sent when David and Melinda were born.

'I'll have an iced tea,' Tess said.

Sam looked at the attractive young woman and wondered what was wrong with her. She was too quiet, too pale.

102

'It's safer to have a martini, honey . . . at least the alcohol might kill some of the germs from the waiter's hands,' Nell suggested.

'Not today, thanks. My stomach's not in very good shape.'

'How long have you been here now?' Sam asked.

'Almost three weeks.'

'You've got the Tripoli Trots, honey. It took me three months to get used to this place and get over 'em,' Nell remarked. 'They won't kill you, but sometimes you'll wish they would.'

'Where are you living?' Veronica asked.

'An apartment in town. My husband applied for base housing, but they said it would take a year. I just wish my household goods would arrive. All we've got are a couple of footlockers and two canvas cots that we borrowed from Supply. I haven't got a stove or a fridge, so I have to come out here every day to eat.'

'We've all been through the same thing, my dear. Just be thankful you don't have kids to feed and take care of too,' Veronica said grandly, and patted Tess's arm.

Tess caught a look of annoyance as it crossed Sam's face. 'Veronica, just how long did you have to wait for your furniture and household goods to get here?' Sam asked with an irritable edge to her voice.

'Well, of course it was different for me. Mine arrived before I did, but I've certainly been through similar situations. Brick's been on active duty for over ten years, you know,' Veronica retorted, annoyed at this woman who didn't know her place. Bob Mulhare was only a major, and it irritated her that he and his family lived so grandly.

Although Sam had tried to structure their life in terms of her husband's rank, she eventually got tired of the

103

austerity and the pretense. Samara had inherited half of Abe Stone's estate shortly after arriving at Wheelus, and she decided to be honest and live like the wealthy woman she was. One day she simply boarded a commercial plane bound for Europe, where she went on a shopping spree of immense proportions. The dollar, 'American green' they called it, was highly prized, and there was an abundance of bargains to be had. She bought Wedgwood china in England and silver from Georg Jensen in Copenhagen, where she also acquired a houseful of sleek contemporary Danish furniture which was all the rage back in the States.

When she was told that she must not overpay her Tripoli employees and risk corrupting them, she promptly doubled the wages of the staff that ran her sumptuous villa. Her cook was Italian and one of the best in town, and her maids were diligent and clean and thrilled to be working for her. Almost everyone else entertained at the officers' club, but Sam had intimately elegant dinner parties in her own spacious dining room. She attended the lunches and parties in designer dresses shipped directly from New York and Paris.

What kept everyone from hating her was her warmth and generosity. If one of the wives was sick or needed help, Sam was there with chicken soup and offers to care for the children. She saw to it that rank was ignored at her parties and yet nobody ever turned down an invitation to her house. Because of her familiarity with the great and the celebrated, she and Bob were invited to social affairs given in town by the diplomats. Everybody in the world, it seemed, was interested in American movies, and Sam's close connection to them made her a desirable guest.

Veronica too lived like royalty in a country that was

poor and impoverished. The commander's residence was a beautiful rambling one-story villa overlooking the Mediterranean, situated in the loveliest spot on the base. Veronica fully expected it to be the center of social power in Tripoli, and she wanted no competition from the wife of a mere major.

The next hand was dealt, and Veronica opened with two hearts. Sam looked at her cards and swore silently. It was loaded with honors. They were obviously going to slam, and reluctantly she bid. Veronica got the contract for six hearts, and she was jubilant when Sam laid out her hand.

'Wonderful . . . wonderful!' Veronica exclaimed as Nell led a diamond. Suddenly Tess dropped her cards.

'Oh, God, I think I'm going to be sick!' Tess exclaimed, pressing her hand over her mouth and standing up quickly, but vertigo set in and she lost her balance.

Sam leapt from her chair and rushed to steady the pale, weaving young woman. 'Come on, I'll take you into the ladies' room and get some cold water on your face.'

'I don't think I can make it,' Tess whispered as she felt her stomach begin to convulse.

Sam grabbed a half-empty pitcher of iced tea from a waiter's hand and stuck it under Tess's chin.

'Keep walking. This'll catch it if anything comes up.'

They made it to the bathroom, and Sam held Tess as she leaned over the toilet and retched for what seemed to her an eternity.

Chili Shaheen was in the stall next to them, and she emerged quickly. 'Anything I can do to help the poor little thing?' she asked.

'Wet some of those paper towels for me, will you, Chili?' Sam asked.

'Just a sec,' Chili replied, and got them quickly. When

105

Tess's stomach was emptied, the two women bathed her face and hands in cool water and spoke soothing words of comfort.

Tess tried to thank them, but they both shrugged it off, and Sam introduced the other benefactor. 'Tess Kipling, meet Chili Shaheen.'

Feeling better and much relieved, Tess managed a weak smile. 'I can't thank you enough. Oh, Lord, I would have been ruined if I'd sat at that table another minute.'

'No you wouldn't, honey, but the cards sure as hell would've been in lousy shape,' Chili retorted. 'I bet you just got here, right?'

Tess nodded and whimpered, 'Three weeks, and I've been sick most of the time.'

'The trots last a long time, but don't worry, you'll get used to it after a while, and then your stomach will be like cast iron. Nothing will bother it,' Sam assured her.

'It's not just that. I'm pregnant too.'

'No kidding? Well, that was fast. It takes most wives at least a month to get that way after arriving here. The big joke is that it's in the water,' Chili remarked, and wryly added, 'Guess I'm drinkin' too much hootch.'

'We got married just ten days before Kip left, and that's when it happened,' Tess said softly, wiping her lips with the rough paper towel that had been moistened with cold water.

'You poor kid,' Sam murmured. 'Come on. I'll drive you home.'

'Won't Mrs Masters be upset if we don't go back and finish the game?' Tess asked.

Sam smiled her Cheshire smile and replied, 'I sure as hell hope so. Mind if I'm the one to tell her?'

106

15

After being driven home by Samara, Tess called Kip to tell him she was at home and wouldn't be having dinner at the officers' club as usual. She insisted that he stay, and asked him to stop at the commissary and buy her a box of crackers and some Seven-Up. Then she undressed and stretched out on the stiff canvas cot and tried to rest. She felt awful, but the apartment was cool and quiet. It had terrazzo floors, high ceilings, and thick walls. Kip had gotten some netting from Supply, and a carpenter was constructing screens for the windows, but now she kept the shutters closed, welcoming the darkness and security. This was the first time she had been alone in the apartment since her arrival.

The hours passed, and she dozed a little. It was almost eight o'clock when she heard Kip pulling the car into the garage below. She wanted to get up to greet him, but she just couldn't bring herself to move.

'Are you okay, hon?' he asked with concern, dropping to his knee beside her.

She reached up and stroked his cheek. 'I'm okay now. I got sick in the middle of Mrs Master's slam hand. I don't think I made a very good impression on her.'

'Well, she knew you were ill, didn't she?' he asked, frowning.

'Sam Mulhare went back to explain to her that I was too sick to continue and that she was taking me home.'

'God, honey, what were you doing with that woman?'

'If it hadn't been for "that woman," I'd probably have thrown up all over the cards,' Tess retorted.

'Don't get mad at me. It's just that there are some things you have to learn about life in the service. Mulhare is on the commander's wife's shit list, understand? And it won't do my career any good for you to get buddy-buddy with her,' he said apologetically.

Tess was shocked. 'Why would Veronica not like Sam? She's a lovely woman.'

'Because she doesn't play by the rules, that's why. You can't go around flaunting your dough. A major's wife is not supposed to have more servants, a fancier villa, or a more expensive car than the base commander's wife has, understand? Even if you've got the dough, you pretend that you don't.'

'That's stupid.'

'Yeah, maybe, but that's how the game's played. And Brick Masters is a tough bastard to work for. He plays a round of golf in the morning, has lunch at home, takes a nap, and arrives at the office about three. Then he rides everybody's ass and calls a staff meeting at five.'

'At quitting time? How can he get away with that?' Tess asked indignantly.

'Because he's the commander here, honey. He's God. By the way I'm flying to Benghazi Wednesday with him in Hall's place. I should be back by Friday evening.'

'You'll be gone two nights?' she asked nervously.

'Yep, and you better start driving tomorrow. Larry will pick me up in the morning. You can sleep in and come out to the base for lunch.'

'Oh, God,' she moaned. 'I hope I don't hit one of those horse-drawn carts that are always pulling out in front of you without warning.'

'They're not lethal, but the Italian drivers are,' Kip

agreed as he undressed and walked naked into the bathroom. 'But you've got to start sometime. It might as well be now.'

It was not long before he was snuggled beside her on her cot. For a long time he kissed her and caressed her, and she felt warm and comforted. There was nothing as reassuring as being in Kip's strong arms, feeling safe and loved and secure. They made love leisurely, and it was wonderfully sensually and fulfilling.

Since the cot was too narrow for them to sleep together, Tess soon found herself alone again, unable to sleep for hours because she was fretful about the coming day.

Kip was gone before she awakened the next morning. He had left the box of saltines by her cot, but they didn't help at all. Ten minutes after she got up, she drank a glass of cool water and then immediately retched. She felt feverish and ill.

She crawled back into bed and was just starting to doze off when the doorbell rang. Startled, she pulled her cotton housecoat on, ran a brush through her tousled hair, and hurried to the front balcony, where she could look down to see who was ringing.

To her disappointment, it was an Arab swathed in a heavy wool barracan that had once been white but which was now encrusted with dirt. He rang the doorbell again, this time more forcefully.

'What do you want?' Tess called down to him.

The old man looked up to where she stood twenty feet above him and whined, 'Baksheesh . . . baksheesh.' He was bent with age, his grizzled beard was matted with dirt, and one eye was milky and opaque. Flies, attracted by the particles of food in his beard, clustered about his face as he raised his arms in supplication. Pitifully he begged, 'Baksheesh, baksheesh,' which translated literally from Arabic meant something for nothing and was one of the few words foreigners learned quickly.

Heeding her husband's admonition never to give, she shook her head and walked inside, closing both the door and the shutters behind her. She knew he would continue to ring, but she had been warned that if she once gave in and tossed even one piastre over the balcony, the house would be marked, and legions of the poor would descend on her. Nevertheless, she felt sorry for the old man. During the Depression, she could remember the countless out-of-work and hungry men knocking on her parents' door. Her mother never turned a single one of them away without giving him at least something to eat or a few coins. Ignoring the man's plea made Tess feel guilty for having so much in the midst of great poverty and not sharing some of it.

She was beginning to feel light-headed again and was just about to lie down on her cot when the telephone rang.

'I was hoping you might have already left,' her husband's voice proclaimed.

'No, I'm feeling really awful today. I think I better stay in bed.'

'Oh, God,' Kip moaned, 'you can't. I'm really sorry, but I just found out that we're expected to make a call at the commander's house between five and six.'

'Not today?' she asked, alarmed.

'Today. Military custom, honey. I'll wear my dress uniform and you have to wear a hat and white gloves. We're expected to have one drink, nibble a canapé, leave our calling cards, and depart exactly fifteen minutes after we arrive.'

'Are you crazy? I can't get all dressed up and go out

110

today!' she snapped, outraged. 'I've still got diarrhea, and I think I'm running a fever. You'll have to go by yourself.'

'You don't understand, Tess. This is a command performance. You have to go.'

She would not give in. 'No! There's just no way I'm taking a chance on getting sick in public again.'

'Look, I'll get Larry to run me home at four-thirty. Rest awhile, and then try to be ready when I get there. I've gotta go.'

When Tess realized that Kip had hung up the phone, she slammed down the receiver in frustration. Goddammit! Why hadn't someone told her she was enlisting in the Air Force when she married an officer?

Frustrated, she threw herself onto the cot and buried her face in the pillow.

The telephone rang half an hour later, and she snatched it up, hoping it was Kip calling to apologize for being so insensitive, but it wasn't.

'How're you feeling today?' Samara Mulhare asked.

'Worse, if that's possible, and now Kip tells me I have to make a formal call at the base commander's residence. I'll never make it.' A sob caught in her throat, and she was humiliated that this stranger might suspect that she was crying, which she was.

'Settle down, now. I'll be right over.'

'No!' Tess tried to protest, but Sam had hung up. Tess looked at her surroundings in despair. She should try to tidy up a bit, but it was hopeless. Their clothes were hung on makeshift racks and stacked in footlockers. Who was she trying to impress anyway?

Within half an hour the doorbell rang again. Tess checked to be sure it really was Sam, and then she walked gingerly down the steep flight of stairs to the door on the street to let her in.

'Sweetie pie, you should have just thrown the keys over the railing. Now, get back upstairs and sit down. I'll be with you in a second. I have some things to carry from the car.'

Tess sat on the edge of her cot as Sam toted a large box up the stairs. She carried it into the kitchen and set it on the sink, took a quick look around the apartment, and nodded her head.

'Just as I suspected. Didn't your orders instruct you to bring a few simple things in your hold baggage, like a hot plate, a few dishes, and a pan or two?'

'I intended to, but Kip told me not to bother. He said we'd just eat all our meals at the club until our household goods arrived.'

Sam shook her head. 'Men!' she sniffed. 'Well, I brought some stuff. I'll connect this hot plate at the sink, and at least you can heat a cup of soup or make yourself some tea.' She opened a mason jar and filled a small pan with broth.

'I keep fresh chicken soup in my fridge at all times. I make the kids eat it at least twice a week. One of these days, scientists are going to discover that it really does have medicinal qualities. I also brought you a jar of peanut butter, a loaf of fresh bread, and a can of tuna. I brought a can opener too.'

As she talked, she hustled about the kitchen, with Tess watching her, wondering how anyone could possibly think badly of this woman.

'You're a saint, Sam. Do you know that?'

'How did you know?' Sam laughed, and then, qualifying her comment, said, 'Well, maybe not really, but that's what Bob called me the first night we met. It was a joke. He still calls me St Sam occasionally.'

When the soup was hot, Sam poured it into a cup and

brought it on a plate to Tess with a few crackers spread with pineapple-flavored cream cheese. She set it on her lap and commanded, 'Now, finish that, every bite of it. One thing I've learned about pregnancy and the trots. You have to keep up your strength with both of them.'

Tess sipped the soup, and it tasted better than anything she'd ever had before. As she ate, they chatted comfortably, and Sam told her the latest base gossip. When Tess complained about having to get dressed up to make a formal call, Sam surprisingly took Kip's side.

'He's absolutely right, my dear. There are some things we wives just have to do. It's true I've bent the rules a bit now and then, but I do it with Bob's blessing, understand? He also enjoys kicking a little dust in the brass's faces.'

'Do you like being an Air Force wife, Sam?' Tess asked.

Samara let out a long sigh. 'Wow, that's a hard one. Do I have a choice? Actually, no, I don't. I have to like it because my husband loves planes and flying, and he loves being in the Air Force in spite of the fact that he's kind of a maverick. I could never force him to choose between me and the work he loves.'

'Couldn't he do something with planes in civilian life?'

'Like being a test pilot? Uh-uh, too risky.'

'A commercial pilot?'

'He says that's like being a bus driver.'

'What's his job here? This is a MATS base, isn't it?' Tess asked.

'Theoretically. At least according to the UN charter we're only allowed to have a transport command here, but since when did Uncle Sam let anybody tell him what he could and couldn't do?' she replied mysteriously, adding, 'One of the diplomats told me that the runways at Wheelus were phenomenally long, capable of taking the largest bomber yet built. Figure it out for yourself.'

Sam took the tray from Tess when the soup and the crackers had been consumed. 'Now, do you feel better?'

Tess nodded sheepishly. 'I think I do.'

'Good. Now, don't you think you'd feel even better if you took a nice, long hot bath?'

'I guess so,' Tess agreed, but there was reluctance in her voice.

'The *scaldabagno* scares the hell out of you, right?'

'Right. I'm sure the thing is going to blow up every time I light it.'

'Nonsense. It's the best, most efficient hot water system ever invented. It heats the water as it flows through its pipes. No need to have big tanks that leak or anything. Come on. Make friends with it.'

When Kip arrived, prepared to haul his pitiful wife off her cot, he found her ready to go, dressed in a trim black-and-white cotton dress, with a little white straw pillbox on her head. The seams on her stockings were straight, her shorty gloves were gleaming white, and her lipstick was bright and red. She didn't look at all sick.

'You look great!' he exclaimed, delighted that she'd capitulated gracefully.

'Thanks to Samara Mulhare, who came over this afternoon and put me together,' she said pointedly.

Kip started to say something and then thought better of it. 'Well . . . she did a good job,' he admitted.

'Let's go,' Tess said, marching toward the door. 'Fifteen minutes is about all the time I can manage to be charming and gracious before I might have to rush to the bathroom.'

16

When the date of the tea for all newly arrived officers' wives came round, Tess was feeling better. Approaching her fifth month of pregnancy and already bursting out of her trousseau clothes, Tess had gone with Sam to a little dressmaker in town, who made her a couple of tentlike maternity dresses so she would be comfortable.

If it weren't for the frequent overnight trips Kip was being assigned, Tess would have been reasonably content with her new life. She tried to be happy for him, since he had been given more responsibility and was getting a lot of flight time, but the lonely nights in the apartment still frightened her, and she was envious of the women who had quarters on the base. Although Sam invited her to sleep overnight at her villa when she was alone, she was afraid to suggest it to Kip since he still hadn't warmed to the idea of her friendship.

The tea was one of the more important affairs of the Officers' Wives' Club, an organization, Kip had informed her, in which it was mandatory that she actively participate. Tess didn't mind at all, since she was homesick and feeling directionless. Most of the wives she had met played golf every day, or bridge, but she didn't see much point in taking up golf now that she was pregnant, and although she enjoyed bridge occasionally, it bored her on a daily basis. She was rapidly reading her way through the selection of novels at the library on the base.

Sam arrived to pick her up promptly at two, and they drove out to Wheelus in Sam's snappy MG sports car with the top down. It was a beautiful day, and the leisurely drive was delightful, especially since Sam seemed to know everything and everybody and kept up a running commentary of gossip.

'I understand the commander intends to crack down on the Dirty Dozen,' Sam remarked, 'although he's such an old goat himself, you wonder why he's getting so pious all of a sudden.'

'What in the world is the Dirty Dozen?'

'You know . . . those women who haunt the club day and night when their husbands are out of town.'

Tess shook her head. 'I never noticed.'

'Well, you've certainly met Aurora Bingham, haven't you? Stringy black hair, always looks like it needs to be brushed or washed. Spends a lot of time at the beach, and her skin looks like leather. Not pleasant, at least to women. She's always on the prowl . . . smokes with a long cigarette holder . . .'

'The one they call the Beast of the Bar?'

'God, I hate to hear anybody labeled like that,' Sam snapped.

'So do I,' Tess agreed.

'You know, it galls me how men denigrate women for playing the same filthy little games that they do. Brick Masters is the biggest skirt-chaser on the base, but he's planning to have all the men whose wives are in the Dirty Dozen reassigned to other commands.'

'What do they do that's so awful?'

'When their husbands are out of town, they pick up officers in the bar and take them home to bed. They have a little score sheet they keep on each man's prowess, and they pass it around their group,' Sam said, chuckling.

'You're kidding! They actually talk about it?' Tess asked in shocked disbelief.

116

'They brag about it, my dear. And if most men weren't such egotists, they'd steer clear of them, but the fools actually think they'll get a high score.'

'How did you find out about this? Do you ever talk to these women?'

'They don't tell women outside their circle any of this stuff. Bob brought home copies of the score sheets. They're a riot.'

'How did he get them?' Tess asked suspiciously.

'Now, now, not the way you think. Everybody talks to Bob because he's likable and funny and never puts anybody down. Anyway, one night he was in the bar waiting for me to arrive at the club for dinner when Aurora tried to pick him up. He declined, of course, but they started talking, and he came straight out and asked her if the rumors were true. She said yes, and to prove it, she pulled some score sheets out of her purse and showed him. The woman who has the most sheets filled out at the end of the month wins, and the rest of the group treats her to dinner at the Del Mehari in town.'

Tess's curiosity won out over her reticence to discuss sexual subjects. 'What kind of . . . things does the form, um . . .'

Sam giggled. 'Well, size, for instance . . . both length and girth. Then there's endurance, and recovery . . . you know, how long it takes him to get it up for a second go-around . . . and satisfaction, which means how many times she got off.'

'Oh my God!' Tess squealed, pressing her hands to her flushed cheeks. 'That's awful! How could they do that?'

'I think it's pretty funny, especially since everybody seems to feel it's okay for men to talk about the size of a woman's breasts.'

'I'd just die if I ever found out that Kip's name appeared on one of their papers,' Tess said quietly.

'Well, I wouldn't die if I ever found out Bob was unfaithful to me, but I'd make sure *he* did,' Sam remarked with a laugh.

As they were waved through the gates at Wheelus, Sam asked, 'Mind if we stop at the base exchange for a minute? I promised Melinda I'd bring her a new box of crayons.'

'Not at all. I'd love to see if they have anything new.'

Inside, the exchange was packed with people. At one counter there was a crowd so large it was impossible to see what was being sold.

'Let's take a guess,' Sam said. 'I'll bet it's Hummel figurines.'

'Well, whatever it is, if that many people want it, we better get in line,' Tess said with a grin.

'That's the spirit. You get us a place, and I'll go buy the stuff I need.'

Twenty minutes later, they were back in the car on their way to the officers' club.

'I don't understand it,' Tess exclaimed in bewilderment. 'People were waiting to buy little brass ashtrays shaped like shoes from India. You can buy that junk at Woolworth's.'

'It's just something to do, that's all. And if they cost a dollar at home, they can probably buy it for less than a quarter here. You learn to find enjoyment in very small adventures in a remote place like Tripoli.'

The club was crowded with women wearing hats and gloves. In a land of deprivation and poverty, it was comforting to dress up and wear hose, drink tea or fruit punch, and eat little cakes and cookies. It was a ritual that brought cohesiveness and reason and a sense of homeland. The British had been doing it for centuries, but it was a new experience for Americans. The base was comforting because it was home territory.

Vernoica Masters stood in the receiving line, and she smiled affectionately as she greeted Tess.

'It's so good to see you looking well again,' she said, clasping her hand firmly. 'Please don't leave before we have a chance to chat. I have a proposal to make to you.'

Sam wandered away to talk to some friends, and Tess went to the table for a cup of fruit punch. It was a ghastly red color that turned her stomach, so she took tea instead.

A hand touched her shoulder from behind, and a low seductive voice said, 'My, my darlin', you sure look pretty now that your face isn't green anymore.'

Whirling around, Tess looked into a pair of dark-fringed blue eyes and smiled. 'Why, hello, Chili. How nice to see you again.'

'What a sharp lady you are to remember my name in spite of the terrible fix you were in that day! I'm sure glad to see you're feelin' better. Tell me, when is the baby due?' she said, poking her finger at Tess's waistline.

'Not until January, although at the rate I'm ballooning, it might be during the Christmas holidays.'

As they chatted, Tess was mesmerized by the woman's soft unfocused beauty. Chili looked as if she'd been painted by Renoir. Her hair was a deep gold-red, shining, thick and wavy. Her skin was pale, translucent, and unblemished, untouched by the sun's rays. Her breasts and hips were full, her waist narrow, and the rayon print dress she wore was tight and low-cut. She had thin, delicate fingers, tipped by long nails that were painted a bright red, and she had a habit of fluttering her hands about to punctuate her conversation. Her eyelashes were thick and dark brown, and her lips were full and sensuous. There was a deep dimple in her left cheek when she smiled, which she did often. She was so voluptuously feminine she made Tess feel almost like a boy, in spite of her protruding pregnant belly.

'How long have you been in Tripoli?' Tess asked.

'Almost a year now. Gam and I came together. I didn't have to wait like most of the wives did, because we were transferred here from Rhein-Main in Germany, dammit.'

'You weren't happy about that?'

The sparkle in Chili's eyes dulled as she replied flatly, 'It was a career move for Gam. His parents are Syrian, and he speaks fluent Arabic. The base liaison officer, Colonel Morelo, is a sweet guy who gets along well with the British and speaks Italian, but they needed someone who could talk to the Arabs in their own language. At least we got housing in the new quarters on the base, but I sure did like Germany. I wish we could have finished our tour there,' Chili said wistfully.

'Do you have children?' Tess asked.

'Not yet, although we sure as hell have been tryin',' she replied, and Tess noticed a quiver of vulnerability in her voice.

Suddenly Veronica Masters descended on Tess like a battleship under full speed. Without preamble, she asked, 'I'm looking for someone to write a little booklet that could be sent to dependents waiting for their orders to come here to Wheelus. Your husband said that you had been an English major in college. Is that right?'

'Yes, but it was in literature. I was planning to get an advanced degree so I could teach. I was never interested in being a writer,' Tess hedged, fearing that Veronica would not be an easy person to please.

'Good,' Veronica responded, ignoring what she didn't want to hear. 'You'll do just fine. Now, if you need any information or help, Brick will see that it's made available to you. I'll have someone move that the Wives' Club pay for this printing, and we'll all be set. Believe me, my dear, this booklet is desperately needed. Most of these women come here completely unprepared.'

'Amen,' Tess replied too softly to be heard.

Mission accomplished, Veronica sailed away, and Tess heard a gentle voice behind her whisper, 'I see you just volunteered for one of the madam's projects.'

Tess turned and saw an attractive and tiny woman smiling at her. 'You heard?'

'I didn't have to. Experience is the key. Hi, I'm Beth Cellini, and you're new here, right?'

'Hi, I'm Tess Kipling, and not really. I've been here for almost two months, but I've been too sick to get around much.'

'It happens to all of us, but mercifully it's not permanent. I hope you're feeling better now. Are you living in town?'

'Yes, and you?'

'Me too. You and your husband must come over for dinner some evening. Do you like Italian food?'

'Love it,' Tess replied, feeling that perhaps she had made a new friend.

On the way home, she asked Sam about Beth.

'Pretty lady, isn't she?' Samara replied. 'Her husband, Joe, is a real sweetheart. You'd never guess his father was a Mafia don, would you?'

Tess gasped. 'Oh, my Lord, how do you know?'

'Hey, don't get me wrong, Joe and Beth are as straight-arrow as they come. You see, his father put him into West Point because he wanted him out and away from the rackets. It was also a good place to keep his only son safe and protected. Joe got hooked on the military and stayed in, which was a good thing, because his father was assassinated in a still-unsolved shooting two years ago.'

'Does he talk about his family?'

'Never, but his name and profession were mentioned in the papers at the time. One thing that he and Beth have mentioned, however, is that their marriage was arranged between their families.'

'Then her family . . .'

'I never asked, and she never volunteered anything except that it was the greatest thing that ever happened to them both. They have a darling little girl, Angela, who is about six, or seven years old. Although Beth's never talked about it, I think they're quite disappointed not to have more children.'

Tess was fascinated. Maybe the Air Force life was going to be more interesting than living in Champaign, Illinois, after all.

17

'I want to do it,' Beth said with finality, 'even if I don't get paid as much as the other teachers.'

Her husband, Captain Joseph Cellini, shook his head. 'Dammit, now. That third-grade class has close to forty kids in it, and God knows when the government will find another teacher to send over here. It could be months.'

'All the more reason I should take the job. Those children haven't had any decent instruction since their teacher quit two months ago, and even if I have no formal training, I'll be better than what they have. Besides, now that Angela is in school, I have lots of time on my hands. You know I don't like bridge or golf, I hate all the busybody girl talk at the club, and I've got more sex than I can handle right here at home, so joining the Dirty Dozen is out. Come on. Give in,' she coaxed him gently.

Beth was a tiny, frail-looking woman. Her hair was dark and so thickly curled it was almost unmanageable, her skin was a golden olive color, and her eyes were large, brown, and slightly tilted up at the outside corners. There was a slight space between her two front teeth, and she had a habit of touching it with the tip of her tongue with her lips slightly parted that was unconsciously sexy.

From the moment he first laid eyes on her, Joe had considered her the most beautiful woman who had ever lived, and he was utterly devoted to her. Because of their family background, he tended, however, to be overly protective of her and their little girl.

Joe was especially uncomfortable with the idea of his

wife working. As gentle and unassuming as he was ordinarily, he intended to stand firm on this point. In the Air Force, a wife was expected to devote all of her time to caring for her husband, her home, and her family. It was a notion he approved, since it was in keeping with the traditions of his Italian family.

'Can't somebody else do it, like your new friend Tess? Her husband, Kip, graduated from the Point five years after I did, and he told me she graduated from college just before she came over here,' Joe insisted.

'I already suggested that, but she's pregnant, you know, and Veronica doesn't want her distracted from working on the book for dependents,' Beth replied as she went to the small gas stove to stir the red sauce she was cooking.

'When do they want you to start?' Joe asked, sensing that the battle was lost. As sweet and soft-spoken as Beth was, she was impossible to move once she set her mind on something.

'Immediately, like tomorrow morning. Go check to see if Dici set the table properly.'

'Where is she? Didn't you tell her she'd have to stay late to clean up tonight?'

'Joe, you know I didn't. I only pay that poor woman twenty dollars a month, she cleans this apartment five days a week, does all the laundry, scrubs the floors every morning, and then goes home to cook and clean for her own husband and four kids. I know the other wives expect the maids to work late and baby-sit, but I'm just not going to do it, not unless I pay her extra, and you won't let me do that.'

'Honey, look, as the base contracting officer, I have to do a lot of business with the people here in town, and everybody's annoyed with us for overpaying the workers. They say the Americans come to town, and prices go up

124

for everybody. If I let you pay Dici extra money, she'll brag to all her friends that she makes more than they do, and I'll be on the carpet within a week . . . or less.'

'You've made your point, darling. Now, go check the table. Gamal and Chili will be here at six. Did you get some gin?'

'I've got two cases of booze in the car. Max made a run to Cypress and brought some back. The price went up, though. I got a case of Canadian Club and a case of Gordon's . . . cost me more than twenty bucks.'

'Each?'

'No, for both.'

'Well, it should last awhile, if you don't start dumping the pitcher when the ice melts in the martinis,' she said pointedly.

'Hey, everybody does that, not just me. Nobody wants a drink full of water.'

'I've got something special tonight,' Beth said, changing the subject.

'What's that?'

'Well, when I went up to the commander's villa to talk to Veronica, a case of avocados had just been shipped in for them, and while we were talking, the maid carried a box in and asked her what they were.'

'Don't tell me the bitch actually parted with one of them?'

'She's not a bitch, Joe . . . a pain maybe, but anyway, she didn't have much choice. My jaw dropped and my eyes glazed over and I said, "Are those really, truly avocados?" Of course, she only gave me one, but I bowed and scraped and drooled my thank-yous as I backed obsequiously out the door. I'm sure that as soon as I left, she informed the maid never to display any of the goodies in front of the peasants. Should I slice it on the salad?'

'With that green leather they call lettuce here?' Joe snorted disdainfully. 'I hate eating that crummy stuff. With every bite, I think about the midnight soil they use for fertilizer. I hope you washed it well in Mikroklene.'

'The BX is all out. They told me to use Clorox,' Beth replied, and giggled at the expression on his face.

'Oh, God, are you kidding? You washed the salad stuff in Clorox? Did you use Tide too?' he asked sarcastically.

'Don't be such a fussbudget. I rinsed it, and I put two extra cloves of garlic in the olive oil, just in case.'

The doorbell rang, and Joe went to answer it. To his surprise, Chili stood there alone.

'Chili, come in. Where's Gamal?'

'He won't be here. That son of a bitch Masters called him in for some kinda conference. I knew Beth'd probably gone to a lot of trouble cookin', so I came by myself. Gam said to tell you he was real sorry.'

As she walked into the apartment, Joe noted that she was a little unsteady on her feet. 'Are you okay, Chili?' he asked.

'Nothin' wrong with me that one of your man-size martinis won't fix. Beth, darlin', you're lookin' prettier than ever. Looks like this Tripoli life is agreein' with you.'

Joe mixed her a martini, but he diluted it with water, hoping he wouldn't have to drive her home.

Beth served dinner immediately, but Chili had no interest in food. She picked at the salad, ignoring the precious bits of avocado, nibbled at the spaghetti, and passed on the bread. The only thing that seemed to interest her was the Chianti, and although Joe poured lightly, she got progressively drunker.

'Damned Air Force. I'm so sick of it all. Gam spends more damned time in Benghazi with the queen than he does with me.'

'He has a big job, smoothing over relations with King Idris and the government. It's a new country, and we have to give them all the help we can. You should be proud of what he's doing, Chili,' Beth said encouragingly.

Chili seemed not to hear. 'Even when he's at home, he never talks to me,' she complained. 'He makes me so mad sometimes that I think to hell with it all. I ought to go back to Texas. At least then I wouldn't have to do any more time on the damned prayer rug,' she mumbled.

A look of concern passed between husband and wife. Chili was too drunk to realize what she was saying, and they had no desire to hear anything she shouldn't be talking about.

Beth immediately got up to bring the coffee, but Chili waved it away, and Joe said, 'Why don't we give you a lift home? Beth, you can drive her in our car, and I'll follow in hers.'

Chili protested that she was perfectly fine, but Joe and Beth were insistent, and once in the car on the unlighted road, she didn't have much to say. As they approached her quarters, it became obvious that she was making a valiant and somewhat successful stretch toward sobriety. There was a touch of fear in her voice as she said confidentially, 'Beth, Gam'd kill me if he found I was too drunk to drive myself home.'

'We won't say a word, I promise.'

'He gets so mad when I drink. He says cheap booze is making alcoholics out of everybody here.'

'He's got a point there,' Beth agreed.

On the way home, Beth expressed her concern. 'Joe, I'm worried about her. I've never seen anybody sober up as fast as she did, and she looked scared to death when

127

she got out of the car. Do you know what she was talking about at the dinner table?'

'Let's just forget about it. There's a lot of stuff going on around here, and I don't want any part of it.'

18

Tess was lying on the beach one Saturday afternoon, waiting for Kip, who had promised to leave the office early and meet her there. Although the workday was officially over at noon, it was past one and he still hadn't arrived. She looked around at the families spreading out their blankets to take advantage of the last of the warm beach weather before the winter rains set in, and she felt singularly alone.

Kip never seemed to have much time for her. His commanding officer, Lieutenant Colonel Nat Hall, who was on Masters' staff, was piling most of the work on Kip and he accepted it without complaint. Tess marveled at the discipline instilled in him at West Point. Educated in a civilian university where she had been taught that it was good to question everything in a quest for truth and understanding, Tess had trouble relating to the military. She rejected the concept of blind obedience to authority and believed that it stunted one's ability to think and reason.

More people arrived to spread out their blankets on the sand, but seeing no one she knew, she felt increasingly isolated. She pulled a pad of paper from her canvas beach bag and began rereading some of the pages she'd written for Veronica's pamphlet. It was almost complete, but she was unsure about the wry humor. Kip had pointed out that it probably couldn't be appreciated by anyone who hadn't lived there yet. She had wanted the material to be

129

upbeat and not reflect her own ambivalent feelings about the place.

She looked up from the paper to gaze upon the beautiful, clear Mediterranean. The sun was shining on its crystal teal swells as they rolled toward the shore, breaking with a splash of sparks so bright and glimmering it seemed as if a thousand Tinker Bells were dancing on the crest of each one. What was wrong with her that she couldn't be happy in such an idyllic setting?

It must be homesickness, she decided, and the words of her old friend Oliver Wendell Holmes seemed to float in on the ocean breeze: 'Where we love is home, home that our feet may leave, but not our hearts.' She missed her mother, and she especially missed her conversations with her father.

She had thought she and Kip would have long talks about ideas, exchange thoughts the way she had with her father, but Kip didn't seem interested in talking much to her anymore. Once she had become his wife, he seemed determined to squeeze her into the mold of the perfect officer's wife, and she didn't fit into it yet. Maybe she would in time. She placed her hand on her swollen belly and waited for the movement that would tell her that her life now had meaning above and beyond her own inadequate self. She was creating a human being, a real person who might possibly grow up to make a difference in the world around him.

'Poor baby. I promise I won't expect you to shoulder the burden of my own discarded dreams. Even if I'm not a very good wife, I'l try to be a good mother,' she murmured.

'Talking to yourself? Tsk, tsk, that's not good,' a gentle voice spoke from above her.

Tess looked up and squinted to make out the face of

the woman standing over her, silhouetted by the bright sun behind her.

'Beth Cellini, hello! It's so good to see you!' Tess exclaimed, happy to be rescued from her dreary solitude.

Tess scooted over to make room on the blanket and asked, 'How's the third grade? Sam told me you had taken on the teaching assignment.'

'I've found I have no talent for it. I wish I'd been pregnant so I could have said no.'

Of course, Tess thought bitterly, they hadn't asked her to do it because of her protruding belly. Perish the thought that a woman with child be allowed to stand up in front of a class and let the kids know what she'd been doing in bed.

'Well, at least you've got a reason to pass up some of the bridge sessions,' she consoled Beth.

'Yep, but it's the biggest, most difficult class in the school. How was I to know that the teacher ran off to save her sanity? I've been sitting bolt upright in bed at night, screaming in my sleep, "Jimmy, sit down!"'

'That's awful,' Tess sympathized.

'That's not the worst. Colonel Royce's wife stopped in to tell me that if I wanted my husband ever to see gold leaves on his shoulders, I'd better make sure that her son, Doug, got promoted next year.'

'She threatened you flat out?' Tess asked, amazed.

'I wanted to tell the bitch off, but I didn't. I just agreed to do my best. She wouldn't have believed anything I said anyway, and Joe would have taken the heat, although I must say I was sorely tempted to comment on the way she and her husband are always taking off for vacations in Europe and leaving their three kids here with Mohammed, the houseboy.'

'I just don't understand how they can do that.'

131

'By the way, I called Kip's office to find out where you were, and he asked me to tell you that he wouldn't be here for another two hours.'

'Oh, no! I can't stay out here for two more hours. I'm already getting pink,' Tess complained.

'Let's go to the club and have lunch. You can call him and tell him to pick you up there.'

'I can't. I've got shorts on, and they're not allowed in the dining room,' Tess pointed out.

'Nobody will be around today. Just carry your beach bag in front of you. That maternity top is almost long enough to be a dress anyway.'

They sat down at a table just inside the entrance to the dining room, and Beth gave Tess a scarf to cover her bare legs, and the two giggled like conspirators.

'If Kip finds out I did this, he'll be furious,' Tess said, looking around the room furtively, hoping to see no one she knew.

'Look, it's not a court-martial offense,' Beth replied, laughing.

Although they had talked together on only one other occasion, the women felt as if they were old friends. Just as they were being served the ubiquitous glass of luke-warm iced tea, Sam Mulhare appeared in the doorway. As soon as she saw them, she came over and sat down at the table.

'Hi, I was hoping I'd find someone to talk to. I just couldn't stay home another minute.' Her hands were shaking, and she asked the waiter to bring her a gin and tonic.

'Isn't it a bit early in the day for that, Sam?' Beth asked disapprovingly.

'Not today. I've been a nervous wreck since Bob told me there'd been a bad plane crash. Two of the fighter

132

pilots collided during target practice. Nobody knows why. Bob was in the tower at the time, and he said they just smashed right into each other and exploded in a fiery ball that plummeted into the sea.'

Any plane crash brought into the open the monstrous fear that was the constant companion of every pilot's wife. It was a creature that lived in their homes, ate at their tables, peered out from the eyes of their children, and slept beside them. When they were making love to their husbands, it perched at the foot of the bed like a vulture, watching, telling them to make it good because this might be the last time.

In the four years that she had been married, Sam Mulhare had often told herself to ignore this monster and not permit it to haunt her. Life was temporary for everyone, she reasoned. She could just as easily be clipped off the vine by a drunken driver or a dreadful disease. And she believed it, until a crash, and then the monster opened its jaws and began to chew on her.

'I suppose that's why Joe couldn't have lunch with me. It's his job to make the mortuary arrangements and inspect the remains,' Beth said, and wanted to bite her tongue for being so insensitive. Joe was not a rated officer, having washed out of flight school when he burst an eardrum. Although the monster did not live in her house, Beth felts its presence in those around her. Furtively she sneaked her rosary from her purse and held it in her hand for comfort.

Tess touched Sam's arm. 'Look, it wasn't Bob, and it wasn't Kip. Let's be thankful for that.'

Sam shook her head. 'I know, but I can't help thinking about the two poor women out there who loved their husbands as much as I love mine.'

The women had lunch and talked quietly. When it was

133

time to leave, Beth suggested that they and their husbands come to dinner at her house that evening, and both women accepted. It was a time to draw together.

As they walked to their cars, Beth remembered the reason she had sought Tess out. 'I almost forgot to tell you why I came looking for you. I found you a maid. A terrific one.'

'I don't need a maid, Beth. I've got a three-room apartment as bare as Mother Hubbard's cupboard.'

Beth insisted, however. 'Tess, my dear, having affordable servants is one of the few compensations for being a service wife overseas. Besides, this woman is a gem, and you'll need her when the baby comes, to mop the tons of dust from the terrazzo floors and wash diapers. You don't have a washing machine, do you?'

Tess shook her head.

'Well, you're getting her the only way you can get a good servant, from an American who's rotating back to the States. The maid's name is Giuseppina Bressani. She's married, so she won't live in, and she speaks only Italian.'

'How'll I talk to her?'

'You'll find a way. Everybody else does. Just think of it as a learning experience. I told her to report to work Monday morning. See you at six-thirty.'

'Can I bring anything?' Tess asked.

'Just your sweet self and your dear husband.'

19

Tess and Kip walked the three blocks to the Cellini apartment with Kip protesting every step of the way.

'Dammit, Tess. You know I don't want to get involved socially with the Mulhares. Why did you accept the Cellinis' invitation?' he grumbled.

'Because I like both Beth and Sam very much, and I should think you'd be happy that I've made some friends here. And please try to make the best of it. One little evening won't damage your career. Besides,' she wheedled, 'you owe me something for standing me up this afternoon. We were supposed to have a lovely day at the beach, remember?'

'I had to stay and brief Masters, because Hall got called on the carpet about something, and he, of course, blamed me. Said I hadn't provided him with the proper information.'

'Was it true?'

'No! The guy's scared to death of Masters, and so he's become a real artist at laying the blame on anyone who works for him. He makes it a point never to take responsibility for anything. Thank God, his tour will be up next year, and with a little luck, maybe I can get Masters to let me have his job.'

'But you're not even a captain yet, Kip, and everyone on the staff is a lieutenant colonel.'

'Look, if Masters wants me, I'll get the job, even if I don't have the rank. I should be a captain by then, anyway.'

Tess knew better than to argue. Besides, what did she know? Her father had been a doctor, and since he practiced alone, he had been answerable to no one except God. She had grown up in a world uncluttered by power and people maneuvering for position, and all the politics seemed childish to her. She sighed audibly.

'What's wrong now?' he asked, irritated.

'I'm not a very good service wife, I'm afraid. I just can't seem to get the hang of it.'

He put his arm around her and hugged her briefly. '*Malish*, sweetheart. You'll learn.'

The walk to the Cellini apartment took only a few minutes, and when they arrived, Joe greeted them warmly.

'Kip, good to see you. I hear that Hall was on your ass again today,' he said. 'Come on in and have a drink. You know the Mulhares, don't you?'

Bob Mulhare pulled his compact, muscular body out of the chair and approached the new arrivals with his hand outstretched. 'Not officially. Nice to meet you, Kip . . . Tess. Sam tells me you're expecting a little one. Congratulations to you both.'

Kip shook hands with him, and in spite of himself, he was disarmed by the warmth of the man's smile and his open and charming manner. Bob Mulhare's bright blue eyes twinkled with a sense of fun, and he seemed genuinely pleased to meet them.

Turning to his wife, Bob said, 'Babydoll, you said she was pretty, but she's not what you call pretty . . . she's a real beauty. Are you Irish, by any chance, colleen?' he asked Tess.

Pleased and somewhat self-conscious, Tess replied. 'Well, only on my mother's side.'

'Aha, I knew it!' he exclaimed in delight, and taking

136

charge, he quickly put everyone at ease and gathered them all into a relaxed, enjoyable social group. Bob knew just how to keep the conversation going, keep it light, and keep everyone interested and involved. Tess watched in fascination as even her husband came under the spell of this handsome, friendly Irishman.

Joe mixed and poured martinis by the pitcherful, throwing them down the sink when they became diluted by the melting ice. When everyone was in serious danger of becoming potted, Beth served up spaghetti that was delicious and rich and sobering. Her guests ate it with gusto, laughing and talking between mouthfuls.

Tess couldn't get enough of the thick, crusty bread. It tasted like nothing she had eaten since she arrived at Wheelus, and she said so. 'Wherever did you buy it?' she asked.

Beth smiled slyly and replied mysteriously, 'I'll tell you after dinner.'

By the time coffee was served, along with a plate of peanut-butter cookies from the commissary, Bob had everyone organized into two teams to play charades. He chose Tess and Joe to be on his team, and Sam joined Beth and Kip.

It was a crazy, hilarious game, and even Kip lost some of his reserve and became a bit raunchy as he tried to act out 'Marilyn Monroe.'

Tutored by Bob, Tess found she had a great knack for the game and her team trounced the other group resoundingly. It was past midnight when Kip finally called a halt.

'I know it's Saturday, but I think my wife's had enough excitement for one night,' he said. Although Tess's color was high and she was enjoying herself immensely, he could tell that she was beginning to tire. 'Besides, we have to walk three blocks to our place. If I'd known we were going to stay this late, I'd have driven the car.'

Bob stood up immediately. 'We've only got a two-seater, but Sam can drive Tess home. Come on, Kip. You and I can get a head start on them and walk. We need the exercise anyway. Let's go. Thanks, Joe . . . Beth. It was terrific. Next Saturday night, our place, okay? I'll give you guys a chance to beat us . . . if you can.' The two men thanked their hosts, and the shorter Bob set a pace that even the long-legged Kip had to hustle to match.

Sam and Tess lingered longer, expressing their appreciation for a delightful evening.

'I don't know when I've had such a good time,' Tess said. 'Of course, I ate too much spaghetti and at least three pieces of bread . . . say, you promised you'd tell me where you got it. I'm getting so sick and tired of holding the commissary bread up to the light in the morning so I can pick out the weevils before I put it in the toaster.'

Beth grinned. 'You know those flat carts you see all over the city . . . the ones piled high with loaves of bread?'

'My God, we just ate that stuff!' Sam exclaimed. 'It sits out on those carts uncovered, attracting flies and God knows what else.'

'I know. But I always wipe it off and heat it in a hot oven. My maid, Dici, buys it for me fresh every morning. It's baked in Italian ovens, you know,' Beth replied defensively. 'It hasn't made us sick yet, and we eat it all the time. It certainly tastes better than the stuff they bake on the base, which, besides being full of critters, tastes musty.'

'Like it was baked in the toilet, you mean,' Sam agreed.

'Well, I'm convinced. Besides, it seems so . . . insular

138

and unfriendly to get everything we consume from the base,' Tess agreed.

After thanking the host and hostess profusely, they drove in silence through the stillness of the darkened streets toward Tess's apartment, and the fun of the evening seemed to evaporate into the night air. As they drove past their two hiking husbands, Tess remarked, 'Beth's lucky that Joe doesn't fly,' but Sam said nothing. The monster was awake again and sitting beside them.

20

Chili slid the key into the door and was just about to open it when it was suddenly wrenched from her grasp and swung wide. Her husband stood inside the doorway looking at her with icy contempt.

'I was at the Cellinis' for dinner,' she said too quickly, caught off guard and wanting to bite off the tip of her tongue for having said something that was so transparently false.

'Oh, really? Again?'

'I was – ' she started to protest, but he cut her off.

'No more lies! I talked to Beth two hours ago, and she said she hadn't seen you since last week when they dropped you off here at the house. Where the hell were you?'

Chili tried to brush past him and get inside the door, but he blocked her way. His dark eyes were black with fury, and he grabbed her wrist and squeezed it until her fingers went numb.

'Let me go! You're hurting me,' she whimpered.

He slammed the door and pulled her farther into the living room of their handsomely furnished quarters.

'Not until you tell me where you've been!' he threatened. Anger was swelling inside him, and he squeezed her wrist more tightly and twisted her arm. 'Tell me!' he demanded.

'I was at the club,' she finally gasped, trying to unwind his fingers from her arm, but he was much too strong for her.

Her words angered him more than her silence, and he swept his free hand into a wide arc that landed in a slap across the side of her head. The blow was so hard and fast it snapped her head to the side, and she felt a sudden wrenching pain down her head and shoulder that was more excruciating than the sting of his hand on her face. She screamed in pain and fear, a scream that was so piercing it was like a shower of ice water extinguishing the flame of his anger. He released her immediately, and she crumpled to the floor moaning and sobbing.

'Dear God, I'm sorry, Chili, I'm so sorry,' he whispered hoarsely as he knelt to the floor beside her. Gently he gathered her into his arms and held her close to him as tears coursed down his cheeks. 'I didn't mean to do it, baby. Forgive me. I'm so sorry.'

Chili continued to sob and moan. Her neck hurt and she was terrified. Gam had never gotten this angry before. He had cursed her, he had shaken her, but never, ever, had he hit her. Suddenly her moody, often glowering lover had become her torturer, and she was unhinged, both by his anger and now by his abject remorse.

When the emotional storm began to subside, they remained locked in each other's arms. Gamal continued to soothe and caress her. He kissed her gently on her hair and her forehead, moving his lips gradually to her cheeks, her mouth, and then to her breasts.

Gamal loved his wife's round, full breasts. He loved to kiss them, touch them, and bury his face in the deep cleavage between them. As he murmured words of love, he unbuttoned the front of the dress she was wearing and slipped his hand around and unhooked her brassiere. Sexual passion suddenly became as intense as his anger had been minutes before, and he began to suck hungrily

141

at her deep red nipples, pulling at them so strongly she felt pain.

'Take me out,' he commanded.

Responding to him as she always did, she quickly unzipped his trousers and pulled the shaft of his manhood free. Holding it tightly with one hand, squeezing and massaging to keep his passion at full power, she pulled away her own panties and guided him quickly into the welcoming wet warmth of her body.

In spite of the pain she still felt, she was no longer afraid, for now she was maneuvering on territory where she was the expert. Quivering with emotion, she begged, 'Oh, Gam, give it to me, baby. I need it now. Now, baby, now.'

As he plunged himself deeper into her, she gasped, 'Harder . . . harder . . . please, baby, please.' Her mouth was open, her eyes were wide, and she writhed beneath him like a woman possessed by the demons of lust and desire, until suddenly her body arched in a spasm of ecstasy. It was an orgasm that rose and fell and rose again, undulating with unbridled energy. When it was over for her, Gamal commanded, 'One more time . . . one more time. I want it one more time,' as he squeezed her breasts in his hands and lengthened his strokes, penetrating her so hard and deep that she thought he might split her apart. In response to his demands, Chili willed herself to let go again, surrendering her being to his will, allowing herself to be carried once more into the vortex of a passion in which she lost all control. As she felt herself nearing that most intense moment when all else falls away but desire, she thought, as she almost always did, that at this moment she would choose death, if death were the price of fulfillment. 'I'm coming, baby, I'm coming again,' she gasped. At last he joined her in the moment of release, as, with one deep and final thrust, he delivered into her body the seeds of his passion.

Exhausted, Gamal rolled away from her and lay stretched on the rich brown Karouan rug, his clothes in disarray. They lay together in silence, and Chili was aware of the moist heaviness of the air around them, the fragrance of spent ardor, the musk of human rapture, and she was content. There wasn't a woman alive who could please her husband as she could. He might neglect her because of his dedication to his job. He might be furious with her because she liked to drink and have a good time, but in the end, she had one thing he needed from her and her alone.

At last he turned toward her and stretched his arm across her waist. 'I really never meant to hit you. Are you okay?'

'I'm okay, darlin', but my jaw hurts and I think I'm goin' to have a stiff neck,' she said softly. 'Why do you get so mad at me?'

'Because I can't stand the thought that you might be out screwing around with some other guy. It makes me so mad I almost want to kill you. Where the hell were you, anyway?'

Chili looked up at the ceiling and after a long pause said wearily, 'Oh, Gam, darlin' . . . I just got so disgusted when you called and said you weren't coming home again . . . that you had to go into town to have dinner with some of those Arabs. I just felt like I was suffocatin'. So I put on a dress and went to the club to see what was cookin' over there. Some fighter pilots here on TDY came in and started tearing the place up, so I left. I stopped in at the base movie and saw *High Noon*, with Gary Cooper. He's always been my favorite star. It's a wonderful movie.'

143

'Then why, for God's sake, did you lie to me if it was as simple as that?' he demanded, bewildered.

'Because you scared me, yelling like you did. I don't know what I'm sayin' sometimes when you get that mad look on your face. And then, when you started twistin' my arm, I got crazy with fear,' she said petulantly.

'I'm sorry, Chili baby. I promise never to do that again.' He pulled her close and kissed her softly on the mouth.

Chili closed her eyes and was thankful that she had gotten off as easily as she had. This had been entirely too close a call, and she knew she would be in mortal danger if Gam ever found out what was really going on. She ran her fingers lightly across her bright red pubic hair and hoped that maybe this might be the time that things would work for her. She just had to get pregnant. All she ever really wanted in this world was to have Gam's baby. And if she got pregnant, it would solve the other problem too.

21

Samara checked the list to make sure she hadn't overlooked anybody in her seating arrangements for the party that evening. Both the American and the French ministers and their wives were coming – Libya did not yet qualify for ambassador status. One of the top men from LATAS, the Libyan-American Technical Aid Service, the organization developing agricultural resources so that the Libyans could feed their people adequately, would be there too. Sam had heard some strange rumors about 'black water' they were finding while digging holes for wells, and she hoped to discover what was going on after enough cocktails had been poured. Sam collected stories and gossip the way others collected stamps. It made life interesting.

Among the Air Force officers, she had included the Cellinis, the Shaheens, and the Kiplings. She hadn't wanted to invite Brick and Veronica, but Bob insisted that it would be foolish to alienate them by leaving them out of her first party of the season. To balance that off, she had also invited the commander of the 580th, the new wing that had a mission rumored to be super-secret. She had also invited Wadie Khouri, who was doing some kind of business with the Americans and was purported to be related in some way to the royal family.

It was now November, and the Wheelus social season was in full swing. Sam looked with despair at the pile of envelopes on her desk. Last season, her first in Tripoli, she had been delighted with the deluge of invitations to cocktail parties at the club, and she attended them all, at least three or four a week, but it hadn't taken more than a few before she realized a sad and painful truth: each party at the club was exactly like every other one. Only the roster of hosts changed. Otherwise the food was the same, the drinks, the ambience, everything. And she found it a bloody bore to stand for hour after hour in a crowded room, balance a drink in one hand, a cigarette in the other, and try to make a stab at the finger foods without spilling cocktail sauce from the frozen shrimp or melted Velveeta on her designer gowns, which would be turned into pulp by the dry cleaner on the base.

Sam decided to do it differently. It was bad enough to have to attend all the parties so they would not offend anyone, but she had no intention of hosting one. Instead, she gave small dinner parties, sometimes once a week.

At Sam's dinners, everybody sat at a table and was served good food and drink by servants she had personally trained to be efficient, quiet, and courteous. Sam's cook was an Italian woman who made thick, tasty sauces and pastas, and Sam herself had learned to make light, delicious desserts from the ingredients available at the commissary. There were always fresh flowers on the tables, which were set handsomely with her fine Belgian linens, Baccarat crystal, English bone china, and heavy Danish silverware.

During the afternoon's preparations, she looked at the clock and saw that it was almost three and she had not yet begun to set the tables because the flowers were nowhere in sight. She went outside into the enclosed garden, where a young Arab was watering the potted plants and patiently letting the children help him. Ali always found time for David and Melinda, and he treated them with the affection of an older brother.

'Ali, did you get the flowers as I asked you to?'

'In kitchen in bucket. Not very nice today. Sorry.'

Ali accepted responsibility as well as any servant she had ever had. He had originally applied for a job as a *shifti*, to watch over the house and the cars and make sure nothing was stolen or vandalized, but he was so bright and affable and eager to learn that he had begun taking care of the garden, running errands, and doing a myriad of indispensable jobs, and so she had elevated him to houseboy. Eventually Sam had allowed him to hire another young man to be the *shifti*, and Ali was pleased with his exalted status, although occasionally she had to reprimand him for his harsh treatment of the underling.

When the flowers were arranged in the sleek Georg Jensen silver bowls, she set the tables and arranged the place cards, being careful to place the people she most wanted to talk with near her and putting Brick Masters in the living room at Bob's table, as far away as possible. She wasn't particularly fond of Veronica, but she found her far more tolerable than the over-bearing and egotistical colonel. Although she knew that Masters would be insulted at being seated away from the diplomats, Sam didn't care, and Bob didn't protest because he knew how much she detested the man.

Since military personnel are trained to be punctual, all of the officers and their wives arrived at seven o'clock on the dot, and the rest of the guests appeared soon after. Trays of manhattans and martinis were passed, and the party was quickly in full swing.

Chili Shaheen arrived on the arm of her dour and stiff husband, who was not very popular with his fellow officers because of his singular lack of warmth and inability to engage in small talk. Chili, however, made up for his drawbacks, since she was a chatterer, always ready to fill

147

in the conversational gaps with her homespun and artless comments.

'My goodness, Sam, your house is simply gorgeous. I love what you've done. You know, I wanted to be an interior decorator. I signed up for a class in night school once, but something was always coming up, and I had to miss too many of them, so I quit. My, I do love that Danish modern. It's so much nicer than that frilly, fancy Early American stuff everybody's buyin' nowadays.'

Sam smiled and listened, although it was obvious that Chili's chatter was making Gamal uncomfortable. Sam interrupted, 'Chili, you look perfectly beautiful in that green satin dress. Have you found a wonderful little dressmaker that you're keeping all to yourself?'

Chili grinned and winked. 'If you'll promise not to tell a soul . . . well, I bought it at the annual sale held by the Rhein-Main Officers' Wives' Club in Germany. The wives bring clothes they're tired of wearing, see, and they sell them to each other. 'Course, it might be a little funny seeing your dresses on somebody else, but since we never stay in one place very long, heck, they're like brand new when you go to a different assignment.'

Barely managing to hide his annoyance with his wife's ingenuous revelations, Gamal said through clenched jaws, 'That's the point, Chili. You're not supposed to tell, are you?'

'On the contrary, Gamal, I find your wife's honesty charming, and it's refreshing to have someone around who calls things as they are,' Sam said, squelching him. Samara hated it when husbands corrected or put down their wives in public. 'Chili, is that your real name?' she said, changing the subject.

Chili finished her manhattan and picked up another from a passing tray. 'Well, they've called me that so long,

I reckon it is, but actually, I was baptized Sarah Lou. My daddy said my hair was the color of chili con carne, and he's the one who started it. Nobody's ever called me Sarah,' she replied, not adding that her mother's second husband often whispered to her in the dark that she was hot as a chili pepper.

Their conversation was suddenly interrupted by the presence of Brick Masters. 'Shaheen, I need to talk to you for a minute in private,' he said tersely, taking Gamal's arm and ignoring the women. He led him to the other side of the room, where they engaged in an intense conversation. Sam's irritation with his rudeness quickly gave way to curiosity, however, when she noticed the stricken look on Chili's face as she stared at the two men talking *sotto voce*.

'What's wrong, Chil?'

'Can you tell what they're talkin' about?' Chili asked in a strangled whisper.

'I'm sure it's nothing very important. Come on, let's go talk to Tess and Kip. He's the lowest-ranked officer here, and we should make him feel at ease.' She tugged on Chili's arm, but she seemed rooted to the spot, paralyzed with anxiety.

Sam eased herself away unnoticed and went quickly to her husband's side. 'Honey, look at Chili,' she whispered. 'Ever since Masters and Gamal started talking, she's been a zombie. What the hell's going on between those two?'

'Something, for damned sure. Got any ideas?'

'No, but you better break it up before she goes into a trance,' Samara urged.

Instantly Bob strode toward the two men and clapped them both on the shoulder. 'Come on, now, Gamal, you mustn't keep the commander from socializing. My wife just hates to have her parties used for business talk.

Colonel, the minister of France particularly wanted to talk to you. Let's go over and join him,' Bob said, making a mental note of the few words he had overheard. Shooting a warning glance at Gamal, Brick allowed himself to be guided toward the diplomats, whom he was always interested in impressing. Diplomats knew politicians, and Brick wanted to impress anyone who could help him win his first star. Wadie Khouri approached Gamal, and they were soon deep in conversation in Arabic.

Sam watched Chili's color and demeanor return to normal gradually, although when she touched her arm, she could feel that Chili was still trembling. 'Are you okay?' she asked.

'I musta had a little dizzy spell,' Chili responded, downing the remains of her manhattan in one gulp, then added, 'Maybe another one of these will make me feel better.'

Another one of those might put you under the table, Sam thought, and replied, 'You won't have time, Chili. I'm just about to call dinner.'

As she herded her guests toward the tables, Sam's mind was occupied with Chili. There was something going on between her and Brick Masters, and she intended to find out what it was. She hated secrets, unless they were hers.

Later, when the guests were just beginning to eat their osso buco, Sam had an opportunity to speak quietly to the man who was the head of LATAS. 'Lars, what's this black water that people are talking about?'

Lars Hendriks replied softly, 'Where in the hell did you hear about that, my dear?'

'Well, from the caddy at the golf course, for one. Come on, tell me. Are you striking oil out there in the desert?' she persisted.

'No, my dear, we are not. That story started when one of the American engineers saw some puddles of oil in the areas where we were drilling for water. He contacted a geologist in France who did extensive studies here a couple of years ago, and he was assured that there was absolutely no oil in this part of the world whatsoever.'

'Then where did it come from?'

'Leaky trucks, that's all. Strictly false alarm.'

Sam looked him straight in the eye. 'I hope you're telling the truth. It would be rather wasteful for us to be spending millions trying to establish an agricultural economy here to help the people, and at the same time hiding from them the information that they're sitting on top of a mine of black gold, now, wouldn't it?'

'It would be ridiculous indeed. If we found oil for them, it would be a very good thing for everybody. Unfortunately, there's just not a word of truth in the rumor. Black water, indeed. What foolish ideas these natives get.' He laughed and turned away to talk to Tess Kipling, who was sitting next to him.

Later that night, after the guests had gone and Bob was turning out the lights, Sam told him about her conversation with Lars Hendriks.

'What do you think about it, honey?' she asked.

'I don't know. I've found that the government often doesn't let the right hand know what the left hand is holding. Then again, there are negotiations going on between the United States and Prime Minister Muntwasser regarding the rights to keep our air base here on Libyan soil. Who knows, maybe they do know there's oil here and want to keep it a secret. Wheelus and its personnel generate a lot of jobs for the Libyans. They might get difficult to deal with if they knew they had oil and didn't need us.'

151

'For a hotshot pilot, you have an uncanny amount of insight, my love,' Sam said admiringly.

'Well, dearie, would it possibly be puttin' you in a sexy mood if I told you another tidbit of a rumor?'

Sam put her arms around Bob's waist and said, 'I don't need it, but I'd like to hear what you have to say.'

'Fair enough,' he replied softly, kissing her on the tip of the nose. 'The 580th's mission is to eavesdrop on the Soviet Union. They're monitoring radio signals and taking air samples.'

'They're looking for smog?' Sam asked sarcastically.

'Sort of. The lethal kind . . . nuclear radiation.'

'How depressing. Bob, will there be a world left for David and Melinda or is our generation going to muck things up for our kids?'

'We've got to have faith, darlin'. If they can manage not to blow the planet to smithereens for another twenty or twenty-five years, surely they'll have found the way to peace and prosperity by then. Atomic energy, I understand, can be harnessed to bring cheap, clean energy to the world, and then nobody will be hungry, and there'll be no need for war. Come now, let's go to bed and let the world take care to its own problems till morning.'

They climbed into bed together and made leisurely, satisfying love, but just before they went to sleep, Bob said something that postponed sleep by putting Sam's senses on alert.

'By the way, darlin', when I went over to break up that little tête-à-tête, I heard somethin' pretty weird.'

'What?' Sam asked anxiously.

'Well, they shut up as soon as they saw me, but I heard Brick say, 'As soon as she gets knocked up.' Pretty weird, uh?'

'Who were they talking about?' Sam asked.

'Haven't the foggiest. G'night, sweetheart.'

22

Tess's household goods arrived just in time for Thanksgiving. She watched eagerly from the balcony as the huge wooden shipping crates were broken open and piece by piece her furniture was unloaded and brought upstairs. Then she and Pina worked hard all day getting her house in order. Tess was learning more new Italian words and phrases every day, and she was enjoying communicating with the feisty, hard-working little woman who cleaned daily for her.

Now, exhausted, she stretched out to rest on the new Beautyrest mattress and box springs. Thank heaven, no more sleeping alone on a canvas cot. Tonight she and Kip would sleep in the same bed, with their arms and legs twined warmly together. He had promised to stop by the commissary and pick up some groceries so they could have their first real dinner at home. She closed her eyes and listened with satisfaction to the humming sound emanating from the kitchen, assuring her that her new Frigidaire was making ice, real ice.

She shivered and looked over at the Aladdin heater to make sure it was still lit. With its high ceilings and thick walls, the apartment had stayed cool in the summer, but it was damp and cold in the winter. She hated the little kerosene heaters. They smelled bad and made her eyes sting, but they were the only kind available. She had an abiding fear of being suffocated in the night, but Kip said she was worrying foolishly. Everybody used them.

Reaching over, she turned her new little radio to the

Air Force station and snuggled down to wait for her husband, happy in her new surroundings. Back home, living in this same apartment, she would feel poor and deprived. But here, in Tripoli, where she had lived for almost four months with nothing, she exulted in her new riches.

Suddenly the baby kicked again, as it did so much lately, and Tess placed her hand on her abdomen. Dr Pepperman, the new obstetrician at the outpatient clinic, had told her that everything was going fine except that she had to restrict her salt intake. Her ankles were swelling badly every afternoon. He also told her she must lie down with her feet propped up as much as possible. She ran her hand lovingly across the quilt her grandmother had made for her years ago, and she was as happy and content as she had been since she arrived in Tripoli. It didn't take long for her to fall into a deep sleep.

With a start, she awakened suddenly. The room was dark. Disoriented, she sat upright and groped for the flashlight she always kept on the floor beside the cot, but it wasn't there. Remembering that she was in her new bed, she reached for the small lamp on the bedside table and turned the switch, but nothing happened. Then she recalled that both the light and the radio had been on when she dozed off, and now she was in darkness and silence, and the hum of the refrigerator was stilled. The power must have gone out! Suddenly there was a flash of lightning and a crack of thunder, and the rain began to pour down in a heavy torrent. God, it was storming!

Because she had been raised in the Midwest, where thunderstorms were ordinary manifestations of nature, she was unfazed by the weather. She had put some candles in the kitchen cupboard, and she felt her way to them quickly. She turned on a burner on the gas stove, lighted a candle from the flame, and checked the time on her watch. Good Lord, it was after eight. Why hadn't Kip come home?

She crept through the apartment, feeling very alone, and picked up the telephone. It too was dead.

At last she found the flashlight, and it comforted her to hold it in her hand. Something must have happened at the base to keep her husband there. Perhaps he was delayed because of the storm. She had no idea how long the telephone had been out, but it was possible that it hadn't been working since morning when she had called Kip to tell him the truck had arrived.

There was another crash of thunder and lightning, and Tess shivered. She opened the balcony shutters to peer out into the dark, liquid night sky. Quickly she closed them again to shut out the cold, wet wind and retreated into the safety of her kitchen. She tried hard to quell the rapidly escalating fear she felt, not for herself but for Kip, who she imagined might be lying hurt on the dark road to Wheelus Field, his car smashed into a tree. That miserable road got slippery with camel dung and dirt when it was wet, and it was dangerous.

She had to get hold of herself. Putting a kettle of water on the stove to boil, she opened a can of Campbell's chicken noodle soup. She had skipped lunch, and both she and the baby needed nourishment. When the soup was hot, she put it into a bowl from her new set of yellow dishes. By the flickering light of a candle she sat down at her new Formica kitchen table with the soup and some crackers and cheese for the first meal in her now-furnished apartment, feeling eerily like a besieged heroine in a horror movie, afraid that any moment something terrible was going to happen.

It was almost eleven before the storm abated and

155

settled down to a steady, quiet downpour of rain. Every ten minutes Tess would check the telephone, hoping in vain that service had been restored, but knowing full well it wouldn't get fixed in the middle of a storm, since it was nearly impossible to get people in Tripoli to fix things even on a bright sunny day.

Tess tried to harness her rising anxiety, because there was undoubtedly a perfectly good reason for Kip's failure to come home as planned. There had to be. And she couldn't permit herself to be frightened needlessly. She undressed and put on a pair of warm flannel pajamas that had arrived with her household goods. Pulling a pair of Kip's sweatsocks on her cold feet, she crawled into her new bed and covered herself with the heavy quilt and then remembered the lighted Aladdin heaters. Dragging her heavy body out of bed, she turned them all off as quickly as she could.

The terrazzo floors were cold and unyielding as she scurried about the apartment, but she was back in bed within minutes. It took hours, however, for her to escape into sleep.

A bell was ringing somewhere far in the distance, and she couldn't shut it out of her dreams. She was back home and Mom was telling her to answer the telephone before it woke up Daddy, who had been at the hospital all night delivering a baby and needed his rest. She didn't want to wake up, didn't want to climb out of her warm bed and hurry to the landing to answer and talk to another sick patient trying to reach her father.

She turned over in bed, and the ringing was replaced by the sound of pounding on the door. Suddenly she was aroused, and she sat up in bed. It was morning! She could see the sun filtering through the shutters, and she realized that someone was knocking at the downstairs door. The memory of the frightening evening and Kip's unexplained absence flooded over her and catapulted her out of bed. Quickly she put on her robe and slippers and raced to the balcony. Flinging open the doors and shutters, she stepped outside to see that it was just Pina trying to get in. Another human being at last! Thank God she wasn't alone anymore.

'Pina! *Un momento!*' she called. She then took the key off the hook in the kitchen and threw it down to her.

When the sturdy little woman got to the top of the stairs and let herself into the apartment, she handed Tess a note that had apparently been slipped under her front door sometime during the night. '*Per la signora?*'

With trembling hands Tess opened the note and noticed with relief that it was in Kip's handwriting.

Darling, sorry to do this to you, but the guy who was supposed to fly with Masters to Tunis this afternoon came down with the trots, and he asked me to fill in. I tried to call you, but the lines were out again. I asked Larry to drop this off to you on his way home.

I picked up a toothbrush and a razor at the BX and got my clean shirts from the laundry, so you don't have to worry about me, I'm all set.

I love you, honey. Have a nice rest on that new mattress. See you day after tomorrow.

Kip

Relief tinged with hurt spread through her. Kip was okay. He hadn't wrecked his car on the road . . . but on the other hand, he had left her stranded without a car, with no food in the house, and no telephone. She turned the envelope over in her hand and saw an additional note scribbled on the outside in a different handwriting: 'Tess, I had such a hard time getting through the flood in Suk El Giuma last night that I forgot to give this to you. Sorry. I hope it didn't cause you any concern. Larry.'

157

23

Sam picked up Tess in the big blue Pontiac, which she had refused to sell when Bob bought an MG, and they drove toward the base. It was a sparkling, clear day. The downpour the night before had washed the streets and the buildings clean. Tess regaled Sam with the story of her night of horror.

'Don't be too hard on Kip. He was in a bind,' Sam reassured her. 'I'm glad I stopped by to see if you wanted a ride. Marilee, who has a villa across the square from me, called this morning to tell me that the commissary was going to have some of those five-pound blocks of jumbo frozen shrimp today, along with some other goodies. Have you met Marilee yet?'

'I think so. Is she the pretty one with the dimples and the southern drawl so thick you can cut it with a knife?'

'Right. Her husband's the commissary officer, and she tips me off when something good comes in. Naturally, her husband would be upset if he knew, but she feels that she's evening the score a little. It annoys her that the good stuff goes automatically to the commander's villa, and whatever's left gets put out for the rest of us.'

'I really miss having fresh milk. Dr Pepperman tells me I should drink it for the calcium, but I can't stomach that awful powdered stuff. Kip brought me a Waring blender from Bahrein, and it does a pretty good job of getting the lumps out, but the junk still tastes, yuck, like chalk,' Tess complained.

'The frozen milk isn't bad. Have you tried that?'

158

Tess groaned. 'Yes, but it separates when it thaws. The blender reconstitutes it pretty well when it's fresh, but forget it when the stuff gets old.'

'I know, and we haven't had a new shipment in months,' Sam agreed. 'You know Veronica's family has plenty of fresh milk all the time.'

'They told us not to drink any of the local stuff, that it wasn't safe,' Tess commented.

'Well, hers is safe, all right. A plane goes to Germany once a week to bring them all the things we don't have, like milk, iceberg lettuce – '

'Iceberg lettuce!' Tess squealed. 'I would lie, steal, or kill for just one head of iceberg lettuce. I'm sick and tired of those weeds we use for salads . . . they're tough to chew and bitter, not to mention being flavored with Mikroklene or Clorox.'

'One day Beth was called to duty at the Masters' villa when there was a bunch of VIPs here from Washington. She was told to bring a big pan of her lasagne and a triple-size string-bean casserole.'

'I thought only staff wives had to do that,' Tess commented.

'Usually that's true, but for some reason or other they needed more help that day. I'd guess some of the wives were getting overburdened, they'd had so many visitors,' Sam conjectured.

'Do they get reimbursed for all that food they take up there?'

'Huh? Are you kidding? Masters has never once offered to repay them, and they have to do it every time a VIP comes to town. Anyway, Veronica's best buddy, Betsy Calhoun, was recovering from an appendectomy and wasn't there to oversee the arrangements. One of the wives who was on duty that day stood guard at the kitchen

159

door and kept watch for Veronica while the rest of them sneaked mouthfuls of lettuce and swigs of fresh milk right from the carton. Pretty funny, eh? There were US Senators dining graciously in one room, and a bunch of officers' wives stealing food in the kitchen not more than twenty feet away.'

When they pulled up at the commissary, they saw a line of woman snaking out the door and around the building.

'Word really travels fast,' Tess exclaimed as they hurried out of the car and got into line.

Tess looked down at her ankles and wondered how long it would take for the flesh to swell so much it would spill out of her shoes. What were they going to be like in two months, when the baby was due?

'Why don't you sit in the car and let me stand in line alone? Surely nobody will complain, you being in a delicate condition and all,' Sam insisted.

'I just can't do that. I'd feel too guilty stepping in front of people who had been waiting. Besides, I'm fine, really I am. I'll spend the rest of the day in bed with these elephant feet propped on pillows. Do you think we could stop at the library before we go home? I'm out of books to read.'

'Sure. How's the writing coming along?'

'I'm having trouble with the printer. He doesn't speak any English, and he makes the strangest mistakes in setting type. We're already correcting the fourth set of galleys, and the end still isn't in sight. I'll be so glad when it's finished. Veronica loves what I've done, however.'

They chatted, and the line moved slowly. It took almost an hour before they got inside the building. It was Tess's turn to get the next grocery cart, and just as she was about to take it, a gray-haired woman dressed in a fashionable black dress and wearing a wide-brimmed black hat and gloves brushed past her and with a muttered 'Excuse me' snatched the cart from Tess's hands and pushed it toward the meat counter.

It took a moment for Tess to realize what had happened, and even then it was difficult to believe that any mere mortal could have so much gall. Who the hell did that bitch think she was! Without considering whom she might be offending, Tess strode toward her and put her hand firmly on the handle of the cart, stopping the woman in her tracks.

'Excuse me!' Tess spit out angrily.

The woman looked at her in surprise and annoyance. 'Please get out of my way. I'm in a hurry,' she snapped haughtily.

'Do you see this belly, ma'am?' Tess asked, and without waiting for an answer continued. 'Well, this belly and I have been standing in that line on these swollen ankles for almost an hour. If I can wait my turn, then so the hell can you. That's my cart!' And wrenching it from the shocked woman's hands, she stomped away with it to the sound of whistles and applause from the people behind.

Mortified, the woman turned and swept out of the commissary. Sam got the next cart, and she hurried to catch up with a flushed and flustered Tess, who was collecting her allotted five pounds of shrimp.

'My God, you're a tough lady. Do you know who that was?' she asked.

'If it's somebody important, don't tell me. I'm already feeling perfectly terrible. I don't know what got into me. I just can't stand pushy people who think they're too important to wait their turn . . . Who was she?'

'The wife of the American minister, Peggy Fletcher. The highest-ranked lady in Tripoli.'

161

Tess put her hands over her face. 'Oh, my God, now what's going to happen?'

'The bitch deserved to be set straight for once. She's always pulling rank. She sends her kids to school on the base in her black Cadillac limousine with the chauffeur, which I think is a bit pretentious here in this poor country. And she sails out here to Wheelus and expects everybody to kowtow to her.'

'You didn't answer my question,' Tess insisted, determined to hear the worst.

'Don't worry about it, probably nothing will happen,' Sam said, trying to be reassuring.

'I can tell by the tone of your voice that you don't believe what you're saying. Was I wrong to do what I did?'

'Morally, no, but to be honest, Kip's probably going to get called on the carpet for it. Unfortunately, when we dependents step over the line, it's our husbands who get raked over the coals. It's not fair, but that's the way the Air Force works.'

'She doesn't know my name. I've never even seen her before,' Tess said with renewed hope.

'That's true,' Sam said brightly, but she knew realistically that Peggy Fletcher would not let the humiliating reprimand pass. Before the day was out, the name of the offender would be known, although Sam vowed it would not be from her.

Kip returned the following afternoon, and he called Tess from his office. She was startled at the unexpected coldness of his voice.

'Tess, I'm back. Are you all right?'

'Oh, Kip, I'm so glad to hear your voice. I can't tell you how worried I was when you didn't come home.

162

Larry forgot to give me the note, and the electricity and the phone went out – '

'Colonel Channing, the base exec, called me into his office and said you'd have to write a letter of apology to the minister's wife for insulting her yesterday. Jesus Christ, what did you say to her, Tess?' he asked and she could tell he was annoyed with her.

'She pushed ahead of me in line, after I had been waiting for almost an hour, and I just told her she should take her turn like the rest of us,' she said weakly. Her heart was beating rapidly, and her hands shook.

'My God, Tess, it's not up to you to tell anybody how to behave, understand? I'm just a lowly lieutenant. Now, write the letter and bring it out to my office this afternoon. I told Channing it would be on his desk by three o'clock so he can send a messenger into town with it.'

Trying to force back the tears, Tess said meekly, 'Can't I just call her on the telephone and grovel? Besides, you've got the car.'

'The car's downstairs in the garage. I asked Talhami to drive it into town and leave it for you night before last. Didn't the *shifti* tell you?'

'No, nobody told me, but it's a good thing I didn't know it was there or I probably would have killed myself driving around in the storm looking for you, because I was so worried,' she said bitterly.

'Hey, look, I have a job to do, you know. And I need you to give me a little cooperation,' he said.

'Please, don't ask me to do this today, Kip. My ankles are as big as watermelons, and I'm supposed to keep my feet elevated.' She tried to suppress the petulant whine she could hear creeping into her voice.

'It can't wait, Tess. If you get right on it, you can be back home in no time at all. And make sure your apology is a good one, because Channing wants to approve it before he sends it out. See you later.'

Tess heard the click, but it was a long time before she could rouse herself enough to put down the telephone. She was outraged at the injustice of it all and hurt by her husband's cold, insensitive manner. Did his career mean more to him than she did? More than his child she was carrying?

Numbly she stretched out on the bed and tried to suppress the feelings rolling inside her. She wanted to scream, to cry, to kick things, but she did nothing. After a while she got up and pulled her little portable Smith-Corona typewriter from the shelf and set it on the kitchen table, rolled a sheet of paper into it, and began the apology that galled her to write.

At exactly 2.57 that afternoon she walked into her husband's office and laid the note on his desk. Although he greeted her warmly, she refused either to look at him or to speak to him, but turned and marched angrily back to the car.

Tess drove directly to the Mulhare Villa. When Sam saw her, she was alarmed. Tess's face was ashen, and her eyes seemed to disappear into deep purplish circles of flesh.

'My Lord, what's happened to you?'

'Sam, I feel awful,' she whispered.

Sam put her arm around Tess's expanded waist and led her inside, guiding her to the guest bedroom, where she helped her onto the bed. Without asking questions, she took the shoes off her swollen, misshapen feet and told the maid to bring a cold, wet cloth and a pot of hot tea.

When Bob got home that evening, he found his wife sitting beside her friend, holding her hand. Tess had finally fallen asleep.

Sam tiptoed silently from the room and closed the door. Quickly she told Bob everything she knew about Tess's lone vigil in the storm, the encounter with Peggy Fletcher, and Tess's sudden frightening and silent appearance on her doorstep.

'Does Kipling know she's here?' Bob asked.

'I doubt it.'

'I'm going to call him.'

Within half an hour Kip appeared at their door.

'God, I was so worried. I didn't know what to think when I got home and she wasn't there. She left the base about three o'clock.'

'She was at the base this afternoon?' Sam asked in alarm. 'I drove her out there early this morning for dependents' sick call. We waited over three hours to see Dr Pepperman about the swelling in her feet, and he told her not to get out of bed until they went down. What was she doing out there again this afternoon?'

'I asked her to bring something to me,' he answered sheepishly. 'She didn't tell me she'd been to the doctor.'

'I hope it was something extremely important,' Sam replied coldly. 'She's very pregnant . . . or hadn't you noticed?'

Bob tried to smooth the situation over. 'Let the poor guy alone, honey. It's none of your business. Kip, why don't we let her sleep for a while? Sam said she was really wiped out when she walked in here. Come on, have some dinner with us.'

'No . . . no, thanks. I'll just . . . uh . . . go on home. I'd appreciate it if you'd call me when she wakes up. I'll take the car with me, and I'll come right back and get her.'

Kip left the house, feeling miserable. It was obvious that Tess was having a hard time being an officer's wife.

He'd just have to try to explain things to her a little more clearly and hope she would love him enough to try harder. He wondered if she realized how much his career in the military meant to him.

He didn't go to bed at all that night. He sat in the kitchen by the telephone, drinking coffee and waiting for the call that never came. Tess did not awaken until morning.

24

Chili was just about to take a shower when the telephone rang and startled her. Her heart started pounding and her breath began to come in rapid little gasps of anxiety. She stared at the noisy black instrument sitting on the hall table with abhorrence. She would as soon pick up the phone and answer it as she would wrap her fingers around the flared hood of a cobra.

Turning away, she dropped her robe onto the floor and stepped into the bathtub. She pulled the thin plastic shower curtain closed, attempting to put a barrier between herself and the persistent ringing of the telephone demanding to be answered.

Without thinking, she plunged her head under the stream of water and realized that in her anxiety she had forgotten to put on her shower cap and had ruined her hairset. To hell with it. She let the water cascade down her face, through her hair, over her shoulders, down, down into the crevices of her body, over her legs and feet and into the drain. She wished she could open her skull and let the water wash through her brain and flush out all the misery lurking there.

She stayed there for a long time – not long enough, never long enough to wash away the filth and deceit and adultery that seemed to cling to her – but long enough, perhaps, for the caller to have conceded defeat and gone away.

As she turned off the water and opened the plastic curtain with its gray spots of mildew peppering the hem, she hesitated, listening, hoping for silence. When she was certain that the telephone was no longer ringing, she stepped out of the tub and began to towel herself dry.

Dusting her body with the Chanel No. 5 talc that she'd gotten from the BX, she felt a small measure of relief. She got into her robe and began to roll her hair into pincurls, a necessary procedure to control her wild and unmanageable mane. When Chili was still a child, her mother had impressed upon her the need to be beautiful and desirable at all times. To celebrate her first period at the age of eleven, her mother had presented her with her first Tangee lipstick, which appeared translucent and pale peach in the tube, but turned into a glorious rose on the lips.

As a young girl, Chili had not been allowed to participate in sports, nor had she learned to swim, because handling a ball would break her long polished nails, and chlorine and the sun would ruin her perfect white skin. Chili had been brought up to be darling. It never occurred to her to want to be anything else.

Perhaps it was the very qualities her mother had instilled in her that ignited her stepfather's unhealthy attraction to her, an attraction that brought about the loss of her virginity at the age of thirteen. Two years later, when her mother learned of it, it was Chili who was blamed and punished and cast out into the world on her own.

Because the only important woman in her early life, her mother, had failed her when she most needed understanding and support, Chili found it difficult to respond to another woman's friendship, and so now when she desperately needed a friend, she had no one to turn to. She dared not tell Gamal, and although she found Beth Cellini and Sam Mulhare to be pleasant and friendly, she was afraid to trust them. She was all alone.

She finished setting her hair and was about to plug in the hair dryer when the telephone began to ring again. She stared at it for a moment, and then she switched on the dryer and let the noise drown out the insistent sound.

It took almost an hour for her thick hair, wound in fat round pincurls, to dry, an hour in which she luxuriated in the isolation the noise of the dryer created.

She brushed out the dried curls into a shining mass. A lot of the wives were going to the Italian hairdressers in town and having their hair cut in short, straight, narrow little styles, but she could never do that. Her hair was her crowning glory, her mother had said, and she would not be as beautiful without it. Fashion was for plain women, she had been taught. A naturally beautiful woman wore only what suited her.

Carefully Chili applied her Pan-Cake makeup, brushed a bit of Maybelline mascara on her thick lashes, and coated her lips with a bright coral lipstick, which she also used to smudge some color on her cheeks. That done, she stepped into a pair of satin panties and donned a Hollywood Vassarette brassiere with circular stitching that lifted her round, soft breasts and moulded them into conical shapes that protruded sharply through the soft green rayon print dress she put on over them. Checking her appearance in the full-length mirror behind the bedroom door, she was satisfied with what she saw. Green really was her best color, she thought, for it reflected in her blue eyes and gave them an emerald tint.

Sliding her feet into a pair of leather flats she had bought at the native market in the Old City, she grabbed her matching leather purse and hurried out the door before the telephone could ring again.

She got behind the wheel of the little green Morris Minor her husband had bought when they arrived at Wheelus, put it into gear, and drove off, happy and relieved because she had escaped. No one could reach her now. No one could tell her that she must be at a certain place at a certain time to do a certain thing. As she drove toward the gate, she made her plans for the day. She would drive into town, browse through the Old City markets for a while, maybe find a trinket or two to buy. The shopkeepers were dazzled by her beauty, and she enjoyed the protracted bargaining and haggling over piastres as much as they did.

She must keep track of time, however, so that she could get back to the base just before dark. Then she could go directly to the club, where there would be people around to shield her, telephone Gam at his office, and arrange to meet him so they could have a quiet dinner together, go home, make love. Wonderful. For the first time that day she felt good. She began to hum Gershwin's "Swonderful' as she tapped her fingers to the rhythm on the steering wheel.

Just as she drew up to the gate, one of the guards on duty hailed her car and stopped it. The handsome young man in his khaki uniform smiled at her politely and said, 'Ma'am, are you Mrs Shaheen?'

Fear and dread clutched so tightly at her throat that it was impossible for her to speak. She nodded mutely.

'Then I have a message for you. Apparently your husband has been trying to call you all morning. Your telephone must be out of order, so he sent a note down to us with your license number and the description of your car and asked us to watch out for you. Here it is, Ma'am.'

With trembling hands Chili took the sealed envelope

170

and dropped it in her lap. Managing a weak smile, she murmured a soft 'Thank you' and drove off. As soon as she was out of sight of the guardhouse, she pulled to the side of the road and with shaking hands looked at the envelope with her name printed in bold letters on the front.

She wanted to rip it up and throw away the pieces. It was not Gam's handwriting on the envelope; the message was not from her husband. Trying to suppress the anger and frustration she felt, she tore open the envelope and read the terse note: 'Answer your damn phone! Five o'clock tonight. You know where.'

There was no signature. It wasn't necessary. She knew who had written it.

Chili crumpled the paper in her hand and put her head down onto the steering wheel. Once more she was overcome with despair. Was there no place for her to hide?

25

When Tess awakened in the strange bed, dawn was just beginning to peek through the closed shutters. She turned over and buried her face in the pillow, trying to shut out the light of today as well as the memory of yesterday. She had experienced no momentary disorientation at the instant her eyes opened; she knew exactly where she was and what events had brought her there the day before. She tried to shut off the flow of sadness that threatened to engulf her. How could she have possibly made such a terrible mess of things?

Love . . . how different it was from her expectations of it. She and her father had spent hours discussing the concept of love and what it meant, but they had never delved into the possibility of mutual love in the absence of mutual respect, or love in which one person controlled the relationship and made no attempt to sheathe his power with affection. How could her husband really love her when he had no respect for her feelings? Kip had condemned her justifiable reaction to a miserably unjust set of circumstances without even trying to understand why she had acted as she had. The wretched truth of it all was that he didn't care how she felt. He only cared that what she had done reflected badly on him.

Raised in a family where her concerns had always been taken seriously, Tess now found that her feelings were of little consequence. She tried to tell herself that Kip was rightly anxious about the effect her behavior would have

172

on his career, but she was also bitterly hurt by the way he had treated her.

If only he had sympathized with her and said he thought she was right, but as a favor to him, would she write the letter and get him off the hook, she would have done it gladly and with love. But he had treated her as a naughty child who must be punished for being impudent, and she was hurt and infuriated. If he should suddenly appear before her on bended knee to apologize, she was not sure that she could forgive him, although she was mature enough to realize that she must make some kind of accommodation. After all, she was married, she was pregnant with Kip's child, and she had made an irrevocable commitment to him and to the marriage. But she was not happy. Was there something wrong with her? Was she an unnatural woman?

An hour passed, and she heard people talking in the kitchen. She must pull her cumbersome body out of the bed and get dressed. She had already imposed too much on the Mulhares' hospitality. It was time to go home.

When she entered the dining room, Sam was sitting at the table drinking a cup of coffee. She was dressed in a soft blue velvet robe trimmed with a wide ecru lace collar. Her snort dark hair was brushed and shining, and even without makeup she was a pretty woman, not in the usual sense of the word, but in her own unique way. Her features were sharp, her chin a bit pointed, but her eyes were large and very dark, and she radiated a zest for life. There was an assurance about her too, a confidence in her own ability, that made her interesting to be near.

Sam smiled. 'Well, good morning, Sleeping Beauty. Your prince was here last night, but I wouldn't let him wake you up. Sit down and have some coffee.'

Tess settled herself in the chair across from Sam and

shook her head. 'No thanks – I'm already nervous as it is – I better not.'

'How about a nice big mug of hot chocolate? I've even got some marshmallows to toss on top.'

'Sounds grand, but I've already gained over twenty pounds and I still have two months to go.'

'Okay . . . hold the marshmallows. Now, how about some scrambled eggs? The protein would be good for you.'

'I don't want you to go to any trouble . . .' Tess protested.

'Hey, I've got a cook to do it, remember? I'll tell her what you want, and then we'll talk.' Sam breezed into the kitchen, and Tess could hear her talking in the pidgin Italian most Americans used to communicate with the locals.

When she was again seated at the table, Sam looked at Tess thoughtfully and asked gently, 'Want to talk about it?'

Tess hesitated. She did not want to gossip or criticize her husband, but she needed someone to hear her side of the story. There was a long silence.

'I know about the letter, Tess, and I think it stinks,' Sam said, breaking the awkward silence and shocking her guest.

'How? Did Kip tell you what happened?'

Sam, shook her head. 'Kip? The great stoneface? Of course not. After he left last night, I called Beth Cellini. She told me.'

'But how . . . how in the world would she know about it?' Tess asked in bewilderment.

'Nell Carson told her at the club last night. Honey, news travels fast around here. Gossip is all we really have to make life interesting. By this time, everybody knows, but don't worry, most people are on your side. I'm sure that any woman who's ever been in line at the commissary when Peggy Fletcher pushed her way in applauded what you did.'

'Maybe,' replied Tess bitterly, 'but would any of them have stooped to write that letter? Would you have done it?' Tess asked.

'Of course I'd have done it, and frankly, I don't know a wife here who would have refused, in spite of being every bit as furious about it as you are. When you're a dependent, you have to submit yourself to all kinds of rotten little duties, but you don't have to let yourself be humiliated by them. It's all part of the system. Military service tends to become a game men play to give them an illusion of control over the world. They set up all kinds of ridiculous little rules about rank and protocol, and they go into a foot-stomping snit if the people around them refuse to play the game their way. What really gripes me most are the wives who try to wear their husband's rank and pull the same kind of stuff.'

Sam took a sip of her coffee before continuing. 'Tess, the only thing you did wrong yesterday was to get out of bed against the doctor's orders. You should have told that husband of yours to drive in and get the letter himself, or if it's still too early in your marriage for that kind of self-assertion, you could have called me and asked me to go for you. Right now that baby is more important than Kip's military ambitions.'

A large mug of hot chocolate was placed on the table in front of Tess, and she wrapped her hands around it to absorb its warmth. In spite of the kerosene heaters in the corner of the room, the air was chilly and damp, but she felt considerably better. She looked up into Sam's twinkly dark eyes and smiled.

'Thanks for being my friend, Sam. And thanks for putting things in perspective. I better write my folks and tell them I forgot to pack my sense of humor and ask them to send it to me.'

'You'll need it to survive. Now, don't you think you ought to call Kip and tell him you're okay? He was really worried about you last night in that stiff-upper-lip way of his. I think he's the one who needs a better sense of humor.'

'My dad said he didn't have one. In fact, at our wedding reception – after Dad had two glasses of champagne, mind you – he told Kip to remember that life was temporary and most people didn't know it and spent too much time being miserable.'

'I think I'd like your dad.

'I think my dad will sleep a lot easier knowing I have a friend like you.'

As soon as Tess was dressed, Sam drove her home. For a while Tess stretched out on the big bed and tried to read, but she couldn't concentrate. She needed to talk to Kip. Finally she gave in to her restlessness and called his office.

'I'm home Kip,' was all she said.

And he replied gently, 'I'll be home early tonight.'

True to his word, he arrived home at five-thirty, bearing two large steaks and a bottle of wine. By candlelight, they had their first meal in their apartment, and they didn't bother to clean up the dishes afterward because they were anxious to sleep on their new mattress.

Cuddling next to her, Kip kissed her gently and said, 'Forgive me for being such a bastard, honey. It's just that I'm trying so hard to be successful, not just for myself but for you and Junior too.'

Running her fingertips across his lips, Tess shushed

him. 'I know, darling, I know. Have patience with me. I'll get the hang of it, I promise.'

Holding her as close as her enormous belly permitted, he kissed her, gently at first, and then more passionately. Tess reached down to take his erection in her hand. Although the doctor had warned her against any more intercourse until after the baby was born, she wanted to do something for this beautiful man who loved her. She lifted the blanket and moved her head downward, but Kip protested softly, 'It's not fair to you, honey.'

'But I want to,' she whispered.

26

Beth Cellini sat in the principal's office and stared furiously at the man charged with the responsibility of administering the school for dependent children of all the Americans in Tripoli. She had been brought up to seek the best in everyone she met, but she was hard-pressed to find one praiseworthy trait in the man sitting before her. From his seedy tweed jacket dusted with dandruff to his unpolished brogues, Mark Clausen was as distasteful in body as he was in spirit.

'Look, Mrs Cellini, you gotta face it. Most of these kids are losers. There's nothin' we can do for 'em, and there's just no use putting that Kenny kid back a grade, because he's never gonna amount to anything anyway. Both his father, Sergeant Kratz, and his mother are alcoholics. They've got six kids, and they don't give a damn – excuse the language – about any of them.' His tone was patronizingly patient and oily.

'If that's true, then we'd better made sure the boy has some skills to fall back on. He can't read, Mr Clausen, at all. With thirty-seven children in the class, I have all I can do just to keep them quiet and working. I have no time for individual instruction. He needs to go back, really, to the first grade and start over.'

'That would be a mistake. If we can't teach the kid to read, then we at least shouldn't stigmatize him socially by demoting him. Sorry.' He turned away from her and began to shuffle the papers on his cluttered desk in an attempt to dismiss her. Beth was not ready to give up.

'Mr Clausen, if we fail to teach Kenny to read, we're not doing what we're being paid to do. Our children deserve better than they're getting. We have overcrowded classrooms, worn and scruffy textbooks that are out-of-date, and very little in the way of supplies. Teaching is not my profession, but – '

'Mrs Cellini, in spite of your lack of teaching credentials, I approved of hiring you, but I think now that perhaps it was a mistake,' he said testily. 'I've had nothing but complaints from you since the day you started. If you'd ever taught in schools Stateside, you'd realize it's not so bad here. Now, I have work to do.' There was a long silence, and then, without looking at her, he said, 'I'm prepared to accept your resignation if you can't work under the present conditions.'

Beth was angered by his bluntness. 'Well, Mr Clausen, you have it. As soon as another teacher can be brought in to take over this class, I will happily make way for her.'

'Fine, Sergeant Wilder's wife just arrived at Wheelus last week and applied for the job. She's had twenty years' experience teaching in grade schools both in the States and in Europe. She's ready to go to work immediately.' He swiveled his chair around, smiling with satisfaction.

'Good,' Beth said angrily. 'I only took this job because Veronica Masters asked me to do it as a personal favor. When can Mrs Wilder begin?'

Through clenched teeth Clausen replied, 'This afternoon. Why don't you go clean out your desk and tell the children good-bye?'

Driving away from the school, Beth was in a state of shock and anger. Although she had just been sacked, she'd get no sympathy from Joe, who had opposed her taking the job in the first place. At the gate she stepped on the gas, anxious to get away from the base and glad that they lived in town. She was fed up with everything connected with the service.

Although the speed limit was twenty miles per hour, Beth had her car up to thirty-five when she suddenly passed a car stopped at the side of the road. From the corner of her eye she got a glimpse of a woman slumped over the steering wheel, and she slammed her foot on the brakes, turned the car around, and drove back to the green Morris Minor. She knocked sharply on the window. There was no mistaking who was under that head of curly red hair.

'Chili, Chili! Are you all right?' she called through the glass.

Chili raised her head just enough so that Beth could see that her eyes were streaked with mascara-tinged tears. She was crying, and she made no movement to open the window. She just shook her head and turned away, but Beth did not intend to be so easily rebuffed. 'Chili, open the window so I won't have to yell at you,' she ordered.

Finally Chili rolled her window. She wiped at her eyes and smiled weakly. 'Hi Beth,' was all she said.

'What are you doing sitting out here all by yourself? You know it's not a good idea. What's wrong?'

'It's nothin', Beth, honest. I just had a little fight with Gam, that's all. I'm fine, really. Goodness, I must look a sight.' She looked at her reflection in the rearview mirror, got a tissue from her purse, and tried to dab away the smudges of black on her cheeks.

'Are you sure?' Beth asked doubtfully. Why in the world would she pick this place to stop for a crying jag?

'Really, I was on my way into town to shop, but I don't feel much like it now. Maybe I'll just head home.'

Beth looked at her watch doubtfully. 'It's almost two, and all the stores will be closed for the afternoon. Why

180

don't you come on home with me? We can have a cup of tea and you can listen to me bitch. I just got fired, can you believe that?'

The note lying in Chili's lap did not go unnoticed, and as Beth talked, she tried to make out its contents, with only partial success. As soon as Chili realized that Beth was looking at the piece of paper, she snatched it up and crumpled it in her hand.

'No, thanks, Beth. I better be gettin' on home. I haven't shopped for Gam's dinner yet, and it's gettin' late. Thanks anyway.' She wiped her eyes, turned on the ignition, and put the car in gear. Beth had no choice but to step back and let her go.

For the rest of the day Beth's anger with Mark Clausen was filtered through her concern for Chili Shaheen. There was something seriously wrong there, she was sure of it. Who could have written her a note that began with 'Answer your damn phone?' And was that the reason she was so upset? Was Chili trying to avoid someone?

At the dinner table that evening Beth told Joe about meeting Chili and seeing the note.

'Does seem strange. Gamal went to Benghazi this morning with Dr Pepperman.'

'The base obstetrician? Is the queen pregnant?'

'I have no idea.'

'Chili said she was going home to fix dinner for him,' Beth ruminated, thinking that she ought to do something to help her but having no idea where to start. She didn't want to meddle in someone's personal affairs. Perhaps she'd call Chili the next morning and invite her for lunch and bridge sometime during the week. She'd recruit Sam Mulhare and Tess Kipling, and perhaps the three of them could figure out what was going on.

181

27

Chili turned the car around and headed home. There was no point in going anywhere now. She hadn't escaped. She would never escape, and if Gamal ever found out what was going on, he would either leave her or kill her, and she wouldn't blame him. If she'd only known how important honor was to her husband, she probably wouldn't have tried to deceive him about her past. Now she was trapped and there was no safe way out.

As soon as she entered her quarters, she went from room to room, closing the venetian blinds, shutting out the light, closing herself off from the world. She had almost three hours before her command performance, three hours to fortify herself with just enough booze to help her through the encounter, but not enough to turn her brain and her legs to slush. But first she had to call and find out exactly what time Gam would be home. She didn't dare walk into the house late again and have him already there.

Gamal's office told Chili he had been called out for some special duty.

'What kind of special duty, Sergeant Gomez?' she asked.

The sergeant, who always seemed to know everything that was going on, lowered his voice as he replies, 'The old man sent him to Benghazi. It was rush-rush, hush-hush, as usual.'

'Benghazi? When will he be back?'

'Tonight. I guess the queen's not feelin' so good, and

the major was asked to accompany the doctor and translate for him.'

Chili breathed a long sigh of relief. 'Do you have any idea how long they'll be there?'

'No, ma'am, but the plane and crew's gonna wait to bring 'em back. They didn't get off till after ten. Dr Pepperman was deliverin' a baby.'

'Thanks, Sergeant. I guess I'd better fix something that won't be ruined if he's late.'

Chili went to the kitchen cabinet where Gam kept the liquor stashed and poured herself a stiff shot of gin. She splashed a little tonic water in it, tossed in a couple of ice cubes, and sat down on the couch. As she sipped the drink, she tried not to think of the coming encounter. It wasn't that she minded the screwing – that didn't bother her much at all. She had screwed so many men in her life that she had learned either to enjoy the moment, or if that wasn't possible, to think about something else until it was over.

What really disgusted her about having to perform on command was that she had thought that part of her life was over forever when she got married. She loved Gamal more than anything in the world and she wanted to have his baby, wanted desperately to be nothing more than a normal wife and a mother. Why couldn't men leave her alone? Maybe Mama had been right to say she was a bad girl and that it was her own fault if men couldn't keep their hands off her.

At five o'clock Chili swallowed the last drop of her second drink. She stood up and shook her head to clear away the mists of alcohol and depression, picked up her keys, and walked out the door. She did not bother to check her hair or her makeup. It didn't matter. The parts of her body that would be used in the next hour or two didn't need to be spruced up.

The parking lot at the officers' club was beginning to fill with cars of the men who had just gotten off work and were headed for the bar, when Chili arrived. She waited until no one was watching and walked around to the side of the building. Just behind a clump of palm trees, hidden by a large trash bin, was a door, locked from the outside by a shiny new hasp and padlock. Using the small key she had been given, Chili unlocked the door and stepped into what was jokingly called, by those in the know, the commander's prayer rug. It was a small dark room, unheated and damp, probably used at one time for storage for the club, now appropriated solely for the commander's use. Before closing the door behind her, she snapped on the overhead light and looked around to make sure there weren't any creepy, crawling things scuttling about on the lush Karouan rugs which were the room's only furnishings, except for a number of tapestry-covered pillows and a pair of huge brass candlesticks.

Chili closed the door, fished through her purse until she found a Zippo lighter, and lit the candles. When the soft flickering light suffused the room, she snapped out the overhead lights. As she undressed, she wondered if any other wives had been called on the carpet by Brick Masters in this little cubbyhole, and how many people knew of the room's existence.

Once she was naked, she stretched out on the rich, thick rug in the center of the room and covered herself with her dress. Gamal could never understand why she had not wanted one of the beautiful Karouan rugs for their quarters. Made without dye, the wool was woven into patterns in the sheep's own colors of black, brown, and white. Because the color was natural, it never faded, and the rugs were incredibly inexpensive in Tripoli. But Chili hated them, because they reminded her of the hours she had spent wrestling on them in this dark little room. Since she couldn't tell Gamal the reason, she finally relented and let him buy one. Unfortunately, all the Americans had at least one or two in their homes, and so it was impossible to avoid them.

It was almost six o'clock before the door opened. The dark, cold air accompanied Brick Masters as he quickly stepped into the room and closed the door behind him.

'It looks like you were on time for a change, eh?' he said as he bolted the lock.

'I was, but you weren't,' Chili said crossly. 'I'm freezing to death in this damn refrigerator. Can't you have a heater put in here?'

'Don't worry about being cold. I'll warm you up in no time. Besides, without any windows, there's not enough ventilation in here. It would be too easy to fall asleep and never wake up.'

'Now, that would cause a stir, wouldn't it? Up-and-coming bird colonel dies in the arms of the base bimbo. Get your clothes off, Brick, and let's get this over with. I don't know what time Gam will get back from Benghazi, and I'd better be home when he arrives. He caught me in a lie the other night, and he was mad as hell.'

Brick Masters sank to one knee and pulled the dress off Chili's body. He ran his fingers across her nipples lightly until they came to attention, and then he spread her legs apart and stroked her vulva until he felt her clitoris begin to harden and swell.

Chili tried to ignore it, tried defiantly to think of something else, but she could not stop the mounting desire she felt. Her body was like a sex machine that she couldn't turn off, and she hated it. She wanted to be true to her husband, to have desire and joy only with him, but the insistent fingers of this man she hated were having the same effect on her as Gam's.

'You want it, don't you baby? But first you gotta show me how much.' He stood up and unzipped his pants and took off his clothes. Then he went around and knelt on the rug behind her head and let his body fall forward. His erect penis rested on her mouth. 'Open up, baby,' he said hoarsely, and she parted her lips.

As she sucked gently, she could feel his mouth exploring her moist and ready recesses, and within a few minutes they were both close to the edge of a climax. Chili wanted to finish as they were, but suddenly Brick pulled away.

'Too easy, too easy,' he commanded.

'Brick, no . . . please,' she begged, but he grabbed her shoulder, turned her over, and quickly dropped on top of her. Sensing that she was losing her passion, he lifted her body and massaged her clitoris rapidly as he sodomized her.

'Am I man enough for you, or do you need two men to fuck you . . . one in your mouth and one in your cunt?' he hissed into her ear.

Chili hated to talk during the sex act, hated to be distracted from the passion that was building up inside her, but Brick needed dirty talk to keep him going.

'Two . . . I need two cocks as big as yours,' Chili gasped, wanting it to be over, wanting release from the terrible need to come, but it was not to be. Suddenly there was a hard, painful thrust that signaled it was all over for him, and with a groan he let the full weight of his body sink down on hers.

Chili tried to move against the rug, tried to bring some satisfaction to herself, but she could not. Brick rolled off and stretched out on the rug beside her, spent and gasping.

Chili curled herself into the fetal position. She felt, as she always did after an illicit sexual coupling, degraded and filled with self-hate. She wished she could be indifferent to the rubbing and poking of men at her body – the way her stepfather had said her mother was. Smart woman. Had she figured out all by herself that sexual satisfaction didn't necessarily mean satisfaction in life?

Reaching out, she pulled at her clothes and started to dress, but Brick stopped her.

'You're not finished yet, baby.'

'Oh yeah? I'm not waitin' around for you to get it up again. That could take hours,' she retorted harshly.

'A friend of mine is here on TDY. I promised him a good piece of ass tonight. He'll be here at six-thirty.'

'You're nuts! You can't pass me around to your buddies. I'm not some two-bit whore!' Chili snapped, pulling on her underpants.

'You'll do anything I tell you to do, understand?' he said menacingly. 'Or I might just call that husband of yours into my office and tell him all about the stuff you've been doing with me. I might even put in his ER that his career has been jeopardized by his alley-cat wife.'

'You bastard!' Chili said, but her words lacked force. Brick Masters held all the cards.

'I just wonder what the proper and upright Major Shaheen would say if he found out that I had him transferred here and given quarters on the base to make it convenient for me to hump his wife?'

'You made me do it,' she said weakly, 'you made me,' but she stopped putting on her clothes and sat on the rug with her face in her hands.

'I didn't make you do anything. I made you a proposition and you accepted it, that's all. In exchange for important duty for your husband – and provided, of course, that I didn't tell him that you were once known as the juiciest piece of ass in San Antonio – you agreed to accommodate me when and wherever I pleased.'

'That doesn't include banging your friends,' Chili said bitterly.

'That agreement includes anything I want it to include, understand?' he snapped. 'It's your own fuckin' fault, you know. You should never have lied to your husband. Don't you know an Arab will kill his woman if another man even sees her face?'

When Brick was fully dressed, he looked at his watch. 'Good timing. It's just six-thirty. Now, have fun, but don't take too long. My wife is expecting Fred at the villa for dinner at eight. Give him a good time, though. He's already got his first star, and he's got more coming.'

There was a soft knock at the door. Brick pulled the bolt to open it, and Chili could hear him say, 'She's warmed up good and she was hot to begin with. Wait'll you see those tits.'

28

Although she had fully intended to sleep in the morning after she'd left her job at the school, Beth was up and about early. The image of Chili's mascara-streaked face had troubled her most of the night. As soon as Joe left for work, she called Sam Mulhare.

'Hi, how come you're not at school, Madam Teach?' Sam asked when she heard Beth's voice.

'I got fired. Well, not exactly fired, but asked to resign. I had a tiff with Clausen,' Beth said, and explained the circumstances.

'You were absolutely right. You didn't really like the job anyway. Come on, what do you say we play bridge today?' Sam asked.

Beth sighed. 'You know how I hate to play cards, Sam. I do want to talk to you, though. Something strange happened yesterday . . .'

'Oooo, goody. Tell me.'

'Not on the phone. Do you think Tess would feel like having lunch?'

'Why don't you call her? I've got the Pontiac today, and I'll pick you both up, and we can check the BX for exotic treasures and then go to the club for lunch,' Sam suggested.

'That'll be fine.'

Two hours later, the three women were settled in Sam's car on their way to the base, and Beth told them of seeing Chili. 'What do you make of it?' she asked when she finished the story.

189

'I think she's in some kind of trouble,' Sam said, remembering the look of horror on Chili's face when she had seen Brick Masters talking to Gamal at her dinner party.

'I do too,' Tess agreed. 'Is there anything we can do for her without poking our noses into her business? All I know about Chili is that she's warm and kind and sweet. She's got a good sense of humor, and in spite of those outrageously sexy dresses she wears, she's a nice woman.'

'She could dress in a nun's habit, and she'd still look sexy,' Beth commented.

'Do you think it's booze?' Sam asked.

Tess shook her head. 'I've never seen her really drunk, have you?'

Beth considered mentioning the night at her house when Chili had had to be driven home, but she refrained, feeling it would add to Chili's problems if the story became generally known.

'Do you think there's some connection with Colonel Masters?' Sam wondered aloud.

'Well, there's always the possibility . . . considering her looks and his reputation,' Beth replied.

Tess was affronted. 'That's an awful thing to suggest, Beth. She wouldn't get herself involved with him.'

'Don't be so naïve, little girl. People are always getting themselves involved. Look at the Dirty Dozen,' Sam said.

'I'd hate to think she was one of them,' Tess commented, and they drove the rest of the way in silence.

They stopped at the base exchange and luckily arrived just as a batch of Hummel figurines were being put out for sale. Tess bought a charming lamp with a small boy climbing up a tree for the baby's room, and Beth got a little girl with an umbrella. Sam passed. 'They're not my cup of tea,' she observed. 'Too cutesy.'

190

They arrived at the club at noon and ordered what Sam called, 'slop du jour.' Now that she was in the latter stages of her pregnancy, Tess's nausea had been replaced by a ravenous appetite. No matter how strong her resolve to eat less, she managed to devour whatever was put in front of her and long for more.

When Nell Carson arrived with a group of friends, Beth said pensively, 'I wonder if I ought to ask Nell what she knows about Chili.'

'If anybody knows anything, it's the wife of the commander's pimp,' Samara said sardonically.

'Kip said that was only a joke,' Tess said uncertainly. 'It is, isn't it?'

'Not really,' Sam countered. 'Hasn't Kip ever told you about the womanizing Brick does when they're on those trips? And that he expects his officers to do the same, because he figures if they're screwing around too, he doesn't have to worry about them telling.'

Tess's heart seemed to drop into her lap. She couldn't stand the thought that Kip might ever be intimate with another woman.

'Kip goes on trips all the time with him,' she whispered hollowly.

Sam quickly put her hand on Tess's arm. 'I didn't say all the guys actually did it. Bob refused to get involved, and I'm sure Kip did too. He probably just didn't tell you about it because he didn't want to upset you,' she said, sorry she had brought up the subject.

'You have to trust your husband, Tess. We all do. Since we spend so much time separated from one another, we can't allow ourselves to be suspicious, or we'll torture ourselves and our marriages to death,' Beth said, adding, 'it just goes with the territory of being a service wife.'

Tess smiled. 'You're absolutely right, Beth. It just

191

shook me up for a minute there,' she said, but she couldn't help thinking that it was odd that Kip was spending so much time traveling with Masters. She hoped his ambition wouldn't make him feel it was necessary to do everything Masters wanted him to do.

Just as they were about to leave the club to head home, Nell Carson spotted them and called out, 'Hey, we need a fourth for bridge. One of you ladies want to join us?'

Tess and Beth shook their heads, and Sam said, 'Sorry, but I'm driving.'

'Go ahead,' Beth insisted. 'If you want to join them, I can take our car home if you'll pick up Joe after work.'

'Do you mind?' Sam asked. 'I might be able to find out something about Chili, okay? Nell has a direct line to the villa, you know.'

'Okay, but you have to promise to call both of us tonight if you find out anything,' Beth said.

'It's a deal.'

Sam drove Joe home that evening, and stopped in to talk to Beth.

'Did you find out anything?' Beth asked.

Sam shook her head. 'Not really. Nell made a sort of rough joke about the commander having a prayer rug. When I asked her if he faced east when he was on it, she giggled a very dirty giggle and said the only direction Brick knew was down. Apparently everybody got the joke except me, because they laughed a lot. Got any ideas?'

Joe shook his head. 'Nope. Hate to make a pun, but I haven't a prayer. Sorry.'

When they were alone, Beth looked at her husband questioningly. 'Why did you lie to Sam?'

'I just don't want to get in trouble, that's all. I've already had one go-around on paying for that damned 'prayer rug,' and if something ever comes up about it, I don't want to be on record as knowing what it was for.'

'Then why didn't you stand up to Masters and refuse to pay for his rotten screwing room with taxpayers' money?' Beth asked angrily. 'He has no right to force you to do anything wrong.'

Joe was defensive. 'I tried, didn't I? And all I got was threats. You know the kind of bastard Masters is. He'd have found some way of getting even. The best I could do was insist that he personally sign the request for funds. Now, I don't want to talk about it anymore.'

Beth did not pursue the subject any further, but more than ever she wished that her husband had stood his ground and refused to kowtow to that bully.

193

29

The fatigue Tess felt climbing the stairs to her apartment was not caused solely by the huge load she was carrying in her abdomen, nor by the incline she was ascending, but by the weight in her heart. It had never occurred to her that Kip might be unfaithful. Often in the months since they had fallen in love and gotten married, some of Kip's characteristics had surprised her and at times annoyed or disappointed her, but never once had she entertained the possibility that her husband might have slept with another woman.

She tried to believe that Kip would stand by his principles and be faithful to her, but would he? He wanted to get ahead. No, it was more than just wanting, he was zealous about moving up in the ranks and becoming a general, just as his father and his grandfather had. His drive was one of the reasons she had been attracted to him. He was so strong and sure of himself, and until this afternoon she had trusted him implicitly.

Having reached the top of the stairs, she unlocked the apartment door and let herself in. It was cold and dark. Pina had left hours before, and the shutters were drawn, the Aladdin heaters unlit. Tess had no energy left. She went immediately into the bedroom, pulled back the covers on the bed, and climbed in. Closing her eyes, she tried to go to sleep, tried to close out of her mind the image of her husband unclothed, lying with a faceless woman, making love to her . . . but the horrifying apparition would not go away, and sleep, cleansing, comforting sleep, would not come.

All the doubts her father had expressed about Kip as her husband came back to torment her. He had warned her that it was a mistake to marry someone from a world so different from her own, but she had loved Kip too much to listen seriously to her father's reservations. She still loved him, perhaps a lot more than he loved her.

The baby moved, and she ran her fingertips over the taut flesh of her abdomen. She must stop this foolish conjecturing. They were going to have a child who would need to be loved, not by one parent but by two.

At six o'clock Kip walked in the door and was immediately alarmed by the silence, the chill, and the darkness. 'Tess, are you all right?' he called, snapping on the light in the entry. There was no reply.

Rushing into the bedroom, he found the lamp switch and turned it on. Seeing the inert form of his wife in the bed, he went to her immediately, concern icing his heart.

'Tess, baby, are you okay?' he said, sitting down beside her and touching her shoulder.

At the sound of his concerned voice, Tess began to cry. She had never been able to handle sympathy without showing emotion.

Kip gathered her in his arms and gently rocked her, crooning words of comfort and affection. 'Honey, I was so worried about you when I walked in. What's wrong? Are you feeling all right?'

The more he talked to her, the more racking her sobs became. 'Come on, now,' he coaxed gently. 'You mustn't upset yourself like this. It's not good for the baby. Tess? Please stop crying, and tell me what's wrong.'

But the only words Tess had to explain her overwrought state were words that would make her out to be a foolish and jealous wife. When her sobbing at last began to subside, Kip released her momentarily, undressed, and quickly got in beside her. It was not the first cold evening they had spent snuggled together under the covers in their bed. He put his arm under her head and pulled her close to him.

'Why've you still got your clothes on, babe?' he asked curiously.

'I had lunch at the club with Beth and Sam, and I was so exhausted when I got up the stairs, I didn't have enough energy left to take them off,' she replied softly.

Kip was not reassured. 'If you feel that tired, then something might be wrong. Maybe we should go see Dr Pepperman tomorrow.'

'It's not that,' she replied, having decided to forge ahead, come what may, and tell him the real reason that she was feeling so terribly depressed. 'Kip, I heard something today, and I need to ask you a question that'll probably make you angry. Will you promise to give me a straight answer without causing a scene?'

'Come on . . . am I as bad as all that?' he asked teasingly, and Tess wished he would always be as warm and human as he was when they were alone and in bed together.

'Have you ever had . . . have you ever been . . . unfaithful to me on those trips with Colonel Masters?'

She braced herself for the answer, which she expected to be glacially hostile, but he did not pull away. With a sigh of regret he said, 'I should have known that one of these days somebody was going to tell you what goes on during those damned trips.'

Suddenly Tess was afraid to hear any more. She didn't want him to confess. What would she do with the rest of her life if she had to turn away from him? She would have no husband, no lover, no father for her unborn child. Who would hold her in the night?

196

'I know I shouldn't have asked you that, but I had to. I need for you to tell me the truth.'

'It's a bad question to ask, Tess,' he said sadly, 'because the only answer you'd believe would be yes, right?'

'I'll believe the truth, whatever it is,' she insisted, feeling utterly miserable. She wished she could pull the accusing words back and erase them forever, but words once spoken can never be unsaid. Kip pulled away from her and lay on his back, staring up at the dark ceiling. The silence in the room grew heavier with each moment.

'Tess, suppose I asked you if I was really the father of the baby you're carrying. How would that make you feel?'

'Angry . . . No . . . more than that, I'd be furious with you. I was a virgin the night we married. You know that. You should know I wouldn't – ' she began, but he interrupted her.

'See? That's how I feel too. What have I ever done to make you think I'd touch another woman?'

'Honestly? Well . . . sometimes you're too eager to please the brass, Kip. I know you work hard, but I've felt – often . . . that your career is more important to you than I am.'

'You hate being a military wife, don't you?'

'Damn, that makes me mad! How come every time I complain about something you accuse me of not being the perfect officer's wife? Kip, let's go back to the subject,' Tess insisted, refusing to be put on the defensive.

'That's my answer,' he said tersely.

'It's not good enough. I want to know how you avoided it, or are you going to tell me that you just told Masters to go to hell, that you weren't going to join the party?'

Suddenly Kip laughed aloud and pulled her close to him. 'What the hell ever happened to the shy little shrinking violet I married? Have I turned you into a tiger?'

'You're not going to answer the question, are you?' she snapped stubbornly, feeling better about herself and more secure than she had felt in months.

'God, even with that belly of yours, you make me horny when I touch you,' he whispered.

'Kip!' she said sharply, refusing to be diverted, demanding an answer to her question.

'Okay, okay. You win, but first let me tell you a little story about Masters that will show you what kind of a creep he is, so you'll appreciate what I'm up against. A wing commander arrived here on TDY with his group for target practice. The guy reported to Masters, and out of the clear blue sky Masters asked, 'Been getting any strange stuff lately?' It's a question he routinely asks, but this time he got the wrong answer. The guy was totally offended and shot back sarcastically, 'Why don't you ask your wife?'

'Oh, God, that's funny! Tell me, what happened to him?' Tess asked. 'I mean after he was hung by his toenails?'

'Masters reported him for practicing unsafe procedures, and he was banned from ever returning here again. I assume it went on his record. Masters is as vindictive as they come.'

'So how did you refuse without making him an enemy?'

'On my first trip, he set me up with some German babe, and I admit I was too chicken to refuse. I gave her five bucks to get lost and went out to dinner by myself. Next morning on the flight home, he asked me what kind of a lay she was, and I started to say 'great' but I just couldn't bring myself to lie. I just couldn't. It was too demeaning. And besides, I couldn't keep on paying whores not to

198

sleep with me. So I told him the truth, that I had no interest in anyone except my wife. He just laughed and said not to worry. That it would wear off in time and I'd be out scrounging 'strange stuff,' as he calls it, just like everybody else.'

'Then why does he continue taking you with him if you don't play his game?'

'Because he knows I can keep my mouth shut, which is true. I didn't even tell you until I had to, did I? And somehow telling the truth and not screwing around has telegraphed to him that I'm a loyal person, and he needs people he can trust. He's ambitious, you know. Very ambitious.'

Tess believed Kip, not just because she wanted to, but because everything he said had the ring of truth, and she was happy.

'Besides,' he continued, 'even though I do all the flying, he takes credit for the flight time. And I'm qualified in jets, which a lot of his older cronies aren't. To make me an accessory, I guess, he put me in charge of bringing the foul-weather gear,' Kip added with a snigger.

'What's the 'foul-weather gear'?' Tess asked.

'Rubbers . . . condoms,' Kip explained. 'Some of the women they mess around with are pretty tough babes. You should have seen the blond. I'm sure she survived the war on her back.'

'How perfectly disgusting,' she said. 'How come you've never told me a thing about any of this?'

'You were already disenchanted with service life. I didn't want to make it look even worse to you. One thing I learned from Dad about getting ahead in the service is that you can put up with quirky COs because they're temporary. Remember that. Change is the constant of military life.'

199

'Are all COs such bastards?' Tess asked.

'I hope not.' He hesitated and then added, 'As long as I've started, I might as well tell you the worst. He tried to borrow money from me.'

'He what?' Tess asked in astonishment.

'He does it all the time, and I hear he never pays it back.'

'How much did he ask for?'

'He asked me for a thousand, but I told him I just didn't have it because of the expense of buying furniture and stuff.'

'But we do, honey. I've still got that savings account of money we got as wedding presents. There's at least twelve hundred dollars still there.'

'I know that, but he doesn't. I didn't have enough guts to say no and report him, so I just pleaded poor. Do you think that was cowardly?' he asked sheepishly.

'I think you were brave to refuse at all.'

'Yeah, but Howard said I should have paid up because he never hits on a junior officer more than once if he gets the dough.'

'What'll you do next time?'

'I don't know, honey. I just don't know.'

'When you were at West Point did they tell you there might be men who would use their rank like this?'

'Nope. They sure as hell didn't. But then, West Point's not the real world.' He sighed and kissed her, and she was content.

30

The morning after Chili's encounter with the visiting general on Brick Masters' 'prayer rug,' she awakened to the grim realization that her life was careening wildly out of control. She had to do something quickly or soon it would be too late. She longed for a close friend in whom she could confide, but there was no one she trusted except Jimmyjohn, and he was a world away. She would write him a letter, she decided, and tell him the whole story. Surely he could give her some advice.

Because she had little education, she was reluctant to put her thoughts down on paper. She was so self-conscious about her penmanship and doubtful of her ability to write coherent sentences with properly spelled words that her letters were stilted and stiff.

'Dear Jimmyjohn, I am well and hope you are the same. Tripoli is nice. The weather is sunny,' she began and then crumpled the paper in her hands and threw it into the wastepaper basket. To hell with the weather and the sunshine. She needed words that would describe the nightmare she was living under the shadow of Brick Masters.

She began again. 'Dear Jimmyjohn, I've got a terrible problem, and I need your advice.' Haltingly she wrote six pages detailing her problems with Brick Masters. She wrote that she still loved her husband and hated lying to him. As she wrote, she began to realize that if she'd just had the courage to tell Gamal the truth about herself and

201

her background, she wouldn't have to screw the black-mailing Brick Masters to keep him from telling. She had tricked Gamal into marrying a woman who didn't exist. It was a depressing thought, but it was time to face the truth.

When she finally finished the laborious task, she closed the letter by saying, 'So, that's the way it is, Jimmyjohn. I took your advice and pretended to be a virgin, and I got Gam. Now I don't know what the hell to do. Your loving cousin, Chili.'

She read the letter over once, wondering if all the words were spelled right, and then she sealed it and addressed the envelope to the house where Jimmyjohn had been rooming when she left San Antonio. Then she got into the car to take the letter to the post office to be sure it went out on the next plane to the States. On the way back, she decided to go to the commissary and buy food to fix for a nice dinner at home for a change.

Just as she put the key into the lock of her quarters, balancing two bags of groceries, she heard the telephone ring. Thinking it was probably her husband calling to say he was on his way home for dinner, she dropped the bags on the table and grabbed the telephone. It was not Gamal's voice, but that of her tormentor.

'Hi,' he said. 'I just called to tell you that my friend was very pleased with the services you provided. He's planning to come back for a visit soon.'

'I'm not gonna do your buddies anymore, understand?' she said angrily. 'It's not part of the deal.'

'You'll do whatever I say.'

'Yeah, well, just suppose I decide to tell Gam everything? Then what?' she asked with more impudence than she felt.

'You wouldn't dare,' he said coldly. 'That Arab you're

202

married to would kick you out of the house . . . if he didn't kill you first. They think women who screw around are better off dead.'

'Maybe I would be better off dead. Maybe I'm gettin' fed up with all the bullshit around here, and maybe, just maybe I might decide to tell your wife before I tell my husband. Two can play this game, you know? Hell, what have I got to lose anyway? It's not like I'm havin' any fun.'

'Listen, you whore, if you ever go near my wife, so help me, I'll ram your filthy cunt so hard you'll never be able to get your legs together again!' he snarled furiously.

Chili heard herself say, 'Promises, promises . . .' and she laughed nastily.

'I want you over there now. In ten minutes, you understand?' he barked, and slammed down the telephone.

Chili walked shakily into the kitchen. Her heart was pounding and her hands shook. What had gotten into her? Even if she told Veronica what was going on, would she believe her? And would Gamal be angry enough to kill her . . . really? He had hit her once. Maybe he would hurt her badly.

Pouring herself a tall, stiff drink of bourbon, she downed it quickly and then poured another. Masters had finally pushed her too far. No matter what happened, she wasn't ever going back to that damned prayer rug again. Not if her life depended on it.

When Gamal arrived home that evening, she was stretched out on the couch unconscious. The grocery bags were still sitting on the table where she had dropped them.

The sight of her and the smell of the booze in the air sickened him, and he whirled on his heel and stomped angrily out of the house. Tomorrow he would give her an ultimatum. Either she quit drinking altogether or he was finished with her. He would not share his life with a lush.

The next morning Chili awoke with an enormous headache, and the inside of her mouth felt like a furry piece of mold on a rotten apple. Gamal had apparently come home, slept, and gone to work. The grocery bags were just where she had left them. She took two aspirin and got into the shower to try to wash some of the toxicity out of her body.

After she made herself a pot of rich black coffee and drank most of it, Chili threw away the now sickeningly fragrant chicken and cleaned up the kitchen. She tried not to think about Brick Masters, but feared what he would do now that she had not obeyed him. Drearily she reflected on her decision not to go and decided it was the right one.

When the bed was made, she did a load of laundry, washed the bathroom sink, and swished Clorox around the toilet bowl. She then dusted the furniture and vacuumed the rugs. Unlike most women, who loathed housework, Chili appreciated the illusion of peace and order it gave her. A clean, tidy house validated her existence and gave her a reason for being, something she desperately needed.

Since she had washed the windows two days before, she refrained from doing that job, but she did polish the mirrors until they were clear and shining. When all that was done, she ran a comb through her hair, put on some lipstick, and drove to the commissary for another chicken. When it was in the oven baking along with a pan of scalloped potatoes, she picked up the telephone to call her husband to apologize.

'Gam, honey,' she said before he had a chance to

204

berate her for her drunkenness, 'I'm real sorry about last night. I promise I'll never take another drink as long as I live. Cross my heart and hope to die. Sometimes I just don't know what gets me goin' with that stuff, but when I start, I just can't seem to help myself. So this mornin' I vowed that the only way to stop it was to quit altogether. Gam, baby, I promise I'll never take another drink as long as I live.'

Gamal sighed. Although he wanted to believe her, he'd heard the same promises too many times and he was no longer sanguine about her ability to change. 'I hope you mean it this time, Chili. I won't live with a common drunk.'

She ignored the threat, because she was sure he didn't mean it. Gamal needed her. 'It won't happen again, Gam. Now, I fixed us a special little dinner tonight. We'll have it by candlelight, and things will be just like they used to be. Okay?'

'I can't. I'm having dinner at the palace. The king is in town and is entertaining several of the ministers, and he invited the CO and asked him to bring me along to translate. I'd have told you about it last night, but you were in no condition to listen.'

Chili was crestfallen. Another damned long evening all by herself. 'I see. Well, the food'll probably be godawful, but I'll keep the dinner warm so we can have a little snack together when you get here before we go to bed,' she suggested, hoping to salvage a little bit of the evening and give herself something to look forward to.

'That won't be necessary. I'll probably be late, so you just go ahead and eat by yourself. Don't bother waiting up for me.'

Chili took the chicken and potatoes out of the oven, placed them in covered dishes, and stuck them in the refrigerator. She had no appetite. All she really needed was a drink, but she kept her promise and drank nothing but a bottle of Coca-Cola. She listened to the armed-forces station on the radio, smoked half a pack of Old Gold cigarettes, and was still pacing the floor like a caged animal when Gamal finally walked into the house. He had ridden all the way into town and back with Brick.

Chili searched Gamal's face for signs of anger or hostility, but there were none. Masters hadn't made good on his threat. Mercy be to God, she had called that son of a bitch's bluff! Why hadn't she thought of it before?

Throwing herself into Gamal's arms joyously, she said, 'I waited for you, honey.' She held him tightly and tried to force his mouth down to hers. Gamal was weary but not angry.

'Not now, Chili, it's been a long night, and I'm dead tired. Just go to bed, will you? And open the window and air this place out. God, I wish you wouldn't smoke in the house.'

Gamal undressed and got into bed. Undaunted, Chili quickly donned a pink satin gown trimmed in black lace. She wanted to celebrate her freedom by making wonderful love to her husband, even if he was too tired. She brushed her teeth and rinsed her mouth with Listerine to wash the tobacco from her breath, then sprayed herself with a mist of Chanel No. 5. Her face scrubbed clean and her hair brushed into a great glowing auburn halo around her head, she walked sinuously toward his side of the bed. She must not let him go to sleep without proving to him that he still needed the touch of her body on his.

'Darlin',' she said softly, 'I know you're tired, but maybe you just need me to make you feel better.' Her fingertips traveled gently from the hollow in his neck down through the black hairiness of his chest, in a straight

206

line toward the object of her desire, but just as she reached his navel, he grasped her wrist and brought the journey to a halt.

'Not tonight, Chili. Can't you understand? I just don't feel like it. Now, get in bed and go to sleep.'

Rebuffed, but not ready to concede defeat, she whispered breathily, 'Come on, darlin'. I'll make it worth your while . . . promise I will.'

Exasperated, Gamal sat up in bed and looked directly at her. 'Chili, grow up, will you? Not every problem in the world can be solved by a good fuck, understand? I've got a lot on my mind right now, and I'd appreciate it if you'd just let me sleep. Good night.'

He turned away from her.

It was a slap that hurt far more than the real one he had once struck. She couldn't remember a time in her whole life that a man had refused to make love to her if she wanted him to.

31

'You're invited to what?' Kip asked in disbelief.

'Beth's new maid, Rima, has invited us to visit an Arab bride tonight. Women only, I'm afraid, because we're going to the women's quarters.'

'How come?'

'I don't know exactly. She went to work for Beth right after Dici left to get a job that paid more. Joe wouldn't let Beth give her the raise she wanted. Anyway, this new one is an Arab, and she and Beth apparently have a good relationship. Beth told her she was interested in knowing more about the Arab way of life. Lucky for me, I was included, as well as Sam Mulhare and Chili Shaheen. I understand their wedding festivities last three to five days, and although they never invite strangers to the wedding night, it's okay to do so earlier. It's really a golden opportunity and I don't want to miss it, even if I do weigh a ton and look like an elephant.'

'Where is it?'

'I'm not sure, but I don't think it's in the Old City.'

'It better not be. The Old City is off limits to personnel after dark. Are you sure you want to do this?'

'Definitely. Here we live in an old culture that's foreign to us, and all we ever do is socialize with our own countrymen. No wonder Americans have so few friends around the world,' Tess declared. It was not the first time she'd complained about the insularity of the Air Force personnel.

'I'll be worried until you get back,' Kip said.

208

'No you won't. I picked up a copy of James Jones's new novel, *From Here to Eternity*, at the library today. They saved it for me because I'm their best customer.'

'You mean you're actually going to let me read a book first for a change?' he asked, teasing.

'Don't get used to it. Now, hurry up and finish so I can clean up the dishes. Chili's coming by to pick me up in half an hour. Okay?'

'I guess so,' Kip relented. 'Just drive carefully, and don't stay out too late, or I'll have the Air Police out looking for you.'

Chili was right on time, and as Tess settled into the car moaning about her clumsiness, Chili said with envy, 'Count your blessin's, honey chile. I wish to hell that big belly was mine.'

'Have you seen Dr Pepperman about the trouble you're having getting pregnant?' Tess asked.

'Yeah, he gave me a thermometer, but Gam wouldn't cooperate. He didn't even want to hear that I talked to the doctor about it. I don't think he even likes the idea of me goin' to the doctor. He's real funny that way.'

'He's Moslem, right?' Tess asked.

'His folks were. I don't think he's much of anything, although I did ask him once about us maybe goin' to church service on Sunday now and then, but he just said for me to go alone. He wasn't interested.'

'Have you ever read any of the Koran, Chili?'

'The Arab Bible? Gosh no, I have a hard enough time readin' the English one.'

'My dad sent me a translation, and it's really fascinating, especially the chapters about women. It says that the reason women are supposed to hide themselves is that Allah has guarded their unseen parts.'

'What in hell does that mean?'

209

'Well, I think it means that nature put women's sex organs inside her and so it was meant that women too should be hidden.'

Chili hooted. 'And a man's winky is hanging out there for everybody to see, so he's allowed out of the house.'

Tess laughed. 'I love you, Chili, you always make me laugh.'

Chili suddenly became serious. 'What else did you read in the Koran?'

'Well, their religion does not condone celibacy at all, whereas Christianity encourages it. In fact, the Arabic word for 'marriage' and 'sexual intercourse' is the same – *nikah*.'

'You're such a smart lady. I sure wish I'd stayed in school. Say, is it true that a man can kill his wife if she, you know, fools around?' Chili asked, trying to be nonchalant.

'Not exactly according to the Koran, but a lot of the subjugation of women has become tribal custom, and it's much worse now than it was in the time of Mohammed. For instance, the honor of a family must be defended by the male members, and a woman doesn't even have to do anything bad to be dishonored. She can be disgraced by just being talked about.'

'Oh yeah?' Chili said, biting her lip.

'Pina tells me that she personally knew of a family where the brother stabbed his sister to death when her husband sent her back because she wasn't a virgin.'

'What did they do to him – the brother, I mean?'

'Pina said they didn't do anything, and in fact the family was proud of the brother for getting rid of her and restoring the family honor, and the authorities found the killing justified. Pina says that the old women treat the young wives pretty badly.'

'You've learned enough Italian to talk like that to your maid?' Chili asked, impressed.

'I studied both Latin and Spanish at school, and Italian has come easily to me. I love using it. Sometimes Pina has trouble getting the housework done because I talk to her so much.'

When they arrived at Beth's house, Sam was already there, and the two American women were standing on the street talking to Rima. Sam volunteered to drive, and they all got into her Pontiac.

'Which way, Rima?' Samara asked.

Rima, who was one of the lower-class Arab women and had worked outside the home all of her life, had never covered her face. Because she had worked for the British before the Americans came onto the scene, she could speak English a little and understood almost everything. She indicated the direction Sam should take, and they drove off.

'I understand that an Arab woman of quality ventures out only three times in her life,' Beth said.

'When's that?' Chili asked curiously.

'When she marries and goes to the home of her husband, when she goes to the funeral of her father, and when she goes to her own funeral,' Tess explained.

'Hard to believe that women stand for that kind of oppression in the fifties, isn't it?' Beth commented.

'That way . . . then turn that way,' Rima interrupted, and the conversation halted so that Sam wouldn't get lost. Winding through the blocks of ancient buildings, turning corners, going down dark, narrow streets, Sam followed Rima's directions. Suddenly Rima told Sam to stop in front of a whitewashed house. 'We go in here,' she commanded.

As they climbed out of the car, Tess whispered to Beth,

'Do you have any idea where we are?' and she replied, 'Not the faintest, but I think we're in the Old City.'

'Lordy, don't let Rima out of your sight,' Chili whispered.

Rima led them, not to one of the doors fronting on the street, but through a tiny, dark alley to the back of the building, up the stairs. She knocked on the door, and as they waited for someone to answer, Tess looked up at the sky. The stars were out and she felt secure and unafraid, so different from the way she had felt that night five months ago when she first arrived in this strange and exotic land.

The door opened and Rima spoke in rapid Arabic to the young woman who greeted them. They entered and passed from the quiet serenity of the night into a chattering babble of joyous women.

Sam whispered into Tess's ear, 'They sure don't act oppressed, do they?'

Most of those rushing about were nubile girls, some children, and even some young mothers with babies nursing at their breasts. Although most of them had dark hair and brown eyes, there were a few with blue eyes and lighter hair.

'Where did those blonds come from?' Chili asked Tess.

'They're probably Berber,' Tess whispered.

'Lordy, look at those redheads. Their hair's brighter than mine,' Chili said, staring at the women around them.

'Henna, Chili. See, they use it as hair color as well as skin decoration.'

'God, you're smart, Tess,' Chili said with admiration. 'You know just about everythin'.'

The visitors were led into the bedroom, where a pretty young girl with dark almond-shaped eyes was having her thick brown hair brushed with some difficulty, for it seemed to have been tightly wrapped in curlers and the brush could not smooth out the kinks. A beautician was putting makeup on the girl's face. The Americans watched as black kohl was drawn around her eyes.

'This the bride,' Rima explained.

'She's just a child,' Beth exclaimed softly, but Rima shook her head. 'No, no, ma'am, she almost fifteen . . . very late. Family very happy she finally getting married.'

The young bride smiled at them, and they smiled back, offering their best wishes in English, and she seemed to understand.

'She looks dead tired. Even before the kohl she had dark shadows under her eyes,' Beth observed.

'She not sleep for three nights. It is custom,' Rima explained.

'What do you mean?' Samara asked.

'Three days, three nights, ladies in family and friends stay here with her, make party, no time for sleep.'

'Why?' Beth asked.

Rima just shrugged her shoulders and led them down the hallway. When they stepped through the door, they found themselves in a long and narrow room. Seated in rows on either side of the room were at least fifty or sixty older women on chairs, benches, and couches. Rima directed her guests to vacant places in the two rows, told them to sit down and wait, and she left.

The older women gathered there were a colorful group. Dressed in traditional Arab dress, their ample bodies were swathed in beautiful barracanos of sheer silk, brocaded pantaloons of varying bright colors, and high-necked embroidered blouses. Fringed and beaded scarves completely covered the women's heads, except for tiny wisps of dark hair that had been pulled forward to frame their faces. Their movements were accompanied by the

213

click of their waist-length necklaces of brightly colored glass beads and gold coins and the many bangle bracelets on their arms.

At first, Tess tried not to stare, but as time passed and everyone just continued to sit quietly, she allowed herself the luxury of inspecting them openly, trying not to gaze at one person too long. The women chatted among themselves, but the talk was subdued and formal, unlike the hubbub in other parts of the house. Tess noticed that most of them had very fair complexions, much whiter than the Arab men and women she had seen in the streets, and wondered if it was simply due to a life sheltered from the sun or a difference in race. A couple of women had African features and black skin; they were extravagantly dressed, and she guessed they might be from the Fezzan, the desert area far to the southwest. Beth had told her that many of the guests were from outlying areas.

Chili, who was interested in cosmetics, was fascinated by the great amount of makeup the women wore. They had lines of black kohl under their eyes and on their eyebrows, bright circles of red rouge on their cheeks, and red lipstick on their mouths. The palms of their hands had been hennaed in a precise pattern that also darkened the little finger and the forefinger, and the whiteness of their skin was enhanced by a dusting of rice powder.

After a while, some of the younger women came into the room, and refreshments were offered. Beth whispered instructions to accept everything offered graciously, that it was a slight to refuse, and so they all drank sugared water and mint tea and ate almond cakes. Time passed slowly, but there was an aura of expectancy that kept everyone alert. Suddenly, surrounded by her friends, sisters, and cousins, the bride was led into the room. She was a vision of exotic beauty, her face covered by a silken scarf, her arms filled with bracelets of gold, and dozens of gold necklaces and beads around her neck. As everyone gathered around her to admire her beauty, wedding chants began, and women started beating out primitive rhythms on gourds. The peaceful decorum now burst into giddy excitement. The bride was seated on a cushion in the middle of the room, and her veil was lifted so that all could admire the beauty of her heavily made-up face. The beautician bowed and accepted congratulations for her work, and then several of the younger women began to gyrate around the bride in a sensual belly dance to the beat of the drummers. As the dancers tired, other women took their places, and the celebration moved into high gear.

Chili whispered to Sam, 'I feel like I just stepped into a harem.'

'You did, Chili. That's where we are.'

At last Rima touched Beth's elbow and said, 'Go now.'

Beth looked at her watch and realized that they had been there more than three hours, and she got up immediately. It was getting late. As the Americans took their leave, the women smiled cordially and touched their arms and their hands, letting the four women know they had been welcome guests.

Once out on the dark street, Rima said, 'I stay, yes?'

'You stay here, no!' Sam protested. 'I have no idea how to get back to Mrs Cellini's.'

'Easy go this way,' Rima said, smiling, and turned and walked toward the corner, indicating that the car should follow her.

At the corner, Rima pointed them in the direction they should go; then she waved good-bye and disappeared into the nearest alley.

'Okay, ladies, we're on our own.' Sam declared. 'Watch for landmarks. Damn, it's dark tonight.'

'Go that way. It's not a very big city, you know – sooner or later one of us is bound to see something familiar,' Beth said, sounding composed.

'I swear to God, Beth Cellini, the end of the world could be comin' and you'd be calm and cool. Don't you ever get upset about anythin'?' Chili asked.

The car careened through the dark and quiet streets, and they hoped they were going in the direction Rima had indicated.

'Why are you driving so fast?' Tess asked.

'I hoped I'd attract the attention of the Air Police, wherever the hell they are.'

'Well, let's not attract the attention of the Libyan police,' Beth warned, and Sam immediately slowed down.

'Good thinking. I sure as hell wouldn't want to deal with them at this hour. Can you just imagine what they would think of four crazy American women driving around in the middle of the night?' Sam commented.

'I'll never forget the evening the police were called to the Ridley's apartment next door after it had been burglarized. I mean, there was nothing left except furniture that was too big to throw out the back window. When Marna Ridley reported that all their clothes were gone, the policeman accused her of lying, because he had seen two shirts and a pair of underwear on the clothesline on the roof. He scratched out the note that there were clothes missing,' Beth related.

'Well, it's all relative, I guess. Most of the Libyans are so poor that what was left seemed like a lot to them,' Tess said. 'So, what did you think of the evening?'

'Well, that little girl is sure gonna be one tired bride.

She'll probably fall asleep the minute she gets in bed. She'll never know what hit her,' Chili said with a laugh.

'Actually the rituals aren't too different from ours. Joe and I had a big wedding, and we were exhausted by the rounds of showers and parties, not to mention the wedding itself and the reception. Then on top of it all, they kept shoving glasses of champagne in our hands and drinking toasts. We were supposed to leave that night to drive up to Connecticut, but we didn't. We got in the car, let them throw rice at us, and then we drove around the corner, checked into the Plaza Hotel, and crawled into bed.'

'You're not gonna tell us you went to sleep, are you?' Sam asked in disbelief.

Beth giggled. 'Joe would die if he knew I told anybody, but that's exactly what we did. Our marriage didn't get consummated until five o'clock the next morning.'

Everyone laughed. 'Well, at least you didn't have the groom's family waiting outside the door for the sheet,' Tess commented.

'What sheet?' Chili asked curiously.

'The nuptial sheet. The one on the marriage bed. Tomorrow night in a private room while the guests are still partying, the bride and groom will consummate their marriage. And there had better be blood on it or the bride will be in big trouble, not only with the groom but with her family.'

'Not all virgins bleed,' Chili said defensively. 'I didn't . . . did you, Tess?'

Beth and Tess giggled self-consciously. Beth said yes, and Tess said, 'It looked like there'd been an ax murder,' and Sam added with a laugh, 'So did I, but you know what that proves, don't you?'

'What?' they asked in unison.

'It only proves that three out of four virgins bleed when they lose their cherries,' she replied, and everyone laughed.

Sam turned a corner, and they suddenly found themselves on the Lungomare. They all cheered as they headed for home, and although they'd had nothing but tea and sugared water, they were high on adventure and camaraderie.

32

One morning, on her way to an emergency meeting of the Wives' Club's fund-raising committee, Sam stopped at the BX to buy a few items. Veronica had called earlier and asked her to attend, even though she was not a member. As she stood in line waiting to pay, she noticed Chili Shaheen, and went to talk to her about their big night at the Arab wedding.

'Chili . . . hi, are you going to the meeting Veronica called this morning?'

As Chili approached, Sam noticed that the redhead seemed listless and pale, though not wan enough to keep the men she passed from looking her over appreciatively. Chili possessed the delectable loveliness of a summer-ripe peach, but Sam suspected she was unaware of the power that gave her.

'Hi, Sam. Yeah, I guess so. Veronica called this morning in a big snit. Somethin's happened to that shipment of clothing for the big fashion show.'

'Are you on the committee?'

'Not really. I was just goin' to be one of the models,' she replied, and there was a detectable lack of interest in her voice and manner, much different from the way she had been just a few nights before.

'Are you okay?' Sam asked with her usual directness.

'Yeah, I guess so. I got my period this mornin' . . . again, dammit. It was late this time and I was hopin' I was p.g. I must look sick, huh?'

'Well, I just miss the sparkle in your smile. You should have been a movie star, you know that, don't you?'

Chili was startled by the unexpected compliment. 'Quit teasin' me, now. I'm just a poor old girl from Texas.'

Sam paid for her purchases, and they walked out of the exchange together.

'I wouldn't kid you, Chili. You're really stunning, and I ought to know. I grew up around the most beautiful stars in the world: Maureen O'Hara, Hedy Lamarr, Rhonda Fleming. I've seen them all, up close and without makeup, and I can tell you that you're right up there with them.'

Chili was overwhelmed. She'd never had a woman say something so nice to her. Men were always complimenting her, but they usually wanted something.

'I don't know what to say, Sam. I feel kinda embarrassed,' Chili replied, the pink returning to her ivory cheeks and the sparkle to her eyes.

'Come on, let's ride over to the club in my car. You can leave yours here,' Sam suggested, and Chili eagerly agreed. It was lovely being near a person who made her feel good, even if she was only a woman.

'Tell me all about Hollywood,' Chili said when they were in Sam's MG.

'What do you want to know?'

'Anythin' and everythin'. You know, before I got married, I used to buy all the movie magazines, but Gam won't let me have them in the house anymore. He says they're trash and I should be tryin' to improve my mind.'

'That's silly. I still read them occasionally, but a lot of things in them aren't true.'

'Gosh, I know that, but they're fun to read anyway. Who's your favorite star?'

'On the screen or in person?' Sam asked.

220

'Both,' Chili said with a giggle. She had never really known someone who had been close to her idols on the silver screen.

'Well, Greg Peck, I guess, is my personal favorite. He's a wonderful actor, but he's also a terrific guy. He's every bit as nice as he looks. I had an enormous crush on him, and whenever he came to the house for dinner, I would switch the place cards so he'd have to sit next to me.'

'Be still, my beatin' heart! He actually came to your house!' Chili squealed with delight.

'Many times,' Sam replied, pleased that Chili had come to life. 'My favorite star on screen, however, has always been Charles Boyer. There's something about those big dark brooding eyes of his that is so sexy. Who's your favorite?'

They arrived at the club and Sam parked the car. Chili walked slowly toward the entrance, reluctant to bring the conversation to an end.

'I've been in love with Gary Cooper ever since I first saw him,' Chili replied. 'Guess that's not so surprisin', since I'm from Texas, huh? Have you ever met him?'

'Chili, I've met just about anybody you could name. My father is a very powerful man in Hollywood.'

After a moment of trying to digest that remark, Chili got up her courage to ask Samara a question. 'Would you have time to have lunch with me when this thing's over today?'

'Sure. Why don't you join Tess Kipling and Beth Cellini and me?'

Chili's eyes lighted up. 'That'd be great. D'ya think they'll mind?'

Sam took her arm and squeezed it affectionately. 'We'd love to have you.'

Veronica Masters took charge of the meeting without

even bothering to observe the protocol of allowing the chairman of the fashion-show committee to conduct it.

'Thank you all for coming out here on such short notice,' Veronica said. 'I know some of you are wondering why I asked you here. Well, we have a problem. We've sold a lot of tickets to the dinner and fashion show on Saturday night, but we don't have any clothes to show. We had planned on making money by auctioning off the dresses during the show, as you know, but there was a slip-up somewhere, and even though my husband has chewed out everybody up and down the line, the sorry truth is that the shipment was lost, and we have nothing to replace it with.'

Everyone groaned in disappointment. Veronica went on. 'We have already publicly committed the funds to refurbish the cemetery where our American marines were buried years ago. It's fallen into disrepair and has become a shabby memorial to those brave men. We must come through for them. May I have some suggestions, please?'

There was an awkward silence while the women looked down at their hands, across the room, anywhere to avoid eye contact with the commander's wife.

'Well,' Veronica continued, 'since no one seems to have a better idea, I'll give you mine. I suggest that each of us donates her very nicest dress to the cause. The base dry cleaners will clean and press them, and I assure you that they will do it properly or they'll have my husband to answer to. These donated dresses will be worn by the models and auctioned off. The proceeds will all then go to the fund. Would someone like to make a motion to that effect?'

Samara raised her hand to speak. 'Veronica, what makes you think people will buy second-hand clothes?'

Veronica smiled. 'Samara, you should be the last to ask

222

that question. There are any number of women who would give their eyeteeth to have one of your designer gowns.'

Tess remarked under her breath to Sam, 'Yeah, but how many of them can squeeze into a size six?'

'Guess why we were invited to solve the problem,' Sam replied. It was obvious that Veronica had shrewdly singled out the women most likely to have desirable clothes to come to this meeting and be fleeced. Nell Carson dutifully made the motion, it passed unanimously, and it was decided that the committee would visit the homes of everyone who wished to make a donation and help make an appropriate choice.

After the meeting adjourned, the four friends went to lunch, and Tess remarked, 'Well, it's obvious why she asked me. All my trousseau things are brand-new. I've been wearing these maternity tents practically since the day I arrived.'

'I don't know why she asked me. I haven't got anything much,' Chili said.

Beth interjected, 'Chili, it doesn't make any difference. You could wear an old flannel nightgown and make it look like an evening gown.'

Beth's comment gave Chili an idea. 'Sam, I've got the most gorgeous pink-satin-and-black-lace nightgown. It's got this long see-through black-lace peignoir that goes with it. It's the sexiest thing you ever saw, and it's practically brand-new. Why don't I donate that?'

'Well, if you also agree to model it, I'll bet the guys will be falling all over themselves to buy it,' Sam commented.

'Sure, I'll model it. Why not?'

'Don't you think you ought to check it out with Gamal before you commit yourself, Chili?' Beth asked dubiously.

'I know Joe would kill me if I ever got up in front of a crowd in lingerie.'

'He won't care,' Chili said with a shrug. 'Gam doesn't like the thing anyway. Besides, I'll wear panties and a bra underneath. The effect won't be quite the same, but I'll be decent.'

They enjoyed a delightful lunch, and everyone was reluctant to leave when it was over. Chili had never known how much fun it could be just talking to a group of women. As they walked toward Sam's car, Chili said shyly to Samara, 'Could we have lunch again sometime?'

'Of course. Call me whenever you like. And remember, if you ever decide you want to be a movie star, I know all the right people.'

Chili went home that afternoon feeling better about herself than she had felt since she entered puberty.

33

The members of the fund-raising committee went about their tasks with an enthusiasm not often seen in the Wives' Club. It wasn't often they were invited to browse through the closets of friends and acquaintances, and they made good use of the opportunity. From Sam's closet they selected a white moiré silk taffeta gown from the house of Dior; from Tess's they chose her favorite little basic black crepe dress with a matching short jacket. Tess hated to part with it, because she had worn it only once, but it was fitted very close, and with her now burgeoning girth, she couldn't imagine ever getting into it again. Although they got a beautiful silk print by Pucci from Beth, they weren't sure they could sell it, since Beth was a size two and there weren't many women tiny enough to wear it.

Chili's offer to donate the nightgown-and-peignoir set and model was greeted with some reservation until Veronica approved. 'It will spice up the show, and if the men have enough liquor under their belts, it'll probably bring in more bids than anything else,' she said, bestowing her blessing with a chuckle.

For the rest of the week Chili had no trouble staying sober. She pitched in with the committee members and helped organize the show. Since she was good with a needle and thread, she mended hems, burst-out seams, and even, in some cases, did a bit of redesigning. She enjoyed that more than anything she'd done since she became a service wife.

Besides, now she had a friend. Samara joined her in the preparations for the fashion show, and they had lunch together every day. For the first time in her life, Chili felt open and at ease with another woman, and she told Sam all the things she could tell no one else. Because Sam had been raised in a town that winked at clandestine liaisons, Chili's stories did not shock her, nor was she judgmental.

Gamal noticed the change in his wife, and since he knew nothing about her friendship with Sam, he assumed that it was his ultimatum to her that had brought it about. He was pleased, and his manner toward her thawed considerably. She did not tell him about the nightgown, because she was afraid he would forbid her to model it. She was confident, however, that he would be proud of her when she was the hit of the show, as Veronica Masters herself had predicted. If it was okay with the commander's wife, he couldn't very well disapprove.

The dining room of the officers' club was filled to capacity for the pre-auction dinner. A ramp had been built down the center of the room for the models to parade across. Bob Mulhare, with his quick wit, was tapped to be the auctioneer. One of the wives had once been a model, and she had rehearsed the women all day on Friday and again on Saturday morning. When the guests arrived, they learned that the bar was charging only ten cents a drink. Veronica wanted to make sure that when the auction started, the bidders would have few inhibitions about spending money.

Tess and Kip shared a table with the Cellinis, the Shaheens, and the Mulhares. Just before dessert was served, Sam, Bob, Beth, and Chili went backstage to get ready. The orchestra played and everyone was having a rousing good time. Tess was glad that her pregnancy kept her from having to model. Just thinking about walking

226

across the platform in front of so many people made her nervous.

When the models were ready, Bob got the crowd's attention in spite of a number of bawdy remarks shouted at him, and the show started. It went well. Beth was noticeably stiff and nervous, but there was a spirited bidding contest between two visiting fighter pilots for the dress, and it drew a commanding bid of a hundred dollars, more than Beth had paid for it.

Subsequent clothes did well but did not bring as much as the Pucci. On several occasions the husbands found it necessary to buy back their wives' own dresses when nobody bid on them. The bidding became active again when Sam came out in her smashing Dior gown, and it brought the astounding figure of two hundred dollars – actually less than half its original cost – not from a Wheelus officer, but a visiting fighter pilot.

The drinks had continued to flow throughout the evening, and the crowd became noisier and louder. Bob was royally heckled, but he handled it with his usual grace and humor and dry wit.

Chili had been saved for the finale, and the house lights were dimmed so that when she stepped forward in the figure-hugging gown with its gossamer lace peignoir floating behind her, there was a gasp of appreciation and surprise. She seemed to float down the ramp so measured and assured and graceful were her movements. With her head held high, she was a delight to behold. Standing in the rear watching, Sam saw the qualities in her that she had seen in many Hollywood stars. In front of an audience, Chili was dynamite, and it was apparent that she was not only at ease, she was in heaven.

She made the walk twice, leisurely, gracefully, not wanting to end her moment of celebrity, and when the houselights went up, Bob asked the crowd, 'How about that for gorgeous? Who wants to open the bidding and take this beautiful gown home to Mama?'

Men all over the room waved their paddles in the air, and although there was much legitimate bidding, there were also a lot of remarks about Chili herself. 'A hundred bucks for the dress . . . a thousand if she stays in it!' 'Forget the gown, I want to take *her* home to Mama.'

Although it was done in fun, with Chili loving every moment of attention, her husband was furious. Raised in a culture where women were expected to reveal themselves only to their husbands, Gamal felt humiliated and degraded. Amid all the joyful noise, he was stonily silent, and his discomfort affected everyone at his table. Kip had been the first to notice Gamal's reaction to Chili's appearance, and he took Tess's hand and squeezed it under the table, indicating that she should take a glance. When Tess saw the expression on Gamal's face, it frightened her. The only word to describe it was murderous.

Heady with success, Chili continued to parade about as the bidding progressed, until Bob finally gaveled down the last bid at an incredible five hundred dollars, close to a month's pay for a nonrated officer. Then Chili did the unthinkable. She walked to the end of the runway, put out her arms for support and allowed herself to be lifted down into the cheering crowd. She then made her way to the top bidder, a full colonel whose squadron was at Wheelus on TDY for target practice. Squeezing his cheeks, she pulled his face down to hers and gave him a big kiss on the lips. He made a quick grab for her, but she was too nimble for him. Whirling about, she dashed away and behind the curtain. The audience went wild with applause. It was a star turn if there ever was one.

Watching from backstage, Sam saw Veronica jump to

her feet and applaud wildly. Her fund-raiser had been an enormous success, and she was thrilled. Sam thought it strange that Veronica's husband, Brick Masters, did not share her excitement. He sat grimly quiet at the table, drinking his highball and taking no part in the tumult of appreciation for Chili's triumphant appearance.

As soon as Chili came backstage, the women gathered around her, congratulating her warmly. Sam hugged her and said, 'Chili, you were meant to be a star! You were sensational!'

'Oh, God, Sam, I've never had such a wonderful thing happen to me in my entire life. I can't believe it! They liked me!' she said breathlessly.

A commanding voice made everyone turn. 'Like hell they liked you, young lady . . . they loved you!' Veronica had rushed backstage to congratulate her. 'Forget Marilyn Monroe, we've got Chili Shaheen,' she added exultantly.

Veronica's enthusiasm encouraged a renewed outpouring of praise. All the women who had been involved in the show shared in the glory of having raised twice as much money as they needed, and Veronica reported that the pictures taken would probably be seen in newspapers throughout the command. They had raised more money in a single night than had ever before been raised by a Wives' Club.

When they had dressed and handed over the clothes to be delivered to the buyers, Beth, Sam, and Chili returned to their table, which was an island of quiet and restraint in a storm of merrymaking. Although many people had gone home, there was still a wild contingent, particularly unescorted males, whooping it up. Chili's appearance was greeted by shouts of approval and applause.

When she saw her husband's face, Chili knew the party was over. Gamal was furious. Sam and Beth saw it too

229

and tried to intervene and change his perspective. 'You must be very proud of your wife, Gamal. She was the hit of the show.'

Bob came up behind them and added his enthusiasm. 'You're the envy of every man in the room, Gamal, old man. Your wife is a real beauty, but I guess you know that.'

Gamal did not reply. Getting to his feet, he took Chili's arm. 'It's getting late. We have to go home.'

Bob tried to stop him. 'I've ordered a bottle of French champagne to drink a toast to our lovely ladies. Don't go yet. We've hardly had a chance to visit, and it's Saturday night.'

Chili looked hopefully up into her husband's eyes, but all she saw there was granite – dark, hard, unyielding granite. 'Sorry,' Gamal said. 'Perhaps another time.' Without another word, he moved his reluctant wife away. Chili called back to Sam, 'I'll call you tomorrow, okay?' And then they were gone, leaving a cloud of depression and gloom behind them.

Tess was the first to speak. 'She's in for it, I'm afraid. He's furious with her.'

Joe tried to explain Gamal's viewpoint. 'Look, most guys would hate to have their wives on display like that. You can hardly blame him for being a little upset.'

Beth would not accept it. 'Joe, you're letting your Italian background show. After all, we're not in the Dark Ages. Women don't belong to their husbands. They're free to do whatever they want. Besides, she hasn't hurt his career a bit. Veronica Masters is thrilled beyond words.'

'Maybe,' Tess said, 'but look at the women here in Tripoli, the Arab women. All but the very poorest still skulk about the streets with everything covered but one

230

eye. Gamal's background has given him a different outlook from ours.'

Although she said nothing, Sam agreed with them both.
From everything Chili had said, it was evident that a crisis
of one kind or another was not far off in that marriage.
The next time she talked to Chili, she'd try to draw her
out more. Sam had a feeling Chili was going to need a lot
of emotional support in the rocky days ahead.

34

Samara thought about calling Chili the day after the auction, but it was Sunday, and she didn't want to annoy Gamal by bothering them on his day off. She was worried about her, however, and promised herself she would touch bases with Chili the next day. Sam and Bob spent a leisurely day at home with the children, and Bob left early on Monday morning for a flight to Tunis. Sam drove him to the field, and when he'd left, went to pick up the mail. It was too early to call Chili, so she sat down to sort through the stack of letters and papers. Since neither she nor Bob corresponded with either of their families, they tended to forget to pick up the mail from the post office, sometimes for days at a time.

Suddenly, her eyes fell on an envelope that sent her heart beating rapidly and her hands trembling with anticipation. It was the pale gray stationery of Silverstone Studios with its embossed silver logo above the return address. God, had something happened to one of her parents?

With shaking hands she tore open the envelope. There was a single sheet of paper inside. She unfolded it and looked at the signature first, and her heart plunged in terror. The letter was not from her father, as she had hoped, but from his secretary, Golda.

Dear Samara,
    I know I shouldn't interfere like this, and I certainly shouldn't betray a confidence, but I could never forgive myself if something happened and you didn't know.

232

Your father has seemed to age very fast in the past years since you left the country and you stopped writing to him. Oh, I know, he never answered any of your letters, but he loved them so. He carried the most recent one in his breast pocket constantly. So many times I caught him reading those letters over and over again, and always with a silly smile on his face.

When he stopped hearing from you, he changed. It was like something inside him died. For the first time in the twenty years I've worked for him he's stopped paying attention to business. Television has hurt our industry badly, but he refuses to make those teenage-beach movies everybody else is doing. I heard him telling someone that maybe it was time to sell the studio and retire to his ranch in Malibu.

I thought you'd want to know how things are.

Love,
Golda

Sam read the letter twice, and the terrible guilt that had weighed on her ever since the day she ignored her parents' pleas and married Bob descended on her, shutting out all light from her soul. Never in all of her youth had her relationship with her mother and father been anything but loving and supportive until she had announced that she wanted to marry outside of the faith.

Going into the kitchen, she poured herself a cup of hot water from the teakettle that was constantly heating on the stove, and dropped a teabag into the cup. She took the tea to her large comfortable bedroom, where she nestled into the womb of a deep black leather egg chair. She rested her head against its smooth wing and closed her eyes. She loved this chair because it was so large she felt hidden in it. It reminded her of the times she had spent hiding under the huge dining-room table in her parents' big house. Her mother always kept the table covered with a heavy Belgian lace cloth that fell almost to the floor, and as a little girl Sam had loved to seclude

233

herself there. She would take her favorite toys with her to play in solitude and secrecy. It was her special place, where she would escape when the world was too much for a little girl to handle.

Sam was not prone to tears. She had grown up trying to emulate her older brother and be tough and strong like he was, like her father wanted him to be. Her mother had seen Sam only as her pretty little princess, and had taught her to be soft-spoken and polite, to wear white gloves and a hat when she went out, and always to sit with her knees tightly together, like a lady.

Such paradoxical training had seemed perfectly normal to Sam until she reached puberty, developed breasts, and discovered boys. Unlike the other girls, she found the notion that she must allow a boy to beat her at tennis or anything else utterly ridiculous. She liked to win. In spite of that, she also loved all the trappings of femininity: beautiful clothes, makeup, and jewelry.

Perhaps it was because he seemed to understand these conflicts in her personality that she found Bob Mulhare so attractive. He was self-assured, unintimidated by her family's position, and yet respectful of her as a woman, totally unlike anyone she had ever met in the Hollywood-Beverly Hills social milieu.

Her father had warned her to stay away from narcissistic actors, who were so self-absorbed that they were rarely able to sustain a balanced relationship. Sam laughed when her father said, 'Remember, honey, if you fall in love with an actor, that'll just make two of you in love with the same person,' but she had agreed with him.

Bob's feelings for her were untainted by any but the obvious motive – he loved her for herself, for her mind and her body. She had never regretted her decision to give up everything she held dear for his love.

Even now, here in this ancient land, miles and centuries removed from the country of her birth, she was content. The rituals of rank that were the burden of every service wife, Sam found amusing, and although she occasionally looked back with nostalgia at the glamour of her girlhood associations, her life with Bob and the children was so rewarding that the feeling was always a fleeting one.

Except last night. When Chili had walked out on the ramp in all her splendid, voluptuous beauty, Sam had felt a nostalgia for the movie industry, and she had longed for the chance to make Chili a star. If ever a woman was made for the spotlight, it was Gamal's wife, and Sam had learned enough of the disturbing circumstances about Chili's background and relationship to her husband to know without a doubt that the marriage was in deep trouble.

When the teacup was empty, Sam went to her desk and pulled the fine Florentine leather writing portfolio from the drawer. She took out a pen and a sheet of her monogrammed stationery and began to write:

Dear Mom and Dad,
Please forgive me for not writing to you for the past year. You have been in my heart and my thoughts constantly. Almost every day I tell David and Melinda some little story about you so that they will know what wonderful grandparents they have. They are beautiful, bright children, and I regret every moment they have missed knowing you, and you them.

Sam continued to write. She filled page after page with details of the past year in Tripoli, drawing upon all her skills as a writer to make the world around her vivid and real to them. She wrote for several hours, stopping only late in the afternoon to play with the children and have dinner with them. As soon as they were in bed for the night, she went back to her writing. She was so absorbed with her thoughts and her memories that after giving her returning husband a quick kiss, she returned to her desk to continue writing. Bob was long asleep when the telephone rang. It was past midnight.

'Sam, I think I'm in labor, and I'm all alone.' She heard Tess's voice over the static of the line.

'Where's Kip?'

'He went on a State Department flight early this morning, and he won't be back for three days. Oh, God, Sam, I'm so scared, and it's pouring rain outside. I hate to ask you, but – '

'I'll be there in ten minutes,' Sam replied. 'No, go lie down till I get there.'

Rushing into the bedroom, she shook Bob and said briskly, 'Sorry, sweetheart, but I need you to get up and go with me.'

A light sleeper, Bob was awake instantly. 'What's up?' he asked, getting to his feet and reaching for a pair of trousers.

'Tess just called. She's in labor and all by herself, and she's scared to death.'

'What a night she picked,' he complained, but Sam retorted, 'I'm sure she didn't choose it. She's about two weeks early, I think. Move, Bob. We've got to get going.'

Before Bob could get his shirt buttoned, Sam was dressed in a wool skirt and sweater. Even though it was cold and damp outside, she slid her bare feet into a pair of tennis shoes and pulled on a raincoat.

'I'll wake up Jetta and tell her where we are so she won't worry. You get the car,' Sam ordered.

'Thank God we've still got the big Pontiac. In case we have to deliver a baby on the road, at least we have a back seat.'

236

They were in the car and on their way when Sam replied to his comment. 'I know you were trying to be funny, dear, but if Suk El Giuma is flooded, we might very well *have* to deliver a baby.'

'Lord have mercy,' Bob said, and stepped on the accelerator.

Tess threw the keys over the balcony to the Mulhares, and they rushed up the stairs.

'How's it going, honey?' Sam asked Tess who was cramped with pain.

'My water broke, and the pains are two minutes apart.'

'Jesus, Mary, and Joseph! Where's the telephone?' Bob demanded.

'Who're you calling?' Sam asked.

'The Air Police. I want an escort to pull us out of the water if we get stuck,' Bob whispered so Tess wouldn't hear.

Tess went into the bedroom with Sam close behind, saying, 'Forget about getting dressed. We'll just put a raincoat over your robe, but you'll need shoes on your feet. Sit down on the bed, and I'll do it for you.'

When they were ready to go, they returned to the kitchen to hear Bob's distressing news.

'Tough luck. Suk El Giuma is impassable. They're sending a jeep to guide us around the back roads. It'll take longer, but it's surer,' he declared.

'Oh, God,' Tess groaned, in the throes of a contraction.

'Let's get her in the car before the next one comes, honey,' Bob urged.

With their help Tess was able to walk downstairs and climb into the back seat of the car, where she stretched out. Sam covered her with the blanket she had snatched off the bed, and the Air Police arrived within minutes.

237

All the way to the hospital, the Mulhares talked gently to Tess, trying to keep her spirits and her courage up. The drive seemed interminable, but they got her to the hospital in plenty of time.

As the nurse wheeled her away, Tess managed to say thanks. 'I'll never forget you, Sam. You're the best friend I ever had,' she whispered, tears streaming down her face.

Sam approached the desk. 'Can't I stay with her? Her husband is away on TDY. This is her first child, and I know she's afraid,' she pleaded.

'They'll examine her and prep her, and if she's not ready, I'm sure Dr Pepperman will let you go in. We have so many women who come in here alone because their husbands are away that the doctor is quite lenient. Get yourself a cup of coffee, and I'll keep you posted.'

Sam was not permitted into the labor room because the doctor himself stayed with Tess. Her cervix wasn't dilating as it should, and he insisted that she grab her knees and push with each contraction. It was excruciatingly hard work, and Tess was racked with pain and close to hysteria. She wanted Kip beside her to hold her hand and comfort her, but he wasn't there. She was alone. Her mother wasn't there, her father wasn't there. She had never felt so isolated and abandoned as she did during those hours of lying on that hard table while in the grip of what seemed like alien forces torturing her to death.

At last the baby began to push its way out, and when Dr Pepperman was assured that it was well on its way, he administered a spinal block to take away the pain.

Dawn was just coming up when the doctor lifted the baby's head out with forceps, and the shoulders and body followed immediately. Tess, released from pain, felt only a tug of pressure as she watched her child born in the reflection of the mirror behind the doctor's head.

'It's a boy!' the doctor announced, holding the baby up so that his mother could get a good look at the red and swollen testicles. A nurse suctioned the mucus from the baby's mouth, and when he let out an indignant yell, the doctor plopped the baby on Tess's belly while he cut the cord. With tears streaming down her face, she tried to lift her hand to touch the bloody little body, but her arms were in restraints and she could not reach him.

'I love you,' she whispered softly, and she yearned for her baby's father to be there to share this incredible moment of joy with her.

35

During the short drive from the officers' club to their quarters on the base, Chili made a dizzying descent from the heights of triumph and adulation down to the depths of despair and humiliation. Because she had never seen herself in any way except as a reflection in men's eyes, she withered under the disgusted gaze of her husband. As soon as they were away from the crowd, Gamal attacked her with a hatred more venomous than the violence wreaked by Handy. Old Handy had merely wanted to destroy her body, but her husband seemed bent on crushing her spirit.

'How could you embarrass me like that in front of everyone?' he asked contemptuously.

'Like what? What did I do?' she asked in bewilderment. 'They liked me . . . I got more money than anyone.'

'You're nothing but a stupid, ignorant little tramp. No woman with any self-respect would get up and parade her body around the stage for men to – '

'Gam, honey, it wasn't like that! I had underwear, even stockings on under that gown. I had on as many clothes as any of the other models,' she pleaded, trying to make him understand.

'You're such a dumb broad. What the hell do you think was in the minds of those men who were whistling and yelling at you? Do you have any idea how I felt knowing that everyone was laughing at me? Poor stupid Shaheen, married to a slut.'

And suddenly, because he was giving voice to an image

that had been engraved on her from childhood, first by her stepfather, then by her mother and by an unending chorus of faceless men with erections, Chili no longer had the will to defend herself. By the time they walked into their quarters, she was weeping and apologizing for her worthlessness, convinced that Gamal was right, promising that she would never do anything like that again to humiliate him.

Having dissipated the heat of his anger by reducing her to tears of remorse, Gamal switched his fury from hot to cold. He made it quite plain that he had nothing more to say to her, not then, not ever. Hell is not hot; it is cold, icy, numbing cold, and Chili found herself frozen out of his affection.

Fearful of reaching out for help, afraid that her friends might have as low an opinion for her as her husband did, she sank further into isolation and despair. Life would have been unendurable without alcohol, and the more she drank, the more her husband detested her.

Because they were involved with their own concerns – Samara with renewed hope of reconciliation with her parents, and Tess with her new baby – Chili's friends were not there to keep her from falling into the abyss. Even if they had thought to call her, she probably wouldn't have been able to answer the telephone. One Saturday morning, however, before she started her daily bout of drinking, the telephone rang and she picked it up.

Startled by the voice of the commander's wife, Chili responded, making a gallant effort to pull herself together and speak clearly. Veronica was so busy talking that she didn't notice the slurred words coming from the other end of the line.

'Chili, my dear, how are you? My, can you believe it's been more than two weeks since the fashion show? I'm so sorry I didn't call you sooner, but I've been awfully busy. We've had such an onslaught of VIPs visiting the base that my head's in a spin. Everybody, it seems, wants to come here for a visit. I told Brick that maybe we shouldn't treat our guests so well. Anyway, my dear, I was disappointed when Gamal came alone to the reception for the Vice-President and Mrs Nixon night before last. I had so wanted them to meet our radiant beauty. Gamal said you were ill. I hope it's nothing serious.'

Chili's mind was clouded, but Veronica's words were breaking through to a clearing.

'Uh . . . why . . . I have been a little under the weather . . . but I'm feelin' better . . . lots better,' she replied, and suddenly it didn't matter anymore what Gamal said about her. Veronica was the CO's wife, and if she approved of her, then obviously Chili had not made a fool of herself or her husband, and she had definitely not hurt his career. In fact, if Veronica had thought enough of her to invite her to meet the Vice-President of the United States, she must be okay – more than okay.

'Oh, good. I'm so glad to hear you're all right. You see, I'm having a dinner party here on Wednesday evening for one of my husband's dearest friends, General Fred Torrance. He's just received his second star, and he's coming down from Germany. I hope you and Gamal will join us. It won't be a terribly big party, just twenty or so.'

'Me?' Chili asked, bewildered. 'Why?'

'Why?' Veronica asked indignantly. 'Why, because, Chili, you are the loveliest lady here at Wheelus, and I want to show you off. Fred, the old goat, has a real eye for beauty.' She chuckled confidentially. 'When he called to say he was coming, I promised him the most gorgeous dinner partner he'd ever had.'

'I see,' Chili said, trying to organize her thoughts.

'Roberta, that's his charming wife, is coming with him. They're stopping to see us on their way back to the Pentagon. You'll like her, Chili. She's a sweet woman, and so unconcerned about her husband's little flirtations. She knows they mean nothing, because Fred is as devoted to her as Brick is to me. You and Gamal be here at six sharp for cocktails, and since you'll be my guests, you won't have to prepare any food this time. Now, wear your prettiest dress and make me proud.'

Long after Veronica had signed off, Chili stood holding the telephone in her hand, trying to make sense of her sudden acceptance into her husband's world. Damn him to hell, he was wrong! She hadn't disgraced herself. She wasn't a total washout as a wife.

Anger coursed through her veins, washing out the dregs of humiliation, and she went to the bathroom to look in the mirror and try to see what Veronica apparently saw in her, but the reflection looking back at her was no beauty; she looked like a crone. Her hair was a tangled mass, there were dark circles beneath eyes that were puffy and red. Thank God, Veronica hadn't seen what a mess she had made of herself. Could she possibly get into good enough shape to go up to the villa Wednesday night? She looked at her shaking hands and decided that what she needed was a good stiff drink to get her body in gear.

Shuffling into the kitchen, she pulled the last bottle of bourbon off the shelf and saw that it was empty. Was it really possible that she had drunk all of it?

There was plenty of vodka, however, and she tilted the bottle to take a good long swallow. As soon as the bitter liquid touched her tongue, however, she was hit by a wave of revulsion, and she leaned over the sink and spat it out. No! She wasn't going to drink anymore. The stuff was killing her.

Gritting her teeth in determination, she forced herself to pour the liquor down the drain to make sure she wasn't tempted again, and then she went back into the bathroom for a long hot shower. With her body and her hair clean, she felt cleansed inside too. After toweling herself dry, she slipped on a robe, covered her hair with another towel, and took four aspirin to dull the throbbing pain in her head. She went into the kitchen to fix herself something to eat, wondering how many days it had been since she'd had any food.

She was just finishing a bowl of Campbell's tomato soup when the telephone rang, and the voice she heard made her regret that she had poured out the booze.

'Don't you show your ass at my house on Wednesday, understand?' Brick Masters barked into her ear.

'Why not?' she asked, steeling herself not to be afraid of him anymore. What could he do to her marriage that she hadn't already done to it herself?

'Because I said so. I will not have some filthy little cunt like you as a guest in my house.'

Suddenly Chili had had enough abuse to last her a lifetime. 'Since you and your crummy little prick will be there, there's no reason for my ass not to be,' she retorted nastily, amazed at her own sass.

'Stay away! That's an order,' he almost shouted at her.

Chili laughed a loud, explosive burst of derision. 'What'll you do, Brick, court-martial me? I'm not one of your piss-scared little officers. I'm comin' to that party, hear? Unless, of course, you have the guts to tell Veronica the real reason you don't want me there.'

'Did she tell you who was coming?' he said, biting off

his words so sharply they sounded as if there were teeth marks in them.

'Why? Is it somebody else you want me to screw?' she asked flippantly.

'You already did . . . the last time he was here.'

Chili snickered. 'No kiddin'? Say, that's swell. I'm lookin' to have a real nice time. I just hope I don't have too much to drink and start pawin' 'im. He's got a great cock, you know, much bigger'n that puny little thing of yours. We'll have lots to talk about, seein' as how we've all rasseled on your prayer rug.' Laughing uproariously, she slammed down the telephone. God, it was great to be on top and be the one doing the screwin'.

She looked at herself in the mirror once more. Her color was high, and the purple circles under her eyes had paled to lavender. She was going to be just fine. Now, she had things to do. First, she wanted to talk to Sam Mulhare and ask her if she had meant what she said about that movie offer. Then, maybe it might be a good idea to fix her hair and get dressed. It was Saturday, and even if Gamal didn't want to go, she was going to have dinner at the officers' club like everybody else did. She'd been out of touch for too long.

Chili went into the kitchen to get a cigarette, but the package was empty. Nuts. If she was going to get through the day without any booze, she sure as hell would need a smoke. She checked the drawer where Gamal usually stashed the cartons but there were none there. Escalating her search, she went through all her purses but found not one single cigarette. She opened Gamal's closet and began to rifle the pockets of his jackets. Surely she could find one measly little cigarette. She felt a lump in the pocket of his best uniform, and hoping she had hit paydirt, pulled out the tiny package. It was not what she was looking for,

245

so she crumpled it in her hand angrily and started to toss it in the garbage.

Suddenly she realized what she had found, and opened her hand slowly to look once more and make sure that she had actually seen what she thought she had. Sure enough. It was a package of condoms, and there were two missing. Condoms! They had never used condoms, not once. What the hell was Gamal doing with condoms?

The question and the answer occurred to her almost simultaneously. Her holier-than-thou bastard of a husband was screwing somebody besides her! So that was why he'd been too tired for her. So that was why he hadn't touched her in weeks. The injustice of it all overwhelmed her. Here she'd been creeping around, feeling more low-down and dirty than a cockroach, while he acted as if he was Jesus Christ himself.

Before the telephone call from Veronica, Chili might have blamed herself, believing that her husband had turned to another woman because his wife simply had not satisfied him, but she knew that wasn't true. Besides, she already had enough guilt to last her a lifetime. She wasn't about to take the blame for anything else.

Gamal arrived home late that Saturday afternoon, feeling there was no need to rush since his wife would undoubtedly be in a drunken stupor. He almost preferred it that way, since then he didn't have to talk to her or deal with her on any level. He was startled, therefore, to walk in the house and see that the magazines and newspapers had been picked up, the rugs vacuumed, and the kitchen cleaned. He went into the bedroom and found Chili sitting on the bed, wearing her black satin kimono, with her hair in pincurls, and painting her fingernails with red polish.

Without looking up, she said. 'You're late.'

'I went back to the office after lunch. You clean up the house?'

'Who else? I'm the only officer's wife on this base who doesn't have a maid, right?'

'That was your choice, not mine,' he said stiffly, taken aback by the sudden change in her, not only in her appearance but also in her attitude.

'I ironed you a shirt, since you didn't seem to have any clean ones in the drawer. I figured we ought to go to the club for dinner tonight. I'm sick of lyin' around this house all the time,' she said, and there was something in her voice that warned him not to cross her.

'Okay,' was his only response, and as he turned toward the bathroom, she called out, 'Wait a sec. Did you bring home any cigarettes? I looked all over the house and couldn't find a one, not even in any of your pockets.'

36

Tess was extremely nervous as she and Kip stood in line at the entrance to the dining room of the officers' club. It was her first time out with the baby, who was sleeping nicely in the basket Kip was holding. She hadn't wanted to go out so soon after Skippy's birth, but Kip had insisted that they take a drive and stop at the club for dinner. Aware that he was tired of spending every single night at home, she agreed. It was Saturday evening, and as usual there was a wait for a table. She felt weak and uncomfortable. Her waistline wasn't anywhere near normal, and she had to resort to wearing a maternity dress, since nothing else fit her. She shifted uncomfortably from one foot to the other.

'Is he all right?' she said, peeking under the tiny crib blanket to make sure the baby was still breathing. Ever since his birth two weeks before, the responsibility of motherhood had weighed heavily on her. What she wouldn't have given to have had her mother with her at this time of her life. Samara and Beth had been inordinately helpful, but still, it wasn't the same.

Chili Shaheen approached them, and though she wore a broad smile, her complexion was the color of gray alabaster and there were deep circles under her eyes. There was also a disturbed and haunted look in them, Tess noticed.

'Tess, darlin', I just this minute found out that you'd had your baby. I'm so sorry I didn't know. I've been awful sick,' she said, putting her arm around Tess and giving her an affectionate hug.

'Are you okay now?' Tess said, hoping that whatever Chili had had wasn't contagious.

'Absolutely fine. Can I have a peek?' she said, and Tess drew the blanket back so she could see Skippy's face. 'Oh, darlin', he's beautiful. Are you feelin' okay?'

Tess smiled wanly. 'Not really. I haven't had much rest, because he doesn't sleep for more than an hour at a time, and I'm so tired.'

'What the hell are you doin' here then?' Chili asked bluntly, looking with disapproval at Kip.

'I thought it would do her good to get out of the house. I didn't realize the place would be so crowded,' Kip said defensively.

'Sugar, there's no need for you to stand in this line. You go right over there to that table in the corner and join us. Go on, now. There's only the two of us and we'd love to have you.' Kip and Tess tried to resist, but Chili would not be denied. She took Tess by the arm and escorted her to the table. Gamal was polite but obviously not enthusiastic about having his privacy invaded, which made Tess and Kip even more uncomfortable.

Chili sensed their strain, and she took over the conversation and chattered animatedly. Tess noticed that her hands shook when she lighted her cigarette. Gamal, who Tess felt had a cold personality and was never given to small talk, was unusually dour that evening. The conversation lurched back and forth awkwardly. Because of the large number of diners, service was slow, and Kip had a couple of drinks, but Tess refrained because she was nursing the baby.

During one lull in the conversation Tess mentioned casually that she'd heard a rumor that the queen was pregnant. 'I figured if anybody knew if it was true, it would be you, Gamal. Is she?'

There was an awkward moment of silence and then Gamal shook his head sullenly and said no. Just as the main course arrived, the baby began to fuss, and Tess picked him up and carried him to the ladies' room to nurse. She sat on a straight backed chair, closed her eyes in peace, and nursed him. Her breasts had filled with milk, and it was a relief to have the baby sucking at them.

Chili arrived shortly, settled herself on another chair, lit a cigarette, and began to chat.

Tess hated to have the smoke curling around her baby, but she didn't want to offend her. 'Chili, please, you'll make me feel terrible if you don't go back and finish your dinner.'

'I had a late lunch. Besides, I'd rather talk to you. Tell me all about the night little Skippy was born.'

When the baby was asleep, Tess and Chili went back to the table. After a few bites of her roast beef and cold mashed potatoes, Tess was able to persuade Kip she was exhausted and they finally went home.

Kip left Monday morning right after Pina arrived. The maid was utterly devoted to the baby she called 'Mio Skippeee.' Every day, bent over a washboard in the bathtub, she scrubbed his clothes, hung them on the line on the roof to dry, and then ironed every piece of clothing that touched his little body, including all his diapers. She wanted nothing harsh or wrinkled near the baby's sensitive skin.

Pina promised Kip that she would watch the baby so Tess could sleep late. At eight-thirty, however, the telephone rang, and she awakened Tess to tell her that her husband wanted to talk to her.

250

'Tess, good grief, where did you get the idea that the queen was pregnant?' he asked.

'What?' she asked sleepily. 'What are you talking about?'

'Colonel Channing, Masters' exec, called me this morning and asked me what kind of rumors my wife was spreading around. Where the hell did you hear that the queen was pregnant?'

Tess was irritated by the coldness of his tone. 'I don't know where I heard it, dammit, and besides, what difference does it make?'

'A lot. Channing wants you in his office at ten-thirty this morning.'

'Me?' she asked indignantly, offended that anyone would try to order her around. 'Well, you just tell him I said to go to hell. I've got a baby to take care of. If he wants to see me, he can damn well drive into town.'

Kip's manner changed immediately. He realized that he had made a mistake in his approach. 'Look, honey, I'm sorry. I tried to talk him out of it, but he told me that it was my responsibility to see that you got here. I know he can't order you to do anything, but he sure as hell can make my life miserable if you don't do as he says.'

Tess knew she was defeated. There was no way she could ever refuse to do what Kip asked when he put it that way.

'Can you come pick me up?'

'Damn, I wish I could, but Larry picked me up this morning, and I left the car at home. Look, tell you what. Drive out here yourself, and I'll take you home right after the meeting. Promise. No waiting. And if you feel like it, I'll take you to the commissary to shop for some groceries.'

Good Lord, this must be important, Tess thought. Kip

hated to shop for groceries and went to the commissary only in the most extreme circumstances.

'It's a deal. I'll bring Pina with me to carry the baby.'

Tess nursed the baby just before they left, and Pina held him in her arms as Tess drove to the base. She arrived in Channing's office a few minutes late, and was escorted in immediately. Defiantly, she chose to carry Skippy with her to let the colonel know what an imposition it was for her to come.

The colonel might have been a nicer man, everyone agreed, if he didn't work for such a miserable commanding officer. Channing, who took his duties seriously, was convinced that it was his job to make the men jump just as high as Brick Masters wanted them to jump. He was not, however, accustomed to calling on the carpet frail young women with tiny babies, and he was uncomfortable.

He welcomed her with the utmost courtesy. 'Please come in, Mrs Kipling, and sit down. Would you like to have a cup of coffee or a glass of water or something?'

'No, thank you,' Tess replied somewhat coldly. She was not going to kowtow.

'Sorry to drag you out here like this,' he apologized. 'Don't you have a servant to take care of the baby for you?'

'Yes, but he's too young to leave. He's not yet three weeks old.'

'Well, he seems to be a fine boy. He's awfully quiet.'

'I nursed him in the car just before I came in so he wouldn't disturb us,' Tess replied, curious as to why they were involved in small talk and worried that Skippy would awaken and begin to fuss.

'Mrs Kipling . . . may I call you Tess? Well, Major Shaheen called me first thing this morning and told me that you had heard the queen was pregnant. I need to know where you heard such a rumor.'

Having had more than an hour to think about what she would say, Tess lied. She was not about to be sandbagged into getting anybody in trouble, particularly her friend Beth.

'Well, I wish I could tell you, but I just don't remember. I recall hearing it mentioned one day when I was playing bridge at the club, and one of the women, I don't have any idea which one, said that she had heard that Dr Pepperman had flown to Benghazi with Major Shaheen to see the queen. She concluded therefore, that the queen was . . .'

'Pregnant!' Colonel Channing finished the sentence for her, and then in frustration he slapped his hand down on his desk, got up, and walked to the window. There was a long pause, and without turning to face Tess, he replied, 'Well, she is, dammit, but it's supposed to be a state secret.'

'Really? Then you probably shouldn't have let people know that the obstetrician was going to see her. People, especially women, are quick to notice things like that.'

'Look, Tess . . . this conversation is top-secret, okay? The king isn't getting any younger, see? He's already in his mid-sixties. According to his religion, he could take other wives, but he refuses. He loves his wife, but she has given him no heirs. If he should die without there being a successor to the throne, God knows what would happen to this country. It would be in turmoil, and the United States has too much at risk here.'

Tess was enjoying the conversation. Colonel Channing was talking to her as if she were an equal for a change, taking her into his confidence, and trusting her discretion.

'If an heir is so important, why is it a secret that she's pregnant?'

'Because she's been pregnant before, and she miscarried. We've brought two specialists in here from the States, and we're doing everything we can, but it'll take a miracle to pull it off. You see, there's a dissident faction of the Senussi clan trying to get the king to designate one of them as the heir, and the king won't do it. If he could just produce a son, it would settle a lot of controversy.'

'Then I guess we better pray that she brings forth a son, right?' Tess said, smiling. 'By the way, Colonel Channing, for your information, none of the Libyans refer to Fatima as the queen. That's our notion. To them she's just the king's wife.'

'Why didn't I know that?' he asked with a grin.

Skippy suddenly awakened in Tess's arms and began to make his presence known.

'Well, thank you for coming in, young lady. Sorry to drag you in here on such short notice. I don't have to tell you that this conversation was strictly between us.'

'You can trust me. It was a pleasure, Colonel Channing. And good luck with the stork.'

'If you see him, put in a good word for us. From the looks of that young fellow, he seems to have done all right by you.'

Tess walked out of the office smiling. It was her first pleasant brush with Air Force officialdom. She wondered if she should tell Kip about it, or if she should just let him wonder. Maybe she'd tell him it was a secret Colonel Channing had entrusted her with and told her not to tell anybody, including her husband. Ha. She could hardly wait to see his face when she said that.

254

37

Tess held the baby to her breast, but just as he started to nurse, the telephone rang. Fortunately, it was close enough to reach.

'I'll get it, Pina,' she called.

'Hi there, sweetface, how's that big boy doin'?' Chili's voice came floating through the line.

'Chili, how nice to hear from you. He's fine, but I'm still kind of tired. Going out to the club for dinner the other night was a very big effort. Then, I had to drive to the base again day before yesterday, so I'm really exhausted. I don't plan to leave the house for a week,' Tess replied. 'How are you doing?'

'I'm fine. I'm just gettin' ready to go into town to see my hairdresser. I've got to get myself all gussied up today. Veronica invited us to one of her VIP dinners tonight, can you believe that?'

'That's great. Who's going to be there?'

'Oh, some friends of his nibs. A two-star general, I hear. He's bringin' his wife.'

'Well, that should be interesting. Lieutenants never get invited to parties like that, so you'll have to tell me all about it,' Tess said, thinking that she really didn't feel like chatting on the telephone.

'Sweetgirl, I just talked to Beth, and she's pickin' me up tomorrow to do some shoppin' at the commissary. If you're feelin' okay, we thought maybe we'd stop in to see that big boy of yours. How much did you say he weighed when he was born?'

'Eight and a half pounds.'

'That musta hurt a mite.' She paused and then continued wistfully, 'You're some lucky woman, Tess. I hope you know that.' The tone of sadness in her voice was unmistakable.

'Don't give up, Chili. One of these days you and Gamal are going to have a baby. I just know it. You'll be such a good mother,' Tess said, although the reassurance in her voice sounded false even to herself.

'Forget that, honey. I don't even want to, not anymore, not with Gam anyway. Him and me are just about done.'

The sudden unheralded confession took Tess completely by surprise. 'Oh . . .' She hesitated, because she was afraid Chili was going to tell her something more that might be even more personal. 'Don't be hasty, Chili. It's probably just a little quarrel that will blow over.'

'Honey, you're such a nice innocent girl. No, this ain't somethin' that's goin' away. I thought when Gam started treatin' me bad, it was somethin' I was doin' wrong . . . that it was my fault for not bein' a good wife . . . but it wasn't me at all. It was him that was doin' wrong.'

'I'm sure this is all a misunderstanding,' Tess said stiffly, wondering how in the world she was going to stop the revelations. Lord, how she hated to get involved in people's intimate lives. They'd tell you things you didn't want to know and then hate you afterward for knowing.

'Uh-uh, I found rubbers in his pocket, can you believe that? And he had the nerve . . .' She stopped, realizing that she was saying far too much. 'Golly, I'm awful sorry about tellin' you this kinda stuff. Listen, forget it, will you? Everything's gonna be squared away in a day or so, and I'm gonna be just fine. So, whatta you think about me gettin' invited to the villa to a VIP party? And did you hear, I don't even have to bring a covered dish?'

Relieved that they were now off the subject of her marriage, Tess replied, 'They tell me that Veronica's been raving about you to everyone. She told Beth that Marilyn Monroe couldn't hold a candle to you.'

'No kiddin'? Wow, that's great,' Chili chortled. 'But it's kinda hard to believe. Gosh, that Marilyn Monroe is the most beautiful woman in the world.'

'No prettier than you are, Chili. Listen, I hate to cut you off, but the baby just dirtied his diaper, and I ought to clean him up.'

'That baby needs you, honey. I'm gonna sign off now. Call me early in the mornin' if you think of anythin' you might need us to bring. Take care.'

'Thanks for calling. And have a nice time at the party tonight.'

'Well, I'm gonna have a time, all right, but I'm not sure it's gonna be nice,' she said wryly.

Tess put the telephone down and carried the baby into the bathroom, where she had set up the little canvas bathinette and changing table Sam had ordered for her from the Sears catalog.

The conversation with Chili had left Tess with an uneasy feeling. She wasn't particularly surprised at the revelation that Gamal had been cheating on his wife. It was just about what she would expect of someone as cold and brooding as he was, although she had to admit she was prejudiced against him for tattling to the brass about her own perfectly innocent remark. If he'd been any kind of a friend at all, he would have simply told her to shut up about Fatima's pregnancy.

But it hadn't been all bad, she reflected. She had actually enjoyed her talk with Colonel Channing. There was something about him that reminded her of her father. Maybe it was because he spoke to her as an equal. The thought made her wince in pain. Why wasn't it that way with Kip?

38

They had overslept and were late getting out of the house. So Beth and Joe were both nervous and agitated. Joe was leaving that morning for Heraklion, and he wouldn't be back for several days. The United States was building 'Project North,' a secret listening post on the island of Crete, and he had to go there to make local building contracts to get construction started.

'Will you drop Angela off at school before you pick up Chili?' Joe asked.

'That's the plan. After we finish shopping, we'll get rid of the groceries, and then we're going to Tess's to see the baby. Then I'll take Chili back home on my way to pick up Angela.'

'Angela could take the bus home,' Joe said, 'and you wouldn't be rushed.'

'Let's not go into that again, honey. Ever since that airman masturbated in front of those little kids, I just can't bear the thought of putting her on that school bus.'

'Look, he was just a smartass trying to get himself shipped out of the service. Thank God it was Kip who presided over his court-martial and not somebody who'd let him off the hook.'

'Maybe, but it was too bad that those poor little kids had to testify,' Beth said. 'I'm not sure I would have let Angela do it.'

'Oh, yes, you would. Look, they were only kindergarteners, and their testimony wasn't the best, but it was pretty obvious he had shown them his 'wee-wee,' and that was enough for Kip. He made sure the guy would do time before he was discharged.'

'Well, I've certainly lost confidence in the people who assigned a creep like that to drive a school bus full of innocent children,' Beth snapped impatiently.

'You can't always predict that kind of thing. Anyway, it's all over now. You shouldn't keep fretting about it.'

'Maybe so, but I intend to keep on driving Angela myself.'

Beth dropped Joe off at his office, and he kissed her good-bye. 'I've got to rush, hon. Bob Mulhare's the pilot, and he hates to be late. He's going to drop me off in Heraklion, refuel, and then go to Cyprus to pick up some British personnel who need to be hospitalized. If you need anything while I'm gone, call Kip. I told him you'd be alone, and he said they'd keep an eye out for you. I'll work real hard and be home Saturday.'

'Don't worry about me. I'll be just fine. Be careful, and come home safe. I love you,' she said, affectionately patting his cheek.

Joe kissed her again, then kissed his daughter. Because he wasn't a pilot, Joe didn't leave his family often, and the parting was difficult for all of them.

Beth drove to the officers' club, where she and Angela had a glass of milk and a doughnut. At nine o'clock, just as she had left her daughter at the school, she heard a plane and looked up to see a DC-3 climbing into the air. There they go, she thought, and making a sign of the cross, she said a short prayer for her husband's safety. When the plane was out of sight, she headed out toward the dependent housing in the back area of the base, a couple of miles from everything, where the Shaheens lived.

Driving slowly through the rows of ranch houses, Beth

checked the house numbers to make sure she stopped at the right one. The neighborhood seemed deserted. All the children were either in school or at the nursery, she presumed, and she was glad that they had decided to keep their town apartment for the duration of the tour. Although the houses here were new and relatively nice, it was a dusty, desert area, with no landscaping. There was something about it this morning that made her feel as if she had just landed on the moon. She much preferred her apartment with its spacious rooms and high ceilings, even if the plumbing was not good.

Because she was a few minutes early, Beth approached Chili's door slowly, looking around, wondering if it was always this quiet. She knocked at the door, but there was no answer. She knocked harder the second time, and when there was still no response, she considered going back to the club and telephoning. First, however, she decided to try the door, and to her surprise, it was unlocked. She pushed it open and called, 'Chili . . . Chili?'

Silence. She stepped inside the house and noted that it was in good order, although there was an odd, unpleasant odor in the air. Liquor? Was it possible that Chili had drunk herself to sleep and hadn't yet awakened?

Walking through the living room to the kitchen, which was sparkling clean, she noticed a letter sitting on the kitchen counter. She stood still and called out once more, 'Chili! Are you here? It's me . . . Beth.' Without really meaning to pry, she let her eyes graze the letter. The handwriting was not very good, but it looked as if it had been written by Chili. It was dated yesterday and began, 'Dear Jimmyjohn, I got your letter today and don't you worry none. I'm going to find some way to get myself out of this fix and come home to take care of you. I'll get there fast as I can. Don't let them . . .'

Suddenly aware that she was poking her nose into someone's private affairs, Beth stepped backward. 'Jesus, Mary, and Joseph, what am I doing?' she said aloud, appalled at her brazen behavior.

She wanted to leave, but there was a presence in the house that stopped her. She sensed strongly that she was not alone. Perhaps Chili was ill and needed help. Moving cautiously, Beth headed toward the bedroom. Confronting a closed door, she hesitated briefly and then slowly turned the knob and pushed it open. She peered inside but could see nothing. The blinds were closed tightly, the room was dark, and the unpleasant menstrual-like odor hanging in the air was much stronger there than it had been in the other rooms.

It took a moment for her eyes to adjust to the dim light, but she was soon able to make out a figure lying on the bed.

'Chili?' she asked softly. 'Are you still asleep?'

There was only silence. Beth went to the window and opened the blinds, and slats of bright sunlight shot instantly across the room, slashing the bed into planes of light and darkness. Beth moved toward the figure, and when she was close enough to see, she gasped in horror.

Chili, dressed in a green satin dress, was lying on the bed, her eyes open, her hand still clutching a revolver that rested on the pillow beside her right temple. There was a hole in her head where the bullet had gone in on the right and another one where it had made its exit on the left, skidding across the white pillowcase, leaving a trail of blood and brain tissue in its wake.

Chili was dead.

261

39

Beth sat in Colonel Channing's office staring numbly at the wall. No matter where she looked, all she could see was Chili's dead body in that bright green satin dress, her eyes glassy and lifeless, her skin gray beneath the stark circles of pink rouge on her cheeks . . . her lipstick bright and red in contrast to the darkness of the smear of blood on the pillow. Colonel Channing was talking to her, but she didn't want to listen anymore. She just wanted to go home.

'Mrs Cellini, I've radioed the field at Heraklion and authorized your husband to return home as soon as possible by commercial aircraft. Sorry one of us didn't think to do it before the plane went on to Cyprus. Are you all right?'

Beth nodded mutely and looked at her watch. It was almost three o'clock, and she realized someone had to pick up Angela.

'I have to go. I have to pick up my daughter at school,' she said, getting to her feet.

'Please sit down. I'll send someone to get her and bring her here. I've called your friend Samara Mulhare, and she'll be here in a little while. You've had a terrible shock, and I don't think you should be alone. I'm sorry I had to ask you so many questions, but . . .' His voice trailed off.

Beth sighed. First, she'd had to tell Major Carson when he arrived, then Air Police had questioned her, then some other men in civilian clothes she had never seen before, then they had brought her here to talk about it some more. There was nothing else she could tell them. Nothing. She had walked into Chili's house and found her dead. Wasn't that enough?

'When Sam gets here, can I go?' she asked.

'You've had quite enough for one day. Would you like to have one of the doctors give you something to help you relax?' Colonel Channing asked solicitously.

Beth shook her head. 'No, thank you. No.'

There was a knock on the door, and Channing's secretary came in to say that Mrs Mulhare was waiting outside.

Beth got to her feet immediately and hurried out to Sam, who put her arm around her.

'Oh, Sam, it was awful,' she said, relieved to be with someone who would understand what a terrible ordeal she'd been through.

'Come on, let's get out of here. I stopped at school and picked up Angela. She's waiting in the car with David and Melinda.'

They drove to Beth's house in silence, not wanting the children to hear anything about the tragedy. At the door, Sam asked, 'Will you be all right while I take the children home? I'll just be a minute. Jetta's there, and she'll give them dinner.'

Beth nodded. 'I'll be fine.' She was so glad to return to the privacy of her own home that she was already feeling better.

By the time Samara was back, Beth was stretched out on the living-room couch with a cup of tea in her hand. Sam poured herself a cup from the pot and sat down.

'Will you be okay here tonight? I'll be happy to stay over . . . really I will. The children will be fine with Jetta, and I'm only a few blocks awa – '

Beth shook her head vigorously. 'I wouldn't think of it.

263

Angela and I will be fine. Right now, it only seems like a bad dream anyway. I just hope Joe gets back soon.'

'Poor Chili. It's hard to understand how a woman can bring herself to do something like that,' Sam reflected.

'Do you think it was the booze?' Beth asked.

'Maybe, maybe not. Although she seemed sober enough when I talked to her at about five yesterday. She said she was late getting dressed for the party at the villa, because something happened with the electricity at the beauty shop and they had trouble getting her hair dry. She promised to give me a call first chance she had,' Sam said thoughtfully, wondering how much she should reveal to Beth. Finally she decided that just because the poor woman was dead, she should not betray her confidence.

'Did she make it to the party?' Beth asked.

Sam shrugged her shoulders. 'I don't know. Let's see, who might have been on food duty last night?'

Beth thought a minute and then suggested, 'I'll bet Marilee was. Veronica thinks she's the best cook on the base, so you know if it was an important visitor, Marilee was told to bring food.'

Sam went to the telephone, saying, 'Only one way to find out.'

When she finished the call, she looked perplexed. 'Marilee was there, all right, but she said Gamal came alone. Veronica was furious with Chili for not showing, because her seating arrangement was shot to hell. Marilee had to fill in for her.'

'Did Gamal say why she didn't come?'

'According to Marilee, he said she had a sudden migraine.' Sam could not restrain the bitterness in her voice. 'She had a headache, all right, a fatal one.'

'I didn't know she had migraines . . . did you?'

Sam shook her head. 'She nevere mentioned it. Does a

264

migraine hurt bad enough to make you blow your brains out?'

'I've never had one. Sam, while Colonel Channing was questioning me, I asked him if Gamal was out of town, and he said no, that Gamal had slept at the BOQ because the party lasted late and he didn't want to disturb Chili. Do you believe that?' Beth asked hesitantly.

'Maybe. I know for a fact that they've had some serious spats,' Sam answered, 'but it sure as hell seems coincidental, doesn't it? If he can prove he was never at home, he's really off the hook.'

'Colonel Channing said that Gamal assured him that he did it all the time, because she often drank herself into unconsciousness and would wet the bed, so he either slept on the couch in the living room or in a spare bed in the BOQ.'

'Oh, God,' Sam moaned. 'I don't want to talk about this anymore.'

The two women sat in silence for a long time, and then Beth insisted that Samara go home to the children. 'Look, I'm fine. They said Joe just might get in late tonight, and besides, Rima is here with us. So don't worry, Sam. I may be tiny, but I'm tough,' she said with a wry smile.

'Okay, but remember, call me if you need me, and I'll be here in five minutes.'

Just as she was leaving, Beth said, 'Sam, have you called Tess yet?'

'No, but Kip knows. I'd rather he told her.'

Kip actually did not tell Tess until he came home for dinner that evening, because he knew she would be extremely upset. For some reason, a reason he did not quite understand, she liked Chili a lot. As pretty as she had been, Gamal's wife had been a little coarse for Kip's taste, and it was obvious she'd had no education. Kip had often wondered why an officer as ambitious as Gamal had married a woman who would be no asset to his career.

When Tess heard the news, he was stunned by her reaction.

'Chili wouldn't kill herself!' she declared emotionally.

'Well, she did, honey, and apparently she'd been planning it for some time, because the weapon she used wasn't something that was lying around the house that she picked up on impulse. Gamal said he didn't have a gun.'

Tess couldn't accept it. 'And everybody believes him? How nice!' Tess snapped sarcastically, and then she sat down on the edge of the bed and started to cry.

Kip put his arms around her. 'Come on, honey. I know it's a shock, but sometimes people are more troubled than you think.'

'I just can't believe she's dead. She was coming to see Skippy today . . . why would she call and tell me she was coming if she was going to kill herself? I talked to her just yesterday, and she sounded fine. Oh, God, she had things on her mind and she obviously wanted to talk, but I just wasn't in the mood to listen.' And in her sorrow, Tess felt as so many do when they hear that someone they know has committed suicide. She felt as though she were somehow responsible. If she had only talked longer . . . if she had said something different . . . if she had been more attentive . . . perhaps it wouldn't have happened.

'I thought she looked kind of spooky at the club the other night. She was sort of pale and the circles under her eyes were unusually dark,' Kip mused.

'She's been sick . . .' she began, but couldn't go on because her grief brought on a torrent of tears.

'Well, if you call going on a long binge being sick. Look, babe, liquor can really screw you up . . . you know that,' he said, and continued to hold her and talk to her

266

gently. When her tears had dried and she was feeling calmer, Kip broached the subject he'd been avoiding.

'Honey, Major Carson called me this afternoon and asked me if you'd mind coming in and answering some questions tomorrow. He's going to have Sam in too. They've already talked to Beth.'

Tess sighed. 'Do I have a choice?' she asked.

Kip avoided her eyes and looked down as he shook his head and answered, 'Not really.'

'Well, okay. But I'm going to tell them what I think.'

'What do you mean?' he asked warily.

'I'm going to ask them why they're so sure it was suicide,' she said defensively.

'Honey, please, for my sake, don't do that.'

'Why not?'

'Do you have a good reason to ask that question? Because if you don't, then you'll just look like an idiot. The OSI is going over everything with a fine tooth comb.'

'Who the devil are they?' she asked contentiously.

'You've seen them skulking around the base. They're part of the Air Force's investigating unit. They wear civilian clothes and are called mister so no one knows what their rank is. Believe me, if there's something wrong, they'll find out about it,' he reassured her. 'Just answer questions, honey. Don't offer opinions.'

Seeing the determined set of Tess's mouth, Kip asked in exasperation, 'Okay, if she didn't blow her own brains out, who did? If you're insinuating that it was Gamal, forget it. He was at the villa, at Masters' dinner party, when it happened. He didn't even go home last night. He slept at the BOQ because Chili was drunk.'

'Are they sure?' she asked uncertainly.

'They're sure.'

That night Tess was unable to get to sleep. She lay on

her bed beside the slumbering Kip, listening to the storm raging outside, and trying to put the pieces of the puzzle together, but she couldn't find a single rational reason for her suspicions. The problem was probably that she just didn't like Gamal. She never had liked him, and Chili's revelation about his cheating had made him seem even more despicable. Dammit to hell, Gamal was to blame for something. He didn't deserve to walk away from this disaster free of a messy marriage and clear of any blame.

40

Tess sat in Colonel Masters' office, clutching Skippy to her breast. Kip stood beside her. She had not had a wink of sleep since she had heard about Chili's death, and she was grieved, angry, and resentful. She had hoped that she would be able to talk with Colonel Channing, but instead she was sitting facing a man she didn't like at all.

Brick Masters tried to mold his face into a smile that was warm and friendly, but it didn't work. He was too tense.

'You're excused, Kipling. Wait outside. I want to talk to your wife alone,' he snapped briskly, 'and take the kid with you.' Kip hesitated, but he had just been given a command, and so after Tess handed Skippy to him, he backed reluctantly from the room. He hated leaving her alone, but Masters hadn't given him a choice. The cold way that Tess avoided his eyes made him feel that he was abandoning her.

Brick Masters eyed the woman in front of him warily and wished he hadn't chosen this particular friend of the dead woman to be the first one he questioned. Channing had misled him. He said she was cooperative and intelligent and easy to talk to, but Masters could tell by the grim set of her mouth and the cool way she looked at him that she would not be intimidated easily. Channing didn't know anything about women. This one was a ball-breaker, if there ever was one.

'Now . . . Mrs Kipling . . . can you give us any possible reason for the tragic death of Mrs Shaheen?'

'I don't understand what you mean,' Tess replied.

Masters clenched his hands and turned away from her hostile gaze. God, he wanted to slap that impertinent look off her face. Where the hell was her humility? He was the commanding officer, and she wasn't giving him the proper respect. Didn't the bitch give a damn about her husband's career?

Stating his words in a measured cadence, he said, 'I want to know everything that you know about Mrs Shaheen. When was the last time you talked to her?'

'The morning before . . . she died,' Tess replied.

'And did she say anything that might give us a clue to her state of mind?' he asked, but Tess just shook her head.

'Look, I know you women gossip about personal things. Did she tell you anything, anything at all, that was bothering her?'

'What difference does it make? She's dead. Since it's been decided that she killed herself, why pry into her personal reasons for being unhappy?'

'Ah, so she told you she was unhappy?' he said, jumping on the word.

'Happy people don't usually kill themselves,' Tess retorted acidly.

'Did she tell you why she was unhappy?' Masters said, moving in closer, wondering how he should react if she revealed that she knew about his relationship with the dead woman. Christ, his whole career could be in this impudent bitch's hands. God knows what kind of fairy tale she might tell the OSI if he let them question her.

Tess looked away from his eyes and down at her hands clenched in her lap, and she regretted telling her husband about Chili's suspicions that Gamal was cheating on her. She regretted even more allowing Kip to persuade her

270

that she should remain silent about it. What did she care if it went on Gamal's record and damaged his chances in the military?

'Yes, she told me,' she blurted out. Dammit, Chili was dead. Somebody was to blame. It wasn't fair for Gamal to get off scot-free.

Masters could not look her in the face anymore. He turned away, not wanting his emotions exposed if she spoke the words he was most afraid of hearing. How stupid he had been to think that redheaded cunt would keep her mouth shut.

'And what exactly did she tell you?' he asked, his voice low.

'She told me that she'd found out that her husband was cheating on her,' Tess said. 'She found condoms in his pocket.'

Masters whirled around to look at Tess in astonishment. 'She what?'

'You heard me,' Tess said stiffly. 'Now, may I go?'

Masters' mind hastily computed the information. Jesus Christ, the mystery was solved! Of course, Chili had killed herself because she thought her husband was screwing around! Women did that kind of stuff all the time.

'That's all she told you? She didn't tell you anything else?' he asked, surprised by the information and finding it hard to believe. But it didn't matter if it was true or not. If Shaheen' wife had convinced this cold bitch, it was a believable motive, one that the boys over at OSI would accept without question. They'd be tickled pink when they found out he'd done all the work for them.

'That's all I know,' Tess said wearily. 'I really don't feel very well, and I can hear my baby crying outside. He needs to nurse; may I go now?' Having laid the blame at Gamal's feet, she felt wretched. Perhaps it hadn't been

271

the truth at all. Perhaps Chili had been mistaken. She hoped to God she hadn't ruined the military career of an innocent man. What would Kip think of her now?

Brick Masters needed a bit more reassurance. 'Do you think he really was . . . cheating on her?' he asked.

'How the devil would I know?'

No longer intimidated by her cold hostility, Masters patted her on the shoulder and in a patronizing manner said, 'You did the right thing, Tess, my dear. It was kind of you to try to protect him. Rest assured, I'll discuss it with him, off the record, of course. If it's true, then he'll have to live with his own conscience, and that will be punishment enough. Now that we have a better understanding of her state of mind, it puts everything into perspective. Thank you for your help. I'll see to it that you're not questioned any further. Go home with your husband and try to forget what's happened.'

Masters went to the door and opened it for her. Kip was waiting anxiously outside.

'We're all finished, Lieutenant. You have a fine lady there, Kipling. Take the rest of the day off. I'll clear it with Colonel Hall,' he declared expansively. The menacing crocodile had suddenly been transformed into a benign pussycat.

41

Samara put down the telephone, confused. Her meeting with Colonel Masters had just been canceled because he was involved with other pressing matters and would contact her later. A curious person, Sam wondered just what matters were more pressing than the investigation of a woman's death. She would be glad when Bob got home this evening. Headquarters had called to say he had been delayed an extra day in Cyprus because the plane had a mechanical problem, but they had assured her he would be back tonight.

Since she was already dressed and ready to go, she decided to drive out to the base and see if there was any mail. She hadn't received a reply to the letter she had sent her parents, and she was still not sure if she would. Maybe she would call Nell Carson and take her to lunch. She had already called Beth, but Joe had come home, and he was staying with her. She'd called Tess too, but no one had answered. Well, visiting with Nell was always interesting, because her husband knew everything that was going on. She had to get out of the house and think of something besides Chili.

Disappointed when there was still no response from her parents at the post office, Sam went to the club to meet Nell at noon. The dining room was busy, as usual, but Nell had already secured a table by the window.

Nell greeted her by announcing, 'I don't know about you, but I'm having a martini. Join me?'

'No, thanks. Drinking before five o'clock wipes out the day for me. But go ahead. I'll stick with iced tea.'

When the drinks were served, Sam lifted her glass and said, 'Let's drink one to Chili, wherever she is.'

They clinked glasses, and Sam asked, 'Do you feel any guilt about her death?'

Nell shook her head vigorously. 'Of course not. I hardly knew her. Why, do you?'

'Unfortunately, I do. Probably because I failed her. She called me the afternoon before she died. I wish I'd talked longer to her.'

'Did she say anything . . . I mean, did she give any indication that she might . . .?' Nell asked curiously.

'No, but she said she needed to talk to me – "serious like" were the words she used. I'd give anything to know what she had on her mind. God, what a waste! She was probably the most beautiful woman I ever knew.' Breathing a deep sigh, she changed the subject. 'So, tell me, what's going on around here that nobody knows but you?'

'What do you mean by that?' Nell asked sharply.

Samara was taken aback by her sudden change in manner. 'Nothing, really, Nell. You just always seem to have the inside track on what's going on around here, and . . .'

'Look, Sam, I don't know any more than anybody else. I just talk too much, that's all.' She took a long swallow of her drink and looked around the room, avoiding Samara's eyes.

Samara stared at her thoughtfully. Why had Nell, who relished gossiping about everything, suddenly become so tight-lipped and uncommunicative?

'Chili's death must be bothering you as much as it is me,' Sam suggested gently.

Nell shrugged her shoulders and replied, 'I know you're

feeling bad about the whole thing, Sam, but let's just drop it, okay? Chili was a drunk, and she messed up her own life. There's no reason for any of us to feel guilty.'

Samara was taken aback by the coldness of Nell's attitude, but there was nothing she could say to dispute her remarks. They finished their lunch in silence, and Sam ruminated on how differently people reacted to a sudden death. Nell was quite obviously as distressed as she was about the tragedy, but her behavior was certainly odd.

After the lunch was over, Sam stayed at the base, checking with Operations to see if there was any news about Bob's plane. When she learned that he had taken off and was on his way, she decided to go home. He had a stop at Benghazi, and would probably be late when he got in, and she didn't want to eat dinner at the club by herself. Besides, the sky had clouded over and Melinda hated storms. She really ought to be with the children.

Later that evening, after David and Melinda were asleep, Sam got out the letter that she had started to her father about Chili and read it over before she tore it into little pieces. She thought about all the foolish ideas she'd had about making Chili a star. Now Chili was dead, and it didn't look as if there would be a reconciliation with her family in any case. It had been almost three weeks since she had written to her parents. God, she was depressed. She always got depressed when Bob was away, but this time it had been particularly bad because of Chili. She went into the living room to pour herself a brandy, but the doorbell rang before she had a chance to taste it.

Her heart lifted. It must be Bob! She called to Jetta that she would answer the door, and with her heart high, she grabbed an umbrella and dashed through the front courtyard to open the heavy door leading onto the street. Without considering that it might be someone other than her husband, she pulled the heavy iron bolt and opened the door.

Standing in the rain were Beth and Joe Cellini, and Tess Kipling, holding the baby under a poncho to keep him dry.

'Hi!' Sam said automatically. 'My God, Tess, what are you doing out in this weather with that baby?'

'Can we come in, Sam?' Joe asked, and there was a seriousness in his voice that panicked her.

'Of course. Come in, come in.'

They picked their way across the puddles in the courtyard and stepped through the door into the warmth of her beautiful villa.

Her hands trembling, Sam took the baby while Tess took off her poncho and head scarf and stepped out of her wet shoes. Everyone was strangely silent. Jetta, the housekeeper, took the wet raincoats and umbrellas and asked if she should make coffee.

'That's a great idea,' Beth said. 'I could use a cup.'

'Let's go into the living room, Sam. We have to talk,' Tess said, taking the baby from Sam and turning him over to Beth.

'It's Bob, isn't it?' Samara asked in a voice that seemed to come from outside her body.

'Don't jump to any conclusions, now. It's too early. The plane is overdue,' Tess said, putting her arm around Sam's shoulders to comfort and support her.

'Oh, my God, no,' Sam whispered, feeling her spirit die within her.

'Kip left just a little while ago. They're sending a lot of people out to search for him. He's out there someplace, I just know it,' Tess said, trying to reassure her.

They were in the large living room, and Tess eased her onto the couch. Joe saw the glass of brandy, and he picked it up and handed it to Sam, but she shook her head.

'No, I couldn't swallow anything. Not now,' she whispered. 'What happened?'

'Bob didn't stop at Benghazi to refuel,' Joe explained. 'He radioed that he had enough fuel and was coming straight to Wheelus. They lost radio contact with him while he was in the middle of the storm, and they think maybe the plane might have been hit by lightning.'

'What does that mean?' Sam asked. Her face was pale and her throat so tightly constricted that she had difficulty getting the words out.

'Just that . . .' Joe searched for words that would explain the situation without terrifying her. '. . . if his radio got knocked out, and he got lost in the storm, he probably won't have enough fuel, so they may have to ditch the plane.'

Tess spoke quickly. 'So you see, that's why we came. It may be a long wait, and I didn't want you to be here by yourself. If they parachuted in the desert, it may take a while to find them.'

Sam put her head on Tess's shoulder, and the long silent vigil began.

42

Early the next morning, word came to the base that the copilot and passengers on Bob's plane had been picked up in the desert by a tribe of bedouins. When Bob's copilot was returned safely to the base, he told them that what they had surmised was true. The plane had been blown far off course by the high winds, and they had run dangerously low on fuel. The plane had, indeed, been hit by lightning, and they had had no radio contact for more than three hours. It was Bob's decision to drop everyone by parachute near the only town where they could see a few lights, and he had insisted on staying with the plane until he was sure it was safely on a course that would take it into the open sea where it could harm no one when it crashed. What had happened then was anybody's most dismal guess.

The search for Bob and the missing C-47 went on for five days, with pilots combing the area in their planes, scanning both the desert and the sea, determined not to abandon the fellow officer who had put the safety of others ahead of his own life. Money was paid to the leaders of many desert tribes, promising more if they could bring any news of the flier, but there was nothing.

Although her heart told her to keep hoping and praying, Sam felt sure that Bob was gone, and she wept through each day that passed until she had no more tears. One morning she awakened and told herself that the time had come to pull herself together. She was no longer a wife. Now she must expend all her energies in being a mother. Without a father, David and Melinda would need all she had to give. She could not squander her resources on grief.

When the search was finally called off and Bob was declared missing and presumed dead, Sam drove to the communications office to send a cable to her parents. She wired them that she would soon be returning to the States and she would let them know when she arrived. She did not tell them she and the children would be traveling alone, or that Bob was dead. Although the Air Force had notified Bob's parents, she cabled them that she would be happy to visit them if they wanted to see Bob's children.

Because Sam was the mother of a son herself, all the bitterness she had felt toward Bob's parents for disowning him faded. How terrible they must feel now that there would be no chance for reconciliation . . . ever. She would not let that happen to her own mother and father. Whether they wanted her or not, she intended to go home and insist that they meet and give their love and support to her fatherless children.

Sam asked Joe and Beth Cellini to talk with the Catholic chaplain and arrange a funeral mass for Bob. Father Cavanaugh insisted that it be held in the base theater. In his wisdom, he knew that Bob had a lot of friends who would want to say good-bye, and he was right. The theater was filled.

Sam and her children sat in the front row. The priest's eulogy was so intimate and heartfelt that it came as a surprise to her, for he seemed to know Bob well. After the services, Father Cavanaugh came to Sam and the children to give them his condolences.

'It was a beautiful service, Father. You spoke as if you knew my husband,' Sam said, hoping to be enlightened.

'But I did, my child. Your husband was one of the

279

finest young men that I've ever been privileged to know. Didn't you know that he came to see me often just to talk?'

Sam was stunned. How could they have had such a close and loving marriage without her knowing that Bob apparently still needed his church? She forced herself to ask stiffly, 'What did you talk about, Father? Was there something bothering him?'

'My child, I cannot betray a confidence. I can only tell you that he was troubled. When you are raised as strongly in the faith as Bob was, it is not easy to break away.'

'I see,' Sam replied. 'Well, thank you for being there to help him with something that I couldn't . . .' Her voice broke.

Father Cavanaugh placed his hand on her shoulder to comfort her. 'Child, don't take this as a failure on your part. Too often we try to be everything to someone we love, but their needs can be greater than we mere mortals can possibly fulfill. Because you and Bob were deprived of the love and support of your families, he looked for reassurance. His search for spiritual guidance in no way diminished his devotion to you and the children. He loved you more than life itself.'

'I didn't get to say good-bye . . . I loved him so much, Father,' Sam said, letting the tears fall freely as she held both children close to her.

'He knew that, and you made him very happy. He has gone on to his reward . . . and you must believe that, my dear. Now it is up to you to raise his children, and my heart goes out to you in the loneliness of your task. You must be very strong.'

'Thank you, Father,' she said, and then in a sudden inspiration she promised, 'I'll make sure that the children are raised in their father's faith.'

'Bless you, my child.'

Riding home in the back seat of the Cellinis' car, Sam was comforted by the impulsive decision she had made. It was the least she could do to honor Bob's memory now that she knew how much the church had meant to him, but the years ahead stretched out before her in a barren eternity. She felt so alone.

43

Tess looked around her beautifully furnished new quarters and felt a bittersweet sense of loss. Dear, generous Sam had insisted on selling Tess her exquisite furniture for a pittance. There had been little that Sam wanted to take back to the States to remind her of the tragedy Tripoli had brought her, and she had confided in Tess that she intended to take her children as far away from the Air Force as was possible. Tess sensed that Sam was not only walking away from the military but also bringing their friendship to a close, probably because it would be too painful to be reminded of the happy times they had shared before Bob's death. Tess hated to see her go, for Samara Mulhare embodied more admirable qualities than any friend she'd ever had, and she had been so much fun to be around.

The week after Tess's conversation with Colonel Masters, Kip had been notified that he was eligible for base housing, which came as a surprise. By his own calculations, Kip estimated that it would take another four or five months to move to the top of the waiting list. When he asked the base housing officer why he had been moved ahead, he was informed that the CO's office had requested it. Tess was suspicious, but she kept her thoughts to herself, because she had an uneasy feeling they were being rewarded for the information she had given Masters about Gamal's infidelity, and she didn't understand why.

Nevertheless, she insisted that they accept. Now that

she had a baby, she was anxious to be close to the health and food services and eager to leave the cold, damp apartment in town. Although she would have preferred assignment to the new housing area, all that was available was a unit in the old quarters of standard row houses, but it was right in the center of the base, close to everything, including Kip's office.

Sam had been gone from Wheelus for more than a month now, and had left no forwarding address. She had promised to write when she was settled, but weeks had passed and no one heard from her.

Tess was about to host for the first time the bridge group they'd joined, and she was nervously separating eggs for an angel food cake. When she finally got the batter into the oven, she set up the card tables and covered them with the Belgian lace cloths that had been a wedding gift from friends of her parents. She put cigarettes in the little silver urns that matched the Ronson table lighters, peanuts in the cut-glass dishes her mother had given her, and flowers in Egyptian brass vases from the BX. One of the primary duties of a service wife was to entertain well, and she wanted her first party in her beautifully furnished home to be a success. Not that it was necessary to have a grand house to give a great party. Service families, Tess had learned, didn't place nearly as much importance on material possessions as civilians did. Their rootless lives made them overlook the ill-fitting draperies, couches that were either too big or too small, and scars on furniture that rarely stayed in one house more than a year or two before being slung onto another van for the next move. Service families also lived with the reality of meager salaries that invariably left too much month at the end of the money.

Ever since the deaths of Chili and Bob, Tess had been

determined to model herself on Beth Cellini, who was her idea of what a good service wife should be. And with the departure of Samara, she also realized that service friendships would not be permanent. People would fade in and out of her life as long as Kip was in the Air Force. She hated the idea that Skippy would not have the same kind of security and continuity in family and friendships that had blessed her childhood. She was not convinced that it was good for children to be forced constantly to make new adjustments. Of course, Kip had been an Army brat, and he had turned out all right. Maybe children who had to move around and make new friends *were* more resilient and outgoing, as Kip maintained. She hoped he was right.

Tess was not as well-organized this afternoon as she'd planned to be. Skippy awakened from his nap feverish and out of sorts, and all he wanted to do was nurse. Whenever she tried to pull him from the breast and put him down, he screamed as if she were beating him. As usual, Kip was late getting home because of Colonel Masters.

Fortunately, Pina had the house in great shape, and although the cake had risen nicely, for some reason the bottled cream refused to whip. In spite of all the work and careful preparation, when Kip arrived home he found the situation chaotic. The Sunbeam mixer was going full speed, probably turning the Avoset to butter, and Skippy was crying and hiccuping between outbursts of screaming.

'Good Lord, Tess, what's going on? The kitchen's a mess! They'll be here in less than an hour, and our dinner isn't even on the table,' he complained.

Tess closed her eyes and counted to ten. She tried to remember how much she loved him, but there were times when she could hardly stand him. Like now. Couldn't he see all the work she'd done? Didn't he have any idea what it was like to take care of a demanding baby?

Instead of lashing back, she replied evenly, 'There's a meatloaf and baked potatoes in the oven. They're undoubtedly dry and overcooked since I expected you home an hour ago. Here, help me put it on the table, and we'll eat quickly. Then you can hold Skippy while I clean up and get dressed.'

Kip let out a long, exasperated sigh. 'Don't try to blame me. I have to work, you know. I don't have a maid like Pina to do my job for me. I'm going to put the liquor away and get changed first, I've had a tough day.' He turned and walked out of the room.

Angered by his cutting remark about Pina, Tess pulled herself out of the chair. The noise of the mixer was irritating her, and she turned it off. The damn stuff was never going to whip because she'd put too much of it in the bowl. She switched the baby to her left breast in order to free her right arm and proceeded to pull the meatloaf and potatoes out of the oven. Working as fast as she could, she set the table for one, and when Kip finally returned, dressed in a sport shirt and slacks, he found his dinner waiting, but that irritated him too.

'Where's your plate? You know I can't enjoy my dinner if you're pouting and acting like a martyr.'

Tess bit her lip and looked at the clock on the stove. In less than forty minutes their guests would arrive. There was no time to argue.

'I had a late lunch, and the Avoset won't whip. I've got to make some other kind of icing for the cake. You go ahead and eat. When you're finished, you can take Skippy and give me a chance to dress.' She was careful to keep her voice smooth so that her anger could not slip through the cracks. No matter how cutting his remarks were to her, she didn't have time for a full-blown argument.

'Okay,' he said, spooning some food on to his plate, 'but I hope he doesn't spit up on my shirt. I hate to smell of sour milk.'

The party was a disaster. The cake still tasted of musty flour, in spite of the extra vanilla she had used, and she could tell that Kip was embarrassed when nobody ate it. They had just sat down to play bridge when Skippy awakened and joined the party, and for the rest of the evening Tess moved back and forth from the bedroom to the living room. She tried to stay in the game, but for the most part she had to let whoever was the dummy play her hand.

The guests left early, but Beth lingered. She put her arm around Tess and whispered, 'Tough day?'

It was the first shred of sympathy Tess had had, and it undid her. Tears suddenly started to course down her cheeks. Understanding, Beth whispered, 'I'll stop by in the morning and we'll talk.'

She tried to hide her tears as she emptied ashtrays and put away the decks of cards, but Kip noticed them.

'Look, it was okay. Really. Next time it'll be better,' he said, putting his arms around her.

Tess tucked her head into his shoulder, and gently he stroked her hair and kissed her on the forehead, murmuring words of love, and soon his mouth was on hers, kissing her passionately. The gentle comfort was now demanding urgency, and Tess felt betrayed. Damn him, now that the evening was over, he expected sex.

'I have to check on Skippy,' she said, pulling away.

'He'll be all right. Come on, let's go to bed,' he insisted. 'It's getting late.'

Tess allowed herself to be led into the bedroom, and

they made love. Long after Kip had fallen asleep, Tess was still awake, sitting in a chair beside the baby's crib, nursing him and thinking about life and love.

Why couldn't Kip ever just hug and kiss her? And why had her mother told her never, ever to say no to her husband? Marriage just seemed so damned one-sided.

Several times she tried to lay Skippy down in his crib, but as soon as he touched the sheet, he would yell and begin to cry angrily, and so she let him nurse. As time passed, his chubby little body began to feel warmer, and she became worried. She had heard other, more experienced mothers say they could guess temperatures by placing their cheeks against their children's backs. Tess tried it, and the hot dryness left no doubt that for the first time in his tiny life, Skippy was spiking a temperature, and a significantly high one.

In his book, Dr Spock had warned about convulsions if a baby's fever got too high. So, following his instructions, Tess quickly removed Skippy's nightgown and gently bathed him in tepid water. She tried to give him a bottle of water, but he shrieked in indignation at the taste of a rubber nipple, and she could only calm him by nursing.

It was a long, frightening night, and she prayed for the sun to come up. Nighttime was always the worst when someone was sick. If she could just hold up until dawn, she was sure Skippy's fever would break and everything would be all right again. So indoctrinated was she with the idea that the baby was solely her responsibility that she didn't disturb Kip to ask for help.

When dawn finally came, it failed to bring the hoped-for relief and comfort. Skippy's indignant screaming had given way to glassy-eyed whimpering and lassitude, and he was very hot to the touch. At six, Tess went into the bedroom and awakened Kip.

'Honey, wake up. We've got to take Skippy to the doctor. He's got a high fever.'

Kip was awake and out of bed immediately. One look at the terrified exhaustion on his wife's face and the limp child in her arms told him all he needed to know.

Quickly he dressed and held the baby while Tess threw on some clothes. By the time they got to the hospital, where the nurse took Skippy's temperature, the fever had reached almost one hundred and five degrees. The doctor checked him over thoroughly and could find nothing obvious that was causing it.

He wrote out a prescription for an antibiotic and said, 'Start him on this as soon as the pharmacy opens at eight. Give him a quarter of an aspirin every four hours. Keep up the sponge baths. If the fever doesn't respond by this afternoon, better bring him to sick call to see the pediatrician.'

They returned to the reception room to wait for the pharmacy to open, when an airman brought them a paper to sign.

'Lieutenant, the doctor forgot to have you sign this release form.'

Looking at the form, Kip saw it was a release stating that if anything happened to the patient, neither the doctor nor the hospital could be held responsible.

'What's this for?' Kip asked in bewilderment.

'That's just regulation, sir. The rules state that no patient can leave the hospital with a temperature of a hundred and two or more without signing a release. If you don't sign, the kid'll have to be admitted to the hospital.'

Kip started to sign the document, but Tess snatched it from him. 'Wait!' she said, then, turning to the airman, asked, 'If they admit him to the hospital, can I stay with him?'

'You have to, ma'am. We're short on nurses, and every kid has to have at least one parent by his bedside at all times.'

'We're not signing,' Tess said quietly.

Kip tried to reason with her, but she was adamant. The duty officer refused to come out of his office to talk to her again, and when the full staff arrived at eight, she was ushered into an office to see the pediatrician.

'Dr Booth,' she said, 'my baby's sick.'

Her instincts had been right. After a thorough examination, Skippy was placed in isolation on the chance he might be contagious. They started an intravenous solution containing a broad-spectrum antibiotic, gave him repeated tepid sponge baths, and waited. Tess did not leave his bedside. Kip came into the room for five minutes twice that day so she could go the bathroom, and have a cup of coffee, but Skippy had his mother's full attention.

It was not until the next morning that the baby's fever finally broke, and although they rejoiced, it was temporary. The fever went back up that night, and so it continued for three days of fear and sleeplessness. Although the doctors did countless tests, they could only guess that the culprit was some strange virus they could not identify. Tess was not encouraged by a doctor's comment that there were a lot of fevers in North Africa they couldn't identify.

When at last Skippy's temperature dropped to normal and stayed there for twenty-four hours, they were able to take him home. Fear bordering on hysteria had kept his mother alert and wakeful throughout the ordeal, but she was exhausted.

Beth came over to watch Skippy so Tess could take a

nap. After two hours of sound sleep, Tess awakened with a start, her heart beating rapidly. She rushed into the living room, where Skippy was resting comfortably in her friend's arms.

'Is he okay?' Tess asked.

'He's fine. Go back to bed. You're going to make yourself sick worrying.'

Tess shook her head and curled up on the couch. 'I'm not sure I'll ever sleep soundly in this place again, Beth. I keep thinking of what might have happened if it had been polio or meningitis and that stupid doctor had sent me home with Skip. He might have died!'

'But it wasn't. Now, stop brooding over it and be thankful he's okay.'

'I've never prayed as hard as I did in that hospital, Beth.'

'They say there's no such thing as an atheist with a sick child,' Beth replied, and Tess added softly, 'Amen,' before she dozed off again, only to dream of taking Skippy home, where he would be safe.

44

For her children's sake, Samara was determined to force a reconciliation with all of their grandparents. She expected to be welcomed home by her own family, but she was not so sure about Bob's parents. All she could really remember about them was their anger. She had heard nothing from them after the Air Force had notified them of their son's heroic death.

A month after Bob's plane had gone down and almost two weeks after he had been declared missing and presumed dead, instead of taking the Air Force flight to which she was entitled, she had flown BOAC from Tripoli to London. Then, several days later, she proceeded to Southampton and boarded the *Queen Elizabeth*. She felt that the leisurely shipboard voyage would be less stressful for everyone, and it would give both her and the children a more gradual segue from the military life to the civilian. While in London, they had been comfortably ensconced at the Grosvenor House Hotel, and Sam made use of the time to interview nannies. Before sailing, she hired a sweet, soft-spoken woman named Margaret Blore, who was in her forties, widowed by World War II, and a seasoned and experienced governess. David and Melinda accepted her readily, which pleased Sam, for she intended to build a large support group of people for her children to love, just in case the grandparents failed her again. She did not want her son and daughter to grow up dependent only on her. Bob's death had taught her how fragile the thread of life was. If, God forbid, something happened to her, she wanted to make sure that her children would have others to whom they could turn.

The voyage was calm, uneventful, and pleasant. Margaret made good use of the week to become acquainted with the children, spending hours reading to them, exploring the ship, and playing games. Sam was always available when they wanted her, but she was relieved to see them exert some independence. Since their father's death they had clung to her much too tightly, and she was glad to let them go a bit.

When they arrived in New York, Sam checked them into the Waldorf-Astoria. While Margaret unpacked, Sam made the telephone call to New Haven that she had rehearsed throughout the trip.

'Hello, Mrs Mulhare? Hi, this is Samara. I'm in New York.'

There was a silence on the line for a long, long moment, and then a voice weak with emotion asked, 'Samara? Are the children with you?'

Sam too felt her vocal cords quaver with emotion as she replied, 'Yes. Would you like for me to bring them to see you?'

'Would you do that, Samara . . . after all the . . .?' Her voice broke, and Sam could hear her sobbing. Suddenly a man took the telephone and said, 'Samara, my wife and I would be very happy if you'd bring our son's children for a visit.'

'We just arrived in the States. We're at the Waldorf in New York City. Just tell us when you'd like us to be there,' Sam replied, her voice now steady.

'Whenever you want to come. Please plan to stay awhile with us. We have plenty of room in this big house, and everyone wants to have time with the children.'

'We have no schedule to meet. Suppose we take the

train there day after tomorrow. Will that give you enough time?'

'Wonderful. Call and let me know which train you'll be on, and we'll meet you.'

'Mr Mulhare, I have the children's nanny with me, but if you prefer, I can leave her here in New York.'

'Bring her along.'

Sam put down the telephone and stood at the window to look out over the skyline of the city, thinking about the strange behavior of supposedly rational adults. Why had Bob had to die to make his family realize how foolish they had been to turn him away just because they didn't approve the religion of the woman he had chosen to love?

Mr and Mrs Mulhare met their train, and Sam was shocked to see how the past years had aged Bob's parents. Had it happened because of the rift, or more recently because of his death?

David and Melinda took to their grandparents right away, sensing the close ties and similarities to their father. At the large, comfortable family home that evening all the relatives came to dinner, and it was a noisy, affectionate group of people. The children were overwhelmed by aunts and uncles who brought them presents and hugged and kissed them. They played with cousins they hadn't even known they had.

Sam stood apart and watched. Although everyone treated her kindly and spoke with love of the man who had been her husband, she knew that she would always be an outsider there. She could never forget how much they had hurt the man she loved, but she would not permit the resentment she felt to deny her children the family they needed.

They stayed for four days, and although the children

would have been content to stay forever, Sam felt it was time to go.

As they waited on the platform for the train that would take them back to New York, Sam decided to tell Bob's parents of her decision about the children.

'Thank you so much for your kindness and hospitality,' she began.

'Samara, please . . . don't say it. Just having Bob's children here with us has made a great difference in our lives. It has, in fact, made everything . . . bearable. David is the image of his father, you know,' Bob's father said, resting his hand on her arm.

'Isn't he, though?' Sam agreed. 'And Melinda looks just like my brother, David,' she added, unable to resist staking her claim to the children's existence too, but immediately regretting it. They did not love David and Melinda because she was their mother, but because Bob was their father. It was only natural.

'I can't tell you how much I appreciate the warmth you've shown us,' Sam said, and then added, 'I just hope my family will welcome us as warmly as you have.'

'Of course they will. After all, they'll be getting their daughter back,' her father-in-law said, but there was no bitterness in his voice. If Catholics could be judged by the Mulhare family, Sam thought, they seemed to have an acceptance of death as a part of life. Perhaps because their religion promised them something beyond.

'Bob never deserted his faith, in spite of what you might think. It was very important to him, and because of that, I've decided to raise the children as Catholics.'

With his eyes misting, Mr Mulhare said quietly, 'You have no idea how much this means to his mother and me.'

'I'm doing it for him. Thank you for your kindness. You will always be welcome in my home to visit, and I hope you'll come often. In any case, I'll make sure that the children visit you.' Although her words were meant to be kind, her manner was formal. Sam would forgive, but she could never forget.

The next day, before they boarded a TWA Constellation for the long flight to Los Angeles, Sam called her father's office. He took her call immediately.

'We'll be arriving in Los Angeles this evening, Dad,' was all she said.

'Thank God. You mother and I will be there to meet you. Will Bob and the children be with you?' he asked.

'Just the children. I'll tell you all about it when I get there.'

She put down the telephone, all doubts erased. She had not wanted to be welcomed back because her husband had died, but because her parents had finally come to their senses about the true meaning of family. God bless them, her parents had passed the test. Now she was free to share the children with them.

45

Sam was dismayed to see how much her own parents had aged in the five years since she had left them. Her father especially seemed to have grown more frail. A small, wiry man who had once radiated power and confidence, he had lost weight and his shoulders were not as square as she remembered them. Holding the children's hands, she walked from the plane to the gate where Reba and Jules stood in the California sunshine waiting to greet them.

Her father stretched out his arms and gathered his daughter and grandchildren into one long, tearful hug. Her mother stood back and allowed her husband the first greeting. But when Jules Silverman picked up the two precious grandchildren in his arms, Reba clasped her daughter to her and began to cry hysterically.

'It's okay, Mama. It's okay. I'm back,' Sam said soothingly. When her mother finally managed to stop sobbing, she reached for the children. She took one look at little David and said, 'My God . . . he's beautiful, Samara! He looks just like David.'

The little boy, who was now four years old and very bright, looked indignant. 'That's because I *am* David,' he replied.

'So you are,' his grandfather agreed, laughing, and lifted him up once more to carry him through the crowd. Sam found it interesting that her parents would think that David looked like her brother, when it was obvious that he looked just like Bob. Melinda was the one who looked like the Silverman side of the family, but no one had remarked on that. It was irritating and comforting at the same time to realize that her parents hadn't really changed. They still cherished sons.

Margaret, who had lagged behind to gather up the toys and games with which she had amused the children throughout the long flight, caught up and was introduced. In a few minutes they were all settled into Jules's long black limousine and on their way to Beverley Hills.

Melinda and David bounced with excitement when they saw the magnificent stone house with its expanse of lawns, its swimming pool, tennis court, and greenhouse where exotic flowers were cultivated for table arrangements. They were especially delighted with the charming two-story playhouse that the studio set designers had built for Sam when she was five years old. Sam had to promise them they could play in it as much as they wanted, but not until they got settled and had time to rest.

The staff assembled to greet them, and Melinda, David, and Margaret were introduced to the butler, the maids, the cook, and the gardeners, and then they were taken upstairs and shown their rooms. David was given his namesake's room, and Sam insisted that Melinda have her old room because it had such a lovely view of the garden. Sam was content to settle herself in the room between them, once used by her governess, and Margaret was assigned to a nearby guest bedroom.

David made everyone smile when he asked, 'Grandpa, is this a hotel?'

'No, son, this is our home . . . and yours whenever you want to come for a visit,' he replied.

'How long can you stay, Samara?' her mother asked after Margaret took the children to their rooms to settle them down for a short rest before dinner.

'That's something we need to talk about. Let's go into the library.'

Settling into the deep, dark green leather chair in which she had often sat as a very young girl, Sam sipped the cup of tea brought to her by the butler. He was not the same one she had known.

'What happened to Martin?' she asked.

'Retired. Went back to England. We miss him, but Kendon is doing fine. He's been here for more than a year. Now, what's all this mystery about your husband? Are you two having some kind of trouble?' her father asked.

His question made breaking the news a little easier. 'I guess you could say that, Dad . . .'

'Well, I could have told – ' her mother began, but her husband silenced her.

'Reba, let's just listen to what Samara has to say.'

Without further preparation, Sam gave it to them straight. 'Bob died in a plane crash a month ago.'

There was a moment of painful and shocked silence before her father exclaimed, 'My God, when . . . Why didn't you call us?'

'I wanted to tell you in person,' she replied softly, and waited for the devastating news to be absorbed before continuing with the details. The first time she'd had to tell anyone about Bob's death had been to the children, and it had been hell explaining why they would never see their father again. This time, it was easier, even though she could not look at her parents as she told them. She was afraid that if she saw even the smallest flicker of joy, she would never be able to forgive them.

There was a long silence. Neither of her parents said a word. At last Sam forced herself to look up at them. Her mother was staring out the window with her eyes full of tears. Her father sat mutely looking down at his hands. Her parents were grieving. Thank God.

Sam went to her mother and sank down to the floor beside her. Resting her head in her lap as she had done when she was a little girl, she began to cry. For a long time she wept as her mother stroked her hair and whispered small words of comfort. It felt so good to be surrounded by her loving family again after the past few weeks of devastating loneliness.

When the storm of grief had spent itself, Sam got to her feet, wiped her eyes, and sat down once more in the leather chair. 'I'm sorry,' she said in a voice husky with tears.

'I'm sorry too, sweetheart. Sorry for a lot of things that happened . . . sorry that now I'll never get to know him. He must have been very special,' Jules said.

'Can you ever forgive us for the terrible way we treated him?' her mother asked.

'Cruel as it was, I have to believe that you were only trying to do what you thought was best for me.'

'I'll never forgive myself, Samara. Never. I can't tell you how many times over the past years I sat down to write you a letter to make things right between us . . . but I could never seem to find the words to tell you how I felt. Then, when your last letter came, I tried again, but all the old pain and the memories of the terrible things we said to each other kept getting in my way . . . now it's too late,' her father said quietly, his words and voice heavy with regret. 'And saying sorry just isn't enough, is it?'

'I know. Isn't it stupid how we go around hurting people, thinking we have all the time in the world to make things right, never thinking of the possibility that fate might intervene and make temporary hurts eternal.

Bob knew how much I loved him, and for that I'm thankful.'

'What are your plans now, honey?' her mother asked.

'She hasn't had time to make any plans, Reba. Come on, now, let's let her go upstairs and get freshened up for dinner. You must be tired from that flight, sweetheart. When did you get back to the States?'

'A week ago. After I got everything squared away at Wheelus, I flew to London, where we stayed while I found Margaret. Then I took the children to New Haven to meet Bob's parents.'

'Everything okay there?' Jules asked.

'They were grateful to see the children, but you know how they feel about losing a son.'

'We certainly do,' Reba said softly.

'Yeah, but at least we were at peace with our son when he died. God bless them. You've gotta make sure that they see David and Melinda often, honey,' Jules said, and Sam knew he was sincere.

She walked upstairs, her arms linked with her parents', saying a silent prayer of thanks that they were still well, grateful to have their presence and their love in her life, not only for her own sake but also for her children's.

46

It was summer again, and Tess was pregnant with her second child. At her insistence, Kip had taken a week's leave, his first since their honeymoon, because she wanted to do some sightseeing with him in the Tripoli area. She had fussed constantly that their tour would be over before she had a real chance to know the place. 'We spend so much time at Wheelus now that we live here, that we might as well be living in Texas,' she complained.

'Okay, where do you want to start?' Kip asked.

'Let's go to the beach this afternoon,' she suggested.

'The beach? Hell, we go to the beach all the time,' he protested.

'Not on the base . . . in town.'

They bypassed Giorgioimpopuli Beach because it was open only to those who could afford to pay ten pounds a season for a bathing cabin and was thus frequented mostly by Libyan and British minor officials. Tess wanted to see what it was like on a truly public beach. She found it crowded with Italian families and Arab men with their children. Because of religious constraints, Arab women were never permitted to go to the beach, and it was strange to see the multitudes of children being cared for efficiently by their fathers alone. Tess loved it, finding it far more interesting than the beach on the base, which was restricted to the American military personnel.

Kip stopped worrying about his office and his career and became again the man with whom she had fallen in love. On leave he was kind, warm, and considerate. They

301

made love in their comfortable bed at night, and during the days, explored the city of Tripoli or drove to Sabratha and Leptis Magna to explore the Roman ruins. Occasionally they left Skippy at home with Pina while they meandered through the Old City, visiting the dark little shops and bargaining for trinkets with the friendly proprietors, who relished the haggling and felt cheated if one paid the asking price. Tess was impressed with the warmth and friendliness of the Libyans.

One day they climbed to the top of the battlements of the old castle, where a couple of ancient, rusty cannon jutted out of its walls, and stood gazing out over the harbor.

'I wonder if those cannon ever fired on the US Navy,' Kip commented, reminding Tess that it was there that Tripoli corsairs had succeeded in capturing an American warship. 'The *Philadelphia* ran aground right near here, trying to get close enough to fire on these very stone fortifications.'

'Tell me about it,' Tess urged. 'I was never very good at remembering historical events.'

'Well, as I recall, Stephen Decatur – '

'Oh, yes, "My country-right-or-wrong Decatur,"' she interjected.

'That was him,' Kip continued. 'Well, he sneaked into the harbor one night and burned the ship right under the pasha's nose. That wasn't the end of it, though. The war went on for a couple more years.'

'How long ago did it happen?' she asked.

'Early nineteenth century.'

'It seems strange that so much of what we learn as history involves battles and wars,' Tess observed, looking out at the lime-washed buildings of the sleepy city.

'That's particularly true at the Academy. I guess

because it's the business we're in. If you don't understand history, you're bound to repeat it, right?'

'But men never do seem to learn, do they?' she remarked, and then quickly changed the subject before they could get into an argument. 'The Wives' Club will soon be starting the restoration of the cemetery where the American marines are buried.' And suddenly her thoughts were again on death and on Chili. The passage of time had not dimmed her sorrow, and she still harbored a depressing feeling that the matter was not over and done with. She wondered if all suicides left such a thick residue of uneasiness.

'Kip, what's happened to Gamal? Has anyone ever heard from him?'

'Let's not ruin our day by bringing up that stuff. It's ancient history, Tess.'

'But I want to know. It's an unfinished chapter in my life. Chili died, Gamal left Wheelus, and . . . nothing,' she insisted. 'Nobody talks about them. It's almost as if they never existed.'

'What else is there to say? They're gone from our lives, honey. That's the way things are.'

'Do you think that what happened will have a bad effect on Gamal's career?'

'Has to. There'll always be a certain cloud of suspicion over him, poor devil.'

'But he's still alive, isn't he?' Tess asked bitterly. 'He's not closed up in a box with a hole through his head, is he?'

'Look, I understand how bad you feel about Chili. After all, she was your friend and you liked her, but keep in mind that suicide is a nasty thing to do to your family and your friends. He didn't pull the trigger, honey. She shot herself.'

Tess started back down to the courtyard. She didn't want to argue with Kip, not now, not when they were enjoying each other so much, but he wouldn't let it go.

'Look, honey, in the long run we all have to take responsibility for our own lives, don't we?' he persisted, determined to make his point.

Suddenly the rage that had been festering deep inside her for months exploded in a torrent of anger. 'Well, that's what I always thought, but there seems to be a different rule of thumb for military wives. It's Chili's fault that her husband's career may be damaged, and it's also her own fault if she's miserable enough to kill herself. If everyone is responsible for himself, why are you always telling me how important it is for me to behave properly and be a good military wife to help your career? Why can't you take responsibility for it yourself and let me be the person I really am?'

She was walking fast now, her heart beating rapidly, and every movement she made radiated resentment and pent-up outrage, much to Kip's dismay.

'I thought when we got married we became a team. What was good for me was good for us all, you, me, and Skippy. If I succeed, we all succeed,' he said softly, crushed by her words and her anger.

The words had no sooner escaped her lips than Tess was sorry for what she had said. She loved Kip, she wanted to be a good wife to him, a good mother to Skippy.

She stopped and turned to him. 'Of course we do, Kip. I'm sorry to be such a bitch. I guess it's being pregnant. Come on, we have a little while until it's time for Skippy to wake up from his nap. Let's stop at the Corso café and have a beer before we go home.'

For once she had said all the right things, and Kip was

pleased. Although he had been trained at the Academy never to display affection in public, he couldn't resist putting his arm around her and holding her close to his side as they strolled out of the Old City. Tess was a hell of a woman, he thought with pride. It was just going to take a while for her to get used to being a service wife, but someday she'd be a terrific general's lady.

Late that night Tess lay sleepless in her husband's arms. It was the first week of Ramadan, and although she could occasionally hear a few drums and the shrill high pipes in a minor key, they were not loud enough to keep her awake. Beth had said that living in town during the month-long Moslem fasting period was a sleepless nightmare, because of the all-night din. During Ramadan, the faithful of Islam were permitted nothing to eat or drink, nor could they have sex during the hours between dawn and sundown, and so the nights were filled with feasting and music and celebration. Tess wondered if the Arab ear found Western music as odd and atonal as she found Eastern music.

Comfortable though it was living on the base, Tess had actually missed living in the city. She felt isolated from the culture of the Libyans, surrounded by everything American, and yet she knew it was more secure and better for Skippy. She was still suspicious of Masters' motive for having moved them ahead of other officers on the waiting list. He wasn't the kind of man who did favors out of the goodness of his heart.

A small ripple in her abdomen made her aware of her pregnancy. It was the first time she had detected the baby's movement. Saying a prayer that this baby would be as healthy and as beautiful as Skippy, she turned over and contentedly fell asleep, but it was not restful slumber. In her dreams, she could hear Chili calling out to her

305

from the grave, begging her to help her, but no matter how fast she ran or far she went, Tess could not seem to reach her. It was the first time she'd had that dream since the week Chili died.

47

There was never a spoken decision that Sam would live at her parents' house; it just happened in the natural course of events. Time passed, and David and Melinda were so happy and content with the arrangement that Sam hesitated to make any move that might upset their lives again.

As her children settled comfortably into their new home, her parents seemed to grow younger. The presence of grandchildren in their lives had given them a fresh outlook and hope. For the first time in his life, Jules Silverman dreaded going to the office, begrudging every moment he was away from the children. He left late in the morning and returned early in the afternoon.

One day when he had come home at three, they were having a drink and Sam suggested he might think about retiring.

'Dad, there's really no reason for you to keep dragging yourself to that office every day. I'm sure you can find someone who could run the place under your direction, or better yet, why don't you put the studio up for sale?'

'That's a good question, sweetheart. I keep asking it myself, but I don't seem to have any good answers. Something inside me just keeps saying no. If I sell it, Silverstone Studios will be gone from our lives. It won't be there for David or Melinda . . . or you.'

'Me?' she asked in astonishment. 'Why would you need to hang on to it for me?'

'You don't realize it, but you're bored stiff hanging around this house all the time. Don't deny it; I've been watching you. You know the kids will be in school all day next year – then what are you going to do? Lunch with your girlfriends? Go shopping?'

'I've got to be here for the children, Dad. Being a mother is a full-time job.'

'Yeah, yeah, maybe it was when you lived in Tripoli, but it isn't here. The kids are surrounded by people to take care of them. Besides the servants, there's Margaret, and don't forget your mother and me. You don't have to cook or shop for groceries, you don't have to wash their socks or iron their clothes. You just have to be there when they need you, and you gotta admit that's not very often nowadays. Give 'em a little room to grow. The truth of it is, you need them a hell of a lot more than they need you right now.'

'That's not true!' she protested.

'Oh, yes it is, honey, and be thankful for it. You want them to grow up independent and self-reliant, don't you? Come on, you need to step out and start living your own life. You can't mourn forever. What do you say? Come to the office with me tomorrow and take a look. I'll teach you everything I know, and then I'll get out of your way. Is it a deal?'

'I don't think so, Dad. It's too all-consuming. Your whole life was wrapped up in that studio. You never played golf, you never had time to travel. I don't think I could live like that.'

'So don't! It'll be your show. Run it any way you want. That's what I did. Hell, I didn't play golf, because I didn't want to. I didn't travel much because I really hate being away from the comforts of my own home. I went to the office because that was where I was happy, understand? Now I come home because that's what I want to do. Sweetheart, the greatest blessing the good Lord can bestow is to make you happy at your work. If I hadn't had that, I don't think I could have survived losing David . . . and then almost losing you.'

'I really don't know that much about the business, Dad. I'm not sure . . .'

'Listen, I can tell you the secret. The whole damn secret of the movie industry – any kind of entertainment, in fact – can be summed up in two little words. "Nobody knows."'

'Nobody knows? What does that mean?'

'Well, when Abe, rest his soul, and I started in this business, everything was so new and exciting that the public was happy with almost anything we dished out. It was almost impossible to make an unprofitable movie, the audience was so hungry. But things are changing, not just because of television, but because the audience is getting choosier. It's tough nowadays to predict what they're gonna go for, and anybody who says he knows is, pardon the expression, full of shit. Nobody knows.'

'Let me think about it, Dad.'

'First you gotta come to the studio and see what it's really like. Then, as they say, make an informed decision,' he said, his eyes twinkling with humor. He was virtually certain he had won her over.

Everyone was surprised to see Sam appear at the breakfast table the next morning dressed in a trim gray suit instead of her usual silk robe. Everyone, that is, except Jules.

'Where are you going, Mommy?' Melinda asked.

'I'm going to the office with Grandpa. He's offered me a job there. Is that okay with you?'

'Are you going to make movies?' David asked curiously.

'I don't know, honey, but I'm thinking about it. You

309

wouldn't mind if I went to the office every day like Grandpa does?'

David shrugged his shoulders and then turned to Jules to pursue a more interesting subject. 'Grandpa, are we going up to the ranch this afternoon? I promised Maybelle I'd bring her some carrots and sugar cubes.'

'Didn't I promise you?' Jules responded, smiling at the little boy. 'If it's okay with your mama, maybe we can go for the weekend and take a little ride on Maybelle in the morning. Whatta you say, Mama?' Jules asked his daughter.

'Can I go too, Mommy, please? I want to feed Maybelle some carrots too,' Melinda pleaded.

'Not this time, honey. David is going with Grandpa alone.'

'That's too bad,' Reba said. 'Would it be all right for Melinda to go if I go with them?'

'Since when did you like going to the ranch in Malibu, Mom? You always said it was too rustic,' Sam protested.

'Oh, that was before your father had the place completely remodeled. Now that we have all those beautiful new bathrooms and that modern kitchen, I enjoy going there. Besides, it's a great place for the children.'

'Well, maybe I should go too,' Sam suggested, reluctant to let the children be away from her overnight.

'You'll be busy at the office, sweetheart. Besides, just for a change, let us have the kids alone for a weekend, will you?' Jules asked. 'I'll have Kendon drive us, and if they get homesick for you, we'll come right home, no matter what time it is. If you'd feel better about it, we'll take Margaret along too. She's a very good rider, you know.'

Reluctantly Sam gave her permission, and she and her father left for the office.

As Jules's limousine drove them through the gates of Silverstone Studios, Sam waved to Harry, the guard who had worked there for more than twenty years. They alighted at the entrance to the long single-story building that had housed the executive offices since the studio was built in the early thirties. Unlike some of the other movie moguls, Jules had kept the studio overhead reasonably low. Now that the business was in a slump, his past thrift was paying dividends. Jules had been able to cut back on expenses and keep the studio going while others were sinking under their own weight.

The long narrow hallway's beige walls were adorned with framed one-sheet posters of the movies that had been made by Silverstone. So, by walking from one end of the corridor to the other, one was able to get a complete history of the studio. As Sam followed her father, her life too seemed to flash before her eyes.

Laughing Ladies had been released the summer of her sweet-sixteen party, and all of her friends had been invited to the premiere. *Change Partners* had opened at Radio City Music Hall, and she had gone to New York with David and her parents for the opening. She remembered the Rockettes dancing on the stage, and taking the boat to see the Statue of Liberty. The World's Fair was in full swing, and although she only vaguely recalled the trylon and the perisphere, she clearly remembered seeing Eleanor Holm swing in Billy Rose's Aquacade, because she returned home and began taking water ballet lessons immediately. She had become a strong swimmer because of that show, and she still was.

Sam's steps slowed as she looked more closely at each poster. There was *Summer Clouds*, the film that was made during the war and was released just before David went into the service, and right next to it was hung the poster for *Storm in the Sky*, the film she was working on when she met Bob.

She took a deep, shuddering breath as her eyes focused on the colorful illustration of a young aviator waving from his plane. God, would the pain never go away? Would every reminder of her dead husband hurt like a knife thrust deep into her soul?

She tore her eyes from the poster and hurried forward. She must not let the memory of Bob invariably fill her with sadness. She owed him more than that. He had met life with a smile, and she must try to do the same.

Stopping at Golda's desk, Sam greeted her father's secretary. Other movie tycoons might have gorgeous long-limbed starlets gracing their front offices, but not Jules. Not Reba's Jules, any way. Reba herself had chosen her husband's secretary, and Golda had served him well for twenty years. She had never misplaced or forgotten a message, nor had anyone ever gotten to her boss unless she permitted it. Short, round, and plain, Golda wore expensive dark suits and comfortable shoes. The only jewelry she wore was the pearl earrings Reba had given her long ago, and she wore them every day. She never took a vacation. She had bought Jules's loyalty early on by asking for a bonus instead of a vacation because she loved her job and hated to travel. It was a sentiment close to her employer's heart.

Golda got up from her desk and approached Sam with her arms open for a hug. Tears of joy filled the woman's eyes, now almost hidden behind thick glasses. Jules's children had been the substitute for a family she had never had.

'Samara, darling! I can hardly believe it. You're here. You're here at last,' she said, patting Sam affectionately. 'When Jules first told me you were coming to work, I

312

thought he was having delusions. What would a nice girl like you want with a business like this? But, God bless you, here you are, just like your father said.'

Sam looked over Golda's shoulder and narrowed her eyes at her father. 'When did Dad tell you I was coming to work, Golda?'

'Let me think,' Golda said, frowning. 'It must have been the week after you came back to Los Angeles with the children. Yes, I'm sure it was that week, because I made a note of it on my calendar. And now, here you are.'

Jules tried to avoid Sam's eyes. 'Yes, well, Dad's a very persuasive man, as you know, Golda. He's made a living out of getting people to do what he wants them to,' she commented dryly.

'Come, come. Let me show you your office. The decorators just finished it yesterday,' Golda said eagerly, throwing all caution to the winds and taking Sam's arm to lead her to the office across the hall.

Jules followed at a distance and watched as Golda opened the door to reveal the beautifully and lavishly done office with pale beige walls, authentic classical furniture, and thick tweed wall-to-wall carpeting. Everything was in place and perfectly done, with a regal and imposing Biedermeier desk dominating the room.

Sam turned and looked at her father. For a long time their eyes were locked in a stare that was so heavy with meaning that it was almost as if a shaft of light connected them.

'This is Uncle Abe's office. I thought you were never going to let anyone use it, Dad. Why me?'

'We had an agreement. David was supposed to get the office of whichever one of us went first. It's just you now, instead of David. It's fine with Abe. Trust me,' he said with a twinkle in his eye. 'I still talk to him, you know. He may be in heaven, but he still needs my advice.'

Sam linked her arm into her father's and kissed him on the cheek. 'Okay, you've got me here, but from now on, no more secrets, and no more manipulating . . . of me, anyway. If I'm going to be of any use to you, I have to know what's going on.'

'No more secrets, sweetheart. Now, go sit in that chair and try it out for size. Isn't that desk something? I don't mind telling you it cost me a fortune. Now, sit. I've got the still photographers coming in to take pictures of you and the desk. Publicity is putting out a press release.'

'It's too soon, Dad, it's way too soon,' she protested.

'Hey, calm down. All we're going to say is that you're coming in as my executive assistant, that's all. No promises, no predictions. We've got to get the word out that you're going to be an executive so you'll be treated accordingly.'

'Why do we have to make an announcement of that?'

'Because, honey, there are no women in the higher levels of this business. One of these pipsqueak producers might ask you to get him a cup of coffee, and then I'd have to fire the son of a bitch. Okay?'

'Okay, Dad.'

'Good, and so that's your lesson for today. Nobody has any power in this industry until it's announced in the trade papers. Sit down. There's a production schedule for the next six months on your desk. Look it over and tell me what you think.'

'How can I tell what to think if I haven't read any of the scripts?'

Jules smiled. 'That's why I'm taking the kids to Malibu this weekend. You'll have lots of peace and quiet at the house. Be sure to take that pile of manuscripts home with you. And don't forget to take notes. We'll talk when I get back.' He turned abruptly and left her, closing the door behind him.

Alone in her new office, Sam swiveled back and forth in the leather chair, opened the desk and looked at the pens and pencils neatly arranged in the top drawer, scanned the rows of buttons on her telephone, and sighed. It was time to get to work, she decided, and picked up the top script to start reading.

48

Beth and Joe sat across from one another in the dining
room of their apartment, silently eating the dinner she
had painstakingly prepared. For the past few months all
her energies had been devoted solely to housekeeping,
cooking, and caring for their young daughter, Angela, as
Beth withdrew from the world to the security of her own
little nest. As children so often do, Angela gave voice to
the stress in the house.

'Mommy, how come you never talk to Daddy anymore?' she asked.

'Wherever did you get such a funny idea, honey? Your
mother and I talk all the time,' Joe responded.

'Not like you used to. Mommy never laughs anymore,'
the little girl insisted.

Beth and Joe looked up at each other, and both smiled
uncertainly. Angela was speaking a truth that both were
too honest to deny.

'Angela, honey, remember when Mommy's friend
died? Well, she's had a hard time getting over that. It's
going to take her a while.'

Angela looked perplexed. 'How come, Mom? Didn't
she go to heaven?'

Beth finally spoke up. 'Sweetheart, sometimes people
die under circumstances that are not . . . well, natural. If
she really died the way everybody said she did, then no,
I'm afraid my friend didn't go to heaven. She couldn't.
She'd be in purgatory, I suppose.'

'Because she killed herself, huh? And Father Cavanaugh says that's a mortal sin, isn't it? Are you praying for her soul, Mommy?'

Beth's eyes filled with tears. 'Yes, I am, darling, and maybe it would help if you'd include her in your prayers too.'

Angela, who was a beautiful little girl, angelic as her name, nodded her head up and down vigorously. 'I'll do it tonight. Maybe then you'll start laughing again.'

Later that evening, when their daughter was asleep, Joe went to the couch in the living room, where Beth was curled up reading, and moved her legs to make room for him to sit down.

'Honey, this brooding of yours has got to stop at some point. Can't you see what effect it's having on all of us? When a child as young as Angela notices, it must be pretty obvious.'

Beth turned away from her husband. She couldn't bring herself to look him in the eyes anymore.

Without responding to his question, Beth changed the subject, as she always did nowadays. In the first few weeks after she had found Chili's body, she had wept and she had raised issues, but when it did no good, she had capitulated and lapsed into silence. Joe refused to see her side of the story, and she was not sure she could forgive him for kowtowing to the powers that be.

'Have our orders been cut yet?' she asked.

'You know they haven't, Beth. Why do you keep on asking? There's no way we're going to get out of this place any sooner. We have at least three more months before my tour is up, and we'll be lucky to leave then. Masters will never let me go until my replacement arrives.'

'I just want to go home, that's all. I need to see my family.'

Joe put his head in his hands. He felt like such an abysmal failure in life. First, he had failed to make the grade as a pilot, and now he had failed Beth, and she was never going to forgive him for not standing by her.

Beth turned back to her book. There was no point in talking about their situation anymore. Joe had allowed her to be dismissed as a hysterical woman when she had gone to Colonel Channing to tell him about the letter Chili had left in her quarters before she killed herself. The Colonel had told her no such letter existed. She insisted that she had seen it and demanded that an investigation be made, but Major Carson had called Joe into his office and assured him that nothing of the kind had been found. He convinced Joe that Beth's mind had been affected by the shock of finding her friend's body, and since it had been only her word against all of theirs, she, of course, had not been believed by anybody . . . not even her husband. And for that, she could not forgive him.

'I know, Beth, that it's hard for you to accept the idea that Chili killed herself, and I understand that. After all, I'm a Catholic too. Suicide is a crime against God, and you don't want her to be guilty of that. In a way, it's more acceptable to believe there was some kind of foul play or cover-up, but – '

'Joe, for God's sake, don't start hammering me with that stuff again! Every time I see Father Cavanaugh, he tells me the same thing, and I'm sick to death of hearing it. He doesn't believe I saw a letter, and neither do you. But it doesn't matter, not anymore. I know what I saw, and I also know in my heart of hearts that there was something in that letter that caused it to disappear,

318

something that somebody wanted kept secret. I wish to God that I had either read all of it or none of it, because I think about it all the time. In the middle of the night I wake up and see that letter. I shut my eyes and try to read the words on the page in my head, but I can barely remember anything about it except that it was addressed to somebody named Jimmyjoe . . . or something like that. Every night before I go to sleep, I pray for the memory of that piece of paper to fade from my mind, but it never does,' Beth said emotionally, and then the energy seemed to drain away, and she muttered, 'And it probably never will.'

Joe had heard about Beth's obsession with that letter over and over and over, and he was growing weary of his wife's obstinacy. 'What do you expect of me, dammit?' he burst out angrily. 'You want me to cause a stink and get myself in trouble? Is that what you want? Well, I can't do it. This is the Air Force, Beth. When the commanding officer tells you to shut up, you shut, if you know what's good for you.'

'Is the Air Force more important than your immortal soul, Joe?' she asked coldly.

'Of course not, but it's what I do, Beth. Can't you understand that? It's what I am. Sure I'd like to have the freedom to tell anybody who disagrees with me to go to hell, but I don't. Without the Air Force, I'm a guy without a job, and you know I'm not just anybody who can go somewhere and fill out an application and get hired. Oh, yeah, Joe Cellini – wasn't his father that mobster? Stay away from him. We don't want hoods like that around here.' He spat the words bitterly. 'I've got to stay in the service, Beth. I told you that before we got married. It's the only place where I can be a normal person, where I'll be judged on my own merits, where nobody cares who I

319

am or who my father was. I can't ever go back to my family, you know that. Would you want Angela dragged into that mess back there? Would you want a life like my mother had?' His anguish was passionate and heartfelt, and when the torrent of emotional words ended, he covered his eyes to hide unbidden tears.

Beth reached out and gently stroked the back of his bowed head. 'Joe, listen to me for once, will you? Listen to my words. I never asked you to do anything except believe me, but you wouldn't. You ganged up with everyone else, trying to make me think I was imagining things. Why was it so hard to believe that I read part of a letter that Chili had written the day before she died, and that it mysteriously disappeared?'

'What kind of a man would I be if I believed something like that and then stood by and did nothing?'

'Just a human being, Joe. No more. No less,' she replied, pulling his head onto her shoulder and comforting him. She had never seen him cry before.

49

Tess awakened in the middle of the night with severe abdominal pains. Although they did not feel the same as her usual heartburn, she reached for the tall blue bottle of Amphogel she kept on her nightside table and took a long swallow. Ordinarily it was like dousing a fire with cool water, but this time it didn't have any effect.

She rolled over on her other side and curled her knees up to her abdomen, since she had the bed to herself. Kip was away on TDY again. Suddenly she felt another sharp crack of pain that stabbed her in the small of the back and then radiated down into her groin. She gasped with pain, and immediately she knew what was happening. God help her, she was in labor, and she was all alone in the house with Skippy!

She wanted to turn on the light but was afraid it might awaken him. He'd been going through a restless phase that seemed to be worse when his father was away from home. Although she would have liked to get out of bed and stretch the crick in her back, walking was the last thing she should do. Perhaps if she could remain calm and serene, the contractions would go away. She was only twenty-nine weeks into her pregnancy, and it was too soon, much, much too soon. If the baby were born now, it would be too young to survive. Closing her eyes, she wrapped her arms around the baby inside her belly and began to talk soothingly to it.

'Not yet, sweetie, not yet. You have to wait a few weeks more. Please, please settle down and go to sleep like a good little baby. You can't come out yet,' she crooned, hoping and praying that she could stop the contractions by sheer force of will.

Suddenly the pain was there again, this time not so sharp. This time it started slowly, gradually intensifying until it wrapped around her and threatened to squeeze the life force out of her. She wanted to scream, but she did not dare, because Skippy's crib was right next to the bed. She had to call someone quickly. She needed help.

When the pain subsided, she sat up and swung her legs to the floor. She moved slowly, supporting her abdomen with her hands so as not to jostle the child inside any more than necessary. She crept toward the telephone, which was in the living room. Her steps were measured and slow, but her mind was racing in panic. She had no idea whom to call. Beth lived in town, too far away. She needed someone immediately.

God, how could this have happened to her? She'd been so careful about resting and taking things easy since Kip had left. Although she had been upset and angry when she found out he was going, she had resigned herself to being alone for two days, but the two days had stretched to four. Jesus Christ, why was he never there when she needed him?

She groped for the light switch in the hallway, trying to think of a name . . . someone nearby who could come to her aid quickly. Marilee? No, she was alone with her six kids. Frank was in Cyprus. Desperately she tried to think, but she couldn't focus, because the pain was engulfing her once more, erasing everything from her mind except its agony. She reached out to grab onto the back of a chair to steady herself, but in the darkness she missed and, losing her balance, fell hard onto the bare concrete floor. A scream for help exploded from deep inside her, piercing

322

the night and awakening Skippy, who began to cry for his mother. Oh, God, what was she going to do?

As the pain faded, hysteria took its place. 'Hold on, hold on,' she gasped, pulling herself to her knees. Afraid to stand up again, she crawled across the room on her hands and knees and pulled herself up onto the couch. She picked up the telephone and dialed Beth. She was far away, but she'd do something to help her.

Joe answered the telephone, but all he could hear was heavy breathing.

'Who the hell is this?' he demanded impatiently.

'It's . . . me . . . Tess. I need help,' she gasped, her voice strangled with panic.

'Tess?' he asked, but suddenly the telephone was snatched from his hand and Beth's voice came on the line.

'What's wrong, Tess?'

The pain was coming again, this time harder and faster. 'I'm in labor . . . I'm all alone . . . with Skippy.'

Beth snapped at Joe, 'Get the car,' and then reassured Tess. 'We'll be there as fast as we can. Now, just calm down. I'll call someone close by to come stay with you till we get there. You'll be fine. Is that Skippy crying?'

'Yes, I fell, and – '

'You fell? Now, listen, you just let him cry. He'll be okay. Don't you move until someone gets there, understand? And don't you dare pick that boy up, you hear me?'

'Hurry, Beth . . . hurry!'

'Hang up the phone, Tess. Now!' Beth ordered, needing the line to be cleared. Quickly she dialed the hospital and asked to speak to the officer of the day.

'Is it an emergency, ma'am?'

'Yes. There's a woman having a baby prematurely over in Quarters 2A. I need an ambulance and a medic sent

323

over there immediately. Her husband is on TDY and she's alone with her little boy,' Beth shouted, trying but failing to speak in forceful, measured tones.

'Sorry, ma'am. The new CI won't let us order out ambulances for dependents anymore. The request's gotta come from him or a staff physician.'

'Look, I haven't got time to argue with you. Now, please call a doctor and get him to send an ambulance to pick her up right away! Now, do it!'

Beth slammed down the telephone, but she was not satisfied with what she had done. Someone had to go to Tess immediately. Who lived closest? She paged rapidly through the base directory and dialed Nell Carson's number. Nell wasn't the most dependable person in the world, but she was just one row of housing away from Tess.

Nell answered groggily, but she was brought sharply awake by the tone of voice in which Beth barked her orders.

'Get up, Nell. Right now! Tess Kipling's in big trouble. Don't wait to get dressed, just throw on a robe and get over there to her immediately. She's all alone. I haven't got time to talk, just do what I say!'

Nell grabbed a raincoat off the hatrack in the hallway and yelled at her husband. 'Get up and get dressed and meet me over at the Kiplings' quarters. Hurry!'

She dashed out barefoot into the rainy night, ran around the corner, and was banging on the door within minutes of the call, but the door was locked.

Tess heard her and called out, 'I'm coming.'

Skippy was screaming at a high pitch, frightened by the terror he sensed around him.

Tess waited for the pain to subside, and then she got up and made her way to the door. Relieved, she moved

324

faster now that she had someone nearby to help her. She opened the door, and Nell stepped inside.

'My God, Tess. What's wrong?' she asked, snapping on the overhead light so she could see the woman hunched over in front of her.

'I'm . . . in labor,' Tess gasped.

Nell dropped the raincoat and moved toward her. She put her arm around her and helped her to the couch. 'Come on, now, relax. It'll be okay. My husband will be here in a minute, and we'll get you over to the hospital. Hang on, now.' Her words were reassuring.

'It's too early,' Tess moaned. 'The baby can't be born yet.'

'It'll be just fine. You're probably only havin' false labor pains, the way I always did. As soon as we get you to the hospital, they'll probably stop. Now, you just sit down right beside me and get yourself together for a minute. Try to calm down . . . everything's gonna be just fine.'

Nell Carson kept her arms around the frightened young woman until Howard walked in the door. Without preamble Nell called out, 'Howard, bring the car around to the front door. We gotta get her to the hospital *subito presto*. Now, move it!'

Major Howard Carson knew better than to question his wife in a crisis. He was out the door and back with the car in less than two minutes. 'All set,' he said.

'Honey, it's rainin' somethin' terrible outside, so I'm gonna wrap this coat around you. Now, Howard and I are gonna help you to the car, and he's gonna drive you right over to the hospital, where they'll take good care of you and your baby.' Her tone of voice was calm and her words were reassuring.

They were a strange sight as the three hobbled down

325

the walkway: Nell Carson, in her bare feet and sheer nightgown, getting soaked to the skin, Tess doubled over in pain and fear, and Howard Carson, clad only in his uniform pants and a sweater, with the rain skidding down his shiny bald head.

As Nell settled the miserable young woman into the front seat of the car, Tess looked up at her and said, 'Nell . . . don't forget Skippy.'

'How could I, with all that noise he's making in there? But don't you worry. I'll take good care of him,' and before another word could be said, Major Carson put the old Ford into gear and drove away.

Half an hour later, Beth and Joe arrived to find Tess's quarters dark and empty. They hurried to talk to Nell, who briefed them while she held Skippy. The little boy had stopped crying and was happily eating a cookie. The Cellinis immediately headed for the hospital, which was only five minutes away.

Beth was furious. 'Can you believe that? The ambulance never came! We could all die as far as that jackass Stark cares.'

'I don't know what we can do about it. Masters doesn't care for him particularly, but doctors are almost above the law in the military, honey, and even the base commander is afraid to take him on. Stark says that the hospital's mission is to care for the men in uniform, and the dependents are here at their own risk.'

'That's a shitty attitude!' she said in disgust, using a word her husband had never heard her say before.

Inside the hospital the airman at the front desk told them that Tess had been admitted immediately and was already in the care of the duty officer.

'Where's Dr Pepperman . . . the obstetrician?' Beth asked.

326

'He and his wife are on vacation. I think they're in Switzerland skiing.'

'Oh, dear God, no!' Beth moaned, pulling her ever-present rosary from her coat pocket.

'Who's the duty officer?' Joe asked.

The airman consulted his chart and then replied, 'I think it's Dr Morgan.'

Before the name had fully escaped his lips, Beth whirled and faced her husband. 'Joe! He's a urologist! What does he know about babies?'

'Look, he's a physician. Surely he's delivered babies before – ' he began, but she interrupted him.

'But this isn't a normal delivery . . . Tess is more than two months early. He needs to do something to stop the labor, not help it along. Dear God, can't we do something?'

Joe put his arm around his wife. She was weeping with anger and frustration, and he felt that he had to act. He couldn't just stand by and let a baby die. After a few moments of hard thinking, he turned to the airman and asked him for a roster of the doctors assigned to the hospital.

'I'm sorry, sir. I can't give you that information.'

'Then get Colonel Stark on the telephone for me.'

'It's against hospital regulations, sir. I'm only allowed to contact the colonel at the request of one of the physicians. Dr Morgan is in charge of the hospital now.'

'Call Brick Masters!' Beth asked her husband.

Joe looked at his wife. 'What am I going to say to him? Be sensible, Beth. He's not going to interfere with the medical decisions here . . . he can't. He'll just get pissed off at me for making him look helpless.'

Frustrated, Beth whirled around and snapped at the airman, 'Where's a telephone I can use?' And following his direction, she marched over to a desk behind him and dialed a number.

'Who are you calling?' Joe asked.

'I'm calling Veronica Masters.'

'Don't – ' Joe began but was silenced by the determination on his wife's face. Clearly there was no way that he could stop her.

Brick Masters answered the telephone.

'Colonel Masters? This is Beth Cellini. I need to talk to your wife. It's an emergency.'

As soon as Veronica was on the line, Beth gave her a quick rundown on the situation. When she finished, Veronica said, 'Look, it's probably not going to do any good, but I'll give Colonel Stark a call and ask him to check it out and make sure Captain Morgan can handle the situation. It looks bad, though, Beth. The hospital has an incubator, but I'm not sure if it's ever even been used. You better prepare yourself for the fact that if she gives birth tonight, the baby probably won't make it.'

'I'm prepared for it, Veronica, but Tess sure as the devil isn't.'

Beth went back to Joe, and they sat down on the couch in the waiting room. Joe put his arm around her, and they settled down for what they expected to be a long night. The wait turned out to be much shorter than they expected.

By the time Tess had reached the hospital, she was dilated too much for the progress of the labor to be halted. The baby was already in transition, and it was even too late to administer an anesthetic. Within minutes, Tess gave birth to a two-pound, one-ounce boy.

There was much excitement and scurrying about by the nurses, readying the incubator, suctioning the fluid from the baby's mouth and trying to get him to breathe on his own. Dr Morgan also had his hands full, because Tess was hemorrhaging heavily and was on the verge of going into shock.

Luckily, Colonel Stark responded to Veronica's plea and arrived on the scene, where his help and support were desperately needed. Stark attended to the needs of the baby while Morgan worked on Tess. The hospital was staffed and equipped only for routine medical situations, not for emergencies. The policy had been to send high-risk patients to Germany, where the Air Force had established large medical centers. Unfortunately for Tess, there had not been time to make that evaluation.

Dr Morgan was able to stop Tess's hemorrhaging. Although she was weak from the loss of blood, her vital signs began to stabilize. One hour after he was born, Tess's baby died.

When the airman at the desk received the news and passed it on to the Cellinis, Beth immediately went to the telephone to call Veronica to ask for further help.

'Veronica, Tess's baby only lived for an hour. I think you should ask your husband to get Lieutenant Kipling back here as fast as he can. His wife needs him more than the Air Force needs him to be wherever the hell he is.'

Veronica replied, 'There's not much that can be done until the weather in Frankfurt clears enough for the flights to take off, but I'll ask Brick to check into it. Please tell Tess that I'm very sorry.'

Weighed down by defeat and again frustrated by her inability to help a friend in distress, Beth went into Joe's arms to weep, not only for Tess and her lost child but also for all the lonely ladies whose destinies were charted by their husbands' careers in the military.

There was no one to hold and comfort Tess.

50

Sam and her father were at odds again. Ever since she had started working at Silverstone, they found themselves disagreeing about almost everything. She couldn't make a decision without having to justify it with facts, figures, and research, and he challenged her every recommendation. At first she hadn't minded, because she was new to the business and learning, but now it just didn't make sense to her, especially in view of the success she'd had in choosing scripts for production.

Lady Light, the first picture made under her supervision, had been brought in on schedule and under budget, and had recouped expenses in four weeks of release. Although it hadn't been a smash hit, it had been well-reviewed and reasonably profitable. The second film she had chosen was *The Lucky Ones*, and although it had not yet been released, its modest budget almost guaranteed that it too would not lose money.

When Sam had started, she'd had no idea how much about the business she had absorbed through the years of living in her father's house, but as the months passed, she realized that she was either a very fast study or had taken in a great deal throughout her childhood. The business fascinated her so thoroughly that she often had to remind herself to go home to be with her children more.

She sat across the desk from Jules Silverman, and they glared at each other. 'You're wrong, Dad. Dead wrong. Television is not a fad, it's the future, and we better make friends with it or the networks are going to eat us alive.'

'They're the enemy, Samara. And when you get in bed with the enemy, you can damn well be sure you're gonna get screwed.' His words were harsh, but there was a twinkle in his eye as he said them.

'It's going to happen, Dad, believe me. Sooner or later, one of the studios is going to break down and begin selling their films to television. They're not going to hold out forever. *Lady Light* is a small film that would work very well on TV, and they've offered us a terrific price for it,' she pleaded.

'I've given my word, Samara. I can't go back on it. Now, how is the advertising campaign going for *Timesteps*?'

'Not good. Nobody can get a handle on the picture. They don't seem to know where the audience is.'

'What are these words? I don't understand that kind of thinking. The audience is out there. Pick a campaign that tells what kind of picture it is, that's all there is to it.'

Sam sighed. She hated to get into an argument with him again, but it was inevitable. Her father just couldn't understand that the market for films was changing.

'Dad, when you and Uncle Abe built this studio, movies were a new and exciting kind of entertainment. It's not that way anymore, and attendance is down because the audience is getting more sophisticated and diverse. We also have more competition for the money the family has to spend on recreation.'

'Make a good picture, the audience will come to see it. It's as simple as that,' he said, closing the discussion. 'Now, I have to leave early today. The circus is in town, and your mother and I are taking David and Melinda. I bought a ticket for you too. How about it?'

David and Melinda had never seen the circus, and Sam wanted to be with them the first time, but she needed to be present at the casting head's meeting with Rosalind Russell's agent. Sam needed to find some way to interest the star in appearing in the film version of *Lover*, a best-selling novel they had just optioned.

'What time does it start?' she asked.

'Seven o'clock, but we have to leave early. I promised to take the children over to Dolores' for hamburgers first.'

Sam laughed. 'Are you kidding? You're going to sit in your limousine at a drive-in and eat hamburgers from a tray stuck on the window?'

'I don't see why not. Every time we pass the place, David wants me to stop. Besides, the french fries are great.'

'You're spoiling the children, Dad. You know that, don't you?'

'I am not,' he declared haughtily. 'Spoiling children means giving them things that make them act bad; it doesn't mean you can't be generous. Besides, David and Melinda are the nicest, most polite kids I've ever seen . . . and that includes you and your brother, rest his soul.'

Sam was touched by her father's ability to mention his lost son with a trace of humor, which would never had been possible without the presence of his grandchildren in his life.

'Is Margaret going too?'

'No, she said she was tired, but I know better. Tonight's the night she watches *I Love Lucy*,' he answered with disgust.

'It's a funny show, Dad.'

'Well, are you going or not?'

'Leave my ticket with Kendon. Have him drop you off and then come back here to pick me up. I may miss the grand parade, but I'll be there. How much should I offer for Roz?'

332

'You found the book and bought it. You decide how much she's worth to the picture.'

'She's worth a lot.'

'Then pay whatever is necessary, not a cent more. See you later, sweetheart.'

Sam went back to her office and spent the afternoon going over the proposed expenditures for the film. This was going to be her first big-budget feature, and she wanted no mistakes.

Late that afternoon her secretary notified her that Rich Wallis wanted to see her. Puzzled, she told her to bring him in. What did he want? He was the head of Galaxy, a new and active young group of artists' agents who had banded together and now collectively represented an impressive roster of stars. She had heard they were tough to deal with.

Quickly Sam checked the mirror in her desk drawer to make sure she looked presentable, and then the door opened and Rich Wallis' presence filled the room. Well, well, she thought, he looks more like a star than most of his clients do. He was tall, very slim, and very tan, with thick blond hair and enormous blue eyes his tortoiseshell glasses could not hide.

He walked gracefully toward her with his hand outstretched and his mouth formed in a smile that revealed perfect white teeth. Good heavens, was he real?

'Hi, Sam . . . isn't that what you're called? I'm Rich Wallis and I thought it was time we met.'

'My friends call me Sam. People I don't know usually call me Mrs Mulhare,' she said icily, taking his hand and wincing at the pressure of his grip.

'Ah, yes. Well, forgive me for being too personal. I feel like I know you.'

'Why?'

'My dear, you're joking. Your influence here at the studio has been written about to exhaustion. Don't you read any of your own press handouts?' he asked, settling himself into the leather chair closest to her desk without waiting to be invited to sit down.

Sam was annoyed and said so. 'Look, Mr Wallis, this is an old-fashioned studio. Our press releases are designed to promote our movies and our stars, not our executives. We are a privately held company, and we need to account to no one.'

He reached into his breast pocket and withdrew a slim gold Cartier cigarette case, opened it, and offered it to her.

She shook her head. 'Thank you. I have my own,' she said, taking a cigarette out of the pack in her desk drawer. Quickly he lighted it with a matching gold lighter before she could do it herself, and then lit his own. Through the smoke haze he squinted and asked, 'What do you think of the researchers who say that cigarettes cause cancer?'

'I hope they're wrong,' she said, feeling awkward. She had taken up smoking during the endless hours of playing bridge while she was an Air Force wife, and although she had often tried to stop in the past year, she hadn't been successful.

'What can I do for you, Mr Wallis?'

'Please call me Rich.'

'Why should I? I hardly know you,' she responded, but with more warmth.

'That's why I'm here. So we can get to know and trust one another.' His smile was radiant and his manner ingratiating.

'That's all well and good, but you're here for a specific reason. Now, why don't you just tell me right out so we can stop wasting time with all this small talk?'

334

'You're much too direct. Every moment of the day doesn't have to be fraught with meaning and accomplishment. I think people need to relax and chat nicely about things like the weather. It makes life more gracious, don't you think?'

He was beginning to exasperate her. 'Yes, I think that's nice at cocktail parties and during dinner, but my hours in the office need to be used for business. Now, is there something you particularly wanted to discuss with me?'

He looked at her quizzically and after a long pause he replied, 'You have the most interesting eyes I've ever seen. Do you know that they give off sparks when you're annoyed?'

'Please get on with it, Mr Wallis. I don't appreciate your sitting here in my office putting me on,' she snapped impatiently.

'Oh, but I'm not putting you on. You're a lovely lady, and nothing like the dragon everybody says you are. Let's have dinner together tonight, shall we?'

'What?' Sam asked in disbelief.

'Dinner . . . at Perino's. I have a regular table there. It's quiet and restful, and we won't have to rush. What do you say?'

Sam stood up to dismiss him. 'Thank you so much for stopping in, Mr Wallis. I'm sorry, but I'm going to the circus with my children tonight. I'm a widow in mourning, and I don't date. Good day.'

He too arose, still sublimely untouched by her curtness. He took her hand and held it in his warm grasp.

'Your husband has been dead for almost two years, lovely lady. Come, let me take you out into the world again.'

'I am in the real world, Mr Wallis, but I suspect you're not. You still haven't told me why you're here.'

Snapping his fingers and looking surprised, he said, 'I haven't, have I? Well, please sit down and I'll tell you.'

'I prefer to stand. Please keep it short. This won't be a long meeting.'

'If that's the way you want it. I represent Laura Huston. You're aware of her work?'

Sam nodded, now interested.

'Well, she's read the Sylvia Maxwell book you just bought, and she wants to play the part of Morgana. She'd be perfect for it.'

'I'm sorry, but Rosalind Russell has already been approached, and I'm meeting with her agent to discuss it today.'

'She won't do it, and if her agent is any good at all, he won't let her,' he replied.

'Why not?' Sam asked, not aware that they had both resumed their seats.

'Because the audience won't accept her in that part. Everybody loves her, and Morgana has a dark side that brings tragedy to everyone around her.'

'You read the book?'

'Of course I read it. What kind of an agent do you think I am?'

'You're probably a very good one,' she conceded, interested in his observations and suspecting that he might very well be right.

'Then you'll have dinner with me?' he asked, and the impertinence was back in his voice.

'Not tonight.'

'Tomorrow night?'

'Tomorrow night,' she agreed with barely a moment's hesitation.

With that, he got to his feet, shook her hand, and left

the room quickly, saying only, 'I'll have my secretary call your secretary in the morning and make the arrangements.'

Later that afternoon, in her discussion with Rosalind Russell's agent, they both agreed that the part was not right for the star, and the agent praised Sam for her insight and sensitivity. Feeling slightly guilty at hearing herself echo Rich Wallis' own words, she accepted his compliments. On the way to the circus that evening, she felt a joy and elation that had been missing in her life since Bob had died, but she tried very hard not to credit it to the handsome young man she had met that afternoon.

51

Tess was not told that her baby had died. Because neither of the doctors wanted her to find out while she was weak and exhausted from the labor and the loss of blood, she had simply been given an injection of a sedative and put to sleep. The charge nurse in the women's ward was told that when Tess awakened and asked for her baby, she was to be given no information until a doctor was summoned to tell her the painful truth.

As the sun began to light the horizon that morning, Tess came slowly to consciousness. Her body felt heavy, so heavy that she could not lift her arms or even turn her head. Through partially open eyes, her lids heavy, she saw in the half-light that she was not in her own bed. Where was she? Suddenly the crisis of the night before sprang into sharp focus, and she remembered being rushed to hospital and hearing the muffled and anxious talk of the people around her. Vaguely she recalled the tumult in the delivery room and the shadowy figures rushing about holding a baby. As the ghostly memories closed in on her, her heart began to beat rapidly and both hands sprang to her abdomen to probe and search vainly for the swelling that would reassure her that the baby was still inside her and that everything had been a dreadful nightmare.

A terrible awareness seeped into her being as blood from a wound oozes through the bandage and stains it bright red. She had lost the baby. Why hadn't someone told her?

338

Without lifting her head or moving her body, she heard a whimpering sound that grew in intensity, and when it became a torrent of despairing tears, she realized the sound was coming from deep inside her. She was sobbing hysterically when the nurse finally heard her and rushed to her side.

'Are you all right, Mrs Kipling?' she asked, reaching for her arm to check her pulse.

Hearing a stranger's voice, Tess began talking rapidly between sobs. When the nurse finally interpreted the jumbled, hysterical words to mean that Tess knew her baby was dead, she left her and summoned the physician on duty. The young doctor, who had entered the service directly from his internship, saw that Tess was hysterical and ordered her sedated immediately.

When the medication took effect, he asked the nurse how she had found out the baby had died.

'I have no idea. When I came on duty this morning, she was still out. The next thing I knew, she was crying and screaming that her baby was dead. Personally, I think it was a mistake not to tell her the truth. She needs to know,' the nurse remarked.

'You're probably right, but Colonel Stark himself wrote those orders, and I certainly don't intend to countermand them. There's not much we can do for her anyway. She needs her husband. Why the hell can't they get him back here to take care of her?'

The nurse shook her head. 'It just doesn't seem right. They bring these women over here with all their kids, and then send their husbands flying off to God knows where on TDY, and expect them to cope all by themselves. By the way, she's got a friend sitting outside waiting to see her. Is it okay if I go out and tell her what's going on in here?'

'Fine with me.'

The nurse found Beth, who had not left her vigil in the waiting room, although Joe had gone home to dress and take Angela to school before reporting to the office.

'Are you here for Mrs Kipling?'

'Yes. Can I go in to see her? Is she awake yet?' Beth asked anxiously.

'In a manner of speaking. She figured out by herself that she'd lost the baby, and she fell apart, I'm afraid. We had to sedate her again.'

'Poor Tess!' Beth said, clutching the rosary that had helped her through the night.

'Any news on her husband? She needs him, you know.'

'My husband says his plane took off from Germany this morning. He should be back this afternoon. How long will she be out?'

'Three hours at the most, but I'm sure the doctor would be happy to recommend another injection to prolong – '

'Please don't do that. Let me stay with her until her husband arrives. She'll be much better off if she has someone near her whom she knows and trusts.'

'I'll check, but I'm sure it will be okay. Go get some breakfast and be back here in two hours. She'll still be out till then.'

Beth hesitated. 'Are you sure?'

'You have plenty of time.'

Beth got into the car, which Joe had left parked out front for her, and drove home as fast as she could. She showered and changed her clothes quickly, and had a fast piece of toast and cup of coffee. She called Nell to report on what had happened and was back at the hospital before the two hours had passed. The nurse brought her a chair, and she sat at Tess's side and held her hand.

It was not long before Tess began to moan and turn her

340

head from side to side on the pillow. Beth spoke to her gently, reassuring and consoling her.

When Tess at last awakened and saw her friend's face, tears began to pour from her eyes; they ran down her cheeks and into her ears, into her hair, and onto her pillow. 'I lost my baby, didn't I?' were her first words.

Beth knew that lying would not serve any purpose. She simply nodded, and her eyes too were full as she reached out to hold her grief-stricken friend and share her sorrow.

The two women cried together, but Tess was not hysterical and out of control as she had been earlier. This time her tears were natural, heartfelt, and cleansing. When at last she calmed down enough to talk, she asked, 'Was it a girl or a boy?'

'It was another little boy. But he was very tiny, Tess. Too tiny to survive.'

'Poor Skippy. Now he'll never have a little brother to play with,' she whispered.

'Of course he will. You'll have other children, Tess. Don't think like that.'

'What did I do wrong?'

'You did nothing wrong . . . nothing! You took good care of yourself. These things just happen sometimes, and we don't know why. That's why we have to have faith.'

There was a long silence before Tess spoke again. 'You know, Beth, all during the pregnancy, something kept telling me to go home. I used to dream about it at night, but it wasn't the baby I was worried about. It was Skippy that haunted me. Ever since Chili killed herself, I've had this terrible feeling that I ought to get on a plane and go home. I've had dreams about my little boy getting sick over here and – '

'Honey, we all have worries like that, but you can't be afraid to live your life. If you'd gotten on a plane and gone home and had lost the baby there, you'd have felt even worse.'

'Maybe. But I'll always wonder if he might have lived if we'd been home, at a big medical center.' Her voice trailed away and tears formed in her eyes again.

'You can't live for what might have been, Tess. You must live life as it is, even though sometimes it can be very grim.'

'Do you think much about Chili, Beth?' Startled by Tess's invocation of a subject that was still very much with her, Beth chose her words carefully. Tess had to be reassured that with time the pain would diminish. 'Sometimes. Not much anymore. I really didn't know her all that well. I know she was unhappy, but it was a terrible thing she did, Tess. In the eyes of the church, it's a sin, you know.'

'I've been dreaming about her, Beth. I've never had a friend die before. You don't suppose it's possible that my thinking about death so much might have caused – ?'

'Now, just get that thought out of your head immediately. What happened to your baby had nothing whatsoever to do with Chili Shaheen's . . . suicide. You've had a lot of medication, and you're getting things all mixed up in your mind, but you've got to hold on . . . understand? You have a beautiful little boy to take care of, and a husband who loves you,' Beth said, putting her arm around Tess and holding her close, hoping to reassure her and give her strength enough to cope.

Beth stayed beside her friend, talking with her, consoling her, and giving her emotional support and encouragement until late that afternoon, when Kip finally arrived from Germany. When he took his wife in his arms to hold her and share the sorrow that was his too, she was tearless and remote. Tess had suffered alone, she had grieved without him, and now she had nothing for him at all.

While Kip held her close, Tess looked across the room and out of the window. She had been alone at her moment of greatest joy, the birth of Skippy, and she had been alone at the moment of her deepest anguish, the death of her second son. She had expected love and marriage to mean sharing, but it had instead brought her more loneliness than she had ever before known.

52

David and Melinda were already at the ranch, enjoying the cool clean air of Malibu, when Sam called early the next evening to find out how everything was going. David told her that he had ridden the old mare, Maybelle, and he was having a wonderful time.

She chatted briefly with her father, bringing him up-to-date on the situation with Rosalind Russell, and he supported her decision. When she suggested that Laura Huston would perhaps be a good choice for the role, Jules was less than enthusiastic.

'It's not an easy story to sell, Samara. You need a big name, and although the Huston woman is a fine actress, she's not box office.'

'Well, it's not exactly a Doris Day part, Dad,' she replied sarcastically, and was immediately sorry. Her father was absolutely right.

'No, but there's another blond who handles the bitch roles real well. Her name is Bette Davis,' he replied, not offended by her remark.

'She would have been wonderful ten years ago, but she's too old. The more I think about it, the more I believe that Morgana should be played very young. There must be an underlying acceptance that she was born this way, not that she's been shaped by life. Do you agree?'

'I think you gotta do what you think is best. Well, dinner's just been announced. We've having chilimack and watermelon. Don't you wish you were here?'

'Not really. I know you love it, but personally, I'd much

344

rather have spaghetti sauce on my spaghetti than chili. Make sure it's not too spicy for the children.'

When she finished the conversation, Sam hung up the phone and checked her appearance in the mirror. She had dressed in a black Schiaparelli dress with bright fuchsia trim. Her hair, which she had let grow long, was pulled back into a figure-eight chignon at the base of her skull, and her makeup was more extreme than usual, with a light mat finish, heavily mascaraed lashes, and clear fuchsia lipstick. She looked austere, stylish, and unapproachable. It was a look that she had evolved over the past few months in her new position at the studio, a look that was designed to keep people at arm's length. In her late twenties, she wanted to look forty, wanted to lay to rest the image of Jules's little girl helping Daddy at the studio. It wasn't easy. She'd had to stifle her natural tendency to be warm, outgoing, and friendly. People were inclined to misjudge friendliness for gullibility, artlessness for naïveté, and they were quick to take advantage.

She picked up her handbag, got a cigarette and started to light it, changed her mind and threw it away. She was smoking too much. She looked at her watch. It was about time to leave. She walked down the wide staircase and saw that Kendon was already waiting with her black wool cape in his hands.

'Will I need that?'

'It's a bit chilly out, but if you'd rather not . . .'

'Is the car out front?'

'Yes, ma'am. Frederick is waiting for you.'

'I won't need the cape then. If anyone needs me, I'll be at Perino's.'

Sitting in the back seat of the Rolls, Sam was glad she hadn't let Rich Wallis pick her up. She wanted to make it absolutely clear that this was not a date but simply a business meeting over dinner. He was obviously pitching his client, Laura Huston, and she wanted it understood that she was fully aware of it.

Rich was waiting for her in one of the circular booths in the middle of the large dining room. She should have known that his regular table would not be at the perimeter, where it would be less obtrusive. Getting her to dine in public with him was a smart move on his part. Nothing would enhance interest in his agency more than the gossip that he had something going with none other than the daughter of Jules Silverman.

He arose and greeted her with a light kiss on the cheek, which took her by surprise and annoyed her. She must be very careful with this man and not let him use her. She sat down immediately and asked coldly, 'Do you kiss Sam Goldwyn on the cheek when you dine with him?'

'No, but only because he's not as pretty as you are. I've taken the liberty of ordering some champagne. Would you prefer a cocktail?'

'Champagne will be fine,' she said, unimpressed. Didn't he know that she had been raised in a home where serving the finest champagne was nothing special?

As soon as the wine had been poured, she picked up the broad, shallow glass and turned to the sommelier.

'I would prefer a Continental glass, if you have one,' she said.

The man looked startled. 'Continental, ma'am?'

'Yes, a tall, thin flute. The sparkle dissipates too quickly in these.'

'I'll see what I can find, ma'am.'

She turned back to Rich, smiled, and tasted the wine. She tasted it again and then set it down. 'It's a little over the edge, don't you think?'

One eyebrow raised, Rich tasted the champagne,

shrugged, and remarked, 'Tastes fine to me, but I bow to your more sensitive taste buds.'

The sommelier returned empty-handed. 'I'm sorry, madam, but – '

'Just bring us a new bottle of wine,' Rich said. 'This one is not satisfactory.'

With a snap of the fingers, another bottle of Dom Perignon was brought, opened, and poured. To the man's relief, Sam pronounced it superb.

As she lifted her glass in a salute to her host, she asked, 'Did you know that the saucerlike champagne glass was created for Marie Antoinette because she wanted to drink out of a glass shaped like her breast?'

'Seriously?' he asked.

'It's true. The modern variation is considerably reduced in size, though,' she said with a twinkle in her eye.

Smiling across the glass, Rich replied, 'Pity.'

She settled herself into the banquette and looked at her dinner partner directly. He had not been the least flustered by her criticism and demands. He was one cool customer.

Wallis was also exceptionally perceptive. Sam Mulhare was staking out her claim to the dominance in this relationship, and he for one didn't intend to concede it to her, not yet, anyway, and particularly not over one little bottle of champagne.

'Well,' he said with a smile. 'I'm glad you noticed that the wine wasn't good. I rarely drink champagne, but most women are impressed when I order it.'

'I was brought up to recognize and appreciate good wines, but I'm not averse to having a martini now and then either. I don't drink much, however. Never more than one cocktail or two glasses of wine.'

'Well, you're a woman of moderation, I see,' he replied. 'Here's to moderation in all things.'

'That's not a very good toast,' Sam said, smiling and shaking her head. 'One can't be moderately in love, one shouldn't be moderately devoted to one's family or country or work. No, let's drink to something less controversial. Let's drink to good health.' She intended to give the arrogant bastard no quarter.

Undefeated, Wallis proposed: 'Good health is too bland for us. Let's have a toast to the beginning of a relationship that will never be bland or taken for granted.'

'Mr Wallis, you and I have no relationship, nor will we,' she retorted, ignoring the toast and sipping from her glass.

'I was talking about the relationship between my agency and Silverstone. Please, nothing personal was intended. This is strictly business.'

It was an enervating evening. The sharpness of their repartee kept both of them on the alert and poised for appropriate parries and thrusts, and neither had time to take notice or enjoy the succession of glorious courses set before them. The light filet of sole, the sublime rack of lamb, and the sprightly cherries jubilee were all barely touched.

When the evening had ended and Sam was in her car on the way home, she had to concede to herself that Rich Wallis had gotten exactly what he wanted, for she had agreed to test Laura Hustom before any other actresses were considered.

Sam didn't feel bested, however, for she would never have agreed if she hadn't thought the actress deserved the chance. If it turned out she was right for Morgana, then they would all be winners.

Above all, Rich Wallis had earned Sam's respect. He was tough and bright and fearless. He was going far here in Hollywood. And he was a damned interesting man to have around.

53

By her own admission, Tess was a klutz in the kitchen. She had to follow recipes exactly or she created disasters, and she had no flair for innovation. To her the only interesting part of cooking was eating the food when it was done. Then why, she asked herself, had she decided to celebrate Kip's promotion to captain with a party in their own house rather than joining with the other newly promoted officers to throw the customary big bash at the club? Why, indeed. Because she was still deep in a depression that had lasted six months since her baby had died, she was forcing herself to join the world again.

Not now, she scolded herself. Not now! She must not think of her lost baby now. There was still too much to be done. She must grit her teeth and think of something else quickly, or she would never, ever get through the evening. The death of her baby still possessed her, and even though she had tried hard to resume a normal life, never a day passed that she didn't think about him – how old he would be at that moment, wondering how he would look, how many teeth he would have, and if he would be sitting up in his high chair eating cereal.

Not now! She must not think again of how often in her dreams she had felt the baby quicken inside her, moving, signaling that he was alive, only to awaken with a start, clutching her flat belly, wanting the dream to be real. What was wrong with her? Other women had lost children and they had carried on. It was warped to cling tenaciously to a child she had seen only for a brief moment as it burst forth prematurely from her womb. God knows, she wanted to let go, she wanted desperately to let go.

Everyone else seemed happy at Wheelus, and most couples were extending their tours for six months, but all Tess could think about was going home. In the darkest weeks after the baby had died, she'd had Beth to talk to, but the Cellinis had been transferred to Montana, and she'd had no one for several months. She used to love to go into the city to shop and explore, to haggle with the merchants in her newly acquired language, but no more. Now she rarely left the sanctuary of the base, because she had become fearful, even more fearful than she had been when she first arrived. She was desperately afraid now, not for herself, but for her only child, terrified that something would happen to him here, and she would never take him home.

She looked at the clock. It was almost four and Kip still wasn't home. Damn him! She closed her eyes and tried to channel her feelings in a more peaceful direction. She must not let every little failure of her husband's arouse all the anger she had felt toward him lately. After all, he had lost a son too.

Just ten minutes before the guests were scheduled to arrive, Kip rushed in to see his wife nude and wet, kneeling on the concrete floor in the bathroom, hurriedly trying to wipe up the mess of Chanel No. 5 bath powder Skippy had spilled while she was in the shower.

'God, why didn't you leave him in the kitchen with Pina?' he asked, and was immediately sorry. 'Here, you finish your shower. I'll do this,' he said, contritely, taking the towel out of her hands.

Tears of humiliation and frustration sprang into her eyes, and her voice quivered as she retorted, 'I couldn't leave him in there because the oven is hot and there are a million things he can get into where he could get hurt! That's why! Where the hell have you been?'

'Honey, I'm sorry about being late. Masters pulled another one of his little games with my boss, and I, naturally, had to stay and provide him with the backup for a briefing. By the way, have you heard the buzz about Indochina?' he said, diverting their conversation away from the anger of the moment.

'What does Indochina have to do with Wheelus?' Tess asked impatiently.

'Remember late last year when all those C-82s came through . . . you know, the planes they call the "flying coffins"? We were ferrying thousands of French paratroopers over there to fight the Vietminh. They stopped here and we fed the guys and fueled the planes. I told you all about that nice Frenchman I met, who had gone to school in the States, didn't I? I ate in the mess hall with him, and we had a long talk. His English was perfect. Anyway, the poor guy was probably slaughtered. Thousands of them were, and Dien Bien Phu fell. Almost ten thousand French troops were captured.'

As a service wife, Tess found herself immediately threatened by the slightest suggestion of war. 'The US won't get involved there, will it?' she asked anxiously.

'Ike's on record as saying that he didn't want to get embroiled in a war in Indochina, but who knows? There, it's all cleaned up,' he said, rinsing the towel in the sink. Tess got back into the shower, glad to let go of her anger. This was going to be a happy night for a change. Everything was going to be fine.

'Now what do you want me to do?' Kip asked, poking his face into the shower and grinning.

'Watch Skippy. I'll be ready in a jiffy.'

When she stepped out of the shower, Kip appraised her

now very slim body. 'You look beautiful,' he said, but Tess quickly covered herself with a towel. She never initiated sexual contact with him anymore, because she was afraid of getting pregnant again. If Kip noticed, he never spoke of it. But then, Kip felt awkward about discussing their sex life, and so if her recent diffidence disturbed him, he would never let her know.

A knock at the door galvanized them both into a frenzy of activity. 'Get your clothes on,' Kip said, picking up Skippy. 'I'll go see who it is.'

'But you're not ready either,' Tess protested, stepping into her panties.

'Hey, if I have to, I can go to the party in my uniform,' he declared as he opened the door to Nell Carson.

'Howard's late as usual, so I decided to come ahead and see if I could help. For God's sake, get yourself ready. Give me the kid's clothes, and I'll dress 'im. Now, move! Tell Tess I'm here if she wants me to do anything else,' Nell said in her direct way.

'Thanks a lot,' Kip said with a smile.

'Oh, by the way, Masters and his wife can't make it. He told Howard to tell you he sends his regrets.'

'More booze for the rest of us peasants,' Kip retorted lightly, but when he was in the bedroom with the door closed, he swore. Tess, who had already put on the brown linen dress she'd had made by a dressmaker in town, looked at him in the mirror and panicked. 'What's wrong?' she asked anxiously. His entire demeanor had changed, and he looked glum.

'Masters and his wife aren't going to show?' he said bitterly.

'So? Who cares?'

'It's a snub. Everybody'll know he doesn't give a shit

353

about me, because he always puts in an appearance at promotion parties if he's in town. It's expected.'

Tess brushed her short hair and applied lipstick, the only cosmetic she ever used. 'He doesn't care about anybody, Kip. Why should he care about you?'

Kip undressed as he talked, but the energy had been drained from him. 'You know what it means, don't you? I'm not getting Hall's job when he rotates next month. That's exactly what it means. They'll bring some guy in who doesn't know shit from Shinola, and I'll still be stuck with all the work.'

'Kip, you knew that was going to happen. Why in the world would Brick Masters want a lieutenant on his staff when he could have a lieutenant colonel or even a major?'

'Captain.'

'Captain. Sorry. I forgot.' Dressed and ready to go, Tess looked sadly at her husband as he stripped. The party that was to be a joyous celebration of Kip's accomplishment had become the harbinger of his disappointment. What a waste.

Alone, Kip stood in front of the wavy mirror hung on the concrete wall over the pitted washbowl in their bathroom and looked at himself. He felt like such an ass. He had traveled thousands of miles with that bastard Masters, flying the plane while Masters slept in the cabin, allowing him to usurp the left-hand seat after landing and take credit for the flight time. On countless occasions he had lied to cover his ass when the CO was drunk and screwing around, and the hints Masters had dropped about giving him Hall's job hadn't been imaginary.

Worst of all, however, he had been away from his wife at the most devastating crisis of their lives. While his second son was being born to die, Kip was dawdling in Germany, waiting for Masters' fucking Leica camera to get fixed. If Tess ever found out the triviality of his mission, she would never forgive him. He had even passed up requesting a compassionate transfer after the baby died, because he was so sure of getting that damned job.

Kip had been an obedient and discreet subordinate. Other officers might snicker and gleefully swap tales about the old man's foibles behind his back, but not loyal jackass Kipling. He had kept his mouth shut. And what had it all been for? Nothing. He wasn't the commander's fair-haired boy at all, he thought in disgust. He was just another boot-licking jerk.

54

Sam had never seen her father more jubilant. He wanted to celebrate, give a party, dance. Senator Joseph McCarthy had been officially censured by the United States Senate, which had previously let him run rampant, tearing the country apart in a vicious witch hunt. His trumpeted motive was to ferret out Communists in America, but in reality McCarthy was on a self-aggrandizing search for power wherein accusation was proof and truth irrelevant. Although he had ruined lives and destroyed reputations, the senator had met his match when he took on the Army, and now he had been stripped of his powers as chairman of the House Un-American Activities Committee. Not even Joe McCarthy was a match for the American military.

It couldn't have come at a better time for Sam. Unknown to anyone but her father, she had hired one of the blacklisted writers to do the screenplay for *Lover* under a pseudonym. Against her father's advice, she had hired Laura Huston to play the lead. Now, tonight, they were having a sneak preview of the film at the Crest Theater in Long Beach to see how it would play with an audience, and she was nervous. Every major decision on the film had been hers, and although she had allowed herself to be persuaded by Rich Wallis when she chose the lead actress, the end result, good or bad, would be her responsibility.

She was grateful that her father was in such a good mood. It was time to go. She picked up her jacket and went into Jules's office, but he was chatting on the telephone, as usual.

She waited patiently for five minutes, but as the conversation droned on, she approached him and pointed to her watch. It was almost six o'clock, they had to stop at the house to pick up Reba, the preview was scheduled for eight, and they had a long drive. There were no freeways to Long Beach, and the thirty-five-mile drive could take as much as an hour and a half. She began to wave at him to get his attention, but he just nodded and carried on. Damn.

Going into Golda's office, she asked who was on the telephone that was so important, but Golda shook her head.

'I have no idea. He placed the call himself. What can I say?'

'Are you going down to Long Beach with us?'

'Are you kidding, honey? I wouldn't miss it. I've seen some of the dailies, and they're dynamite.'

'The story doesn't bother you at all?'

'Why should it?' Golda asked, surprised.

'You know . . . the relationship between the two women. It isn't explicit, but there's feeling there that goes beyond friendship.'

'It's very subtle. I doubt that anyone in the Hays Office will even pick up on it.'

'Dad thinks Laura Huston is too good. She sends messages to the audience with every word and every movement.'

'Sam, darling, don't trouble trouble till trouble troubles you. Let the audience decided. Oops, the light went out. He's off the telephone. Maybe we can finally get this show on the road.'

Both women descended on Jules, who apologized.

'Sorry, ladies. That was an old friend of mine in Washington. I called him up to tell him thanks.'

'Now, don't tell me, let me guess. It was . . .'

'None of your business, little girl. I'm just happy to say that finally someone I donated money to voted the right way. Is that car out front?'

'Has been for fifteen minutes, Dad.'

'Then let's go.'

Reba got into the car with a picnic basket, and while they rode, they ate fried chicken and drank white burgundy. Samara was too nervous for anything but wine.

They had decided to sneak *Lover* with *Magnificent Obsession*, the Jane Wyman, Rock Hudson film that was considered a woman's picture and would have the kind of audience their film expected to attract. They were gratified to see a line of people waiting to buy tickets for the preview. Long Beach was a reliable sneak-preview town: close enough to Los Angeles so they didn't have to travel far, but far enough away to keep industry people from flooding in and influencing the audience response. It was Jules's favorite place to try out pictures, because he said that the citizens of Long Beach were closer to mainstream America than the Los Angelenos.

They waited outside until the theater lights went down, and then they slipped into seats in the last row, which had been cordoned off for them. The director was there, as were the heads of the distribution and publicity departments. No actors had been notified. It was a true sneak preview. Even the ticket seller didn't know the name of the film being screened.

It was probably the longest, most agonizing ninety minutes Sam had ever sat through. The audience was respectful and quiet, and when it was over, response cards

358

were given out, although few people bothered to return them.

'What do you think, Dad?' Sam asked on their way home.

'Honey, you can't hit a home run every time you step up to the plate.'

'Why do you say that, Dad? I didn't see a mass of people getting up and walking out,' she protested.

'The audience was uncomfortable, couldn't you feel it?'

'Uncomfortable about what?'

'Women aren't supposed to act like that,' Reba added, disapproval dripping from her words.

'Like what, Mother? What are you talking about?'

'I'm not blind. Anybody with half a grain of intelligence could tell that those women . . . they were the real lovers. It was a story about them, not about the man who was crazy about the girl,' Reba insisted.

'Even in the book it was only suggested, and we were extremely careful not to indicate anything of the kind.'

'I think we ought to shelve it,' Jules said flatly.

'Dad, we've got almost two million dollars tied up in that film,' Sam protested, trying to appeal to his fiscal pride.

'Win some, lose some,' he replied stoically, and Sam suspected the battle was lost. When Jules Silverman made a decision, he rarely retreated from it.

For two days, Sam argued, cajoled, and tried to talk her father into a limited release at selected theaters, but he wouldn't listen to her. She tried to drum up support from those around him, but no one would disagree with her father.

When she finally conceded that the film would forever lie dormant on the shelf, she called Rich Wallis to tell him the news. It was only the second time she had talked to him since they had made the deal for Laura Huston's services.

'Sam, it's great to hear your voice. What's new?' he asked.

'Bad news, Rich. The studio is shelving *Lover*.'

'Why, for God's sake?' he asked incredulously.

'It's a long story. Do you want to tell Laura, or shall I?'

'Wait, wait. Hold on a minute. This is going a little too fast for me. Look, let's have a drink together, okay. I need all the details.'

Sam knew she owed him at least that much. 'Sure, but I'd rather not talk about this in public. Every waiter in town is an actor looking for a job, with ears pricked up for information.'

'Fine, wherever you say.'

'Well, I'd invite you to the house, but I live with my parents.'

'Then how about my place? I have an apartment on Wilshire. What do you say, seven . . . eight . . . tonight?'

'Seven will be fine.' She took down the address, and when she replaced the receiver, she sat staring disconsolately at the wall.

'Bob,' she whispered, 'I need you to say something funny . . . make me laugh. Children are starving all over the world and I'm crying over a damn movie.'

Sam arrived at Wallis' apartment exactly at seven, and he was waiting for her. Dressed in a gray silk sport shirt and white flannel slacks, he looked beautiful enough to have just stepped from a sophisticated drawing-room comedy.

'Come in,' he said with a smile, gesturing toward the spacious and luxuriously appointed apartment. Sam brushed past him, strode across the white marble floors to the broad expanse of windows, and looked out over the lights of the low-rise city stretching out before them.

'What a beautiful view you have,' she exclaimed.

'Yes, isn't it? I was really happy when I found this place. May I take your stole?'

Slipping the long swatch of lavender mohair that matched her Hattie Carnegie suit from her shoulder, she handed it to him.

'How about the jacket? I have a fire going in the fireplace, and you might be warm,' he suggested.

'You're right.' She unbuttoned the jacket and took it off, revealing a pale pink silk blouse underneath. She settled herself on a down-filled white sofa, took a cigarette from her purse and lighted it, and tried to relax.

'I envy you this apartment. One of these days I'm going to get one for myself just like it,' she remarked, looking around at the exquisite accessories. 'Who decorated it?'

'Well, I did all the choosing myself, but Libby Marcus did all the legwork. She's very good. Here, I just opened a bottle of Moët – will you check it out?' he asked with a smile.

'I'm sure it's fine.' She took the glass and sipped the sparkling wine.

Rich poured a glass for himself, set the silver bucket on the table between them, and sat down on the sofa across from her. 'The place right across the hall is going to be vacant. It's even bigger than this one. Would you like me to call the owner for you?'

'I can't. I have two children, and we live with my parents. The children are very happy there. I wouldn't think of uprooting them again.'

'Do you think it's wise to tailor your life to suit your children?'

Sam looked into her glass and replied, 'They're all I live for.'

'I don't buy that for a minute. You love your work,' he protested.

'Maybe, but I could be out of a job shortly. At the moment, my father is disenchanted with me.' She emptied her glass and held it out for a refill.

'Tell me about it,' he said, and Sam did. She told him in great detail about the filming, the editing, and the scoring of the picture, all of which she had supervised closely. Then she recounted the reaction to it, as well as the final decision to shelve it.

'God, you must feel terrible,' he sympathized. 'I know how bad I feel about having the client I expected to make into a star wind up in an unreleasable picture. When word gets around, nobody in town will hire her for a leading role.'

'But she's brilliant in the picture, Rich. There's not a single overt expression of sexuality between the women in that movie. I swear to you that Laura Huston conveyed it by just thinking it was there. Even my mother felt it, and I'm not sure she knows what the word "lesbian" means. Laura didn't fail us, we failed her,' she said passionately.

'I know, but producers are wary of actresses who are too powerful on the screen. It's not what they want to project nowadays,' he said bitterly.

'Well, I'd use her again if I ever got the chance, which isn't likely, I'm afraid. I have a feeling that any interest I show in a project will be like the kiss of death.'

'Just don't lose confidence in yourself, Sam. If you do, you'll really be finished,' he advised her, refilling her glass and then moving over to sit beside her.

They talked for a long time, but there was no sparring this time. They had become partners in a failure.

When the first bottle of champagne was gone, another appeared as if by magic. Samara became more and more relaxed. The fire burned brighter, the room became warm. Without realizing quite what was happening, she let Rich unbutton her blouse, and when at last she found herself naked on the rug in front of the fireplace in his arms, it seemed natural and desirable. He made love to her tenderly and gently, and after more than two years of celibacy she welcomed his body into hers. Making love with him was like slaking a bone-dry thirst with a tall, cool glass of water.

At two o'clock in the morning she awakened with a start. The fire had become red embers, and the room was chilly. The spell of the wine was gone, leaving in its aftermath a leaden skull too heavy for her slim neck to support. Rich had covered her with his jacket before he too had fallen asleep. She tried to pull away without awakening him, but he was a light sleeper and his eyes opened the moment she moved.

'I've got to go! My family will be hysterical with worry.'

'Don't leave. Call them and tell them you're fine and you'll see them tomorrow,' he said. 'You don't have to answer to them.'

'I can't do that,' she replied, but he held her arm.

'I hope you're not sorry, Sam . . . I'm not. It was wonderful.'

The room was now so dark that she could barely make out the features on his face, but she ran her fingertips gently across his cheek as she whispered, 'I had a lovely time, Rich . . . really I did, but I must leave.'

She dressed quickly and ran downstairs to her car. It was not more than a ten-minute drive home, and to her chagrin, the lights in the house were still on. God, she hoped they hadn't called the police yet.

Her mother and father were sitting in the library in their robes when she entered. Just as she was about to make an excuse, her father lifted his hand to silence her.

'Samara, you're an adult. You do not have to tell us where you've been, but from now on your mother and I would appreciate it if you would let us know when you're going to be late. Now that we know you're all right, we're going to bed.' Having delivered his message, he and Reba walked solemnly from the room, leaving Sam thoroughly abashed, wishing she had at least been given a chance to assert her own independence.

Utterly chastened, she took a shower and got into bed. She turned out the light and talked to Bob as she did every night. 'Darling, please don't judge me too harshly. I still love only you, but God forgive me, it felt so good to hold a man in my arms again.'

55

Now that the time had come to leave, Tess was apprehensive. The packers were doing their work in the midst of one of the worst ghiblis she had seen since her arrival in Libya. During a ghibli, the winds switched course, and instead of flowing inland from the sea, they swept down on the oasis of Tripoli from the vast Sahara desert and filled the air with dust and grit. The thin, powdery sand blotted out the sun and turned the daylight to a thick yellow haze. Even the blue Mediterranean looked as muddy as the Mississippi. If the winds blew hard enough, it was hazardous to venture outside, for visibility was nil, the air was impossible to breathe, and one's eyes, lungs, and flesh, as well as the paint on one's car, were put at serious risk.

Tess watched in despair as minute particles of dust made their way into their quarters through the cracks around the windows and under the door. Although the packers stayed inside, occasionally one would find it necessary to return to the truck for more supplies, and each time a door was opened, a gale of grit rushed into the house. She looked at the lovely oiled teak furniture and wondered how much damage a ton of sand packed into the boxes would to it. When the sandstorm had started that morning, Kip suggested that they postpone the packers until it stopped, but she would not hear of it. It was time to go home. Their orders were cut. Kip was directed to proceed to an assignment at Wright Patterson Air Force Base in Ohio, and Tess was deliriously grateful, because it was not far from her parents. She wanted to do nothing that would interfere with their getting back to the States as soon as possible.

Beth and Joe Cellini had been gone for months, as had Marilee and Frank. The only other wife with whom she was friendly was Nell Carson, but Nell and Howard were close to no one, really, because they were always at the beck and call of Veronica and Brick. Although they bitched constantly, it was a situation the Carsons really enjoyed.

Pina was running about the house directing the men and periodically clasping her head with her hands and wailing, 'Madonna! Madonna!' whenever a packer mishandled a piece of glass or china. Although she cloaked her unhappiness in a bustle of activity, Pina had on more than one occasion wept openly at the thought of 'Mio Skippee' leaving her, never to return. Tess assured her that she would write and send pictures, but she could not promise to return. It was possible that in some distant future Skippy might want to see the land where he was born, but Tess knew that the separation was, for her, quite permanent. Kip too had said that the possibility of his ever being reassigned to Wheelus was remote.

Tess looked at the clock. Good heavens, she had to hurry and dress. Several of the staff wives were giving a going-away tea for her at the club. When Kip told her it was being planned, she tried to find an excuse to decline, but he said it would be considered a slight to refuse. She hurriedly showered, put on the same navy crepe dress that she had worn for every special occasion since she had arrived, her navy felt wide-brimmed sailor hat, and navy pumps. She looked in the mirror as she applied her lipstick and wondered what her parents would say when they met her. How much of a change would they see?

366

Her hair was no longer curled. On her first visit to an Italian hairdresser in town, it had been trimmed into a very short neckline cut, straight, tailored, and easy to manage, and she liked it. Although she was still trim, two pregnancies had left her waistline a little thicker, her breasts a bit heavier. There were two razor-thin lines between her eyebrows that had not been there before she had lost her baby, and she hoped that returning home would erase the skittish fear that peeked through her eyes.

Skippy, who was now almost two, was scooting about the house, excitedly gathering up everything in sight, and throwing it into the corrugated packing boxes. Whenever she or Pina tried to stop him, he yelped, 'Skippy helping!'

Finally, in desperation, Tess said to Pina, 'Why don't I drop him off at the day nursery while I'm at the club? Then he won't be under your feet.' Pina shook her head vigorously. 'No, *per favore, signora*, no,' she pleaded, picking the long-legged little boy up in her arms and hugging him close.

Tess hadn't the heart to take him away from her. She just hoped that Pina could watch the workers and Skippy at the same time. She'd heard the story about the packers who had done exactly as they were told when the wife told them to pack everything in the kitchen, and they had wrapped up the garbage neatly and included it with the dishes. On the other hand, she had also heard that it was important to keep a sharp watch to make sure that everything was put into the boxes and sealed before they left the house, because often things disappeared, and four months and thousands of miles later, there was no way of tracing them.

'*Guarda muy buono*, Pina. *Capisch?*'

'*Si, signora*. I watch good.' Since Skip's birth, Pina had

made great strides in her ability to speak English, just as Tess had become fairly fluent in Italian.

Tess was just as happy to leave Skip at home. It seemed that almost every time she had left him at the nursery, he had gotten ill, and she certainly didn't want to take a sick child on that long transatlantic flight.

'I'll be back as soon as I can,' she said, and ran out into the desert storm to the car, parked across the street. In seconds her eyes began to hurt from the bombardment of tiny particles of sand, and although she kept her mouth shut and held her breath as she ran, her teeth and tongue felt gritty.

The reception did not last long, for few guests attended. The ghibli was too severe for the women in town to drive to the base, and most of them knew Tess only slightly anyway. As a going-away gift, the Wives' Club presented her with a sleek cut-glass Dior lipstick case with eighteen different-colored refills. She had just finished saying her thank yous when Nell Carson engaged her in conversation, preventing Tess from making a fast getaway.

'Tess, dear, have you heard the terrible news?' she asked.

'No, I haven't,' Tess replied, not much caring about any bits of gossip Nell might want to dish out, since Wheelus Field was soon to be a thing of her past.

Lowering her voice and looking about to make sure no one else could hear, Nell said, 'My dear, hasn't Kip told you?'

'About what?'

'Lieutenant Colonel Slauson . . . your husband's new CO.'

'He seems very nice. I've only talked to him a couple of times since he got here last month.'

'Hmf, "sweet" might be a better word than "nice,"' Nell retorted.

Something told Tess that she didn't want to hear whatever else Nell had to say.

'It was a lovely party, Nell, but I must hurry home. The packers are there.'

'Say, about tonight, I'm afraid I'm going to have to cancel. Howard and I have to be at the villa this evening. Can you come to dinner day after tomorrow instead?'

'I don't think so. That's the day we're leaving,' Tess said, smiling. God, those words tasted wonderful in her mouth.

'You're kidding! Whatever gave me the idea you'd be around awhile?' Nell asked, looking genuinely perplexed.

'Afraid not. Well, if I shouldn't see you again before then, take care, and thanks for everything, Nell. I'll never forget the night you and Howard came to my rescue.'

'We military wives never say good-bye, Tess, just *au revoir* . . . until we meet again.'

Tess hurried home. Less than forty-eight hours to go, and she had a lot to do. The footlocker of hold baggage that was supposed to go by immediate air to their next assignment hadn't been packed yet, and neither had their suitcases.

The ghibli had begun to subside, leaving the streets covered with sand, and the sun eventually managed to break through the thick air. As soon as she got home, Tess changed clothes and began to help the packers and hurry them along. She had an unsettled feeling deep inside her, a sense of foreboding that she tried to obliterate with a flurry of activity.

As soon as the boxes were packed, they were loaded on the truck to be taken to the warehouse with the furniture, where everything would be crated and placed in the hold of a ship. By the end of the day her quarters were empty of almost everything except their bed, which she had sold to the same newly arrived couple who had bought their old Ford. Several times in the last few months Tess had noticed some bugs that looked suspiciously like bedbugs scuttling around at the base of the bed, and she had no desire to take home an infested mattress. Skippy's crib was still there too, on loan from a couple who superstitiously believed that a crib in the hand prevented a baby in the womb.

By the time Kip got home from the office, the place was almost clear. Pina had stayed late and was mopping the floor. Without the Karouan rugs and the nice furniture Sam had sold her, the old quarters with their dark green walls and gray concrete floors looked pretty dismal.

Kip whistled. 'Wow, I had no idea they'd get out of here so fast.'

'I think the weather worked in our favor. It was too sandy outside for them to take tea breaks, so they really hustled. I hope they packed the stuff so it doesn't break. Do you mind if we drive Pina home? The bus has already gone, and she wanted to stay till they finished.'

'No problem, but we better get going. Aren't we supposed to go to the Carsons' for dinner at six-thirty?'

'We were, but this afternoon at the tea Nell canceled. It seems she and hubby will be on duty at the villa tonight.'

'Typical,' Kip said with disgust. 'Howard glories in being the court jester. Every time Masters snaps his fingers, he jumps.'

Tess permitted herself a small smile of sardonic amusement, thinking how much Kip's attitude had changed since his realization that there would be no slot on the staff for him.

370

They all drove Pina into town and stopped at the club on their way back to have dinner. Both Tess and Kip were full of joy and hope. Tess's parents were boarding a train the next morning to go to Westover Air Force Base. Although George's doctor had expressed reservations about his making the trip because he'd had a stroke six months before, he and Martha were determined to greet their grandchild the moment he first set foot on American soil.

Happily Tess and Kip chatted about their plans to buy a new car and drive down to Orlando, Florida, where Kip's father and mother had settled after retiring. It was a happy evening, and when they got into bed together in the almost empty house, they made love.

Snuggled in her husband's arms, Tess felt almost secure. Almost, but not quite. Their tour of duty in Tripoli still had thirty-six hours to go.

56

Jules called his daughter into his office late the next afternoon when the activities of the day were winding down, and told her that he wanted to talk privately.

'Samara, I know you don't agree with me, but I feel I must share with you the benefit of my experience,' he began.

Sam bristled. The set of her mouth and the arch of her eyebrows indicated that she was ready to defend her privacy and her independence. She was a widow, the mother of two children. She might be living in her father's house, but she would not live under his thumb.

'What do you mean?' she asked.

'I just don't want you to make another mistake like – '

'Dad, please don't interfere with my personal life. We got into trouble once before, as you'll recall, when you foolishly passed judgment on the man I intended to marry. I didn't tolerate it then and I won't tolerate it now.' Her words were clipped and edged with frost.

Jules responded sharply. 'Get off your high horse, young lady. What you do with your personal life is your own business, although I personally feel you better be careful with that Wallis guy, but that's not what I want to talk about. It's your movie that's under discussion here.'

Samara cursed herself for jumping at the wrong bait. Damn. Now it would be harder than ever to recover the high ground on the most important subject of all, *Lover*.

'I think you're wrong not to release it, Dad.'

Jules sat back in his chair. 'Okay, Samara. Convince me.'

Her almost dead hopes for her film suddenly sprang to life, and she eagerly snatched the opportunity to plead her case anew. 'Because it's so good, Dad, that's why.'

Jules shook his head. 'It'll make the audience uncomfortable. They'll stay away. I was uncomfortable, and I don't live in Nebraska and Iowa, where nobody even talks about such things.'

'You weren't bored, though, were you? Did you once fidget in your seat? Weren't you absolutely mesmerized by every frame?' she asked insistently.

'So it's not boring. It's not boring to watch a dog humping a bitch in heat, but I wouldn't put it on the screen. What else?'

'Is there a single infraction of the decency code?'

'Well . . . the actors don't do or say anything actually explicit . . . it's just . . . I don't know, shocking.'

'And that's exactly why it'll do business. We didn't make it in CinemaScope or wide-screen glorious color. We didn't rely on any of the tricks others are using to lure the audience away from their television sets to go out and buy a ticket to a movie. Instead, we went over the edge dramatically and artistically. We made a film that's titillating and a little shocking, but it's all in the viewer's head. That's the hook. There's nothing on the screen that they can point to and say: There, that's dirty! And they could never see it on television. That's why they'll come to the theaters, Dad.'

Jules watched his daughter with pride. She was not only beautiful in her passionate pleading, she was making an almost convincing case for her film.

'Will you agree to a test market in, say, Salt Lake City?' he asked slyly.

Samara did not jump at the suggestion. 'No, the Mormon church is too powerful there. But Chicago or St Louis or Kansas City, sure.'

'You're on. Get going on it. I'll let you approve all the ads, just so you can't blame anything on me when the picture bombs.'

'It won't bomb. So, if I'm right? Then what?'

'Then we'll release it.'

Samara returned to her office and telephoned Rich immediately with the exciting news, but his secretary put her on hold and left her there for quite a while, which took some of the edge off her excitement. Damnation, when would she learn to let her secretary place all calls for her, even to someone she'd slept with? When he finally answered, she announced immediately, 'Great news. Jules has agreed to test-market *Lover*.'

His response was less than enthusiastic. 'How come you agreed to that?'

'Why not? If we have faith in the movie, then we ought to be ready to take risks with it.'

'Well, I guess it's better than nothing. When can I see the film?'

'Whenever you want to. Just let me know so I can book a screening room,' she replied, feeling disappointed and annoyed with the coldness of his response.

'My schedule is filled today, but maybe I could come over to your home this evening.'

Samara felt as if she were being backed into a corner. Rich was maneuvering his way into her home, where Bob's children were, and she wasn't ready for that. Not in any way. No, she might have slept with Rich Wallis and enjoyed it, but there was a part of her that was still very much married to Bob Mulhare.

'I . . . uh, don't think that would be a good idea. Why

don't we screen the film here at the studio this evening, and then go somewhere for a late supper . . . alone.'

'If that's what you want. I'll be there by six-thirty,' he said curtly, letting her know he felt rebuffed.

'Fine,' she said equally curtly. 'It'll be my treat for dinner tonight.'

'That's not necessary,' he said, his tone softening.

'Yes, it is, Rich. Yes, it is.'

After the call, Samara sat in her chair stunned. It was the first time she had spoken to Rich since she left his apartment, and she was simply not prepared for a business-as-usual response. She had slept with Bob, and they had fallen in love and gotten married. She'd been intimate with Rich, but their relationship apparently hadn't changed a bit, at least not as far as he was concerned.

She was angry with herself for feeling used. What in the hell did she expect of him anyway? Had she actually been so naïve as to believe that he would fall head over heels in love with her just because he'd bedded her? Did she want him to?

It wasn't important now anyway. She had work to do, and when she saw him tonight, she'd know better what his true feelings were. And perhaps she'd have a better understanding of her own.

57

Tess had left too many things out when her household goods were packed and she couldn't fit them all into the suitcases they would take with them on the plane or the one footlocker that would be their hold baggage. She began to unpack the footlocker and start all over again, doubtful that she would ever manage to stuff everything in.

She was all alone in their quarters, since Kip had gone to work and Pina had taken Skippy for a walk. It would be her maid's last day with the little boy she loved as if he were her own, and Tess wanted to give Pina as much time with him as possible. For the past week Pina's eyes had been tearing every time she looked at Skippy. Tess was sad for her but even more so for Skippy, who would certainly feel the loss of this gentle woman who had been a constant source of love and affection to him throughout his young life.

Tess had just laid the clothing for the biggest suitcase out on the bed when the telephone rang. It was Kip.

'Honey, we've got big problems. Can you drive over to the office and pick me up now?'

'I'll be right there,' Tess replied, suddenly filled with dread and apprehension. Good Lord, what could possibly have happened now?

She rummaged around until she found the car keys in the clutter and dashed out the door. Kip was agitatedly pacing outside the low-lying whitewashed building where he had worked for two and a half years, and the expression on his face was grim.

As soon as he was in the car, she asked anxiously, 'What's going on?'

'Masters says I can't go home. He wants me to extend for six months . . . at the convenience of the government,' he snapped.

'Oh, my God! Can he do that?' Tess exclaimed, looking at her husband in dismay. Distracted, she swerved the car to avoid hitting a palm tree.

'Channing called me into his office this morning and told me the bad news, and at first I said no, of course, that our household goods had already been picked up and your family was on the way to meet us.'

Tess pulled the car over to the curb. She was driving so erratically that she was going to kill them both if she didn't stop.

'And did he accept that?'

Kip shook his head. 'You know Masters better than that. Channing told me I'd done a helluva job while I was here. That I'd been given outstanding efficiency reports the whole time and that I shouldn't blow it all away for a lousy six months more.'

'It's so unfair!' Tess exclaimed. 'Why are they doing this to us now . . . when everything's arranged for us to leave?'

'The Air Police caught Slauson in town with one of the Italians who works in the Air Base Group.'

'So? I don't understand. What was he doing?'

'Screwing him – the guy's a homosexual, Tess.'

'Oh, my God! He seemed so nice.'

'He is a nice guy, a helluva lot nicer to work for than Hall was. Poor bastard.'

'What's going to happen to him?'

'He'll lose his commission. I think maybe they'll just let him resign quietly. At least, I hope so. Anyway, he's gone already. Masters shipped him out this morning.'

Tess started the car again, and they headed home. She was not at all reassured by Kip's refusal. She detected a certain ambivalence in his manner, a lack of sufficient outrage at the assault on their departure plans.

As soon as they were in their quarters, Tess returned to her sorting and packing. 'What are you going to do, Kip?' she asked, and there was an edge of hostility in her voice. 'Are you going home with Skippy and me? Or are you going to do as Masters wants . . . as usual?' For the first time in her married life, she intended to take a stand. She could not continue never having a say in anything. Before Kip made a decision, she had to let him know she would not be a silent partner in this marriage anymore.

Kip put his hands on her shoulders and turned her around to face him, but she couldn't look up into his eyes.

'Don't do this to me, Tess, please. Let's solve this problem together.'

'Together? Together? Don't take me for a fool, Kip. By "together" you mean that you decide and I agree with your decision. You don't want to hear what I really feel. You want me to be a good little officer's wife and lie,' she declared angrily, and before Kip could respond, she asked, 'I suppose he promised you the job on his staff, the one you always wanted, if you agreed to extend. He did, didn't he?'

'Yes, he did,' Kip replied, but with the grace to let some of his guilt show through his demeanor.

'How're we going to live? All our furniture, everything is gone,' Tess said, switching from her emotional mode to a more pragmatic one.

'Channing said that if it hadn't been already been

378

loaded onto a ship, which it probably hasn't, he'd arrange to have it all returned, and he would personally take responsibility for seeing that everything was put back exactly as it was. There'll be no cost to us at all.'

'How generous of them!' she snapped. 'What about our car and our bed and all the other stuff we sold? Are they going to replace them for us with taxpayers' dollars?'

She closed her eyes and took a deep breath, and her voice trembled as she declared. 'All right, Kip. Here's what I think you should do. I think you should say no, that for once, just once, you'll put your family first . . . ahead of your career. I want to go home. I need to go home, not in six months, but now. We've served our time here. We've got a right to go.'

As she took her stand, Kip listened stoically, and when she paused, he said, 'Masters will be my enemy, Tess, if I insist on my rights. You know him well enough to realize that.'

Hearing his words, Tess knew that she had lost the battle when the first shot was fired, and she was angry. 'If you already knew what you were going to do, why in the hell did you go through that miserable charade? I'm just the little woman, right? Go ahead, tell me I have to stay. Go ahead!' she dared him.

'If I stay, will you stay with me?'

'When you tell me your decision, I'll tell you mine,' she said bitterly.

'If I go now, Masters will get back at me somehow, some way. Just one rotten efficiency report could haunt me forever. It could be the one thing that might delay a promotion and put me behind my contemporaries. Don't ask me to risk my career for just six more months in a place most dependents consider to be paradise . . . please, honey, think about it.' As he pleaded with her, he held

379

her tightly in his arms, refusing to let her pull away, although she was trying hard to do just that.

She looked up into his eyes and said, 'I've tried, Kip, I've really tried to be a good wife to you ... a good officer's wife. I've made a home here, I've borne two children here, and I've lost one of them.' Her throat was suddenly closed by a sob as the tears began to roll down her cheeks. 'If I don't go home now, my father will be devastated, and he's not well, Kip. You know that. Besides, ever since my baby died, I've lived with a terrible fear of something happening to Skippy before we get him home. Even if I wanted to stay here, I couldn't, Kip. I'm going home. I want you to come with me, but if you don't ...' Her voice trailed off, leaving the ultimatum unsaid but nevertheless quite clear.

'Your home is with me, Tess.'

Pulling away from him at last, Tess answered. 'Not if you stay here, Kip. Give me a sign that you love Skippy and me more than you love your ambition.'

'A wife shouldn't ask her husband to make that kind of choice,' Kip responded, his voice shaded slightly with remonstrance. When she did not reply, he asked, 'Where will you go?'

'I don't know. This isn't a decision I ever planned to make.'

'If you really loved me, you wouldn't go, Tess.'

Tess looked up into eyes that were as tear-filled as her own, and replied, 'If you really loved me, you wouldn't ask me to stay.'

58

Sam waited in her office for Rich to arrive at the studio, but he was more than half an hour late and she was growing impatient. She had met that afternoon with the distribution and ad/pub departments about *Lover*, and it had been agreed to try the film out in St Louis, a big urban city with much of the same sensibilities as towns with smaller populations. The film had been booked into the Loew's State Theater in downtown, to follow *Dial M for Murder*, which would open the following week. If *Dial M* was a hit, they would have plenty of time to devise a campaign, but if the Ray Milland-Grace Kelly film was not well-received, they'd have to rush *Lover*. Sam desperately hoped that Warner Brothers had a hit on its hands.

The clock on her desk showed that it was already seven-fifteen. Damn, she hated to be kept waiting. She picked up the telephone and dialed Rich's office, but the answering service picked up. Either he was on his way or he wasn't coming. She would give him fifteen minutes more, and then she would send the projectionist home and cancel the evening, including the eight-thirty reservation at Scandia.

She actually waited almost an hour, however, before she gave up on him, furious that he hadn't even bothered to call. She strode out of the building and got into her MG sports car, which she had brought to the States from Tripoli because Bob had loved it so much. As she headed home, she felt rejected, foolish, and angry. Her fury was directed as much at herself as it was at Rich Wallis. She should know better than to get involved with a Hollywood hustler.

She got home in time to tuck the children in bed and read them a story, and although she wasn't hungry, she forced herself to eat a piece of chicken left over from dinner and drink a glass of milk. Later, chatting with her parents, she complained of a stomachache, and her father advised her not to take everything so seriously.

'Samara, this business will kill you if you let it. Don't agonize so much. It's a big game, remember that. The one who survives, wins.'

Later that night she lay in her bed sleepless. As she looked at the darkened ceiling above, she made a vow never to allow herself to get entangled emotionally with another man again. Because Bob Mulhare had been such a rare person – so loving and trustworthy – she had lost the cynicism that had armed her against the feculent behavior of climbers in the movie industry. Rich Wallis, however, had given it all back to her, in spades.

The next morning when Rich's call came in, she took it out of curiosity. What kind of slick, sleazy, trumped-up excuse would he use to get back in her good graces?

'Sam, I'm so sorry about last night. I just talked to my secretary, and she told me she'd forgotten to call you. I hope you didn't wait too long,' he said.

'When you weren't here at seven, I went on home to be with the children,' she lied, wondering just what was coming next.

'Good. I'd have really felt terrible if you'd hung around waiting. Sorry I couldn't see the film, but would you do me a favor and show it to Laura Huston. She's in a real state of hysteria and needs a little cheering up.' His voice sounded muffled and thick.

'I would think as her agent you'd have the decency to

find time in your busy schedule to see it too,' Sam said testily.

'Oh, God, you haven't heard? I'm calling from Cedars. I'm in the hospital. My damn appendix burst yesterday afternoon, and they rushed me here by ambulance. I was right in the middle of closing a deal with Paramount when I suddenly felt this massive pain in my gut.'

It took a moment for her to absorb the startling information. 'Oh, Rich! How awful! Are you all right?' she asked, horrified and feeling terribly guilty.

'Yeah, but I'm so full of junk that I can't think straight.'

'Is there anything I can do for you?' Please, she thought, let there be something she could do to make up for all the nasty, hateful thoughts she'd been thinking.

'Right now I need somebody to hold my head. I've got to go, babe, I'm going to be sick again.'

The line went dead, and Samara covered her face with her hands in shame. Good Lord, what was happening to her? Where had the compassionate woman that Bob Mulhare loved gone? Getting up and walking to the window, she looked out at the workers rushing about. If she was going to continue in the movie business, she decided, she had to get some balance in her life.

After a few minutes of reflection, she rang for her secretary. 'Call ad/pub and tell them that if they have any preliminary sketches or copy for *Lover* to send them to you before they leave for the day. I'm going now, and I probably won't be back. You can reach me in Rich Wallis' room at Cedars. Please put everything that I should see in a large envelope and send it home so I can look it over tonight. Is Dad in his office?'

'No, he's already gone for the day. Golda said something about him taking the children to Malibu for the afternoon because David had some carrots for Maybelle.'

'Right. Well, you know where to find me. Call Gregory's and tell them to have a large bouquet of red roses ready for me to pick up in half an hour. Oh, yes, and order a car and driver. I don't want to have to bother about parking at the hospital. Now, get me Laura Huston on the line.'

Sam went back to her desk to scan the production charts and daily budget sheets to make sure that everything was on schedule and there were no problems to confront before she left the lot. One thing she had learned about working for her father was that while he had given her a great deal of responsibility, he had kept most of the authority for himself.

It was early afternoon when she tiptoed into Rich's room at the hospital. He was sleeping, and his private-duty nurse got out of her chair beside his bed, gesturing for Sam to come outside to talk.

When they were out in the hall, Sam asked, 'How is he?'

'A little better, I think. He was very sick, you know. He has a slight fever, but he's on antibiotics. It's just going to take some time. I gave him a pain shot about half an hour ago, so he'll be out for a while, I'm afraid.'

'Why don't you take a little walk and let me sit with him?' Sam suggested.

'I wouldn't mind a breath of fresh air,' the nurse commented, and just before she left the room she asked, 'You must be the Kathy he keeps talking about in his sleep, hmm?'

Sam shook her head and said stiffly, 'Not really.'

'Oh, I'm so sorry. I should never have said that. Besides, people are always saying crazy things when they come out of the anesthetic,' she said, flustered.

'It's fine, really. Mr Wallis and I are associated in business only,' Sam reassured her.

Rich Wallis slept for a long time. By the time he awakened at last, Sam was a much different woman from the eager person who had walked into his room earlier. While Rich slept, Sam had had time to put her emotional house in order. Rich Wallis probably had dozens of women friends. He was far too handsome not to have. The sex they'd had was pleasurable, but then, he'd no doubt had a lot of practice in the art of seduction.

Why, then, had she allowed herself to get carried away by romantic notions like a schoolgirl? Because I don't know everything yet, she counseled herself, but I'm learning fast. With Bob, she'd had the best that life could offer, and now she could never settle for less. As for Rich Wallis, she had to decide whether she wanted him as a sometime lover or as an astute and clever business colleague. It was an easy decision.

Weeks later, after they had finished a long and difficult negotiation, she asked casually who Kathy was, and Rich responded with irritation, 'Just what gossipmonger is filling your head with tales about me and that round-heeled floozy?'

'I have my sources,' Sam replied enigmatically.

'Well, she means nothing to me, understand? She's just a nice piece of ass, that's all.'

Later, when she was alone and thinking about his response, Sam said thankfully, 'Bless you, Kathy, whoever you are.'

Samara Silverman Mulhare never intended to be anybody's nice piece of ass.

59

Although the flight back to the United States aboard a
Navy transport plane was shorter than her flight to
Tripoli, for Tess, traveling alone with her little boy, it
seemed like an eternity. The plane was more comfortable
than that earlier one; it had commercial passenger seats,
facing the rear for safety, and carried a number of other
dependent families returning to the States. Skippy was
well-behaved, and other passengers played with him and
helped her on and off the plane when it stopped at the
Azores for refueling.

Tess, however, was miserable every mile of the way.
Her emotions alternated between doubt and rage, confu-
sion and anger, self-pity and heartbreak. At one moment
she would regret her decision to leave without Kip; at the
next she would be angry with him for not coming with
her. Overlying all her anxieties and doubts, however, was
the deep-seated and heartfelt belief that the time had
come to go home. Staying in Tripoli six months beyond
their allotted time was emotionally impossible, and she
hated Brick Masters for dangling an irresistible lure in
front of her husband, just as she resented Kip for not
refusing it.

At what point in a marriage, she pondered again and
again, does a woman have the right to say this far and no
more? Was it imperative for her always to agree, never to
veto anything involving the family's financial resources,
or were her husband's career choices his and his alone?

As Skippy lay sleeping on her lap, she closed her eyes,

hoping for a moment of peace. Now that she had made this drastic decision, could they ever go back again, or had she ended not only her tour of duty as a dependent in Libya but her marriage as well?

Once the decision had been made, Kip tried no more to dissuade her, but instead did everything he could to help her get ready to leave. And she, in turn, made no more demands of him. There were no further recriminations or bitter words between them, but the atmosphere had been dense with regret.

It was a cold, overcast winter morning when their plane landed at Westover Air Force Base in Massachusetts, and Tess held Skippy's little body close to hers. Snow flurries filled the sky, and she realized that neither she nor Skippy was dressed warmly enough. Customs waved them past without question, and suddenly Tess found herself in her father's arms.

'Mom! Dad!' she cried joyously, and with hugs and kisses and tears, she was happily reunited with her parents. There was much laughing and admiration of the fine young grandson she had brought home with her, and it was all very heartwarming until her mother asked, 'Is Kip getting the luggage, honey?'

'No, Mom, he didn't come. He stayed in Tripoli.'

'Well, will he be on the next plane?' Martha asked, sensing there was something wrong.

'No, he won't. Look, can we talk about this later? It's a long story, and I don't want to discuss it standing out here in the cold.'

'Of course. Now, do you have anything warm for this little guy to wear?' George asked, kneeling to cuddle Skippy with his one good arm. Tess noted that her father leaned heavily on his cane, and silently she said a small prayer of thanks that he was alive to see Skippy.

'We're not used to winter, Dad. No, I don't.'

'Then we'll just have the cabdriver stop at a store where we can buy him a snowsuit. What about you?'

'I'll be fine. Let's just get going.'

Late that evening, after Skippy had been put to bed in a hotel crib, Tess told her parents what had happened. Without elaborating too much, she also told them about her second pregnancy and the death of her child, a story she had kept from them because she hadn't wanted them to worry.

While she talked, she sat on the edge of the bed in her parents' room and wept. She was barely twenty-four years old, she had borne two children and lost one, she had been a wife in a foreign land for over two years, and now it looked as if she would be without a husband.

George and Martha Marshall's hearts ached for their daughter, and they wept openly with her. When she finished her story, however, her parents' reactions were not what she had expected.

'You did what you had to do, honey, just as Kip did what he thought was best. Don't blame yourself, and don't put too much blame on him,' her father said. 'A man has to be concerned about his career and supporting his family.'

'That's a bunch of you-know-what!' her mother snapped. 'Kip owed it to his family to stay with them! He had a lot of nerve putting her on that plane all alone with that little boy. I think it stinks!'

Tess was surprised. Her father had disapproved of the marriage, but now he was making excuses for Kip's behavior. Her mother had enthusiastically encouraged her romance with Kip, and now she was condemning him.

Before she had time to analyze their responses, suddenly her father was on to other things. 'Okay, Martha, we get the picture. The important thing is what Tess is going to do now. Have you thought about it, little girl?'

Tess smiled at the term. She'd always be her father's little girl, she supposed. 'Not really . . . but if it's all right with you, I thought maybe Skippy and I could live with you until Kip comes back to the States in the spring. Okay?'

'Sensible decision,' her father pronounced immediately, as he picked up the telephone to make Pullman reservations for the train home the next day. That night when he went to bed, George Marshall said a prayer of thanks. The last lonely years had not been in vain. Now he not only had his sweet daughter back, he had a glorious little grandson too. He would not think beyond the blessings of the moment.

60

Samara went to St Louis to sit in the back of the Loew's State Theater and watch *Lover* with an audience, a real audience, untainted by the jaded affiliates of the film industry in Los Angeles. Once was not enough. She stayed in St Louis and went to the theater every day that weekend. She could not get enough of it. The audience reacted exactly as the director had intended. They laughed in all the right places, there was a deathly quietness in the moments of highest drama and revelation, and above all, there were tears at the end. Tears not of sadness but of joy. The first night, she worried when the audience filed out so silently, fearing that perhaps they had not been moved, but on the second night she realized that they were quiet because they were thoughtful. They were not leaving the story there in the theater, but taking it home with them.

Awash with triumph and anticipation, she boarded the TWA Constellation and flew home. *Lover* might not draw the huge crowds of a CinemaScope epic, but it would go down in history as a breakthrough anyway, a film that dared to go to the brink of human emotions without falling into the abyss. In the years to come, film historians would write about its daring, its tasteful delineation of feelings that were both universal and unique, and its creation of a superstar. Laura Huston was magic.

Each night Sam had called both her father and Rich to report in detail. It had been almost six weeks since Rich's appendectomy, and he was back at his office, working hard, determined to build a clientele to rival even Metro's golden roster of stars.

Lover was released in a few weeks, and it was a success, in spite of the fact that the Seal of Approval had been withheld because the film suggested that one woman was in love with another. Nevertheless, the audiences understood the humanity in the film and liked it. It was a turning point in Sam's relationship with her father. Jules had disapproved of the picture, had resisted strongly the decision to release a film without a seal, and he had been proved wrong.

The day after the weekend box-office totals were reviewed and it became apparent that *Lover* was going to be a hit, Jules called Samara into his office for one of their private consultations. He did not waste time getting to the heart of the matter. He had made his decision, and he wanted to start the process while Samara was being praised by everyone for her courage in pushing the film through.

'Congratulations, sweetheart, you were right about your movie. Have you got that Huston actress signed to a long-term contract?'

Sam shook her head. 'No, dammit. We get one more picture out of her and that's it.'

Jules smiled and wagged his finger at her. 'Shame on you. You're letting your personal life interfere with business. Rich Wallis put one over on you.'

She had expected a reprimand, and she was prepared with an answer.

'Wrong, Dad, dead wrong. Rich counseled Laura to sign the seven-year contract with excellent elevator clauses tied to box office, but she wouldn't do it. She said she had to be free to choose the right roles wherever they were. She refused to be "held in bondage," as she called it, because she feels she's an artist, not just a contract player. And she is, Dad. She really is. She's more than a star.'

'Okay, okay, I concede the point. Maybe that's why it's time for me to go. I'm a walking anachronism around here.'

Samara was quick to take issue. 'That's not true! You know more about this industry than anyone else.'

'Yeah, yeah, sure, maybe. But it's not the same. I can see big changes coming, and frankly, I have no interest. All I seem to care about anymore is David and Melinda. I resent every hour I spend here when I could be at home with them. I know there are a lot of old war-horses out there who still think they have all the answers, but, honey, I'm not one of them.'

Suddenly Sam's heart did a flip-flop. Good Lord, he wasn't going to tell her that he was selling the studio? Not now! 'What are you planning to do?' she asked.

'I'm gonna kick myself upstairs and let you run the show. We've got a few problems with financing, and I'll work on that angle, but you . . . you're going to be the boss.'

Samara was taken completely by surprise. There had been times, of course, when she wondered what his intentions toward her were, but she had never imagined that the power would fall into her lap so suddenly . . . so soon.

'Dad,' she said, remembering that her father had just had his annual physical checkup, 'are you okay? I mean, are you feeling all right?'

'I'm fine, don't worry about that. I just have to give up the cigars . . . that's all.'

'What does that mean?'

'Doc Rosen said I should take things a little easier. The

392

blood pressure is up, but it's nothing to worry about now. It just made me start thinking that maybe I'm not gonna live forever, like I thought. Maybe I should start doing things I want to do.'

Sam closed her eyes to try to blink away the tears. She must take him at his word. He intended his decision to be a triumphant declaration of his faith in her. She would not turn it into a maudlin display of sentiment.

'I hope I can live up to your expectations, Dad.'

'You already have, sweetheart. Now, have fun, just the way I did, and don't take it too seriously. Remember, we're only making movies, and it's only reels of celluloid.'

Samara went back to her office intending to begin her plan of attack. There were so many things she wanted to do, changes she wanted to make, but she couldn't concentrate on business. All she could think of was her father. Jules Silverman would never willingly relinquish control of the studio that had been his life, not unless he had a very good reason. And although she wanted to believe he had done it only because he had faith in her, she knew better. Her father was a precise man, and he was obviously taking steps to put his affairs in order.

Sam was right. That was exactly what Jules had started out to do, but it was too late. Three weeks from the day that his daughter became the head of Silverstone Studios, Jules Silverman lay down for a short afternoon nap, perhaps the first one he had ever taken, and died of a massive heart attack.

61
1962

Tess was later than usual arriving home from her Monday-afternoon English-literature seminar. She had stopped at the grocery store to pick up milk and bread, and she hoped that Agnes had not forgotten to put the chicken in the oven to begin roasting. As usual, the television in the living room was on, and Skip was in front of it watching the news. He was the only nine-year-old boy she had ever known who was fascinated by current events.

'Mom, hurry up. President Kennedy's just announced that he's ordered a naval and air blockade of Cuba!'

'What?' she asked, dropping her packages and joining him on the couch.

'The Russians are building a missile base in Cuba . . . that's why!' Skip's eyes were bright with excitement as he gave her a quick summary of the situation and then informed her, 'I called Dad at the office as soon as I heard, and he promised to call me later tonight when he has more information.'

'You called your father in Washington, Skip? You're not supposed to do that unless I give you permission. Our telephone bill last month was horrendous, and my salary at the university just isn't going to make it if we're not careful,' Tess admonished.

'It didn't cost anything. I placed a person-to-person for General Stonewall Kipling. That's my secret code to Dad to call me back. Besides, what difference will a phone bill make if the Russians start a nuclear war?'

Tess sighed. Of course he was right, but it was often

difficult to get exercised about national affairs when she had so many other problems. As she listened to the President speak, however, she noticed the stress in his voice, and realized that the crisis was palpably real. The United States was facing the Russians down, daring them to respond. She felt a small wound of terror open itself deep inside her. Dear God, what would she do? They lived in a small apartment near the university, on the second floor. The basement flooded every time there was a heavy rain and would be a sorry bomb shelter, but then, why would anyone drop a bomb on Champaign, Illinois? Of course, there was Chicago, not too far away . . . or St Louis . . . and maybe their aim wouldn't be too good. And what good, really, was a shelter against nuclear weapons?

The President finished speaking, and the commentators took over. She watched Walter Cronkite, but was not comforted by his velvet voice and fatherly demeanor. Skip, on the other hand, was stimulated by it all. Tess observed the tautness of his strong young body and the coarse sand-colored hair topping the head that looked so much like his father's.

'D'ya think Dad'll go down there, Mom?'

'Where?' Tess asked.

'Mom,' he exclaimed in exasperation, 'Cuba! Haven't you been listening to what they've been saying? They're gonna send planes and ships to stop the Russians from bringin' any more missiles in there. Boy, is this exciting!'

'It's not exactly something to be happy about, honey. It's pretty frightening.'

'Gosh, I wish I was old enough to fly one of those fighter planes. Dad's so lucky.'

The telephone rang, and Skip raced to pick it up,

hoping it was his father calling him back, but it was his grandfather.

'You watching the news, Grandpa?' Skip asked.

'Looks pretty bad, doesn't it?' Dr Marshall remarked.

'Bad? I think it's great! Nobody's gonna push the United States around,' the young boy replied smugly.

'Of course. Is your mother there?'

As soon as Tess was on the phone, her father remarked in disgust, 'When he gets a little older, I'm going to make him spend one night in the emergency room at the hospital. I think it would be good for his character to see what happens to people's bodies when they're smashed up and wounded.'

As usual, Tess sprang to her son's defense. 'He's just a little boy, Dad. You shouldn't expect him not to find all this exciting.'

'It's that father of his. Skip thinks he walks on water.'

'That's healthy, Dad, especially since his father feels the same way about him. They're very important to each other. Kip's an extraordinary person, Dad, even if you don't approve of him, but he's a military man, and a good one. He was the first graduate of his class to become a major.'

'Big deal,' her father said sourly. His son-in-law still represented a threat to him. Tess had stubbornly refused to get a divorce, even though they were still separated. She said there was no need for it and it was ridiculous to waste the time or the money. Having failed to convince his daughter, George secretly hoped that one day Kip would find someone else and initiate the action himself, but a lot of years had passed and that hadn't happened either.

He blamed his son-in-law for the fact that Tess had moved out of their house into the tiny apartment while she was in graduate school. Both he and Martha had done everything to persuade her to stay in the big house with them, but Tess refused, and he was sure it was because when Kip came for a visit, he stayed with his wife and son.

Both Dr Marshall and his wife disapproved of the arrangement, and their friends thought it extremely odd. It didn't seem right for two people to live apart, yet apparently be able to pick up their marriage only on vacations. Whenever the doctor broached the subject, his daughter became tight-lipped and grim and refused to talk about it. Any discussion of Kip was strictly off-limits to both her mother and him, and it was annoying and frustrating to both parents.

'Why don't you and Skip come over for dinner this evening, honey?' Dr Marshall suggested. 'Your mother bought too big a roast, as usual, and I'll be eating leftovers for days if you don't.'

'That sounds great, Dad, but I just got the first batch of papers in my American-lit class, and I need to start reading them.'

'Come on, now Tess. You hardly ever spend the evenings here with us anymore. I know it was rough teaching and doing graduate work at the same time, but now that you've finally passed the orals for your Ph.D., I think you ought to ease up a little.'

Tess knew her father was right. She seemd to work all the time nowadays, and she still had to finish her dissertation. 'Let me ask Skip . . . Honey, want to go to Grandma's for dinner this evening? She's making a roast.'

Ordinarily Skip was eager to visit his grandparents because they treated him like a god, and there was always a lot of delicious food to eat. He had a big appetite. Meals

397

at home were simple and nutritious, but always lacked dessert.

'Suppose Dad calls?' He was reluctant to leave the apartment – in case.

'He'll keep calling until somebody answers. He always does, you know,' she reassured him.

'Yeah, okay. Find out what kind of pie Grandma made.'

Tess chuckled. 'Dad, it all depends on the pie.'

Pleased, Dr Marshall replied, 'Tell him apple. And we'll drive over to the store when he gets here for the à la mode.'

Kip did not return his son's call until six days later, right after President Kennedy announced that the Russians had agreed to dismantle the missiles in return for the United States promise not to invade Cuba, and a tacit assurance that the American missiles in Turkey would eventually be removed. Tess answered the telephone.

'Kip, we've been so worried about you. Skip was certain you were flying one of those planes down there near Cuba.'

'Not quite, but we've been on complete military alert, and it's been hell around here. Have you any idea how close we came this time?'

'Don't tell me. Nobody's talked of anything else. The level of interest among the students was amazing. For once the hot topic of conversation was not *Bonanza* or Saturday's game. They were extremely worried.'

'Skip doing okay?'

'He's fine, but he'll be disappointed to hear that you weren't bombing the daylights out of the Russians. I'm beginning to think this predilection for soldiering is genetic. He's not here right now. Today's his Cub Scout meeting.'

'Damn, I forgot. Look Tess, would it be convenient if I came for a visit next week? I really need to spend some time with Skip.'

Tess sensed a certain amount of anxiety in his voice. 'You can come see us anytime you want, Kip, you know that. What's going on?'

'I'm on my way to Vietnam. I've been assigned to one of the military advisory units there.'

'Oh, no!' Tess said. 'Do you have to go?'

''Fraid so. The Air Force issues orders, babe, not suggestions.'

'How do you feel about it?'

'Ambivalent. I don't really know what the mission is supposed to be, and I can't forget all those Frenchmen who stopped at Wheelus on their way to be slaughtered there. I also worry about not being around while Skip is growing up.' There was a long pause, and then he said very softly. 'I'll be gone at least a year, Tess.'

Tess closed her eyes and tried to compose herself quickly before asking, 'When will you be here?'

'My leave starts a week from Monday, but I can pick up a military flight and be there on Saturday . . . okay?'

'How long can you stay?'

'Two weeks, if you can put up with me that long.'

'We'll manage.'

Late that evening, after Skip was asleep, Tess sat in front of the television watching Jack Paar's new show, but none of it penetrated her worried thoughts. Skip had taken the news of his father's overseas assignment too calmly, which was a clear sign that he was shaken by it. Dear God, for my son's sake, please don't let anything happen to Kip, Tess prayed silently, knowing full well that the prayer was for herself as well.

62
1967

Samara sat in her office watching all of her three television sets, each tuned to a different network. David was in his freshman year at Berkeley, and she was absolutely certain he was one of the antiwar protesters with Joan Baez at the Oakland Selective Service Center. She had tried to convince him not get involved, not to risk being arrested and possibly shadowed for the rest of his life by a jail conviction. Damn, what was going wrong with this world?

The telephone on her desk rang, and it was Rich.

'Sam, the overnight ratings on *Benders* are bad news. I don't think anybody was watching it,' he snapped in exasperation.

'It's a good show, Rich. Convince the network to give it some time,' she said distractedly, her eyes darting from one television screen to the other, dreading the thought that she might see her son in that mob of people.

'I've already tried, but they're down on it . . . way, way down.'

'Don't be greedy, Rich, our studio has five hours of prime time this season. That's as big a chunk as anybody else has. Losing one half-hour won't be fatal.'

'That's just what I needed, honey, to cheer me up. That show was going to be our money maker. We've got the best deals with the actors on any of 'em, and it was the cheapest to make.'

'You get what you pay for, friend.'

'Jesus! What's with you today?'

'I'm worried about David. I should never have agreed to let him go to Berkeley,' she confessed.

'It's a great school, and he's a big boy. If anybody can take care of himself, it's David. He's got the niftiest line of gab I've ever heard. He'll smooth-talk the pants off all those luscious young coeds up there.'

'You should know, Rich. You're the expert,' she said sarcastically.

'Hey! Knock it off, will you? You could have had me all to yourself, you know. Can I help it if you cut me off the line and threw me back into a sea just filled with tender young fish?'

Samara laughed, as she usually did when they were needling one another. Rich was one of the most important people in her life. After her father's death, she had found out that the studio was in financial trouble. Almost before she had time to worry, Rich had raised enough capital to buy in and save it for them both. As a working team, they were a perfect fit, and she was glad she hadn't undercut their professional relationship with emotional garbage. Together they had built the company into one of the most successful producers of prime-time television programs. They still made an occasional feature movie, but all the elements had to be just right or it was a no-go. She trusted Rich's instincts, and he trusted her judgment.

'Want to have dinner with me?' he asked.

'Don't tell me you haven't got a date with another of those vapid bimbos trying to get a part on one of our shows?'

'As a matter of fact, I do, but I think you need me tonight more than she does. I can tell you're really upset. Hang up, I'm coming over.'

Within seconds he was in her office. He walked over to

the television sets, turned them off, then plopped himself down on the white couch and said, 'Tell me about it.'

Samara looked at the clock on her desk. 'It's after five, want a drink?'

'Sure. Why not?'

Sam fixed two Scotch-on-the-rocks from the sleek bar hidden in a credenza and handed one to him. She took a sip and then said, 'God, it's an awful time to be raising kids, Rich. The world is going crazy.'

'Is Melinda okay?'

'This is her last year of high school, and she doesn't want to go to college. She says it's irrelevant. She wants to travel and see the world and commune with the forces and rhythms of life. I can hardly keep a straight face when she starts spouting that crapoloney.'

'Has she got a boyfriend?'

'Unfortunately, and he's awful. He always needs a haircut and a shave, and he reeks of hash. He's a philosophy student at UCLA.'

'Ah, a college man.'

'I guess so. Funny, in my day that conjured up an image of gray flannel slacks, argyle socks, and cashmere sweaters. Now a college man wears filthy jeans, a shirt hanging out, has long dirty hair and fingernails, and a beard. And instead of smoking a pipe, he's rolling a joint.'

'What are you compaigning for, Conservative of the Month or the Barry Goldwater prize for reactionism?'

Sam glared at him. 'Easy for you to say. You haven't got any kids to worry about. My pretty little daughter looks like an angel, but she spends half her time with her hair on an ironing board while she tries to press out the curls, and when she talks, the foulest words come out of those rosy pink lips. And as for my son, well, I'm terrified that he's going to get killed or ruin his life forever in those protest demonstrations.'

Rich shook his head in despair. 'Sam, my dear, I feel like a father to both David and Melinda, so take my advice: Cool it, will you? Don't align yourself on the opposite side of issues from your kids. Listen to them. The things they're saying make sense. I wish to hell the whole world would make love, not war.'

'Well, you're certainly doing your part.'

'You know what you need?'

'If you say "A good fuck," so help me, I'll stab you in the balls with my letter opener!'

'Okay . . . then I won't say that. Instead, how about going to a party with me in Malibu tonight?'

'Are you kidding? I don't do that touchy-feely scene, and I'm not interested in pot or LDS or – '

'LSD, sweetie. LDS stands for Latter-Day Saints – Mormons, honey – and I don't take them either. No, I want you to meet a friend of mine. He's got great karma, and he really puts you into a peaceful place,' he coaxed her.

Sam hesitated. 'Well . . .'

'Look, if you want to stay home and watch *The Beverly Hillbillies* on television, it's okay with me.'

'On second thoughts, Malibu sounds great. What should I wear?'

'Have you got a pair of jeans?'

63

1971

Tess went into her bedroom to tidy up. The cleaning woman would soon arrive to strip the sheets and change them, and she needed to get her things put away or she'd never be able to find them again. Everything was in a terrible clutter. Kip had been visiting for a week so he could attend his son's high-school graduation, and it had been a difficult week for her.

She had felt awkward asking him to wear civilian clothes to the campus, but she had to do it because a uniform was an invitation to student jeers, demonstrations, and name-calling. The last thing she wanted was to have an incident involving her own husband. Now that she was acting dean of women, she wanted to minimize controversy and keep the confidence of the students. Having to explain why her son had accepted an appointment to the Air Force Academy at Colorado Springs was difficult enough, without flaunting the fact that his father was a one-star general. Kip not only had a chestful of combat citations, including a Purple Heart, but also had done two tours of duty in Vietnam.

She heard the door burst open and then slam shut. Her young athlete had apparently finished his three-mile run. She closed her eyes and listened as Skip dashed into the bathroom and turned on the shower. Less than two weeks, that's all she had, and then he'd be gone to soldiers. The house would be so still . . . so empty. He would never live with her again. Of course, there would be visits, but he would be gone from her daily life, and she wasn't sure how well she was going to cope with being alone. She had never in her life lived alone.

She went into the kitchen to fix breakfast. Skip loved to have her scramble eggs for him. As she took the food out of the refrigerator, she heard him singing 'Benny Havens Oh,' the West Point song his father had taught him when he was just a little boy.

By the time the eggs, toast, and orange juice were ready, Skip was at the table with the newspaper in his hands. He was so different from most of the other young men of his generation. His hair was short and trim, he was immaculately clean-shaven, and he was even more beautiful physically than his father. Tall, broad shoulders, narrow waist. The only trait he seemed to have inherited from her was the sprinkling of freckles across his face. He was so like his father, it was almost as if she had contributed nothing to his creation.

She set the plate of eggs in front of him and then put her arms around him from behind and gave him a hug.

'Where did you and Betsy go last night?'

'To some dumb party her brother and his friends had. We didn't stay. Everybody was so stoned they couldn't make decent conversation, so we left and took in a movie.'

How typical, Tess thought ruefully. Every day she commiserated with parents who were pained by their children's revolt against all their established values. A whole generation was turning off and dropping out. All except her own son, who had never marched in step with his contemporaries.

Skip had been an honor student all through high school, and the star of the basketball team. After school, he had worked as a box boy at the grocery store. He'd paid for his own car and insurance, and he was totally honest and

405

dependable. If he said he would do something, he would do it.

Tess might have worried more about him if he hadn't been so utterly in control of his life and happy with it. Unlike many of the young men at the university, who had no direction, Skip knew exactly what he wanted – to be just like his father, do just what his father did. Even the girl he dated steadily was every mother's dream daughter-in-law. She was pretty, soft-spoken, very bright, and hopelessly in love with Skip. On the few occasions Tess had tried to engage her in a consciousness-raising discussion of women's rights, Betsy had just looked at her quizzically, unable to relate on any level. She and Skip were such a pristine pair that Tess often wondered wickedly if Betsy were on the pill or if they were both saving themselves for marriage.

She sat down across from her son and drank her coffee. Now that the semester was over, she could take time to relax.

'What movie did you see?'

'Kubrick's *A Clockwork Orange*. Weird.'

'I heard it was really imaginative and frightening. Did you like it?'

'Not really. Mom, do you mind if we watch the news?'

Tess reached over and turned on the small television set that Kip had bought her for the kitchen at Christmas. She was always so busy reading or correcting papers, she had little time for TV, but Skip often watched it.

The newscaster announced that a judge had halted the New York *Times*'s publication of the Pentagon Papers. Skip listened intently, and when they cut back to the game show, he commented, 'Well, I would think so. They've got some nerve, releasing that top-secret stuff.

Imagine how those poor guys slogging through the jungles in Nam feel about it.'

Tess could not let the remark pass. 'It's only temporary, Skip. The Supreme Court will never allow such a gross infringement on freedom of the press.'

Kip finished his toast, gulped down his tall glass of milk, and got up from the table. Squeezing his mother's shoulder affectionately, he teased her, 'Good Lord, Mom, people are supposed to get more conservative as they get older, but you're turning into a bleeding-heart liberal.'

'It's a dirty job, but somebody in this family has to do it, what with you two gung-ho military types. Just remember, the world isn't going to be saved by war. It never has been, and it never will be.'

Kip grinned. 'Peacenik,' he accused gently.

'Warmonger,' she replied, but her tone was bantering.

'Dove!' he countered.

'Hawk!' she accused, and then they both laughed.

'Gotta go. I promised a guy I'd bring my car over and let him try it out. I'm hoping he'll buy it. By the way, I'm having dinner at Betsy's tonight, so don't worry about cooking for me. Did you pick up the dry cleaning?'

Tess shook her head. A sudden lump appeared in her throat and she couldn't speak.

'I'll get it myself. See ya later, Mom.'

When the door slammed behind him, Tess picked up her coffee cup, but her hand was shaking so much she set it down immediately.

She got up and left the tiny kitchen, where she had cooked and served so many meals for her child. She went into the hallway and stopped to peer at her image in the mirror. Before her was the reflection of a woman, almost forty, a woman with an important job, a fine education . . . a few gray hairs and some wrinkles around her eyes.

She could begin to see a faint likeness to her father, now dead for more than four years. Did she feel now as he must have felt when she suddenly left the nest, married a stranger, and flew away to the other side of the earth? Perhaps . . . perhaps not.

But she had come back home, and she had not left her parents again while they lived. It would not be that way with Skip. When he left on the first of July, it would be forever.

64
1975

Samara closed *Ragtime*, the book she was reading, and looked out the window of the plane, down to the thick bank of clouds beneath her. She loved to visit New York, but it was always so tiring. Every moment of her visit was filled with meetings, lunches, dinners . . . business, business, business. Still, it had been a successful trip. Silverstone-Galaxy was on a roll, and both she and Rich were riding the crest of the television explosion.

She wondered if Jules were watching, and she often wished that he could have lived long enough to see what she had done. He would have been so pleased and proud that his daughter had succeeded, not just modestly, but grandly.

'Not bad for a girl, eh, Dad?' she often found herself whispering.

When the plane landed in New York, she was met by the limousine and driven directly to her office. Rich had asked her to get there as soon as possible to attend a meeting with a producer who was looking to make new and more lucrative alliances. Rich hoped to bring him into the company, but Sam was reluctant. She knew Calvin Schilling and felt he'd bring trouble. He had been too successful too fast, and his luck was going to run out soon. The odds were against him, and besides, he wanted too big a piece of the take.

She picked up the car telephone and dialed her daughter's number. The maid answered, but as soon as she heard Sam's voice, she summoned Melinda.

'Mom . . . are you back?' Melinda asked, and her voice sounded far away and weary.

'Just got in five minutes ago. I'm on my way to the office. How are you feeling?'

'Awful. Do you think you could come over when you're through?'

'Where's Allen?'

'He's got a Bar Association dinner tonight. He's not coming home.'

Sam was extremely tired, but she had never been able to say no to either of her children, especially Melinda.

'I'll be there as soon as I can, honey.'

'Can you get here in time for dinner?'

'I'm not sure,' Sam replied, feeling the pressure. 'Why, can't Margarita feed the children for you?'

'She has to leave early. One of her own kids is sick.'

'I'll do the best I can, honey. Hang in there.'

Sam put down the telephone and sighed. Pity. She had been looking forward to a long hot bath and then getting into bed and clicking around the dial on the television to check out the competition until she went to sleep. Ah, well, there were more important things to do. Jeremy and Jessica would be delighted to see her, as she would be to see them. She just hoped that after this next baby Melinda would go on the damn pill. Her daughter had been married less than four years and had been pregnant for most of them.

Sam reminded herself one more time to try to be grateful that Melinda had married such an ambitious, independent young man, but she couldn't help being annoyed with him for not letting her provide her daughter with a proper nanny for the children. And God forgive her, but she also wished he wasn't such a rigidly religious Catholic. How was it possible that her daughter, the

410

rebellious, assertive young woman of the sixties, could turn into a downtrodden housewife of the seventies.

Because the plane had arrived on schedule and she had made good time from the airport, Sam arrived at the office before Calvin Schilling appeared. Rich met her with open arms.

'God, I'm glad you're back. We've got a million things to discuss, but first, can you believe this . . . Megan Manchester walked off the show!'

'Good riddance. We were paying her too much anyway. Find another good body with lots of red hair to replace her, and this time, make sure she can act!'

'That's why I need you around, sweetie, to curb my generous instincts. I offered her more money to come back.'

'Are you kidding?' she exploded.

Rich raised his hands to fend off her fury. 'Down, girl, down! She refused. She says what she really wants is script approval . . . too!'

'You lucked out,' Sam snapped, too tired for tact.

'If the world only knew that I am really the patsy in this partnership and you are the barracuda,' Rich said, teasing her.

'I'm sure the world knows. Didn't you see that picture of me in the *Inquirer* with the fangs and the horns?'

'Well, actually, I was planning to have it blown up and framed for my office. Don't you know that in spite of all this women's-lib propaganda, the world hates a woman who wins all the time? Unless she's Billie Jean King, of course. So, what did you think of *A Chorus Line*?'

'I loved it.'

'Will it make into a movie?'

'No way. Some things are meant for the stage only . . .

411

and that's one of them. I did read *Ragtime* and liked it. Has it been optioned yet?'

'I'll check it out.'

'By the way, I invited David to sit in on our meeting with Schilling,' Sam said.

'Fine . . . any particular reason?'

'Not really. It's just that I think he's getting bored with what he's doing. He's supervising those shows well, and they're doing fine, but he's a creative young man. Even though he's my son, I suspect he could be lured away by a more exciting offer.'

'Come on, you don't believe that, do you . . . really?'

'I most certainly do. He's too much like his father. I think he craves excitement. I've seen his eyes glow when he talks about politics, and he's very active in fund-raising for the Democratic party. I've never seen him show that much enthusiasm for one of our shows.'

'I told you not to send him to Berkeley.'

'You did not! Besides, it was a great experience for him. Even now he speaks with pride of the times he got tear-gassed. He still wants to make the world a better place to live.'

'Maybe he ought to run for President.'

'Maybe he will someday. Some guy named Jimmy Carter, governor of Georgia, walked off a peanut farm and thinks he's going to be the President.'

'Sure he does,' Rich said sarcastically.

'He's not your cup of tea, is he?' she asked.

'I just don't relate to down-home folks.'

The secretary called to announce that Calvin Schilling and retinue had arrived to negotiate. Sam told her to summon David and take everyone into the conference room.

Rich lifted his eyebrows in suprise.

'Tactic,' Sam said with a smile. 'They sit on the sides of the table, you and I sit at the head.'

'Come on, Sam. These little power games of yours won't work on this boy. He's as tough as they come.'

'Not as tough as I am, my friend . . . and you know why?'

'Why?'

'Because I don't give a damn if this deal goes down or not. In fact, I'm hoping it won't. It'll be my way or not at all . . . understand?'

Rich nodded and followed silently as she walked out of the office. This guy Schilling had no idea what he was getting into, Rich thought. When it came to negotiation, Sam Silverman Mulhare had written the book.

65
1976

Tess checked into the Broadmoor Hotel in Colorado Springs on Wednesday, as she had promised Beth she would. She had a reservation back to Los Angeles the next morning, with a connecting flight to the university, but she was really worried that she wouldn't make the dinner with the trustees of Christopher University. When she had told Chancellor Harris that she had to go out of town, he had shaken his head in frustration and tried to impress upon her how vital her appearance at the dinner was, as if she didn't already know. More than once in the past two days she had seriously thought of not coming to Colorado Springs, but something inside her told her that she must. Beth had said it was urgent, and Tess believed her.

She looked at her watch and saw that it was just about time for Kip's plane to arrive. He hadn't been terribly enthusiastic about dropping everything on short notice, but his curiosity too, was piqued. They had decided not to contact Skip until they had found out what the meeting was about, because they might not have time to visit him.

The telephone rang, and it was Beth. 'Beth, well, here I am. Kip will be here this afternoon,' Tess said in greeting.

'Good. Sam came in by private jet late last night, and we had breakfast together. I'm on my way to the airport to pick up Nell Carson now.'

'I was so sorry to learn of Howard's death,' Tess commented.

'It happened just before they pulled the American troops out of Vietnam, but she'll tell you all about it. She still hasn't quite recovered.'

'I'm so sorry,' Tess said, wondering if Kip had known.

'She's very bitter about it, Tess. She's changed a lot. You won't recognize her.' Beth paused for a moment. 'Listen, Sam has the biggest suite in the hotel, and she insisted that we be her guests there for dinner tonight.'

Tess chuckled. 'Same old Sam.'

'Yep, still giving the parties. She looks great. You know she's been very successful,' Beth commented.

'She deserved every good thing she's gotten. How are you doing alone, Beth?' Tess asked.

'Managing, but that's about it. I miss Joe every minute of every day . . . But we have a lot to talk about, Tess. I'll see you at seven.'

Eager to get the show on the road, Tess was five minutes early, but Beth and Nell were already there. The moment Tess stepped past the door, the intervening years fell away, and there was much hugging and kissing and joy. It seemed more like a reunion of sisters than just a gathering of women who had been friends two decades before. Although they had kept in contact only with Christmas cards and children's wedding and grandchildren's birth announcements, their paths had not once crossed after Tripoli.

'My God, Sam, you look great!' Tess exclaimed. 'I can't believe that white hair.'

Sam, looking especially striking in a white wool Halston, grinned and replied, 'It's been that way for almost ten years. Don't you have any gray hair at all, Tess?'

'A strand here and there. I wish I had more. It would make me look more distinguished and scholarly. Beth, you haven't aged a day.'

415

Beth's dark eyes seemed even larger now that her black curls were salt-and-pepper gray. She laughed the same deep throaty laugh they all remembered as she replied, 'On the outside, maybe, but inside I feel like I'm a hundred.'

No one commented on Nell's appearance. Beth had been right, Tess decided. It was almost impossible to believe that the lean, rawboned, nervously attractive Nell was hiding somewhere inside that great abundance of flesh.

'Beth told me about Howard. I'm so sorry,' Tess said, putting her arm around the shoulder of the woman who seemed like a stranger to her. 'You know, I'll never forget how kind you were the night . . . the night I lost my baby.' Even after all these years, it still hurt Tess to remember.

'I always felt bad that we weren't able to help you more than we did,' Nell said wistfully.

'How about a martini, for old times' sake?' Sam asked, hoping for a more cheerful tone.

'I haven't drunk one of those things in years,' Tess demurred. 'Faculty members only have an occasional glass of wine, you know, but I'll have one if you will, Sam . . . but only one.'

They sipped their drinks and chatted comfortably as they waited for Kip. Tess described her rise from associate professor of English at the University of Illinois to dean of women at Christopher. She did not tell them of her imminent hopes to climb higher. Sam talked more about her children and grandchildren than the studio, and Beth described her life as a military wife.

'I actually got into it, I guess,' Beth said, 'once I accepted the fact that Joe wanted to stay in the Air Force. Angela used to tease me, said I got so used to moving

416

that if we stayed in one place too long, I got restless and started moving the furniture around. I was lucky, you see, Joe and I were never separated for long periods of time . . . until now.'

'What about you, Nell?' Tess asked.

'I loved it, every bit of it, until Howard got sent to Vietnam. I tried to talk him into taking retirement and not going, but an old friend in high places convinced him that a tour there would get him a star for sure, and Howard wanted so bad to retire as a general.' She finished her martini and held her glass toward Sam for more. 'He didn't even die a hero. Can you believe that? He got blown to bits while he was standing in a bar. Nobody knows for sure how it happened, because everybody who was close enough to see was killed. He'd been in Saigon less than a month, and he'd been sick from the day he arrived there.' Her voice reflected the depth of her anger.

'Where are you living now?' Sam asked.

'I couldn't afford to stay in the apartment in Virginia, so I moved back to Ohio, near Wright Patterson. I never had any kids, you know. The Air Force is all the family I've got.'

'You're the only one of us who opted out by choice, Tess. Any regrets?' Sam inquired, deciding it was time to change the subject before Nell succeeded in depressing everyone completely.

'I'm glad you asked that question before Kip arrives. The answer is . . . some. Now that Skip is a big strong, strapping young man, it would be easy to say I should have stayed. But without the benefit of hindsight, I would have to admit that I'd probably leave again. I was obsessed with getting my child home safely.'

'I was surprised that you never remarried and neither did Kip,' Beth commented.

'We were never divorced,' Tess said quietly.

'Really? How extraordinary! Why?' Sam asked.

'There didn't seem to be any reason to. Through the years we've both had friends . . . dates, I suppose you'd call them, but neither of us was ever seriously interested in anyone else.'

'No kidding?' Sam remarked, then asked hesitantly, 'Well, I know I shouldn't ask such a personal question, but do you . . . do you, um . . . act like man and wife . . .'

'Say it, Sam. Do we sleep together? That's what you want to know, right?'

'My God, have you changed! The proper young Tess I knew would have died rather than say that. Okay, well, do you?' Sam grinned.

'Dealing with today's let-it-all-hang-out college kids does that to one. But to answer your question, we do. Kip has always visited me whenever possible. Skip and I spent school vacations wherever Kip was stationed, except in Vietnam, of course. And I took a six-month sabbatical when he was assigned to Germany, and Skip and I had a wonderful time there. Every time we see each other, it's like a honeymoon. I wouldn't recommend the arrangement to everyone, but it's worked for us.'

'Good Lord, if I made a Movie of the Week with that story, the critics would laugh it off the tube,' Sam exclaimed. 'Wouldn't it have been easier just to get together again?'

This was the part that Tess always hated, because it made her sound selfish and self-centered. 'I have my own life to live. Kip's life is the Air Force, and I found out in Tripoli that I just wasn't cut out to be a military dependent. You know how much a woman must subordinate herself to be a good service wife. You get bounced from one place to another; you can get a job, maybe, but you can't have anything like a real career.'

'Good Lord!' Sam exclaimed. 'I can't believe it. You're actually into women's lib! You, of all people.'

'Why me "of all people," Sam? I've been a feminist ever since I was just a little girl and my dad told me how women were treated as second-class citizens.'

'Good for you,' Nell commented encouragingly. 'Do you march and burn your bra and that stuff?'

Tess shook her head impatiently. 'No, I don't, but I support those who do.' She paused, wondering what they thought of her. 'You see, I love academia, and although Kip hasn't had a little woman beside him to take care of life's annoyances and attend Wives Club meetings, it hasn't hurt his career, obviously. He was the first in his class to get a star.'

'Joe thought that Kip would eventually be Chief of the Air Force. Do you think he will?' Beth asked.

'I wouldn't have any idea. You'll have to ask him. What about you, Sam? You never remarried,' Tess said, anxious to turn the conversation away from herself.

'For one brief moment years ago I thought I might, but better sense prevailed, and the guy became my business partner instead. It was a good decision, because we've been very successful and he's my best friend.' After a short thoughtful pause she continued. 'I know it sounds silly, but I've always had this secret hope that Bob was still alive somewhere out there, maybe picked up by a freighter in the ocean and carried to distant lands . . . or captured by a band of bedouins and forced to roam the desert for years on end, trying to escape. Even now, whenever a door opens or the telephone rings, there's still some part of me that hopes it might just be him . . . home at last.' She laughed self-consciously. 'You can see that

419

the movie business has affected me mentally. I fantasize in screenplay clichés.'

Tess was just about to allow her cocktail glass to be refilled when Kip was ushered into the room. Even out of uniform, in his crisply tailored navy-blue blazer, starched white shirt, striped tie, and gray slacks, every inch of his bearing exuded command. The atmosphere in the room changed immediately, as he became the women's cynosure.

He greeted Sam, Beth, and Nell cordially but stiffly. It was only when he greeted Tess, that he seemed to unbend. He opened his arms and she went to him for a warm hug, and the moment was a poignant one for the three widows watching them, realizing that there were no more such husband's embraces for themselves.

Kip took his drink to the table so that dinner could be served immediately, and they chatted about the Air Force, current events, Vietnam, and Watergate, although there was an air of anticipation hovering over their conversation.

When coffee was poured, Sam asked the waiter to leave so that they could get on with the business of their conclave.

'Well, I can't postpone this any longer,' Beth said, extracting a letter from her purse. 'I have something to read to you. But first I want you to know that Nell made this meeting possible.' Without elaborating, she continued, 'Twenty years ago, twenty-two years actually, when I walked into Chili Shaheen's quarters and found her body, I saw a letter lying on the kitchen counter. I scanned the top of the page but didn't touch it. After her death was found to be a suicide, I asked Joe to find out what was in the letter, if it had provided any clue as to why she had killed herself. Joe was told that there had been no letter, and it was suggested, rather forcefully, that I was hysterical and had only imagined seeing it.'

Nell interrupted. 'Howard was the officer who talked to Joe. He warned him to get Beth to shut up about the imaginary letter or Masters would have her shipped back to the States because she was emotionally unbalanced. Although it was kept quiet, there had been a second suicide days after Chili's, you see, and an attempt by another wife that failed. Copycat suicides, they called them, and both were committed by noncommissioned officers' wives with a history of alcoholism.'

'What happened then?' Sam asked.

'Joe was afraid of what Brick Masters might do to him if I didn't shut up. Please, don't think Joe was a coward, because he wasn't, but it was vitally important to Joe that he stay in the Air Force. Anyway, I finally did shut up, and I never mentioned it again. Needless to say, it has weighed very heavily on my conscience.'

Nell spoke up. 'There really was a letter, and I have it. Then, just a few days ago, I was visited by an FBI investigator who was making a background check on Brick Masters, because the President is planning to appoint him to a big position in the White House. I was so upset about it that I telephoned Beth and read the letter to her. I decided I had kept quiet too long.'

'As soon as I heard the entire letter, I knew we had no time to waste,' Beth said.

'Right,' Nell agreed. 'We decided there and then to call all of you to help us put all the pieces of the puzzle together and decide what we could, or should, do. You see, Howard told me everything that was going on at the time, and he swore me to secrecy, but I can't keep my mouth shut any longer.'

'How come Howard had the letter?' Kip asked.

'He was the first one on the scene that morning. Beth probably doesn't remember, but she called the Air Police, who had strict orders to report all serious emergencies to the CO's office immediately. Howard picked up the letter and stuck it in his pocket while the APs were checking out the bedroom,' Nell explained.

'Why did he hide it?' Kip asked sternly.

'You know what a patsy he was for Masters. Without even reading it, he picked it up, thinking if it was okay, he could always produce it later. When Masters saw it, however, he ordered him to destroy it, but Howard didn't. He kept it to protect himself, just in case.'

'Whom was the letter written to?' Tess asked.

'A person named Jimmyjohn, and I have no idea who he is except that he was apparently very close to Chili,' Beth explained.

'He was her cousin, I believe,' Sam said. 'I vaguely remember her telling me about him once. I honestly haven't given Chili's death much thought since then, though I liked her.'

'That's not surprising. Bob disappeared right after Chili died,' Tess said gently.

'I called Gamal Shaheen and asked him to join us here, but he refused. He got married again just three months after Chili's death. He resigned his commission shortly after that, and he works for the UN in New York. He has four children,' Beth stated flatly.

'Why wouldn't he come?' Sam asked.

Beth let out a deep sigh of disgust. 'He said as far as he was concerned, his marriage to Chili never happened. He didn't want to talk about her or think about her ever again. Neither his wife nor his children know he was married before.'

'Nice guy,' Kip remarked sarcastically.

Samara spoke up impatiently. 'Beth, for God's sake, read the damned letter so we all know what we're dealing with.'

'Well, here goes,' Beth said with a sigh, slipping the yellowed page out of the envelope.

66

Dear Jimmyjohn,

I got your letter today and don't you worry none, I'm going to find some way to get myself out of this fix and come home to take care of you. I'll get there fast as I can. Don't let them put you into no hospittel. Tell them I'm coming. I asked Gam for the money to buy a ticket on a commershil plane so I wouldn't have to wait for orders, but the bastard told me to go to hell. I got so mad I told him everything about you and me and all those other guys. What do I care? He treats me like some kinda dog shit anyway. Now I have to leave no matter what. I told this bum who's been giving me a hard time to bring me some money or I tell his wife what he's been doing. He better show up pretty soon or his party tonite just might turn out to be a big surprise party. You just hang on till I get there. You won't never have nothing to worry about, because I'm gonna be a big star someday. I got a friend whose family is real important in Hollywood and she told me so. I'll take good care of you, and we'll be on easy street. Our time is coming.

> Your loving cousin,
> Chili

There was a long silence, and Beth handed the letter to Kip to read for himself. When he finished, he gave it to Tess, and she in turn passed it to Samara, who was greatly distressed. Putting her hands over her face she said in a low, pained voice, 'Dear Lord, I only wanted to help her.'

'That wasn't written by a woman on the verge of suicide,' Tess stated numbly. 'I had trouble believing she killed herself, but I never thought someone murdered her . . . until now.'

'Who was the man she was waiting for?' Kip asked Beth.

'I'm sure it was Brick Masters,' Samara responded immediately, her memory of the days just prior to Bob's death now suddenly in sharp focus. 'It had to be him. She told me he'd threatened to tell her husband about her past affairs unless she . . . put out. He even made her service one of his buddies. You see, Chili and I got quite friendly during that fashion-show thing, and one day at lunch she just blurted out the whole story.'

'So . . . if it wasn't suicide,' Kip asked, 'who shot her?'

'She was already dead when she was shot.' Nell's words, spoken in a monotone, nevertheless echoed in the room like the report of a rifle.

'What killed her, then?' Tess asked.

'She was strangled. Howard saw the bruises on her neck,' Nell said, her voice muffled with shame.

'What did the autopsy report say?' Kip asked.

'They didn't have one. Chili's body was shipped out the next day to a mortuary in San Antonio, where she was immediately cremated, at her husband's request.'

'I'm sure there was some kind of an investigation,' Kip protested, 'either by the Air Police or the OSI.'

'Hey, those guys weren't in the FBI, you know, Kip. The dum-dums did whatever Masters told them to do,' Nell insisted. 'I remember Howard telling me it was a cinch. He himself covered her body with a sheet right off, and nobody at the scene that morning even got a good look at her.'

'Seems hard to believe,' Kip said doubtfully.

'Have you forgotten how powerful Masters was over there, Kip?' Nell reminded him. 'He was God, for Christ's sake.'

'Then whoever strangled her shot her in the head to make it look like suicide?' Tess asked.

'Right, but he made a mistake. Anybody who knew

Chili could have figured it out with no trouble at all,' Nell said. 'Howard did, but he didn't tell anybody, except me, of course.'

Beth forced herself to recall the horrible vision of Chili in death, a vision that she had deliberately erased from her mind years ago, and suddenly it was there again in all its gruesome detail. But there was something wrong with the picture now. There had always been something wrong with the picture. She gasped, and her hand went to her mouth as her eyes widened.

'Oh, my God!' she exclaimed. 'The gun was in her right hand!'

Instantly the women in the room understood, but Samara said it: 'Chili was left-handed!'

'Exactly. She had some kind of nerve damage in her arm. Remember that long scar? Anyway, her right hand was very weak. One day when she was working on the fashion show, I handed her a full mug of coffee, and she dropped it. She said she couldn't hold anything heavy in that hand,' Tess said, remembering the incident.

Beth was extremely upset. Her hands were shaking and her voice quivered. 'How could I have forgotten something as important as that?'

'Don't be so hard on yourself, Beth. Nobody noticed but Howard,' Nell continued, relieved at last to be sharing the long-held burden of secrecy. 'He told Brick right away that he thought it might not be suicide, but Brick ordered Howard to keep quiet about it . . . said Chili was just a whore anyway, and any one of a dozen guys she'd been screwing around with could have done it. He said he didn't want the thing blown out of all proportion and risk harm to the base's mission or to his own command. He said a dependent suicide wouldn't be noticed much . . . hysterical women were always killing themselves.'

Samara was furious. 'Brick Masters is a damned liar, and Howard was an ass to be taken in like that. I'll bet my bottom dollar that the only "screwing around" Chili was doing was with Brick Masters himself.'

'Nell, why in the world would Howard go along with Brick? Why did you let him?' Tess asked angrily.

Nell replied softly, 'He never listened to me when it came to the Air Force. He said I was just a dumb housewife who couldn't earn a living, and he was right. What did I know anyway about high-level stuff and secrecy? I was never very smart. I had trouble even finishing high school. He didn't tell me everything that was going on, because he knew I'd give him a hard time. He told me about Chili, though, because he was scared. Real scared. He kept the letter to protect himself. You see, he never crossed Brick Masters on anything.'

'But why? Why did he do everything Masters told him to do?' Samara asked.

'Why did all those people around Nixon do the things they did? Because they hitched their wagons to a star, that's why. Howard believed that Brick was on his way to the top, and he went along for the ride. He was ambitious, that's all,' Nell responded, 'like just about everybody else.'

'So you think that Masters strangled Chili and then tried to make it look like a suicide?' Beth asked.

'I certainly do, but I ought to warn you that I'm biased,' Nell responded. 'You see, I tried so hard to keep Howard from going to Vietnam, but he went because Brick told him it was the smart thing to do career-wise. Still, I probably would have gone to my grave being a loyal wife if it hadn't been for that FBI man visiting me. Something inside me just started churning when I thought of that miserable bastard being appointed to something big.'

'The investigator didn't tell you what the appointment was, did he?' Kip asked skeptically.

Nell shook her head. 'No, but as soon as he left, I called up Brick Masters himself, acting real friendly-like. I told him I had given him a real good recommendation, and he lapped it up. He was so damn proud of himself I didn't even have to ask him. He came right out and bragged about how he was going to the White House as head of the National Security Council. He said he'd finally made it to the top where the real power was.'

'My God,' Sam exclaimed. 'We've got to do something. We can't let him get away with murder!'

'Wait a minute,' Tess said. 'We have to think about this some more. I know Masters looks like the logical person, but what about Gamal? Isn't it possible that he might have killed her in a blind rage after she told him the truth about herself?'

Samara disagreed. 'I understand what you're saying, Tess, but it wouldn't make sense for Masters to orchestrate a cover-up if he hadn't been involved in it himself some way.'

'Sam, don't forget that Masters would have suppressed that letter whether he was guilty or not,' Kip pointed out. 'It would have been easy for anyone to figure out just who the person was that Chili fingered in her letter. A lot of people on the base knew about that damned "prayer rug" of his, not to mention his shenanigans when he was out of town. It was a lot safer for him to have it be suicide and get it over and done with. He wouldn't have given a damn about finding her killer. All he was interested in was keeping the waters oiled and smooth so there would be no hitch in his own career plans.'

After a long, thoughtful silence, Tess had something

new to add. 'Kip, remember when Masters called me into his office to talk to me about Chili's death?'

Kip nodded. 'I remember he wouldn't let me stay in the office with you.'

'You didn't want me to tell him about the telephone conversation I had with Chili a couple of days before she died, remember that?'

Kip nodded that he remembered.

'I thought it was wrong to conceal anything, and so I told him that Chili was upset because she found condoms in her husband's pocket and she was sure he had a girlfriend because they had never used them. She was trying hard to get pregnant.'

'Gamal was fooling around?' Beth asked.

'Brick thought so. He said that was probably why she killed herself. He was extremely pleased about it.' Tess closed her eyes and murmured. 'Dear God, I must have unwittingly provided him with a reason to declare it suicide.'

Nell spoke up. 'You sure did, even though Brick knew exactly why Gamal had those condoms, but your version suited his purposes just fine. As a matter of fact, Masters hated having Gamal along on a trip because he was so damned disapproving of the men screwin' around that he made everybody uncomfortable. Gamal Shaheen was definitely not one of the boys.'

'What about the condoms, then?' Tess asked.

'The US was trying to help King Idris get his wife pregnant so he'd have an heir,' Kip said, and turning to Tess added, 'That was the real reason I didn't want you to say anything to Masters about the condoms. It was a top-secret operation, and I was afraid he'd think I'd broken security.'

Kip looked down at his hands thoughtfully. 'The new

government of Libya would have been in serious trouble if word got out what we were doing, you see. There were a lot of political factions pressing Idris to name certain people as successors to the throne.'

'What did Gamal have to do with it?' Sam asked.

'They brought in some experts from the States. Since the king refused to take another wife because he loved Fatima, they decided to artificially inseminate her with sperm from a younger, more potent male. Gamal was the donor,' Nell explained with a slight smirk.

'Because he was an American who could be trusted to keep his mouth shut, but he was also an Arab whose parents were followers of Islam,' Samara added.

'You knew about it too?' Tess asked in surprise.

Samara shook her head. 'Not at all. It just makes sense. He would be the logical choice. Where did the condoms come in?'

'You want to tell it, Kip, or do you want me to?' Nell asked with a snigger.

'Be my guest,' Kip said, and got up to pour himself another brandy.

'Okay, well, whenever the thermometer said the queen was in heat, so to speak, poor Gamal had to go either to the palace in Tripoli or Benghazi, wherever she was. The poor guy would go into a room near the royal bedchamber and ejaculate into a condom, which he'd hand off to the doctor, who would inject the semen into her uterus. The process was crude in those days, but it worked. Whether by the efforts of her husband or Gamal – nobody would ever know exactly, you see. . . she finally got pregnant and gave birth to a little boy prematurely at the Wheelus hospital. Unfortunately, he only lived one day.'

Tess was particularly fascinated by the story, and

remembered her conversation with Colonel Channing. 'Did they try again?'

'I don't know, but later I heard that Fatima decided it wasn't Allah's will that she bear a child. King Idris finally broke down and took another wife, an Egyptian whom the people never really accepted. When she didn't have a kid either, he divorced her. Kip, pour me one of those brandies . . . a big one,' Nell said. 'This story makes me feel like a very ugly American.'

'Well, I personally think it was a damned good idea,' Sam remarked. 'If it had worked, we might not have Quaddafi and we might still have a base in Libya.'

'You're right, Sam. Ever since we were forced to withdraw from Wheelus, he's been moving that country closer to the Soviets,' Kip added.

Changing the subject, Tess asked, 'If Masters killed Chili, why didn't Gamal raise any questions about it? Surely he knew the gun was in the wrong hand.'

'When I asked Howard about that, he said that Gamal probably had his reasons. That's all I know,' Nell replied.

'What should we do now?' Tess asked.

'There's not much point in creating a scandal unless we can nail her killer, whoever he is. It could get us into a lot of trouble and expose us to a lawsuit,' Sam warned.

'I have nothing to lose,' Beth said, and Nell added, 'Neither do I.'

'Well, I'd hate it if things got nasty, because the media would be all over me,' Sam said. 'I've got a higher profile than most, and I do have grandchildren to think about. What about you, Tess.'

'First, let's figure out if there's anything we can do. Any ideas, Kip?' Tess asked. She decided not to mention the impending chancellorship, because she didn't want her own ambitions to influence their decision.

431

'It's going to be tough. We don't exactly have a smoking gun with fingerprints, and I can almost guarantee there'll be nothing in the files,' Kip commented. 'Remember, we were a world away from the Pentagon, and if Masters were guilty, he had the power to cover his tracks. Besides, it could be an embarrassment to the Air Force, perhaps even to the country, if all this stuff about Gamal and the king came out. Brick Masters had an impressive career. He retired as a major general right after heading up the Ballistic Missile Center and went immediately into the president's chair of one of the prime missile-parts contractors in San Diego. Talk about influence peddling. He's got a hell of a lot of friends in high places, and if we're to judge by the impending appointment, that includes the President himself.'

Sam spoke up. 'Suppose I call up Mike Wallace and ask him to put a couple of reporters on it. If they think it's a good enough story, they'll go with it for *60 Minutes*. It would be right up their alley. What do you think?'

Beth shook her head. 'I don't like it. It's too sensational. We may wind up destroying ourselves and making him look like a hero. You know how strange the public can be. They make heroes out of the most unlikely people.'

Samara observed Tess and Kip closely, and said, 'I think it's up to the Kiplings to decide what we should do, if anything. They have the most to lose. Kip still has a lot ahead of him in his service life, and Tess is on the faculty at Christopher, not to mention that Skip is about to graduate from the Air Force Academy.'

Tess and Kip looked at each other for a long weighted moment. It would so easy to walk away from this and go on with their lives. Only a brief moment passed before Kip reached across the table and took Tess's hand. As the women watched, wordlessly they came to a decision. Their eyes said that although it wasn't the time or the issue they would have chosen, they would live with the moment fate had assigned them. If their lives were to have any meaning, they would have to take a stand. It was Tess who spoke first. 'I agree with Beth. I can't go along with the television thing, not yet anyway, but I am willing to take our case to the Air Force and ask for an investigation.'

'So am I,' Kip said. 'Who knows? Maybe we'll get lucky.'

'Where do we start?' Beth asked.

'I'll call the Staff Judge Advocate and talk to a man I know there first thing in the morning. If he wants to see us, are you all available to go back to DC with me tomorrow?' Kip asked.

'Will he see us so soon?' Nell asked doubtfully.

'He will if I ask him to,' Kip responded. 'I have a few friends in high places too, you know. Besides, I think it would hurt our case if we waited any longer.'

Beth put another question to them. 'Does anyone doubt that Chili was murdered?'

No one said a word.

67

It was a subdued group that gathered for a late breakfast in Samara's suite. Kip had arisen at five that morning to call Washington, and he was about to make a report on what he'd learned.

'I talked to Bert Stankowski and gave him a brief sketch of what we had and what our suspicions were about Masters. Bert's a sharp guy, and he put his people to work on it immediately to see if they could track down any of the files on the operation at Wheelus at the time it happened. He called me back a few minutes ago and said they couldn't find anything, but that wasn't unusual, because they often order sensitive files destroyed when the host country is hostile, which Quaddafi was at the time we withdrew in 1970.'

'Now what do we do?' Beth asked, not expecting any kind of hopeful answer.

'Bert says we don't have nearly enough to open an inquiry of any kind, although he's willing to look at any further information we can gather. We're at the end of a blind alley.'

'Did you tell him we were thinking of going to *60 Minutes*?' Samara asked.

'Yeah, I mentioned it, but of course he wasn't happy with that. He said they wouldn't cooperate with any sensationalism whatsoever,' Kip said.

'Now what?' Tess asked.

'Well, we've just got to start getting some hard evidence, that's all,' Samara said.

434

'How do we do that?' Tess asked.

'I think we need to start in Los Angeles. I know there are some really great private detectives there that we could hire to track down this Jimmyjohn and Gamal,' Samara suggested.

'I know where Gamal lives,' Beth said. 'I've got his address back in my apartment, but I think the detective idea is a good one.'

'Give me Gamal's number, and I'll call him myself and talk to him,' Samara suggested. 'And if you all want to go to LA, I'll have the jet return to pick us up this afternoon.'

'I hope you'll have more success with him than I did,' Beth replied.

After breakfast, as Tess and Kip were driving to the Air Force Academy to visit their son, Kip took Tess's hand in his and squeezed it.

'I miss you so much, babe, I really do. The nights just get longer and longer,' he said softly.

'Kip, I miss you too. I often wish things were different.' She thought a moment and then decided to tell him about the dinner party she was missing that night. When she finished, he asked abruptly, 'What time does your flight leave?' and when she responded, 'They'll probably be boarding the plane in fifteen minutes,' he whipped the car into a U-turn and accelerated so rapidly that she had to cling to the seat.

'What are you doing?' she gasped.

'Getting you to the airport. There's no earthly reason for you to miss that dinner tonight. Why in the hell didn't you say something?'

'But my suitcase . . . I left everything in my room,' she protested.

'I'll bring it to Los Angeles. Listen, my dear, didn't you learn anything at all about ambitions and careers from

435

me? When you want to achieve something, go for it. Don't let anybody stand in your way. Now, get yourself home, attend the dinner and I'll give you a call late tonight and let you know where we're staying so you can join us there tomorrow . . . after you knock 'em dead tonight. Okay?'

'Kip . . . I don't know what to say,' she stammered, astonished that he was actually trying to help her succeed in a career he had always resented.

'How about "I love you"?' he responded with a smile.

68

Later that day, Kip, Beth, Sam, and Nell boarded the Silverstone-Galaxy Lear jet, which Sam had ordered to return to Colorado Springs to pick them up. Noticing that Nell had been particularly quiet at breakfast that morning, Sam sat down beside her.

'Nell, something's bothering you, isn't it?' she asked. 'You didn't have a thing to say this morning. Don't you believe we're doing the right thing?'

'I'm just feelin' real guilty, Sam,' she said, looking out the window pensively. 'Howard told me that the quickest way to success in the Air Force was to kiss the ass of every s.o.b. who ranked us, and look where it got us. My husband's pushing up daisies, and I'm old and fat and ugly and alone and it serves us both right. Maybe if we'd thought more about what was right than what was good for us, Howard wouldn't have been so damn quick to accommodate Brick. The only reason he got away with so much was that he was surrounded by a bunch of jerks who let him.'

'We're all geniuses in hindsight, Nell. But you eventually came to the right decision, and you did it all on your own. Even if we fail, you should feel good about trying to make things right. I do believe God works in mysterious ways, and I think the part you're playing in this little drama is the way it was supposed to be,' Sam said.

'Dammit, Sam. You always did have a way of making people feel good,' Nell replied with a wan smile.

'I just tell the truth, that's all.'

When the plane landed in Los Angeles, a limousine picked them up and took them all to Sam's home. It wasn't the huge estate left to her by her parents, but it was a luxurious house in Bel Air. Refusing to listen to their protests about going to a hotel, she put Kip in the guest house by himself and settled Beth and Nell into guest bedrooms in the main house. It was a sunny warm California day, and she told everyone to relax and enjoy the pool while she attended to some business.

Once alone in her study, she placed a long-distance telephone call to Gamal Shaheen. It was a tense but effective conversation.

Dinner that evening was served in the richly appointed dining room of Sam's home. Sitting on the silk damask chairs, eating from white bisque Rosenthal china rimmed with gold, and sipping Mouton-Rothschild '61 from Baccarat glasses, Sam's pampered guests heard her news.

'Well, friends, you may have to stay here a day or two longer than you planned. Kip, I know this might be a greater hardship for you than for the others, but trust me, in the end it will be worthwhile.' She paused briefly and then continued.

'I talked to Gamal this afternoon, and he's agreed to join us here tomorrow. I'm having a first-class plane ticket delivered to him tonight. I also left a message with Tess's secretary that I'd send the plane for her whenever her business is concluded at Christopher.'

'My God, how did you talk him into it?' Beth asked, astounded. 'He stonewalled me.'

'Never underestimate the power of television. It's changed the way the world works,' Sam began. 'I told him that my company was doing an in-depth documentary about the frequent cover-up of crime in the military, and I intended to use his wife's alleged suicide, which was of

438

particular interest to me because she was my friend. I told him that you, Kip, a general, had consented to be interviewed on camera, and that I had a special team of investigators working hand-in-glove with anonymous military men who had agreed to open certain files for us.'

'My God, Sam,' Beth exlaimed, 'that's all a lie!'

'Who the hell cares?' Nell chortled. 'It worked, didn't it?'

Gloating, Sam picked up her wineglass and tasted the velvety liquid, and when the import of her opening had settled in, she went on. 'There's more. I asked Gamal point-blank if he had any information about Chili's death, and he said he did.'

'And . . . and . . . go on!' Beth urged.

'He wouldn't tell me any more on the telephone. So, let's have a toast to old friends and to justice,' Sam said, lifting her glass.

'Better late than never,' Nell replied with a wry smile.

69

Tess was only ten minutes late for the chancellor's dinner party, and when she explained that she had just gotten in from Colorado Springs and hadn't even had time to go home to change, everyone was quite understanding. She was glad she had put on her best blue wool suit for the visit with Skip that never happened.

It was a pleasant dinner, but Tess had trouble keeping her mind on the conversation, because she kept thinking about Kip and Beth, Nell and Sam. Being in a group with them all, after more than twenty years, had been almost a mystical experience for her, and the dilemma in which they all found themselves seemed so much more important than this dinner party. Why, she wasn't sure. Maybe it wasn't vital that they succeed in bringing Chili Shaheen's murderer to justice. Maybe it was sufficient that they cared enough to try.

'I beg your pardon?' Tess said, realizing that the gentleman sitting next to her had posed a question to her.

'I just asked how you thought school adminstrators should deal with these unruly young people,' the man repeated, and Tess suddenly remembered that he was Avery Hammond, the president of the board of trustees.

Without hesitating, Tess replied, 'I think we should listen to them.'

'You mean we should encourage them to demonstrate and break the rules and destroy property?' Hammond asked indignantly.

'I didn't mean it in that way at all,' Tess replied evenly.

'I believe the ultimate goal of education is not only to train people to be good engineers or architects or whatever, but also to teach students to be thinking, inquiring citizens. Questioning the rules is part of that process, and while I'm opposed to violence, I am also opposed to the suppression of thought or speech, especially in a university where all thought and action are subject to exploration.'

The others at the dinner table had become quiet, and her voice carried across the room. Hammond was quick to take advantage, and he laughed a short bark of a laugh and said, 'Then I hope to God I never hire one of your students to design a house or build a bridge for me.'

Tess glanced over to Chancellor Harris and saw by the look on his face that she had just quashed her chance of being selected, if she had ever really had one, and she was disgusted with herself for being there. She should have known there was no room for her at the head of this university, and if she hadn't let the blindness of her ambition cloud her mind, she would have seen that they were just using her. Damn them all! If she was going down, she would go in flames.

'On the contrary, Mr Hammond, you would be smart to choose someone who had been taught the value of honest and open inquiry . . . someone who respected the work he was doing and who took pride in it,' she said. 'Then you wouldn't have to worry about his cutting costs by putting too much sand in the cement or inferior steel in the supports,' she added, enunciating her words sharply and lifting her voice just enough so that no one at the table could fail to understand every one of them.

The silence in the room was deathly. Avery Hammond was a builder with a stranglehold on every important contract in the county, and it was rumored that he had made his millions by using shoddy materials and paying off union bosses, although no one had ever been able to prove anything.

Tess looked around, aware that she had just committed professional suicide. Not only had she killed any hope of ever being chosen chancellor, but she had probably thrown away her job security. Frank Higbee would be the new chancellor, and her career at this school would be history.

The conversation at the table teetered gradually back to a semblance of normality, but no one talked to Tess anymore, and she was left to contemplate her own dreary future.

What demon of conscience had gotten into her? One meeting with her old friends from Tripoli, and she had undone twenty years of hard work.

Immediately after coffee was served, the members of the board said their good-byes and departed hurriedly. It was an evening they wished to forget but which they would always remember. Tess lingered to apologize to her mentor.

When they were alone, the elderly chancellor put his arm around her shoulder and squeezed it. 'What's going on with you, my dear?' he asked. 'Why didn't you tell me you didn't want the job?'

'But I did want it. I really did,' Tess said, close to tears. 'I guess maybe I never really believed I had a chance.'

'So you turned them down before they could turn you down, right?'

'I wasn't a serious possibility anyway, was I?' Tess asked. 'Everybody decided it would just look good to pretend that I was. Isn't that the way it was . . . really?'

'Honestly?' He pulled his ever-present pipe from his jacket pocket and began to fill it with tobacco.

'Honestly, truly, really.'

'I was trying to ram you down their throats, Tess. That's the brutal truth. I know you're the best choice for troubled times like this because you're honest and you're fair and the kids love you. But the board wants somebody who'll kick ass. Most of the trustees feel I'm too easygoing,' he said with a rueful smile, 'and that there wouldn't be any demonstrations if I were tougher on the troublemakers. So, don't feel bad about tonight. You were great, my dear. The look on their faces is a memory I'll cherish to the end of my days. And if you decide to seek employment elsewhere, you can count on an outstanding recommendation from me.'

'I suppose I'd better give it serious consideration, hmm?'

'I would if I were you. Christopher was lucky to have you, Tess, and I'm really sorry we don't seem to be ready for a strong woman who's not afraid to say what she thinks.'

Tess sighed, a long, quivering sigh of disappointment. 'I really wanted to make it here, you know, not only because it's a fine school but also because it's such a damned bastion of male dominance.'

'In my opinion, you did, Tess. And don't you forget it. You've made me feel as if I were Diogenes, finally finding an honest man. Only it turned out she was a woman.'

443

70

Tess arrived at Samara's home just shortly before Gamal was scheduled to arrive. The group was gathered in the solarium waiting. Getting up to greet her, Sam gave Tess a quick hug.

'I hope your dinner was a triumph, darling,' she said.

'Not exactly, but I'll tell you about that later. I need a tall, cold drink of water, and then I'll have a glass of the wine. Sam, your house is gorgeous . . . and I loved the plane ride. It was my first trip by private jet. It's really the only way to fly.'

'I'm glad you like it, dear. It won't be your last. I've had your bags put in the guest house where Kip is staying,' she said with a wink.

Kip went to Tess immediately, gave her a little hug and kiss. 'What happened?' he whispered.

'As the guys on LSD say, darling, it was a bad trip, a real bad trip. I'll tell you all about it later.'

Gamal's arrival was announced, and the group sat down to await his entrance. When he arrived, Gamal stopped to look around the room apprehensively. A quiet, secretive man, he hated being the center of attention. Samara and Kip rose to greet him, and then he made the rounds, smiling stiffly and saying little. His hair was quite gray, as was the mustache that had been acquired after he left Wheelus. His olive skin was deeply lined, but he was still thin, and his carriage was just as erect as ever. When Samara offered him a drink, he smiled a very small smile

444

and replied, 'I still don't drink, Samara. I never have. But a glass of iced tea would be most welcome.'

As soon as he had been served and settled comfortably in one of the wicker chairs, Samara got down to business.

'Gamal, I want you to read this letter and tell us if you believe it was written by your wife . . . your dead wife, Chili.' Beth got up and handed him the letter.

A tense silence filled the bright, sunlit room. The grass-green carpet, white wicker chairs upholstered in ivy-printed white canvas, and walls of leaded glass that curved up to the ceiling made the room seem an extension of the garden beyond. The butler, who had been serving the drinks from the long bar, left at a signal from Samara. Gamal read the letter stoically and then handed it back to Beth. 'I'm sure that was written by Chili. She didn't have much education, you know.'

Samara snapped, 'We're not interested in the grammar and punctuation, Gamal. Does that read like it was written by a woman just a few moments away from shooting herself in the head?'

'She didn't kill herself,' he said, not looking directly into the eyes of anyone in the room.

'What do you mean?'

'We didn't have a gun in the house. She was deathly afraid of them.'

'If you knew she didn't do it, why in the hell didn't you say so?' Nell Carson asked.

He looked directly at Nell and retorted, 'For the same damned reason your husband said nothing. He knew exactly what happened that night. He was part of it!'

The room was hushed with expectancy. 'Tell us what you know, Gamal,' Samara urged.

'Howard called me at about six o'clock that evening. I was in the bedroom having an argument with my wife.

445

She'd received a letter from her cousin that day. He said he was having blackouts and couldn't take care of himself anymore. From the minute she got the letter, she started hounding me for the money to fly home to take care of him, but I said no. I didn't give a damn if she went – I was sick to death of her anyway – but damned if I was going to spend my hard-earned dough for a plane ticket when she could wait a few weeks and fly back for nothing. From the minute I walked in the door that night, she was on my back about it. Then the telephone rang, and Howard told me that Brick wanted me to come to the office immediately.'

He paused for a swig of iced tea and continued.

'I left the house thinking it was an emergency. Brick was always rushing me in for something or other. I figured it must be urgent or he wouldn't be coming to the office half an hour before his party. Howard was the only one there. We sat around for a few minutes and talked, I can't remember what it was about, then he got a telephone call and said he had to leave, but I was to wait there. He said if he didn't come back in a half-hour or so, I could go on to the party. I must have waited . . . oh, maybe forty-five minutes all by myself there. Finally I figured Brick wasn't coming and so I went directly to the villa. I was sure that Chili had gone on by herself because she was all gussied up and anxious to go to the party when I left her.'

'But she wasn't there, was she?' Kip asked. 'Weren't you worried about her not showing?'

Gamal took a pack of cigarettes out of his pocket, lighted one, and replied, 'Worried? No, why should I have been? I was curious, maybe. Definitely relieved not to have to put up with her chatter and her flirting. When Veronica said Chili had called and talked to Brick and told him that she couldn't come because she had a headache, I thought maybe she was just miffed and trying to get back at me. I knew she didn't really have a headache. Chili was fine when I left her.'

Everyone was hanging on each word he spoke. 'After the party, I went home, walked into the house prepared for a fight . . . and saw her lying on the bed, dead. I checked her pulse, but she was already growing cold. I saw the finger marks on her neck, and I realized she'd been killed while I was sitting in Masters' office all by myself . . . alone . . . no alibi. I figured I'd been set up. I left the house just as I found it, made sure nobody saw me, and went to the BOQ to sleep, which I'd done on several other occasions when she was drunk.'

Nell's face was white with fury. 'Are you insinuating that my husband helped Masters plan to kill her . . . that he was an accessory to murder?'

'I'm telling you what happened,' he replied testily. 'The next morning I went into Masters' office and accused him, but he told me if I didn't keep my mouth shut he'd see to it that I was arrested. He said if I played ball, he'd make sure her death was declared a suicide, and both of us would be rid of her. He said she was nothing but a tramp, and certainly not worth either of us sacrificing ourselves. I had to go along with him. Who in the United States Air Force would take the word of a follower of Islam over that of a red-blooded American war hero like Masters?'

'You're contemptible, you know that, Shaheen?' Kip said angrily.

'How do we know this isn't a story to take the blame off yourself and lay it on Masters?' Tess asked.

'It's my word against his now that his brown-nosing toady Carson is dead and can't lie for him.'

'How did you know my husband was dead?' Nell asked.

'Samara told me. That's why I agreed to come here.

447

I've always wanted to tell my side of the story to someone who was there. It would have been stupid of me to shoot off my mouth while Howard was still alive to alibi for his buddy Masters. If there was a chance of seeing the guy hang, I'd be all for it, but the trail is cold. Any evidence that might incriminate either of us has been destroyed. I was ordered to have her body cremated without autopsy. I had the ashes sent to her cousin, because that's what she'd have wanted.'

'God help us,' Nell said, covering her face.

Sam looked thoughtfully at her for a long moment and then said, 'Nell, there had to be something for Howard in all this conspiracy. I can't believe he was just a simple-minded patsy for Masters. Was he?'

Nell didn't look up as she replied in a tone that was heavy with bitterness and shame. 'Not really, I guess. Brick always took good care of us. Whenever Howard got an assignment he didn't like, one call to his good buddy, and we were on our way to Hawaii or Florida or California. The higher up Masters went in rank, the better our assignments. I looked the other way on a lot of things. It was comfortable for me to delude myself into believing Masters was nice because he appreciated all the favors Howard had done for him at Wheelus.'

'That's just about what it was,' Tess responded with rancor.

'It stinks!' Kip exclaimed angrily. 'Every one of you was a disgrace to the uniform you wore, you know that?'

'I'm not proud of what happened,' Gamal replied defensively, 'but I have a family to think of now. My wife didn't even know I'd been married before, but thanks to Mrs Mulhare here, she knows now. Veronica and Brick have children and grandchildren. Go ahead. Stir up a stew of garbage, if it makes you feel better, but Chili's

448

murderer will never pay for his crime. Mark my words, you'll only succeed in destroying a lot of innocent people.'

Gamal got up to leave. 'I have nothing more to say. Thanks for the plane ticket, Samara. I'll be going home now. Oh, yes, and if you go looking for Jimmyjohn Jensen, you'll be wasting your time. He died ten years ago. I went to see him when I got back to the States, and I told him my side of the story. He believed me, and he wanted revenge. He swore he was going to kill Brick Masters himself, but he was a sick man. You may not believe it, but I've never lied to anybody in my entire life. Under other circumstances, I might have been a good husband to Chili. I did a lot better the second time around.'

He turned on his heel and left them.

'Dear God,' Beth exclaimed, 'now what!'

71

Walking hand in hand through the lighted garden, past the swimming pool, Tess and Kip headed for the guest cottage at the back of Samara's property. It was a tiny house with a sitting room, bedroom, and bath. Decorated in floral chintz, it possessed a charming, cozy, fairy-tale ambience.

'What a lovely place,' Tess exclaimed. 'You know, for the life of me, I couldn't tell you a thing about the main house, I was so wrapped up in what was going on. My God, what an experience the last couple of days have been.'

'I see there's a bottle of port on the tray over there, and wood laid in the fireplace. Why don't I light it and pour us each a glass of wine? I want to hear how your dinner went.'

'I'd love a glass,' Tess said, dropping onto the love seat in front of the fireplace. 'In fact, I might need two of them.'

The logs blazed immediately, illuminating the room with a warm golden light. Kip poured two glasses of the rich purple wine and snapped off the lights before he joined her on the couch. They clinked glasses, and Kip said softly, 'To us.' Then, before taking a sip, he kissed her gently on the lips.

Tess took off her shoes and tucked her legs under her as she snuggled close to him, feeling secure and comforted and loved. When they were together, she never wanted him to leave. As the years passed, he seemed to mellow, and now he was dearer to her than ever. The differences they'd had in the early years had long ago faded into insignificance.

'I'm going to quit my job, Kip.'

'Are you kidding? How can that be?' he asked in astonishment.

'I behaved unspeakably last night. I don't know what got into me, but I insulted Avery Hammond, the chairman of the board of trustees.'

'Why, for God's sake?' Kip said, leaning back so that he could look into her eyes.

'I've been trying to figure it out. I guess it was my conscience telling me it was time to stop toadying to other people just to get ahead. The man is a crook, Kip. Everybody knows it, but he's got so much money and influence that he gets away with murder.'

'There's a lot of that going around, it seems.'

Tess tried to put into words the thoughts that were swirling around in her head. 'It had something to do with Chili, I'm certain of it, my behaving that way. A little voice inside me said it was time for honesty. I had to start saying what I believed, no matter what effect it had on my career. I suddenly saw myself being guilty of the same ambition that I detested in you when we were in Tripoli, and I was ashamed of myself.'

'I know just how you feel. I can't tell you how often I've kicked myself for letting you get on that plane in Tripoli without me. I guess I was just too young and too hungry to get ahead to realize that having someone to love is all that really matters in life. I also had this stubborn and stupid idea that a good wife supported her husband no matter what her own feelings were. It never occurred to me that I had an obligation to support you and your feelings too. If I had it to do over again, I'd tell

451

Masters to take his job and shove it and get on that plane with you and Skip.'

'And you'd probably never forgive me for ruining your career,' Tess said knowingly.

'Hey, it wouldn't have ruined my career!' he protested with feigned hauteur. 'I've been an outstanding officer, my love. I'd have survived and triumphed. I just wish I'd had the confidence in myself then that I have now.'

'I don't regret my life, Kip . . . and neither do you. We both had things we needed to do, and we did them without losing each other entirely. We were very lucky. I'm sorry I was insensitive to your yearnings. I just didn't have enough experience to understand them then, but I do now.'

'Speaking of yearnings,' he whispered, his lips gently brushing hers, 'I have a powerful yearning to ravish you.'

'Sounds good to me. Shall we have a go at it on that rug in front of the fire?' she suggested coyly.

Kip looked doubtful. 'Well, if you really want to . . . but couldn't I ravish you just as well on that nice comfortable bed over there?'

72

Kip and Tess were getting ready to go to breakfast the next morning when the telephone in the guest house rang. It was Kip's office in Washington calling. Tess handed him the telephone and watched the expression on his face as he listened.

'What is it?' she asked, certain that something important was about to happen.

'I've just been appointed commander of the Air Force in Europe. General Holden has decided to retire.'

'What does that mean? Are you happy about it?' she asked, perplexed by his lack of excitement.

'Confused, Tess. Last night, while you were sleeping in my arms, I decided that I was going to take early retirement so we could be together.'

'And now you're having second thoughts?' she asked. 'Don't even think of retiring. You want this job, darling. You've worked for it, you deserve it, and the country needs good leaders.'

'I need you with me on this, Tess. Give me the next four years, and I'll give you the rest of my life, I promise you.'

Tess smiled wanly, thinking that four years out of the academic mainstream might be fatal to her own ambitions, but she could not say no, not yet.

'We'll talk about it later, when we have more time. Let's go have breakfast with the others. We still have to solve the problem of Brick Masters.'

The women were already eating their grapefruit when

Tess and Kip joined them. The gloom and doom of the night before were gone, replaced by the electricity of action.

'Good morning, lovebirds,' Sam greeted them. 'Sit down and listen.' She was ebullient.

'It sounds as if you have some good news,' Kip said.

'Great news. We three lonely ladies sat up until almost three in the morning talking. We decided that what we needed was one witness to corroborate Gamal's story, because we think he was telling the truth. Who could that be? Veronica? She knew that her husband left the house for a while just before the party that night, but she certainly would never tell anything that might harm her husband. How about the guest of honor?'

'Who was it? Nell, do you know?' Tess asked.

'I sure as hell do. It was General Torrance – Fred, I think, was his first name. He and his wife were on their way back to the States. Did you know him, Kip?'

'Everybody knew him. He was a crackerjack pilot and tough as nails, but highly respected. He's been retired for over ten years. I guess he's still alive.'

'Dear God, please let him be alive,' Beth said fervently.

'The telephone's in the study, Kip. You can eat later,' Sam insisted, shooshing him out of his chair impatiently.

Kip was on the telephone for almost an hour. The women floated in and out of the room anxiously, filling his coffee cup and listening for any hint of what he was hearing. At last he finished and returned to the living room, where they all were waiting impatiently.

'Well?' Sam asked eagerly.

'He's alive and well. In fact, he's the president of a large corporation in Cleveland. I had a long talk with him. He's really a sharp guy.'

That afternoon, Sam, Beth, Nell, Tess, and Kip

boarded Sam's plane and headed for Washington, DC, with a stopover in Cleveland to pick up their star witness.

The next morning all six of them met in the office of General Horace Benton to lay out the case of the murder of Chili Shaheen by General Brick Masters. When they told him what they suspected, General Benton took a deep breath.

'Whew! Even in the military, there is no statute of limitations on murder. Are you all willing to testify in a court-martial?' he asked. 'If General Masters gets a good attorney, it could be messy, it could take a long time, and we might fail. Are you prepared for that?'

Kip spoke for them all. 'Yes we are, Horace. No matter what it costs us personally. I think it's also important to go on record with something that will hold up his appointment to the National Security Council. I don't think any of us would sleep well if he were that close to the seat of power in this country.'

'That's a troubling point, Kip. You can't very well sully his professional reputation without solid evidence to support your claims. You'd be exposing yourselves to suit,' General Benton warned.

'God, I hope you all believe I had no idea when I was invited to . . . have sex . . . with that beautiful young woman on Brick's "prayer rug" that she had been coerced,' General Torrance said, obviously distressed at the part he had played in the affair. 'Brick told me she just liked to have a good time, and I believed him. I would never force a woman to have sex with me.'

Fred Torrance spoke with a conviction that no one doubted. He would be a powerful witness, and he would be believed.

He continued, 'When Kip called me yesterday and told me what he knew about this situation, I remembered something that seemed to have no significance whatsoever at the time. A few minutes before the guests were to arrive on the night of my last visit to Tripoli, I was dressed and ready before anybody else at the villa, so I fixed myself a drink and went outside to look at that beautiful view of the Mediterranean. It was incredible, you know. While I was standing there, I heard the sound of wheels on the pavement, and I went around to the front of the house and saw Brick getting out of his car. He was disheveled, I distinctly remember, because it was unusual to see him that way. You know what a spit-and-polish man he was. Before I had a chance to say anything, he told me he had to hurry inside and change out of his uniform because he'd lost a button. It seemed a little odd that he'd be making excuses about his uniform when I was wearing civilian clothes. As I recall, he winked at me and said, "Just collecting a little strange stuff, Fred." We both laughed, and he rushed inside. My wife and I left early the next morning and returned to the States. Not once, on any of the occasions when we met Veronica and Brick over the years, did I ever hear of that young woman's death. It's a big Air Force, you know. We don't know what's going on everywhere, and one wife's suicide wouldn't make many waves. Yes, if I'm needed, I will testify to what I saw. I believe that a man who is capable of forcing a woman against her will is also capable of killing her. Any airman in my command convicted of rape was always given the maximum penalty.'

The group stayed in Washington for three days, telling their stories and searching their memories for names of other witnesses who might be called to testify. When he was officially contacted, even Gamal agreed to come forward and tell his side of the story.

The outcome of the investigation was disheartening.

456

General Benton called them into his office to discuss the findings. 'We've gone over everything as fast as we possibly could without tipping our hand what was gong on, but there just isn't enough concrete evidence to accuse the man. I concede you have cause for suspicion, but that's all it is. Maybe if Mrs Carson's husband were still alive to attest to what he knows, we'd have something, but the trail is over twenty years cold. We have no fingerprints, no body to exhume, no weapon, no records of any kind. There's so little, as a matter of fact, that we wouldn't dare even try to stop his White House appointment.'

'Just exactly what would you need to nail him?' Samara asked.

'Well, I'm afraid the only eyewitness to the crime – if there were one – is General Masters himself, and there's not much chance of getting him to testify . . . or confess,' he replied. 'My advice to all of you is to try to forget about it. You did all that you could.'

The four women returned alone to Los Angeles. Kip stayed in Washington to prepare for his assignment to Europe, and General Torrance went his own way. On the return flight, Samara announced that she wasn't going to give up so easily, but intended to hire the best private investigator she could find.

Tess expressed some reservations. 'What can a private investigator possibly do that the entire government couldn't do?'

'Get Brick Masters to confess,' Sam said.

'Just how the hell are we going to do that?' Nell asked cynically.

'Funny you should ask,' Sam answered with a glint in her eyes, 'because you're the one who's going to get it for us, Nell. I've seen it done in the movies. Let's see if it'll work in real life. Now, listen closely. This is what we're going to do . . .'

457

73

Nell sat in the van listening as Henry Ellis gave her her instructions. Samara, Beth, Tess, and a sound technician were in the van too.

'There's nothing to worry about, understand? The mike is in your purse. If you can possibly do it, just lay the purse on his desk when you sit down. That way, we should get a good clear signal. Now, I've put a beeper in there, and if for some reason you get into his office and we don't have a clear signal, I'll beep it once. Turn around and go to the ladies' room at the end of the hall near his office. Mrs Mulhare will be in there with an identical purse to exchange with you, but I don't think that's gonna happen, because I've carried the purse right up to the office door and everything was clear as a bell.'

'God, I'm so nervous,' Nell said. 'I hope I don't blow this whole thing.'

'Can't I do it?' Tess asked. 'I'd love the chance to go in there and trip him up.'

Samara shook her head. 'He'd be on his guard with any of us, and we'd never get a thing out of him. It has to be Nell. She's the only one who has a prayer. Okay, Nell. Our hopes are riding on you.'

'I'll do the best I can,' she said nervously.

Henry Ellis, who had been recommended to Sam as the best electronic snoop in town, helped Nell out of the van and walked her across the street to the steel-and-glass building where Brick Masters' office was located.

'You're about ten minutes early for the appointment,

but that's fine. And it's okay to look nervous, understand? Now, I'm going to leave you at the elevator. Go to the third floor and tell the receptionist that you have an appointment with him. Mrs Mulhare will follow you on the next elevator. I had a key made so she could get into the ladies' room with the backup equipment. She'll stay there for ten minutes, in case you have any problems. Just knock on the door, and she'll let you in. Now, Masters has never seen me, so I'll hang around on the third floor just in case you need me. Okay?'

Nell took a deep breath and said okay.

The executive offices of the Stilton-Chambers Aeroposition Company were luxurious. Walking across the thick gray plush carpeting, Nell felt her legs wobble with nervousness. She told the receptionist her name, and she was asked to sit down on one of the blue mohair couches and wait. A long ten minutes later, an attractive young woman with a svelte waistline and a mane of long straight blond hair came out to escort Nell to Brick's office.

Brick's greeting was effusive. 'Well, well, Nell, how nice to see you again. Put on a little weight, I see. It's been a long time, now. Let's see, about . . .'

'Exactly three and a half years, Brick. Just before Howard left for Vietnam. And that little going-away dinner you had for him in Virginia,' she said, clipping her words. 'How's Veronica?'

'Have a seat there, Nell. Would you like a cup of coffee?'

Nell settled herself in one of the chairs facing his desk and said she would love one. He buzzed, and within moments the blond woman appeared with a cup of coffee on a silver tray. Her hands shaking, Nell put her purse on Brick's huge walnut desk and took the cup. When they were alone again, Brick answered her question.

'I guess you haven't heard about me and Veronica, then? Well, we finally came to a parting of the ways, can you believe that? After all these years.'

Nell was genuinely shocked and said so. In response to her asking why, he replied 'Well, it was just one of those things, you know. It happens to marriages sometimes, one partner continues to grow and expand his horizons, and the other just . . . well, stagnates.'

'I guess it was Veronica who stagnated, right, Brick? It certainly wasn't you.' She let her eyes roll around the room, taking in every luxurious detail, and added, 'You seem to be doing all right. They must be paying you a bundle to keep Uncle Sam's money rolling in, huh?'

Brick laughed easily. 'You got it, Nell. I've brought in a lot of bucks, more than enough to pay back the gold they've showered on me, but, as you know, I've got bigger things on tap now. So what brings you here?'

'Funny you should mention money, because that's why I dropped in to see you. I'm getting sick and tired of being poor. My widow's pension barely keeps me out of poverty, so after I heard about your new appointment, I figured it was time you paid off on some of the debt you owe Howard.'

Masters' eyes narrowed. 'What the hell are you talking about?' he asked coolly.

'I have some documents that could be very embarrassing to you. Documents pertaining to the death of a young woman named Chili Shaheen. Remember her, Brick?'

'Why should I remember her?' he asked.

Nell sipped on her coffee and noticed that her hands had stopped shaking. 'Because you killed her, that's why!'

'Are you nuts?' he said, but he kept his voice quite low. 'She killed herself.'

'Look, don't play innocent with me, Brick. I know

460

exactly what you did. Howard made copies of every affidavit that you told him to destroy. He wrote out a complete confession of his part in the whole thing . . . all about luring Gamal to your office and leaving him there so he wouldn't have an alibi. He even took snapshots of the bruises on her neck. Lots of stuff. He didn't trust you, Brick. You didn't know that, did you? You thought he was just a dumb flunky.'

'You're crazy. There are no affidavits to tie me in with the murder . . . uh, suicide,' he snapped, and Nell saw that now his hands were shaking.

She smiled spitefully. 'Oh, yes, there are. Like the letter she wrote that day. Howard picked it up before the Air Police came, and you told him to destroy it, but he didn't. Remember what it said?'

'What did it say?' he asked, and there were large beads of perspiration on his forehead.

'Oooo, let's see,' she began, rolling her eyes. 'It said she was going to tell your wife at the party that night all about how you were making her fuck you unless you showed up with the money she needed . . . or something like that.'

'She was a no-good cunt.'

'Sure she was, and she made you so mad you wrapped your fingers around her pretty little throat and squeezed the life out of her. Then you laid her on the bed, put a gun in her hand – the wrong hand, by the way, Brick . . . she was left-handed – and with her own lifeless finger, you pulled the trigger and put a bullet through her head. Then you called Howard, who was keeping Gamal in your office while you visited his wife, and told him to get the hell out and leave Gamal there. That way the poor jerk wouldn't have an alibi. Then you raced home, ran into your good buddy, General Torrance, and told him you'd been out getting laid.'

461

'How the hell do you know all that?' he asked, dropping his guard.

'Shame on you, Brick, you're not listening. Remember, I said I had it all written down, signed, sealed, and witnessed. Howard was very thorough, or have you forgotten so soon what a good officer he was? He wanted to make sure that in case the suicide business didn't work, you wouldn't try to pin anything on him.'

'And just what good would all that junk do you if I told you to go fuck yourself? Who's gonna believe that twenty-year-old crap anyway? I'll say that your husband was a jerk who would have gotten thrown out of the Air Force on his ear if I hadn't felt sorry for him,' he said belligerently.

'Well, maybe you're right. Maybe it's too late for the government to nail you . . . unless I goose them up a little bit. You see, Samara Mulhare happens to be a very good friend of mine. I met her at a little reunion last week, and I told her I might have an interesting exposé that would make a terrific story for *60 Minutes*. She said to call her anytime and she'd arrange a meeting with her good friend Mike Wallace. Wouldn't they just love to get hold of a story like that about a man the President is considering bringing into the White House as head of the National Security Council?'

'I should never have told you about that,' he said, his face crimson with suppressed anger and fear.

'You made the mistake of believing that I was as loyal to you as Howard was,' she said acidly, 'but I'm not.'

Getting up from his desk, Masters walked over to the window and asked, 'How much do you want?'

Afraid that he was now too far away from her purse to be heard clearly, Nell did not respond. Brick repeated the question and she said, 'Did you say something? I'm afraid my hearing isn't what it used to be.'

He returned to his desk, sat down on the edge of it opposite her and said, 'Okay, how much do you want for the papers . . . all of them, once and for all. No coming back for more when this is spent, understand?'

'A hundred and fifty thousand dollars!' she snapped.

'You're out of your mind! I don't have that kind of money,' he shouted. 'The most I can scrape together is twenty thousand. Take it or leave it.'

'No deal,' she said flatly.

'Look, Nell . . . I'd give you the money if I had it, but I just don't. You know how hard it is to save money in the military.' He began to plead.

'Tough shit! You've got your general's retirement pay, and from the looks of this place, I'd say you've got a fancy salary too. If you haven't got it, borrow it! I'm sure your credit is good.' Nell was really into the scene now. 'Or do you want the whole world to know what a real asshole you are?'

'Jesus Christ, Nell . . . have some pity. I've got four kids . . . and six grandchildren . . . think what it will do to them to find out about that dead bitch. It'll ruin their lives.'

'You already had those kids when you choked that poor girl to death. You should have thought about them then!'

'Look, it was an accident, honest to God it was. I just took that damned gun with me to scare her a little. I would never have shot her with it. I just got so mad when she started threatening me that I took a swing at her. She started to scream and I tried to shut her up, and pretty soon . . . well, it just happened . . . and then I had to do something to cover myself. Look, give me some time to get the money together.'

Nell got to her feet, picked up the purse gently, and said, 'Sure, Brick, I'll give you all the time you need. I'm not an unreasonable person, like Chili was. I just want a little security for myself, that's all. I'm staying with a friend in LA. I'll call you before the end of the week.'

'Why don't you let me know where you'll be, and I'll get in touch with you as soon as I get my hands on the dough,' he said.

Nell shook her head. 'I don't think so, Brick. Not that I don't trust you, but I don't intend to wind up on a slab at the morgue. You don't need to know where I'll be. Get the money together, and I'll contact you in a couple of days.'

Nell walked to the door of his office, put her hand on the knob, and turned back to face him for one parting shot.

'Don't feel bad, Brick. Your cover-up held for more than twenty years. That's better than even President Nixon could manage.'

74

'We're not finished,' Henry Ellis said after he and the four women conspirators listened to the tape Nell had so skillfully obtained.

'Why not?' Samara asked. 'Brick admitted he strangled her . . . and he agreed to pay the blackmail to keep her quiet. If that's not a confession . . .'

'We need more, Mrs Mulhare,' the sharp-featured man insisted. 'He could easily deny it by saying he was just humoring a hysterical woman to get rid of her. We've got to collect the money, and when we do, we've got to arrest him on the spot.'

'Oh, no,' Nell groaned. 'I have to go back there and face him again?'

'Afraid so, but we'll be right outside the door this time. Rats like this often attack when they're cornered,' he replied darkly.

'We can't let Nell take such a risk,' Beth said.

'Don't worry about it, honey. I'm not scared of him. He'll pay off, maybe not as much as I asked for, but he'll pay something. Money is not what he's about,' Nell explained. 'He's got a mighty lust for power. That's why the thought of him in the White House scares the hell out of me.'

'That's very perceptive of you, Nell,' Samara commented, impressed by Nell's insight.

'Nell, where did you ever get the idea that you weren't smart?' Tess asked. 'You're absolutely right about him. His compulsive abuse of women stems from his need to assert power over them, and has little to do with his libido. He detests women more than he likes the sex act.'

'Spoken like a true women's-libber,' Sam said.

'Don't make fun of me, Samara,' Tess said with a grin. 'I'm just trying to open people's minds, not that I think yours is closed. After all, you've made it in a man's world.'

'So, now what do we do?' Beth asked the detective, who sat waiting for their decision.

'I think it's time to bring in the Air Force,' he suggested.

'Why not the police?' Nell asked.

'Of course, them too, but the crime was committed by a military officer on active duty and took place on an Air Force base. It's their jurisdiction.'

Tess got to her feet. 'Let me call Kip and bring him up-to-date. He'll help us with the next step.'

Three days later, everything was in place and ready for Nell to call Brick and make an appointment to collect the money. With members of the Air Force security police listening and recording the conversation, Nell dialed his number.

Brick took the call immediately.

'It's me, your old friend from Wheelus,' Nell said. 'Have you got a present for me?'

'That depends,' he said. 'What have you got for me?'

'The stuff you want,' she replied. 'Do you have everything I asked for?'

'Not quite, but I did the best I could.'

'Well, maybe I better give you a few more days,' she said with a nasty edge to her voice.

'Look, you've got to settle for half. That's all I could get. Veronica took me for everything when we got divorced, and I'm borrowed to the hilt.' There was desperation in his voice.

Nell looked up questioningly at the detective and the military men, and they all nodded that she should agree to his terms.

'Are you sure that's the best you can do?' she said, not wanting to give in too easily.

'I swear to God, that's it. Take it or leave it.'

'Okay, it's better than nothin', I guess. I'll bring it to your office this afternoon. Have it ready.'

'Wait, wait . . . let's meet someplace else,' he said quickly.

Nell looked up, and Henry shook his head.

'No way, Brick. I'm not meetin' you someplace where I might not be safe. It's your office, or the deal's off,' she responded.

'Okay. Be here at five-thirty. The office staff'll be gone then, and I want to look over that stuff before I turn over the money.'

Henry shook his head again.

'Listen, Brick, I'm taking a big chance coming there all alone and bringing this stuff with me, so there'll be no dilly-dallying. When I hand it over, I get the cash. You can inspect the merchandise after I leave. I'm not hanging around there, understand?'

'How do I know you haven't made copies and won't come back at me again after you've spent everything?' he asked.

'You don't. You'll just have to take my word that when I walk out of that office, you'll be free and clear.'

'Five-thirty,' he said, hanging up on her.

When Nell put down the telephone, her hands were shaking.

'You did fine, Mrs Carson,' the head of the security police complimented her.

'You're a brave woman, Nell,' Sam said admiringly. 'How about coming to work for me?'

Nell looked surprised. 'Don't kid me, Sam. I might take you up on the offer.'

'I meant it. I'd like you to work at the studio.'

'Gosh, what do I know about making movies?' Nell asked.

'You'll learn fast, my dear. You're a quick study,' Sam replied.

At exactly five-thirty, Nell entered the building where Brick Masters had his office. She was followed closely by Henry Ellis, and as soon as they stepped off the elevator, they were joined by two security men from the Air Force and two detectives from the city police department who had positioned themselves on Brick's floor earlier in the day. There were a lot of people moving about in the building, and men in military uniform were a common sight because the bulk of the company's business was in defense contracts.

Nell was wearing a wire, and her every word and movement were monitored by the men who remained in the hallway, just outside the door. She walked through the door alone, past the vacant reception desk and secretaries' empty chairs, and turned the knob on the door to Brick's private office. It was not locked.

Brick was sitting behind his desk waiting for her.

'Right on time, I see,' he said.

'Didn't want to be late for the biggest payoff of my life,' she said with a rueful smile. 'I could really get into this kind of work.'

Brick took a thick envelope out of the drawer and tossed it on the desk. 'There it is. Want to count it?'

468

'I trust you,' she said, picking it up and checking to be sure the envelope was filled with money. 'Just one question before I head for Hawaii. Why the hell did you do it? Veronica already knew you were screwing around,' she said, drawing him into conversation, as she had been told to do.

'I didn't plan to do it. I only meant to scare Chili so she'd get off my back. She started screeching at me, and I lost my temper. Who the hell cares, anyway? She was nothin' but a whore, you know,' he said flatly.

'You really believe that, Brick?' she asked, astounded by his callous disregard for a human life.

'Look, I'm sorry I killed her, but she wasn't worth anything anyway. Jesus, even her husband was glad to get rid of her. You've got your blood money. Now hand over the papers,' he commanded.

'You know what your biggest mistake was, Brick?' she asked.

'What?' he asked sarcastically.

'You should have kept Howard out of Vietnam and alive. He would never have let me do what I'm doing right now.' Slowly Nell opened her large purse, wondering where in the hell the police were. Wasn't this the moment they were supposed to step into the room and arrest him?

'What are you going to do with the evidence?' she asked, delaying.

Brick took his Zippo lighter out of his pocket and rolled the flint wheel, igniting a bright flame of fire. 'Well, after I have a quick look, I'm going to burn it. What are you waiting for? Hand it over!' he said, holding out his hand.

As she took the envelope containing Chili's letter from her purse, the door burst open and the military men strode into the room.

'You're under arrest for the murder of Chili Shaheen, sir,' one of them said to the shocked Masters. 'You have a right to remain silent . . .'

Nell stepped back out of their way.

75

In the light of the accusation and the evidence against him, Brick Masters was recalled to active duty and tried by court-martial. At an administrative hearing a military magistrate ordered him to be confined at Norton Air Force Base until trial. Unlike the slow process of civilian courts, military justice is swift. The trial took place within two months and it lasted only a few days.

Other officers who had served under Masters at Wheelus testified, as did General Fred Torrance, Kip, Gamal Shaheen, Nell, Tess, Samara, Beth, Henry Ellis, and the arresting officers. He was found guilty of second-degree murder, stripped of his rank, his retirement pay, and his commission. He was sentenced to Leavenworth for ten years. It was never revealed publicly that he had been under consideration for a White House appointment.

When it was all over, the four women who had brought Masters to justice gathered at Sam's home to celebrate the success of their venture. Kip had already left for his new post in Germany, and so he was not able to be with them.

'Now, listen, you all, I'm gonna stuff myself tonight for the last time, so help me God,' Nell announced, digging into the bowl of beluga caviar. 'I'm going to get thin again. You just wait and see.'

'You promised me you would,' Samara said, and then added, 'Nell's coming to work for me as my personal assistant. I don't think I've ever met anybody cooler under fire.'

'That's great, Nell. When do you start?' Beth asked.

'Right after I get back from the Golden Door. Sam's sending me down there for two weeks to get myself into gear.'

'What's the Golden Door?' Tess asked.

'It's a fat farm. A real high-priced one. I'm gonna be pampered and massaged and – '

'And thin, Nell. Don't forget,' Sam interjected. 'You're going to have to fit into the Hollywood scene.'

'Absolutely, starting tomorrow.'

'So, Tess, what happened with your job at the university?' Sam asked.

'Professor Higbee is going to be the new chancellor, which isn't a surprise,' Tess said, 'and I'm not sure I can stay on there. I know he doesn't want me on his faculty. He says he's going to get rid of all the radicals, and that includes me, I suppose.'

'Good Lord, how could anybody consider you a radical?' Samara exclaimed.

'What'll you do?' Beth asked.

'I'm seriously thinking about taking a leave of absence and going to Germany with Kip.'

'Hey, great idea, Tess. You'll really be top dog there in Germany, with your husband the big cheese. All those little ladies'll be kissing the hem of your skirt,' Nell remarked with a grin.

'I've already told Kip that if I go, I'm not going to be a typical commander's wife,' Tess said with a slight grimace.

'You've never been a typical anything, Tess,' Beth agreed.

'What about your career?' Sam asked.

'Ask me a year from now. So, Beth, are you staying in Colorado Springs?' she asked, turning the attention away from herself.

'Funny, but I'm not sure what I'm going to do. There's such a big emptiness in my life now that Joe is gone and Angela is married. I need to do something to fill it. There's a group of nuns that have a lovely convent in Phoenix. I've been waiting for this nastiness with Brick to end so that I could go back there again and do some serious meditating.'

'You're not gonna be a nun, are you?' Nell asked.

'Who knows what will happen? Now, I want to propose a toast,' Beth said, smiling.

'Good idea. What to?' Sam asked.

'I want to drink a toast to five determined women,' Beth said quietly.

'Five?' Tess asked, perplexed.

'Somehow I believe that Chili is here with us now, as she's always been, and I hope she's happy with what we've done,' Beth explained.

Tears glistened in their eyes as the women raised their glasses and said, 'To the five of us.'

76

The Present

Tess and Kip alighted from the Pan Am jumbo jet to find Samara waiting for them at the gate.

'Welcome to Los Angeles, world travelers!' Sam said, opening her arms so that she could hug them both. 'How was the trip?'

'Okay, I guess,' Kip said, 'but I'm really getting sick of airline food.'

'Well, that's what you get for being a big celebrity author. I see that your book's at the top of the New York *Times* best-seller list . . . how many weeks now?' she asked as the three walked arm in arm toward the baggage-claim area.

'Three weeks,' Tess said. 'It's hard to believe that so many people want to read a book called *The Military-Industrial Complex, the Inside Story*.'

'Look, even I read it, and I haven't read a nonfiction book for years. Scared hell out of me. But I'm tickled to death that you came out here on your book tour. Our friend Sister Elizabeth arrived last night from Phoenix, and Nell and Charlie will be joining us at the house for dinner.'

Once the baggage had been retrieved from the conveyor belt, the three friends settled into Samara's silver Cadillac limousine and headed for her home.

'How long has it been now since our last reunion dinner?' Sam asked. 'It seems like ages.'

'It's been almost thirteen years . . . and we vowed to

get together annually. So much for good intentions,' Tess said. 'How's the movie business?'

'Don't ask. Network television's in a slump, and we've had to go back to making theatrical films again. We've come full circle, and I'm beginning to understand how my father must have felt. It's a whole different ball game, and I'm getting too old to learn new rules. Thank God for David. After his one unsuccessful bid to unseat our incumbent representative in Congress, he gave up politics and came back to the business. He's actually been running the show ever since Rich Wallis died last year. I should probably retire altogether, but I just don't know what I'd do with myself if I couldn't go to that office every morning. So, Tess, what have you been up to?'

'Well, I stayed in Germany with Kip for the whole four years, and I enjoyed the freedom I had to read and to travel. At his level of command, we were associating with the people who really run the world. It was heady stuff. I wanted him to take the job as Chief of Staff when it was offered, but he wanted to retire.'

'It's true,' Kip interjected. 'Not only were there a lot of things going down that irked me, but I figured I ought to leave something for Skip to aspire to . . . a level of command higher than his dad's. He's a better man than I am, anyway.'

'I wouldn't say that,' Tess said, smiling and taking her husband's hand.

'You're prejudiced,' Kip said, leaning over to kiss her lightly on the cheek. 'Anyway, Sam, I wanted to write this book. The American public has no idea what's really being done with most of their tax dollars, and I wanted them to know.'

Sam whistled and said, 'Well, you sure did that. Can you still go back to class reunions at West Point?'

'I'm getting too old to go to reunions, Sam. I don't want to look at somebody else's wrinkles and be reminded that I'm wearing them too. Besides, the only ones who might be angry with me are those who haven't read the book for themselves.'

'Well, that big scandal in the Pentagon came at a perfect time for us. That's one of the reasons for all the interest in his book,' Tess said. 'Everyone wants to know how such a thing could happen.'

'Kip, did you know that Brick Masters died last year?' Sam asked.

'No, I hadn't heard.'

'Nell still keeps in touch with a lot of her old friends, and she learned that Veronica took him back when he got out of jail. Can you believe that? She was the perfect officer's wife, right up to the end,' Sam continued.

The limousine pulled into the driveway of Samara's house, and Beth was standing on the steps waiting for them. In her street-length nun's habit, Beth looked almost youthful. Tess and Kip got out of the car and hugged her.

'Beth, you haven't aged a day!' Tess exclaimed.

'That's because I'm so happy . . . but you two look as beautiful as ever. You've always been the handsomest couple I've ever seen.'

After they were settled in the guest house, Kip and Tess joined Beth and Sam in the library, where wine was being poured.

'Just a small glass for me,' Tess said. 'I rarely drink, and it goes right to my head.'

'If you don't mind, I'll just have a glass of designer water, Sam. I don't drink at all anymore,' Kip said.

'How come?' Sam asked.

'I figured I drank my life quota while I was on active duty. When I retired, I swore off.'

476

As they chatted, Tess told Samara the details of her activities that hadn't quite fit onto her annual Christmas cards.

'We decided to settle in the Washington area because Skip and Betsy were assigned to the Pentagon at the time, and Kip had loads of friends there. It gave us a chance to get well-acquainted with the grandchildren, and I got involved with a consumer-advocacy organization. I never did really get my career going again, because I just didn't want to be tied down to a regular job and not be able to travel whenever I pleased. I had twenty years of dedication and work, and I guess I just wanted some freedom.'

'Thank God for me she made that decision,' Kip added. 'I couldn't have done that book without her. She was my live-in editor, and a pretty nasty one too.'

'I'm not much of a writer, but I've got a sharp critical eye. I enjoyed the process as much as Kip did.'

'When's Nell coming?' Beth asked.

'Any minute now. Wait'll you see her. She spends every cent she makes. . .well, almost every cent – on plastic surgery, hairdressers, and clothes, and she looks like my daughter, which is a good thing, because her husband is fifteen years younger than she is,' Sam said.

When Nell appeared it was obvious that Sam's description had been understated. Nell's figure was bone-thin, except for her breasts, which had been augmented with silicone implants, as had her cheekbones and her chin. Her hair was now blond and styled in the full, unruly mode of the time, her nails were red acrylic talons, and she was clothed head to toe in Chanel. Her husband, Charlie, was a good-looking, white-suited man in his late forties who wore his dyed brown hair combed over to cover a bald spot.

After the huggings and the greeting were over, they all

settled down to talk about Tripoli, Chili, and old times. Charlie, who worked in the accounting department at Silverstone, was a pleasant, courteous man who seemed content to sit quietly and listen.

'Well, it looks like Hollywood was the right place for you after all,' Tess remarked to Nell, amazed at the change in the woman.

'She's done a great job for us in several divisions,' Sam added. 'I've just put her in charge of our game shows, and she's perfect for the job.'

Nell chuckled. 'That's because I had so much experience playing bingo and bridge when I was married to Howard. I know what kind of games people like to play.'

Late that night, as Nell and her husband prepared to leave, she said, 'Gosh, it was sure great to see all of you looking so healthy and happy. I just wish you could stay over so I could throw a party for you at Spago's.'

'I do too, Nell,' Tess said, 'but Kip's got a batch of interviews tomorrow, and then we have to be in San Diego on Wednesday, San Francisco on Thursday, and Dallas on Friday. I'm just grateful we could get everybody together for the one night we were here in Los Angeles.'

'Well, one of these days I'm going to DC to visit you and some of my other Air Force friends who settled in Virginia. Sam, see you at the office tomorrow. Beth, say a prayer for me, will you?' Nell said as she and her husband were about to breeze out the door.

'I don't think you need it, but I will anyway, Nell,' Beth said gently.

'Wait, haven't you forgotten what you told me when I left Tripoli?' Tess asked Nell.

'Tess, you never forget anything. What did I say?'

'Military wives never say good-bye.'

NEWS ITEM

WASHINGTON, DC, Sept. 17, 1987
(Associated Press)

The Air Force, ensnarled in a controversy over its attitude toward working wives, is convening a task force to investigate whether it is exerting too much pressure on women to support their husbands' service careers.